HIGH PRAISE FOR LINDA BARNES'S
COLD CASE

"A SATISFYINGLY COMPLEX TALE!"
—*Entertainment Weekly*

"A MUST FOR EVERY MYSTERY FAN. Barnes is a master storyteller, and her latest—in a series that just keeps getting better—is a riveting read that is at once poignant, funny, sad, suspenseful, and hopeful."
—*Booklist*

"BARNES CONTINUES TO WRITE SOME OF THE BEST FEMALE DETECTIVE MYSTERIES ON THE MARKET TODAY. Readers will dive into the action from start to finish. Carlotta is a great female sleuth and the supporting cast adds dichotomous local color to the tale."
—Harriet Klausner, *Painted Rock Reviews*

"ENGROSSING . . . The pages keep turning."
—*Publishers Weekly*

"COMPELLING."—*Kirkus Reviews*

"ABSORBING . . . Barnes keeps readers flipping pages . . . The quickly paced tale neatly balances thought and action, past events and present consequences."—*Orlando Sentinel*

"*COLD CASE* IS AS GOOD AS IT GETS! Linda Barnes is one of today's best authors, mystery or not. Each new book gives us the best in writing, plot and character development."—*Kate's Mystery Books*

Please turn the page for more extraordinary acclaim. . . .

Carlotta Carlyle Books by Linda Barnes

COLD CASE

LINDA BARNES

A Dell Book

Published by
Dell Publishing
a division of
Bantam Doubleday Dell Publishing Group, Inc.
1540 Broadway
New York, New York 10036

The trademark Dell® is registered in the U.S. Patent and Trademark Office.

ISBN: 0-440-21226-X

Reprinted by arrangement with Delacorte Press

Printed in the United States of America

Published simultaneously in Canada

April 1998

10 9 8 7 6 5 4 3 2 1

OPM

For Susan Linn,
my matchmaker,
my friend

ACKNOWLEDGMENTS

The author thanks her faithful first reader, Richard Barnes, for his kindness, generosity, and unflagging belief. The early readers also deserve great credit for their collective insight, patience, and tolerance; they include James Morrow, Morgan Rose, Chris Smither, and Cinda Van Deursen. To each, a heartfelt thanks.

Gina Maccoby, my agent, did double-duty on this one, joining the reading committee in addition to admirably performing all the other tasks that smooth the path for Carlotta and me.

Officer Daniel J. Daley of the Boston Police, and Thomas G. Gutheil, M.D., answered all my questions—concerning police procedure and memory respectively. Books and articles written by Dr. Lenore Terr and Dr. Elizabeth Loftus also helped illuminate various aspects of memory.

Cynthia Mark-Hummel and John Hummel remain active on the ever-important T-shirt squad.

And at Delacorte, Carole Baron kept the ball rolling while Tracy Devine held my hand.

"The past is never dead. It isn't even past."

WILLIAM FAULKNER

PART ONE

She knows not what the curse may be,
And so she weaveth steadily,
And little other care hath she,
The Lady of Shalott.

ALFRED, LORD TENNYSON

August

*S*he wasn't home, which was just what he'd hoped after his casual telephoned question about her weekend plans. She'd never been one to volunteer information.

He patted his jeans, fingering the tiny half-pocket over his right hipbone. The outline of the little key felt hot, even through denim. He kept the larger house key on a five-and-dime chain, a pair of lucky dice balancing the weight of the ring. Rigged, oversized dice, but they always came up boxcars.

The neighbors on the run-down street were used to him. If she left for a few unexplained days, he'd cruise by, pick up the mail. Like a faithful mutt, he could be counted on to perform such services. Why not? He'd followed, dumb and dutiful, all his life.

For a moment, he saw himself as she must see him,

frozen like a bug in amber, trapped at some younger age. When had he stopped growing in her eyes? At fifteen, sixteen? With narrow shoulders, skinny arms, unkempt hair.

One thing: she'd frozen him before he got his full height. She hardly ever lifted her head anymore to meet his gaze. Instead, her eyes stayed fastened somewhere on his chest, as though she were communicating with a shadow boy, not a man.

Before he'd moved out, if he was working around the house, doing chores, he'd deliberately slip off his shirt. He'd wanted her to notice the dark hair on his chest, the taut, wiry muscles in his arms.

A man, twenty-two, even if he still had to show his driver's license at every bar in Seattle.

He yanked the small key from his hip pocket, grasped it tightly in his sweaty palm. Six nights ago, after spaghetti and meatballs and meaningless conversation, he'd stolen it from her jewelry box.

He aimed his motorbike up the narrow driveway, parked it, walked across the faded grass, his boots leaving no impression on the hard turf. Quickly he used the house key, walked through the living room and down the hall without noticing either peeling paint or crooked wallpaper, straight to the side door that led to the narrow garage. Pressed the button.

The garage door, one of those old wooden jobs converted for an automatic opener, shrieked in protest. He wished he'd thought to oil the springs.

He unloaded the wasp spray from his saddlebag, fastened a plastic jar of premixed poison to a metal cylinder with a long red handle, like a tire pump.

She was unpredictable, capricious. If she suddenly came home, he'd need a good cover story. She'd asked him to eliminate the wasps, even if it was way last spring. Shame he'd put it off so long. The insects would fold up their tents and leave once the cool weather came. Why shouldn't they live another day? Die from Northwest chill? Why should he, the executioner, get stung for his trouble?

The metal footlocker had been with them since the beginning. When they moved, it came along, no matter how cramped the space. Often it took two to carry it, two of the semi-strangers who loaded the rent-a-car, the borrowed van, the rusty Cherokee.

Growing up on the move, a nomad, never staying more than a year at each grammar school, finally two years so he wouldn't have to be the new kid his senior year of high school, objects from the early days were scarce—like friends, and ready cash, and gas for the old motorbike he'd bought secondhand with the money he'd saved from mowing lawns.

He could lift the footlocker easily. He swallowed the fear that he'd find it empty. It seemed light only because he was strong now. Stronger than those guys she had known when he was a kid. They'd seemed enormous then. If one of them had been his dad, he'd probably have grown taller, wider, maybe developed a beer gut.

He remembered a trip to Disneyland, a rare time out, a normal-kid day. She'd paid for his silhouette, cut on the scene with a quick snip of tiny scissors, smell of cotton candy. His profile was hers, a duplicate. Same broad forehead, full lips. Shape of his nose had changed after a schoolyard brawl. He didn't look effeminate, though. No way. Girls at the junior college could testify to that. But never the right girl. Maybe the local JC wasn't exactly the place to spot Miss Wonderful.

A racehorse with no papers, no pedigree, couldn't

enter a decent race, sure couldn't aim for the Triple Crown.

Even horses had papers.

His, he was certain, would be in the footlocker, carried so carefully through Tennessee, Arkansas, New York State, Illinois, Montana. Towns he'd forgotten, never known. He examined the footlocker, gray and black metal, studded leather at the corners. Hadn't come from any dime store.

Brass lock, like the gas tank on his motorbike. Small keys, both. Use a hairpin on it, a junior college girl had said, stifling a giggle behind a hand full of rings, hiding an overbite.

His hands were really sweating now, fingers slippery. Photos, he thought. Letters. From my dad. Stuff about me. My birth certificate. Dad's birth certificate.

The key turned easily. He choked down his disappointment at the contents. Row after row of tightly packed notebooks. No photo albums. She rarely snapped pictures, casually stepped aside to escape a pointed Kodak. No legal documents embossed with notary stamps.

He stuffed the contents of the locker into his saddlebags for later study. Whatever the locker held was his, due him in unearned wages, unanswered questions. He flipped through a notebook, pages silky smooth, covered with words. Reminded him of stuff he'd read in high school.

He stared at his lucky key ring. Maybe it was time to start gambling on himself, instead of dogs and horses, cards and dice.

He relocked the footlocker, hurriedly returned the key to its velvet-lined cell. Stopped in the kitchen. Drank a tall glass of water, cool from the faucet.

He could have left, but he went back for the wasps. He was careful, methodical, pulling the plunger all the way out, shoving it in, listening to the whoosh of liquid death as he soaked the mud-brown nests. He'd always been good with his hands. The mindless exercise gave him time to think. The wasps died silently, en masse. Not a single one escaped to warn the others.

1

August, one year later

"If his word were a bridge, I'd be afraid to cross." Or as my *bubbe,* my mother's mother might have said, in Yiddish rather than English, *"Oyb zayn vort volt gedint als brik volt men moyre gehat aribertsugeyn."*

Trust me; it's funnier in Yiddish. I know. I also know that Yiddish is the voice of exile, the tongue of ghettos, but, believe me, I'll shed a tear when it joins ancient Greek and dead Latin. For gossip and insult, you can't beat Yiddish.

I imagined that shaky bridge the entire time I was talking on the phone. Caught a glimpse of it later that evening, while interviewing my client. But that's getting ahead of the story, something my *bubbe* would never do. *"A gute haskhole iz shoyn a halbe arbet,"* she'd say: "A good beginning is the job half done."

* * *

The lawyer's voice oozed condescension over a long-distance connection so choppy it made me wonder if Fidel Castro were personally eavesdropping.

"Excuse me," he said firmly, the words a polite substitution for "shut up." Enunciating as though attempting communication with a dull-witted four-year-old, he said, "I believe this conversation would be better suited to a pay phone. I'll ring you in, say, half an hour."

I've never met Thurman W. Vandenburg, Esq. My mind snapped an imaginary photo: the tanned, lined face of a man fighting middle age, a smile that displayed perfectly capped teeth, pointed like a barracuda's.

"The same phone we used before. I have the number, *if* you can remember the location—" he continued.

I stopped him with, "I'm sitting in that very booth, mister. And you're eating my dwindling change pile. I don't want trouble. I want the shipments to stop. *¿M'entiendes?*"

There: I'd managed five sentences without interruption. I'd included the key words: Trouble, shipments, stop. I hadn't said "money." He'd understand I meant money.

"I'll call back in ten minutes," he replied tersely.

"Wait! No! I have a client, an appointment—"

Click.

I white-knuckled the receiver. I hate it when sleazy lawyers hang up on me. Hell, I hate it when genteel lawyers hang up on me, not that I have much occasion to chat with any. Classy lawyers with plush offices and desks the size of skating rinks are not exactly a dying breed. It's just that I don't come into contact with the cream of the crop in the normal run of my business.

I compared my Timex with the wall-mounted model

over the pharmacist's counter. *If* he actually called within ten minutes, and *if* my after-hours client ran on the late side, I might barely squeak in the door with minutes to spare.

I wish drugstores still had soda fountains. I could have relaxed on a red vinyl stool, spinning a salute to my childhood, sipping a cherry Coke while reviewing my potential client's hastily phone-sketched plight, a situation distinguished more by his breathless, excited voice than the unique nature of his problem. I sighed at the thought of disappointing him face-to-face. Missing persons are a dime a dozen. Amazing the number of people in this anonymous big-city world who think they can make a fresh start elsewhere, wipe their blotted slates clean.

There was no soda fountain, so I lurked the aisles, for all the world a shoplifter, or a woman too chicken-shit to buy a box of Trojans from a pimple-faced teen-aged clerk. The newsrack provided momentary diversion. The *Star* trumpeted DEATH ROW INMATE GIVES BIRTH TO ALIEN TRIPLETS! in uppercase twenty-four-point bold.

The *Herald* led with a heavily hyped local story: WILL VOTERS GO FOR DIVORCED MAN WED TO WOMAN 19 YEARS YOUNGER? *Boston* magazine handled the same sludge more tastefully, focusing on the upcoming gubernatorial race with a simple, CAMERON: THE MAN WHO WOULD BE KING.

By the time the phone rang nine minutes and forty-five seconds later, I'd guiltily spent eighty-nine cents on a pack of spearmint Tic Tacs. Thurman W. Vandenburg, aka Miami Sleaze, might not be my idea of an upstanding member of the bar, but he was prompt.

"Nothing I can do," he said, not waiting for me to speak.

"Well, I can do plenty," I replied quickly. "Expect a large package of cash in the mail. I'll bet you know dodges the IRS hasn't heard more than a million times."

"The situation is somewhat delicate."

"Sure it is, buddy, but I'm out. I've managed to invest Paolina's cash so far. Legit. It ends here. *No más.*"

"There's no evidence that she's his daughter," the lawyer snapped.

"Except he sends money," I replied dryly. "For her, through me. What's your problem? Afraid he can't pay your fees?"

"He's missing," Vandenburg said softly.

It took a minute for the words to sink in.

"No names," Vandenburg insisted.

"Jesus Christ," I murmured slowly. "Ooops, that's a name. Sorry."

Total silence followed by a muffled eruption. Could have been Vandenburg chuckling. Could have been Castro swallowing his cigar.

"No names," I repeated.

"I've been out of touch with our mutual friend," Vandenburg said, "for a certain number of days. That sets off a chain of events, financial and otherwise. I don't think you'll be bothered."

"Is he dead?"

"I have no idea."

"Don't blow me off. I need to know. *Is he dead?*"

Thurman W. Vandenburg terminated the call. No doubt he'd been clocking it with a stopwatch. No doubt he knew exactly how long it would take the DEA to get a lock on the pay phone.

The drugstore on Huron Avenue boasts one of the last of the true phone booths, with a tiny seat and a bifold door, a poignant reminder that once upon a time phone calls were considered private conversations. Ma Bell installed it and NYNEX obviously hasn't found it yet. If they had, they'd have ripped it out, gone for the handy-dandy wall model.

I automatically scanned the aisles before exiting. I assumed the Drug Enforcement Agency would be all over Vandenburg's calls, simply because word is out: If you get nailed on possession of a narcotic substance in the great state of Florida, Vandenburg's your man.

So I wasn't surprised to see the guy. Dismayed, yes, but not surprised. He wasn't watching me, wasn't waiting like a total fool, artillery bristling. He was strolling the aisles and his mild-mannered browser routine might have worked if not for the incredibly hot weather, which surely wasn't his fault. His windbreaker drew my attention like a red flag. The bulge under his armpit riveted my glance. The outline of a holstered gun is unmistakable.

I had no desire to explain my Miami connection to the DEA. My fingertips touched 911 as I slid slowly to the floor of the booth, my T-shirt riding up in back, cool plasterboard tingling my sweaty skin.

The Cambridge emergency dispatcher answered on a single ring. That-a-girl!

I pitched my voice deliberately high, lisped, and paused in a childlike way. "Um, uh, there's a man with a gun," I said cheerfully.

I heard a muted thud, as though the woman had set down a coffee cup in a hurry. "Where, honey? Now, don't you hang up, child," she said.

"In the drugstore," I replied in my singsong little

voice. "Mark's Drugs, I think. On Huron Avenue. I'm with Mommy and the man has a gun, just like on TV."

"Good girl, honey. What's your name? Can you leave the phone off the hook—"

I didn't hear the rest of her advice because I was crawling toward the door behind the pharmacy counter. The front door sports a string of bells to signal customer entrances and exits. The back door doesn't. I wedged my ass through the opening and slithered from air-conditioned cool into the inverted air mass that had hovered over Boston for the best part of early August, holding temperatures above eighty, redlining the pollution index. A street lamp cast a yellowish haze. The night air hung thick and noxious: recycled exhaust fumes, heavy and sticky as a steam bath.

Somebody ought to sweep the damned alley, I thought. Clear away the busted beer bottles. I inched forward. Glass, or maybe a sharp pebble, pierced my right knee. I felt for smoother pavement, glanced up.

No visible observers. Distant approaching sirens. I'd have loved to hang around, listening to the Cambridge cops dispute territorial rights with the DEA. Instead I stood, quickly brushing my kneecaps, and walked home, thankful I'd dipped into my savings for Paolina's three-week stay at a YWCA-run camp on a perfect New Hampshire lake. No chance she'd see a newspaper in the back woods. If anything dreadful had happened to her dad, she wouldn't run across some gruesome death-scene photo unprepared . . .

I'd never told Paolina, my little sister from the Big Sisters Association, that her biological father, the alleged drug baron Carlos Roldan Gonzales, had been in touch. It had never come up in conversation. I'd never mentioned his irregular cash shipments.

I found myself hoping Roldan Gonzales *was* dead, then trying to take back the thought as if it had the power to do the deed. His death would make my life easier, no doubt about that. I'd never have to explain. I could present Paolina with the money as a gift, me to her, no intermediary, no ugly stain on cash that must surely have come from the drug trade. It could be what I'd named it for the IRS's benefit: track winnings. Simple luck, passed on with love from Big Sister to little sister. College. Travel. An apartment of her own when she turned eighteen . . .

Except it would all be a lie without Carlos Roldan Gonzales's name attached.

Lies don't usually bother me much, but I try not to lie to Paolina. She means too much to me. And lies have a sneaky way of tiptoeing back to haunt you.

I glanced at my watch and doubled my pace, vaulting a fence, cutting diagonally through my backyard.

I wondered if the guy had really been DEA or just a casual drugstore holdup man. The cops would go a hell of a lot tougher on him if he were DEA. I know; I used to be a cop. They hate federal poachers.

Safely in my kitchen, I downed an icy Pepsi straight from the can, standing in front of the open refrigerator to bring my temperature down from boil. I stuck my hair in a stretchy cloth band, bobby-pinning it haphazardly to the top of my head. I was dabbing my sweaty neck with a wadded paper towel when the doorbell rang.

A prompt sleazy lawyer followed by a prompt potential client. What more could a private investigator want?

2

As I marched toward the front door, I wondered what lies Vandenburg, the sleaze, had slipped by me, what half-truths he'd told.

What lies would this client try?

With a touch—hell, a wallop—of vanity, I consider myself an expert in the field of lies, a collector, if you will. I've seen liars as fresh and obvious as newborn babes; a quick twitch of the eye, a sudden glance at the floor immediately giving the game away. I've interviewed practiced, skilled liars, blessed with the impeccable timing of ace stand-up comics. I don't know why I recognize lies. Somebody will be shooting his mouth, and I'll feel or hear a change of tone, a shift of pace. Maybe it's instinct. Maybe I got so used to lies when I was a cop that I suspect everyone.

I'd rather trust people. Given the choice.

My potential client beamed a hundred-watt smile when I opened the door, bounding into the foyer like an overgrown puppy. Even if he'd been a much younger man I'd have found his enthusiasm strange, since the number of people pleased to visit a private investigator is noticeably fewer than the number eagerly anticipating gum surgery.

He'd seemed both agitated and exhilarated on the phone that afternoon, otherwise I wouldn't have agreed to a Sunday evening appointment. He'd mentioned a missing person, given his name with no hint of reluctance. I'd checked with the Boston police; there was no 3501, i.e., missing person file, currently devoted to anyone sharing a last name with Mr. Adam Mayhew. Which left a ton of possibilities. The person in question could have been reported as a 2633, the current code for a runaway child. Could have had a different last name. Hadn't been absent the required twenty-four hours. The missing individual might be considered a voluntary—a walkaway or runaway adult.

Possibly my client-to-be knew exactly where the missing person could be found. Quick case; low fee.

Which would be too bad, because the sixtyish gentleman currently shifting his weight from one foot to the other as though testing my wooden floorboards looked like he could donate megabucks to the worthy cause of my upkeep and not miss a single dollar. His shoes were Bally or a damned good imitation, slip-on tassle loafers with neither a too-new nor a too-used sheen. Well-maintained classics, indicating a man with more than one pair of shoes to his wardrobe. A man with quietly expensive taste and access to a good dry cleaning establishment. A formal soul, rigged out in full business attire on a shirtsleeves, sweat-hot evening.

No wedding band. Inconclusive. A class ring, the Harvard *Veritas*, common enough around here, worn with casual pride.

Hair silvering nicely, hairline receding. Height: five-nine, which made it easy for me, from my six-one vantage, to note that his crown was not yet thinning.

Fingernails buffed and filed. Hands well cared for. Prosperous. My kind of client. A lawyer? A professor? A respected businessman? The speed from phone call to initial appointment had curtailed my research.

"Mr. Mayhew?"

"Yes," he agreed cheerfully. "And you're Miss Carlyle."

He'd been eyeing me as carefully as I'd been observing him. I wondered what conclusions he'd drawn from my disheveled appearance.

If Paolina's unexpected package of cash hadn't arrived, if I'd skipped the Miami phone call, if said phone call hadn't taken such a daunting chunk of time, I might have attempted to dress for success. Worn a little makeup to accent my green—well, hazel, really, almost green—eyes, and belittle my thrice-broken nose. I'd have done battle with my tangled red curls.

I opened my mouth to utter polite excuses, realized that Mr. Mayhew didn't seem to expect them. I liked the way his level glance concentrated on my eyes, as though the measure of a woman were not in her clothes or her curves, but hidden in a secret compartment beyond all external gifts and curses.

I nodded him down the single step to my living room-cum-office.

"You may call me Adam," he said.

"Carlotta," I replied. I liked his lived-in, good-humored face—lines, pouches, bags, and all. His eyes were blue behind bifocal lenses, and seemed shy and oddly defenseless, as though the glass barrier were necessary for protection as well as visual acuity.

He toted a battered monogrammed briefcase of caramel-colored leather. Forty years ago, it might have been a college graduation gift.

"I've wanted to do this for so long," he said as he settled into the upright chair next to my desk.

"Excuse me," I said. "You've wanted to do what for so long? Visit a PI's office?"

If the guy was a flake I wanted him out. He didn't seem like a thrill-seeker. He seemed genuine. Sympathetic. So sympathetic I was tempted to tell him my troubles with Paolina and the drug money. I shook myself out of it.

"On the phone—" I began.

"Do you remember Thea Janis?" he said at the same time, glancing at me expectantly. "The writer."

"Writer" jogged my memory.

"It was a long time ago," I said, struggling to recall a faint whisper of ancient scandal relegated to some distant storage locker in my mind like so much cast-off furniture. "I remember reading her book."

"Not when it was published," he said. "You're too young."

"When I was fifteen, maybe sixteen." Over half a lifetime ago. My mother had bought it for me three months before she died. Did I still have it? The title hovered tantalizingly out of reach, a ripe fruit on a high branch.

"Thea was younger than that when she wrote it," he

said. He could have uttered the words dismissively. Or flippantly. But he spoke with longing, with fervency and desire. Triumph, as he added, "She was fourteen. Imagine. Fourteen. The critics didn't know that, at first. Unqualified praise. When they learned the book had been penned by a child, a teenager, the bouquets turned a bit thorny, almost as if some critics felt they'd been duped, not given the real goods somehow. Jealousy. Nothing more than jealousy."

"Why do you say that?"

"She was the goods," he answered simply. "A prodigy. Nietzsche wrote like an adult at twelve. We find it more acceptable in music. Mozart."

"Thea Janis was a literary Mozart?"

"See? You can't keep the skepticism out of your voice. It's automatic. Cinematic prodigies, okay. Visual arts, okay, with reservations. We prefer the paintings of a Grandma Moses. We glorify poets and authors who begin careers in their fifties, or later. I wonder if it's endemic to the beast," he continued softly, almost as though he were speaking to himself, "a way in which humans maintain belief in their own potential: Someday I'll write a brilliant novel, paint a great picture . . . A way to keep the essential meaninglessness at bay."

"We seem to have wandered a bit from Thea Janis," I said.

"Excuse me. Please."

The thought washed over me like a wave of ice water.

"She's not the missing person you talked about on the phone, is she?" I asked.

"Yes," he said. "Of course it's Thea."

"But she's been missing for—"

"Twenty-four years," he said.

"Twenty-four years!" I echoed.

"Yes," he said, quite calmly. *Twenty-four years,* as if it were the same as twenty-four hours.

3

Twenty-four years . . .

Guess I could have given myself an extra ten minutes, circled the block to make sure no DEA agent was tailing me, taken evasive action if necessary. Stopped at another drugstore and bought some Extra-Strength Tylenol for the headache gripping the base of my skull.

I sucked air, blew it out in a sigh.

"Twenty-four years," I repeated, tempted to add a pungent curse, the way I would have when I was a cop. A mere glance at the silver-haired man with his grave expression and hopeful eyes kept my language pure.

"Yes," he said.

"So why the rush?" I asked quietly, leaning my elbows on the desk, my chin on clasped and ringless hands. "Why the eager-beaver phone call, the immediate appointment?"

"Thea Janis is back," the man said vehemently, stepping on the tail of my question.

"And you've seen her," I said matter-of-factly.

I could feel my eyebrows creeping up my forehead, registering disbelief. I tried to force them down. I was totally prepared for a positive response. Everybody looks like somebody. He'd spotted Thea's double, her sister, her distant cousin, waiting at a bus stop. He'd squealed his brakes a moment too late; his vision had taken wing.

"I have not *seen* her."

The man had a way of surprising me.

Memories of Thea Janis, of her disappearance—wait just a minute, her *death*—floated through my mind like half-forgotten song lyrics. I was pretty certain there was more to this business than a runaway teen genius.

Death.

"Wasn't it suicide?" I asked harshly, because I was hot and sweaty from my quick march home, because I was growing more irritated by the second. Finding the dead is not my forte. They tend not to reappear, even after twenty-four years. Unless we're talking Elvis. "Didn't someone find her clothes on a beach?"

"There may have been clothing on some beach," he said angrily, "but no one ever proved it was Thea's, not absolutely. Not to my satisfaction." He slid his rump to the edge of his chair, assuming a defensive posture.

I smiled and made nice, kept my voice low. "You haven't seen her in over twenty years. Right? So what makes you think I can find her?" I asked gently. "Now? After a lifetime?"

"Look for yourself." He opened the caramel briefcase, shuffled papers, extracted a manila envelope, and placed it on my desk, carefully aligning it with the edge of the blotter. I've seen priests handle the Host with less reverence.

"Tell me about it," I said, keeping my hands tightly folded. Some lessons, once learned, become automatic: Don't touch anything that might retain fingerprints.

"Do you have a copy of *Nightmare's Dawn*?"

Thea's book. Thank God he'd named it, or I'd have been up all night obsessing about the title. Haunting images. Prose blended with poetry. A brilliant and unpopular girl's vision of prep school hell. Angry. Upsetting. Unsettling. The *Bell Jar* of her generation. Was it because Sylvia Plath had stuck her head in the oven and turned on the gas that Thea and death were so firmly linked in my mind?

"Somewhere," I said. "In the attic . . ."

"I should have brought my copy." His smile was endearing, an elderly baby's glee. "My treasure. I keep it plastic-wrapped, in a glass display case. She wrote in it, inscribed a first edition, a very special dedication. I've been offered over five thousand dollars for that book."

"You've received something," I reminded him, indicating the envelope. "A written communication—from someone purporting to be Thea."

I don't use words like "purporting." Honestly, I don't. Haven't since I gave up the badge. The twisted linguistics of cop-speak came out of my mouth unwelcome and unbidden. The wretched police vocabulary— "perpetrator" for "thief," "incident" for "rape," "missing" for "stolen"—has some merit. It grants a certain immunity. Distance might be a better way to put it . . . primarily distance . . . distance from pain. I found myself slipping into the lingo because the man seated across from me appeared so transparent, so easily hurt. And he desperately wanted to believe he'd heard from a woman whose scoured bones had probably decorated the ocean floor for two decades.

Why was I so certain she'd drowned? I hadn't lived in Boston any twenty-four years. Had Thea Janis's death made national news?

"I'm not a doddering fool," Mayhew stated firmly, as if he could read my thoughts. "I am sixty-two years old. I am gainfully employed. I am not hallucinating, nor do I take drugs."

"Twenty-four years is a long time," I said. "What exactly would I find in that envelope?"

"Chapter One," he said, trying and failing to keep a beatific smile off his face. "The beginning of the book, the *new* book. Written by Thea and no one else. It's proof, absolute proof. In spite of everything, I could never bring myself to believe she was dead. She was so —vibrant, so real. But then the . . . the silence, the silence almost made me believe. A talent like Thea's— you couldn't keep her from pen and paper. It was the way she related to the world. Her way of talking. And that voice, that voice. If she were alive, no one could quiet that amazing voice. And she *is* alive. She is."

"In spite of everything," I repeated slowly. "Would you care to expand on that, Mr. Mayhew?" I continued, borrowing his words. "I'd hate to take this case if there's proof, *absolute* proof that Thea Janis is dead."

"Just look at what I've brought you, Miss Carlyle. Use your eyes."

"Right, Mr. Mayhew," I said with a curt nod in his direction. Dammit, I hate to give potential paying clients the heave-ho. Our abrupt return to formality knifed through the air. I modulated my tone and my words, trying to get back to friendly if not trusting ground. "Adam, let's say that whatever you have *is* Thea's. It could be something she wrote before she disappeared. It could be a find, a major discovery of an old unpublished work—"

"No!" he insisted. "It looks almost new. A cream-colored sketch pad, like she always used. Her handwriting . . ."

"Well preserved," I said. "A library archive—"

"All of Thea's work was donated to Boston University's Twentieth Century Collection."

"Something may have escaped their attention. It's possible."

"Twenty-four years ago, would Thea have written about the destruction of the Berlin Wall?"

"Not unless she was psychic," I admitted.

In addition to being a prodigy and a genius.

He nodded his satisfaction. "Find her," he said.

I made another attempt to dissuade him. "Someone's imitating her style, as in 'Imitation is the sincerest form of flattery.' "

"Someone who knows Thea wrote in longhand on a particular kind of paper, using a calligrapher's pen? Someone with Thea's handwriting? Someone with—"

"Okay," I said, holding up both hands, palms outward, in surrender. "Have you gone to the police? Missing Persons would be my first recommendation—"

"No," he said flatly.

"Why?"

"The police have hundreds of cases. Do you?"

"Not hundreds," I said.

"It's worth a try," he said firmly. "If only you'd known her. Thea was . . . no, Thea *is* indescribable.

In my whole life, I never met anyone like her. She was quick, bright, but there was so much more to her than that. She was *determined*. She'd tunnel through a mountain with a nail file if what she wanted was on the other side. She could—"

During an initial interview I generally grant a potential client plenty of space, enough rope to hang himself if he's not on the level. It was time to crack down, to narrow the focus on this bird.

"Who exactly are you?" My voice took on an edge and I let it. Twenty-four years is twenty-four years. If the woman was alive and wanted to be found, she'd had ample opportunity to come in from the cold. My headache was building into a doozy.

"Adam Mayhew. I introduced myself—"

"And who is Adam Mayhew? Of all the people in the world, why would Thea Janis choose you as her reentry point? Are you a publisher?"

"I'm her uncle, her mother's half-brother," he said, showing little reaction to my sarcasm, just a mild attitude of apology. "I should have explained. I'm here to represent the family."

"Why?"

"Why what?"

"Why *not* her mother? Her father? What does 'represent' mean? Are you a lawyer?"

His lips tightened as he pondered his response. "Franklin, Thea's father, died almost twenty years ago. He'd . . . accepted his daughter's death. Thea's mother . . . has come to rely on me."

I leaned over and stared at the manila envelope. It was lying face-up. Bare. No address. No stamp. No postmark.

"How did you get this?"

"It was mailed to Thea's home. To the family home."

"You live there?"

"It's a big place. Rambling," he murmured, staring at the floor.

It could have been his first direct lie. Or his first avoidance of a direct lie.

"The Janis house," I said, urging him on.

"Thea's surname was never Janis. That was her literary persona, her *nom de plume.*" He certainly felt more comfortable talking about Thea than talking about her home.

"I'd need her real name."

"Cameron." He flinched, as though flashbulbs might pop when he mentioned the name.

It took effort to keep my eyebrows from hitting my hairline. "As in the Cameron running for governor? As in 'The Man Who Would Be King'?"

He nodded. "Garnet Cameron is Thea's brother. That title was ill-chosen," he said ruefully. "Garnet's not like that at all."

Memory came flooding back, a deluge, a tsunami. "Start from the beginning," I said. "I remember bits and pieces, a lot of tempting little bits and pieces, Mr. Mayhew."

"I may be going about this all wrong," he said helplessly.

"I've got time," I said.

"Thea was born Dorothy Cameron."

"Cameron," I repeated.

"Yes," he said wearily. "The Myopia Polo Club Camerons, the political Camerons, the literary Camerons. Her mother, Tessa—my half-sister—is Italian. Raised in Florence. Minor royalty, no less. She always called Dorothy 'Dorothea.' " He pronounced it with no "th" sound. Do-ro-tay-ah. "Hence Thea."

"And Janis?"

"Thea's contribution."

"The connection to the Cameron family came out."

"Almost immediately. No one could believe the author was so young. And some snip of a publicist, determined to make hay from Thea's youth, discovered which school she attended. Avon Hill had no idea they were going against the family's wishes."

"Were they?" My tone must have inched back into the skeptical range because he jumped on my question.

"The Camerons have never sought publicity unless it was clearly for political ends. Thea's talent had nothing to do with politics. She'd already told her mother and father about the book; she couldn't contain her joy when the first reviews appeared. They were so positive. . . . Her parents decided, helped her decide, that she should keep silent as to her true identity."

"How did Thea feel about that?"

"All she wanted was freedom to write."

"Freedom to write. That's an odd choice of words."

"Is it?" He stared at his manicured nails, smoothed a sliver of cuticle. "She may have been under some pressure. She'd been schooled at home, along with her brother and sister. She'd hated her first year at Avon Hill, felt that their requirements frittered away her time with extraneous trivia, endeavors that detracted from her writing."

"Such as?"

"Gym class," he said. "Pep rallies. Foreign languages. Thea spoke fluent Italian, but they wouldn't accept it as a substitute for French, German, or Russian. Dramatics. They insisted she attend Friday evening social dances. For a girl who'd been allowed to do exactly what she chose exactly when she chose to do it, the schedule at Avon Hill was onerous."

Avon Hill is as ritzy as Cambridge private schools get. Most local academies reflect the area's left-wing political makeup, but not Avon Hill, where uniforms are required to this day. The kids stick out in Harvard Square, where jeans and tie-dye war with slinky black and studded heavy metal. Pristine white shirts. Navy blue slacks, skirts, sweaters, and jackets. Ties. I had no idea what Avon Hill's headmaster or headmistress might consider appropriate attire for "social dances."

"So once upon a time a young girl ran away from Avon Hill and didn't contact a soul for twenty-four years," I said. "That's your story?"

He bit his lip. "It's possible," he said with great dignity.

"But improbable," I said.

"She did call home," he offered.

"When?"

"The last day. April 8, 1971."

He seemed to have no trouble recalling the date.

"The cruelest month," he murmured, staring at his glossy shoes. " 'April is the cruellest month.' T. S. Eliot . . ."

"What did Thea say? On the phone."

"Nothing portentous. That she'd be spending the night with a girlfriend who lived near school."

"That's all?"

"She'd never stayed away before." His Adam's apple bobbed as he swallowed. "I never saw her again."

I glanced at the manila envelope. "Why break the silence now?" I asked.

"Money?" he said, with a slight shrug of his shoulders.

"Tired of supporting herself?"

"Money is freedom to write."

Among other things.

"If she's been gone for twenty-four years," I said, "what makes you think she wants you to find her?"

"Please listen to me, Miss Carlyle—Carlotta. I have waited to hear from Thea for twenty-four years. Twenty-four years," he repeated forcefully. "And now —mercifully, magically—I have. If she doesn't want to see her family, fine. If she does, fine. I—we only want to know that she's all right."

He seemed utterly sincere. I tapped the fingers of my left hand on my blotter. My right hand went automatically to a strand of red hair, twisting it into a fat candlestick. Habits die hard. Like using a favorite calligraphy pen, paper of a certain weight and texture.

I needed the work. I liked the man. I considered my caseload, my financial status. I live rent-free courtesy of my aunt Bea, who willed me the oversized Cambridge Victorian I call home as well as office.

Taxes must be paid.

I was under no illusion that Mr. Adam Mayhew was telling me the truth, the whole truth, and nothing but. On the other hand, my living room-cum-office does not resemble a courthouse. And everybody lies.

"I see two ways to track her," I said. "Through the new work, or through the past."

"Through the work," he said decisively.

"How was it delivered?"

"What?"

I tapped the precious manila envelope with the eraser end of a pencil. "This didn't travel through the mail."

No response.

"Mice leave it on your doorstep?"

"No. And I don't appreciate your tone."

My headache hammered. "Is the mailing envelope inside?"

"No."

"Where is it?"

"There is a secretary who opens the family correspondence. She, being unaware of the envelope's value, threw it away."

"Surely someone went through the trash," I said reasonably, "in the hope of finding Thea's address."

"The envelope could not be located."

"Is there a return address inside the envelope? A cover page?"

"No." Another quick glance at the ground. Another lie?

"Is this all there is? A single chapter?"

"No," he said quickly. "There's an entire novel, a whole new book."

"You've seen it?"

"Parts of it."

"Where?"

He bit his lip. "I can't say."

"Is this some kind of publicity stunt? 'PI searches for missing manuscript? Press hot on the trail?'"

"No. No. I assure you. The first chapter is all I can show you at this time. You have my word that the novel exists."

His word. He peered at me solemnly from behind his protective lenses.

"I always thought they made a mistake," he said quietly.

"What kind of mistake?" I asked.

"A mistake . . . Never mind. It's getting late. What was I saying?"

"I was saying that with no address for Thea, I'd have to consider the writing a dead end. I'd have to start at the beginning."

"What do you mean?"

"I'd need to go back to her disappearance. And I'm not going to kid you: It would be practically impossible. By now, if she's alive, she's established another name, another identity, another life. She could be anyone. She's had time to establish a whole new set of bona fides."

"The rest of the family might object to reopening the investigation," he said pensively. "Old wounds . . ."

"Where would you suggest I start?" I asked.

He stared at me. "You could begin by authenticating the chapter, I suppose. I can get you a sample of Thea's handwriting . . ."

"I'm not a graphologist," I said. "I'm not a forensic archivist."

"I know, I know."

"First you say you *know* she's alive. Now you're asking me to make sure the work is genuine. Am I being hired to locate a missing person? To prove Thea's alive? Dead? What?"

He threw up his hands. "I don't know! I don't know the whys and wherefores. I only—I *feel* that Thea is out there. Possibly desperate—"

"Did you bring a photo?"

"Yes, but it's so old—"

"I'll need it."

The aged briefcase creaked as it opened. Mayhew hesitated, then passed over a large leather folder with a mute glance of appeal, as though he wanted to beg me not to lose Thea's photo. I wondered if it was his only copy.

"What's the setting for the new novel?" I asked. "Is it local?"

"Yes," he said eagerly. "A small town, not far from here."

"Which town?"

"She's changed the details—creative license—but it's probably recognizable."

If I could nail the locale, I thought, I might visit, hang out in the places mentioned.

"Will you, at least, try to find her?" Mayhew demanded. "*Can* you find her?"

First he hit me in the pride. *Can you find her?* Then he appealed to my pocketbook. With ten hundred-dollar bills that he peeled off a fat roll.

"I'd prefer a check," I said. A check with his name printed on it, his address.

"But wouldn't that slow things down?" he said. "I stopped at my bank to get cash, so you could begin immediately."

"Which bank?" I inquired.

His posture didn't alter but his chin seemed suddenly firmer. "BayBank, my dear," he said, his voice calm and level. "I imagine it is your business to mistrust. I'm glad it isn't mine."

I felt shamed by his clear blue eyes. But I didn't take his cash. I said I'd think it over. Missing persons work is dicey at best. Finding someone who's had better than a twenty-year head start and may not want to be found . . . I tried to make it clear that I felt he was asking the impossible.

"Improbable, my dear," he said disarmingly. "Not

impossible. And I will pay for your time. Generously. It is—it could be—so very important."

"I'll need to keep the chapter," I said.

"We'll copy it," he said immediately. "Have you got a machine?"

"No."

"I'll zip into the Square. Those places stay open all hours."

"Mr. Mayhew, if you want me to establish the work's authenticity, I'll have to use the original. It could have fingerprints on it, prints that match Thea's."

Or don't.

For a minute I assumed the deal was off. Then he fixed me with a glance that seemed to see through me and beyond.

"I'll need a receipt," he said.

"No problem."

"I'll write one."

I said, "I'll sign it."

He removed pen and paper from his briefcase in record time. As long as he was in the mood, and since his stationery bore no inscribed return address, I had him print his name, address, and phone number on a Rolodex card. He didn't offer a printed business card, but he happily accepted one of mine.

He practically shook my arm off before he left, his puppy enthusiasm fully restored.

4

I'm prepared. I keep a box of latex examining-room gloves in a desk drawer. Before tilting the contents of the manila envelope onto the blotter, I donned a pair. I'd expected loose pages. Instead, a notebook emerged, the color of milk chocolate with "Strathmore Calligraphy" printed on the cover below an elaborate "S" that could have been part of a fifteenth-century illuminated manuscript. The notebook was eight and a half by eleven inches, bound on the shorter side with a strip of stuff that looked like grosgrain ribbon. Nothing bent, frayed, or aged, as far as I could see.

I lifted it to my face and sniffed. Cigarette smoke. Opened it to the first page. Blank. The off-white paper was not what I'd call cream. When I held it to the light, each sheet seemed divided into six vertical columns with tiny horizontal lines rushing across, like waves on a sandy beach. Fifty sheets, the cover declared in plain print.

The writer had worked with the binding to the left, treating it like a bound book instead of a collection of removable pages. The second page was also blank. The third had a tiny numeral one circled in the upper-right-hand corner. The fourth was the title page: Two words surrounded by blank space. *Callused Bone.*

The fifth page was covered with the kind of elegant script used on fancy wedding invitations, with skinny downstrokes and fat T-crosses. After a hasty riffle, I got up, yanked the gloves off my sweaty hands, and went in search of my ancient copy of *Nightmare's Dawn.*

I found it in the attic along with the eighteen neatly boxed and unopened cartons of "mementos" my aunt Bea left when she died.

I always promise myself I'll cull through them. I never get around to it. My aunt was such a private woman; she guarded her secrets so diligently I never realized she had any till she died. The locket she always wore, even in bed with her high-necked nightgowns, has two sepia photographs inside. Two gentlemen in stiff collars and stiffer poses. As far as I know, Aunt Bea never married. I have no idea who those two men are, or what they meant to her.

I'm not sure I want to know.

I fled the musty attic, clasping the dusty book. Returned to Thea's world.

Knopf had published *Nightmare's Dawn* in a handsome navy edition with a simple jacket. The title's words, in flowing twisted strokes, set in cream against a swirling midnight blue, like lightning in a storm. Had Thea, the calligrapher, suggested the format?

Gloves on.

I suffer from insomnia. Sometimes I benefit from it, depending on your point of view. It wasn't hard for me to stay up late into the steamy night, rereading Thea's brilliant first novel, tackling her "new" chapter.

I can read a forensics report and tell you if the same revolver fired two bullets; I can't read two poems written more than twenty years apart and tell you if the same author wrote both.

The new chapter, like the published book, was a hybrid, poetry mixed with prose. It read like a journal, like notes a woman might write to herself. Nothing seemed quite polished enough for publication, but I enjoyed what I read. The author had used initials in place of names. The locale Adam Mayhew had mentioned was a made-up resort town somewhere on Cape Ann, a haven for painters and yachtsmen. Tension seethed between the year-round folk—fishermen, shopkeepers—and the well-heeled vacationers, who considered the town their private playground. A fictionalized version of Rockport, possibly Marblehead?

Not a single landmark to fix on. I wouldn't mind hanging out on Cape Ann if I had a real lead. But a single chapter of fiction, after twenty-four years . . .

Two restaurants were mentioned by name. I punched the buttons for NYNEX information, requested each eatery in Rockport, then in Marblehead. Nothing. Restaurants are always in the city phone directory. Either Thea'd changed the names to protect the chefs or she'd created the places in her head.

Maybe I'd guessed the wrong towns. Maybe it was a conglomeration of towns. Whatever, Thea was using it as the backdrop for a family drama.

The family in question was rich, prominent in poli-

tics and the arts. Their fabulous wealth stemmed from
the unhappy union of a burly sea captain and a delicate
heiress of China trade millions.

How had the Camerons earned their pile?

The girl in the opening pages of the story seemed
about the same age as Thea when she'd disappeared.
She was referred to as "d." "d" for Dorothy? Was the
journal a memoir? An autobiography? A *roman à clef*?

I'm no expert on modern poetry although the names
of poets, especially women poets, Rich and Lorde and
Plath, are not strangers to me. My aunt owned an extensive modern poetry collection. During her last year, I
read to her.

I remember disjointed phrases, lines. June Jordan's
poem about a boy who died: "So Brooklyn has become
a holy place." That was one of my aunt's favorites. She
said that Jordan's bitter words gave her peace. I don't
know why, but Thea's words gave me peace as well. I
found myself picking up my old National Steel guitar,
trying to find an accompaniment that might do them
justice.

Thea's words awoke in me a demon curiosity. At
fourteen she'd written:

> the mind remembers lonely
> long after
> in dark places of memory
> as a pit of blankness
> of black
> of cold
> and cries at night the name
> with questioning thought
> are you there are you there
> remembers

      and cannot forget
    as a taste of bitterness
      and shiver
      and fear

I couldn't sing it, but I could almost hear someone chant it, a vaguely Chasidic melody wafting from the *bema*, the pulpit of a synagogue.

I wondered what kind of music Thea'd enjoyed. Sixties protest? Folk? The stuff she'd danced to at Avon Hill's Friday night socials?

I spoke the poem out loud.

Jazz.

In her new chapter she wrote, or might have written:

the mind can destroy what the mind possesses:
      and you are there
      before me,
in dusty armour and tarnished silver,
      away from the wars,
      undestroyed

      (you must not be mine).

After so many earlier questions and fears, now solid answers, like blocks of stone. "the mind remembers . . . the mind can destroy."

To whom was she speaking? To whom had she cried, "are you there are you there"? Who stood before her now in "dusty armour"?

Why she'd written the first poem was no clearer to me than why she'd written the second.

If she had . . .

The absence of capital letters, the random placement

of words on lines, the use of commas, seemed similar in both pieces. That was all I could say, except that I liked her work enough to read it aloud. To wonder what Aunt Bea would have said if she sat rocking in her needlepoint-cushioned chair, listening.

My attempt to set Thea's verses to music failed. I play Delta blues. The old stuff, written by slaves and sharecroppers, people with names like Blind Blake, Smilin' Cora, Robert L.

I got a new pair of surgical gloves from the box, slid them on my hands, working the fingers down into the finger holes till my hands were clasped like I was praying. First I shook the manila envelope, then gently squeezed it open, peered inside. Nothing. No hint of where it had come from, whether it had been protected in plastic or stacked on a shelf. I grasped the chocolate notebook by the binding, using thumb and index finger to dangle it over my desk. A loose sheet drifted to the floor like a spent paper airplane.

More poetry, a brief verse.

> berlin, now
>   without a wall
>   can
>   you break down
>   the glistening gates?
> always
>   keep the western wall,
>   the body cries
>   for wailing walls
>
>   (not in jerusalem)

It was Mayhew's cited proof: "berlin, *now,* without a wall." Must have been written in or after 1989. The glorious penmanship seemed the same, the paper identical. Why was this one sheet detached? Had Mayhew added it, separating it from a later notebook, part of a series that made up the complete manuscript?

Thirty-five pages of the notebook had been used to write Chapter One. Fifteen remained blank. The Berlin page was extra, an addition. Was a single poem sufficient to pinpoint a year? Couldn't the young Thea have visualized Berlin without a wall?

"berlin, *now*"

I replaced the page in the notebook, the notebook in the envelope, locked the whole shebang in my desk drawer. Peeled off the gloves and tossed them in the trash.

Before I went to sleep, I called a Web-connected friend on the coast and got a home listing for Thurman W. Vandenburg. I dialed his number, just for the pleasure of waking him, breathing heavily, and hanging up.

Whoops, shouldn't do that, I thought, replacing the receiver as though my hand were on fire. DEA might have a bug on his phone, a high-tech trace. Vandenburg might have a phone that flashed the caller's number. If I boasted a clientele like Vandenburg's, I'd get myself every available gadget; cost—no object.

I'd have to find another method to get information on Carlos Roldan Gonzales, another way to convince his attorney to share.

5

Early the next morning I found Roz—my tenant, housecleaner, and sometime assistant—sniffing around my desk as though she could smell the cash I'd rejected the night before. Roz started out simply as my tenant, then requested reduced rent in exchange for housecleaning, a task I despise. I accepted, immediately and gratefully. Had I tested her cleaning skills, she'd be paying more for her room. Had she left in a snit, I'd have been deprived of her karate training, post-punk art, and intuitive computer expertise. Not to mention her wide range of ever-changing fashion images.

Dressed in shiny black bike shorts and a tie-dye halter salvaged from a sixties headshop, she was updated for the nineties with cone-shaped inserts à la Madonna-does-Dietrich and hand-scrawled graffiti. "Boobs are

Back," she'd lettered across her left breast. A tattoo of sexually entwined eagles decorated her awesome cleavage. She was barefoot so I could appreciate her toenails, each a different shade of green: chartreuse to forest and beyond.

"Paying client?" she inquired, totally unabashed at being caught in apparent espionage. Maybe she'd crack a locked drawer or two while I watched. Roz has no shame.

"What makes you think so?"

"I heard you chatting last night. You coulda been talking to yourself, I guess. In two voices. Maybe you've got multiple personality disorder."

Roz watches daytime TV talk shows. I try not to hold it against her, but I figure it contributes to her general delinquency.

"Privacy is nice," I said.

"I wasn't eavesdropping," she replied, a bit huffily for somebody practically ransacking my desk. "I was setting camera angles."

"What?"

"Never mind. The guy want to hire you?"

"Yeah," I said.

"Retainer?"

"Not yet."

"Carlotta, ya gotta get the bucks up front," she said.

"Man's good for it," I replied.

"Something I could help out on?"

"Hard up for cash?" It's wise to know in advance when your tenant can't make the rent. Roz has never had financial problems before; far as I know she's a trust-fund baby whose fabulously rich parents will ante up any amount provided she doesn't appear at their fancy digs with magenta-and-blue striped hair, tattoos, and multiple nose rings.

"It's not like I'm flat broke," she muttered. "I have a hanging."

"A hanging?"

"A gallery show. At Yola's in the South End. Woman's crazy about my stuff. Says I'm gonna be the next Boston artist to score."

"Score as in money?"

"Like I must be doing something wrong," she said sadly. "I told the lady, yeah, like she can sell this batch of shit, but I'm never doing anything remotely resembling it again. I'd take it all back, but, like, I need bucks because of the film."

"The film," I echoed.

"I'm branching out," Roz said.

"Into cinema?"

"Sort of."

"You have actors?"

"Me."

"Ah," I said, repenting my foolish query. Who more could she need?

"I priced rentals. Cameras are like totally out-of-this-world expensive. Editing equipment, bummer."

"The show, the 'hanging,' won't bring enough?"

"It's consignment. She may not sell a single item."

"Ya gotta get the cash up front, Roz," I echoed cheerfully. I did not ask what the all-purpose word "item" entailed. I don't discuss Roz's appearance. I don't discuss the content, shape, or form of her art-work. I'm scared if I ever got started I'd never stop. I'm still suffering from her *art trouvé* period. Loosely translated: found art, and she found most of her stuff in my kitchen. I didn't think I'd attend this particular opening. It would be disconcerting to find my cheese grater hanging on the wall with a price tag on it. And I can't figure out where the hell else that cheese grater could have gone. I'm an investigator. I find things; I don't lose them.

"So you want work?" I asked Roz.

"Anything."

"Run a check on an Adam Mayhew. Here's the address and phone. Brother-in-law of the posh Dover Camerons. Check the whole family. One's running for governor so it's not exactly low profile."

She rubbed her thumb and forefingers in an international moolah gesture that allowed me full view of her fingernails, the reds and oranges clashing wildly with the toenail greens. "You get in good with *those* Camerons you can start a whole new game here. Rent an office. Pay your operatives a living wage."

I handed over the precious manila envelope containing the possible Thea manuscript. I'd dusted the whole business for prints. The shiny paper and smooth cardboard cover defeated me. Not even a smudge to offer a more experienced technician. The rough manila envelope boasted plenty of prints. Alas, when I compared them to prints on the leatherbound folder Mayhew had reluctantly given me, they matched in so many particulars that I knew I'd detected my client's presence. I'd expected as much. In fact, I'd only done the fingerprint bit as an exercise. Used it as an excuse to keep the original documents. Where, precisely, was I supposed to come up with a genuine twenty-four-year-old Thea Janis print?

Maybe nobody'd cleaned her room since she'd left.

"While you're out," I said to Roz, "Xerox this. Two copies. Don't lose it, okay?"

"Handle the Camerons right," Roz advised, "and you can buy your own Xerox machine. The super-duper color model. Print your own money."

"CopyCop's barely half a mile from here."

"Line's half a mile long, too."

"Then don't let me waste your precious time."

"Lend me a Widener ID card."

Widener is Harvard's main library.

"They allow you in the hallowed doors dressed like that?" I asked, tongue in cheek.

"You kidding? Half the Harvard kids look tons weirder than I do. I pick up style pointers."

"I find that hard to believe," I said, gazing at her attire.

"Believe it." She sighed. "Money. Root of all evil, hah! You can get some good shit with it, I'm telling you."

"Money is not the root of all evil," I informed her automatically. "The desire or lust for money is—"

"Same thing, right?"

"Not exactly."

"Picky, picky," she said.

"Wear shoes," I suggested. "The pavement's hot."

"Right," she said.

"Roz." I was suddenly reluctant to let the notebook out of my sight. "I'll do the copying."

"I didn't mean to bitch and moan. I really need a few bills. I'll do it, Carlotta."

"Check the Camerons. Emphasis on the uncle, Adam Mayhew." I fished another phony university ID card out of my collection. "Then head over to B.U., make like a grad student, and Xerox a few pages of genuine manuscript, if you can, handwritten by Thea Janis. Got it? Thea Janis."

Roz thrust both cards into her cleavage. "Truly, I don't mind CopyCop. Line or no line."

"Nothing personal," I said, taking possession of the envelope.

Some things you need to do yourself. Roz is basically reliable. But "basically" didn't seem strong enough for Thea Janis's first message to the land of the living in twenty-four years.

6

Roz departed, stepping over a morning *Globe* that the delivery boy had forgotten to toss in the bushes. Balanced precariously in high-heeled mules that hid the weird toenail polish and accentuated everything else, Roz didn't bother to pick it up. I did. Picked it up and carried it into my office, where I searched each column for mention of the mysterious disappearance of Paolina's dad, the reputed Colombian drug lord, Carlos Roldan Gonzales. I double-checked every two-inch foreign news brief. For all the details Vandenburg Esquire had dished, the man could have been murdered in Sri Lanka.

Nothing on Roldan Gonzales.

The Camerons owned the front page, everything except the headline and a slim right-hand column, which were duly devoted to the latest Balkan disaster. Boston's other paper, the *Herald,* wouldn't have bothered to give the Balkans the lead. They'd have plunged straight to the nitty-gritty: Was Marissa Cameron ditching her husband in the midst of a gubernatorial race?

And who was I to criticize the *Herald?* I didn't even scan Serbs vs. Croats before wallowing in the details of Garnet Cameron's domestic brouhaha. I especially enjoyed the article's lofty tone, with the *Globe* earnestly implying that it merely covered such sordid fare because other, lowlier, tabloids considered it newsworthy. I wondered when the *Globe* would start picking up on the pregnant-by-aliens death row inmates.

Normally I can leave the peccadilloes of the rich and famous alone, thank you very much. But this same Garnet Cameron, who couldn't seem to hang onto his second wife, was brother to the missing Thea. So I took a gulp of orange juice and waded in.

At twenty-three, Marissa Gates Moore Cameron had been wed two years. Before that she'd briefly attended an Ivy League college, and taken stabs at acting, modeling, and singing careers. A photo caught her campaigning in her "trademark yellow dress," a blond Miss America type, the girl-next-door with pizazz. Dazzling smile, sweet perfection, she looked as if she could twirl a baton while jogging as far as the nearest Elizabeth Arden spa.

Yesterday, she'd missed a scheduled interview for a glossy women's magazine, as well as the opening of a pet-project senior citizens center in Brockton.

Sounded to me like she was throwing a spoiled-brat tantrum. Maybe Garnet forgot to send her flowers. Maybe her yellow dress had a ketchup stain acquired at a campaign-sponsored weenie roast.

Her family background—the toney yet sporadic education, the European travels, the near-misses at film stardom—was all trotted out as though she were a fledgling Princess Di. The *Globe* got in another dig at the other paper by suggesting that a recent *Herald* column speculating on the state of the Camerons' May-December marriage might have been the last straw in this perilous Would-they-stay-together-for-the-sake-of-the-campaign? drama.

I tried to care. My folks didn't even stay together for the sake of the kid. They did try to avoid divorce for the sake of the money—my mother being too poor to support us, my dad knowing he'd have to shell out more for separate accommodations than he did for rent on our crummy Detroit apartment.

I doubted Marissa or Garnet found continuing financial stability an overwhelming concern.

I downed a third glass of orange juice. I could have used more sleep. I get nasty when I don't sleep.

Thea's curious novel-cum-journal had kept me awake. Both her prose and her poetry had a strange uneasy power. Thirty-six pages made me want to know everything about her, discover the smallest detail about her disappearance.

Or death.

No smiling author's face decorated the dust jacket of *Nightmare's Dawn*. The photo Adam Mayhew had given me was professional work. A thin, waiflike creature stared forth from an arty black-and-white eight-by-ten, all wistful eyes and exquisite cheekbones. It wasn't a perfect face. It had flaws. The lips were immensely wide, full, pouty. The chin was too small to balance the mouth. She wore a short white dress, a flowered sun hat, a knowing look that contrasted sharply with her virginal knees-together pose.

It was a photo that seethed with complexity: sexual, sensual, oddly innocent. Marissa Cameron's, admittedly a grainy news shot, seemed by contrast as simple as a fifties sitcom.

I stared at Thea's photo. Computers might be able to age it, but I didn't have the necessary equipment or the right program. Roz could probably do better than any machine. Age the photo in a variety of ways. Thea grown up wealthy, Thea grown up poor, Thea aging, plump and thin, healthy and ill. Roz has the eye, the gift.

And me, well, I took another quick glance at the front page and revised my morning. I've learned enough not to stomp into a hornets' nest of reporters. No visit to the Cameron estate today. I'd have to work my best source first, sneak in the back door of my former place of business.

I ran an icy shower—a good short-term sleep substitute—donned a sleeveless tank top and khaki shorts for a visit to the cop house. I figured I'd flaunt my lightweight attire, let the uniforms sizzle in envy and suffocating heat. Freedom to dress as I choose is one of the few perks of my job.

Of course, as a homicide cop, a plainclothes detective, I'd enjoyed similar liberty. I just hadn't exercised it. I'd known bone-deep that had I come to work dressed "unprofessionally," it would have been another black mark against one of the few women on the force, an offense that might well have led to a dreaded return to uniformed pavement pounding. The only time the uniforms seemed to appreciate my presence was when they assigned me to phony hooker patrol, preferably in winter, out of "concern" for the poor sidewalk strutters: Get 'em the hell in jail so they wouldn't freeze to death. No such concern for me, stuck wearing a crotch-high miniskirt with the wind-chill way below zero. Some guys really got off on it, vetoing heavy tights in favor of sheer panty hose, remarking that I might do better business if I stuffed my bra with Kleenex.

And if I didn't take it with a smile, I had no fucking sense of humor. Right.

I'd told them I'd be happy to stuff my bra, provided they'd arrest the johns who tried to hustle me, instead of the working girls I was supposed to pal up with, then betray.

Maybe if I'd lasted longer on the streets I could have made a difference. Maybe pigs could juggle billiard balls.

Hell, I thought, calm down. I was getting overheated just remembering. It wasn't the whole squad, just a few loudmouthed wrongheaded jerks. I glanced in the mirror, splashed cold water on my face, changed to a more conservative shirt and longer, looser shorts.

Why alienate the good guys when there are so many bad guys around?

I decided to walk into Harvard Square, take the T to South Station. A breeze might be blowing off the ocean. And I didn't feel like getting another parking ticket, which I do almost every time I try to stow my car near the Area D cop house.

I stuffed the manila envelope containing Thea's notebook into a plastic grocery sack, hung it over my left wrist, and took off.

Strolling toward Huron Ave., I turned abruptly, for no reason, just one of the things you do, and saw him. The same man who'd been casing the drugstore yesterday. Today he wore a denim jacket, a baseball cap, shades, and a bulge under his arm. Overdressed for the heat wave.

I knew it was the same guy because of his ears. Ears and fingers are what they teach you at the police academy. Anybody can buy dark glasses, a wig, a mustache. Gnarled stubby fingers don't change. Neither do thin dangling earlobes.

Instead of turning left and heading toward Harvard, I hung a right and veered into the Mount Auburn Cemetery. It may not sound like a pleasant side trip, but I'd been intending to visit. The old burial ground is no modern run-the-power-mower-over-the-flat-tombstones affair. It's a real park, with fountains, trees, sculpture, and glorious landscaping, as well as the graves of Edwin Booth, premier actor of his day and brother of the man who shot Lincoln; Fannie Farmer, the cooking maven; Mary Baker Eddy, the Christian Science lady who is not really buried with a telephone, but it makes such a good story; Winslow Homer, the painter; Buckminster Fuller; and Henry Wadsworth Longfellow. It's also rumored to be the burial site of both Sacco and Vanzetti, but nobody talks about them.

I knew the layout, the location of stone angels and tall monuments behind which I could hide and observe my observer, provided he took the bait and followed me into the park.

I ducked under the stone archway leading to the main section of the cemetery. Across Coolidge Avenue, the less notable are laid to rest in the City of Cambridge Cemetery. I decided to stick to the tourist routes, at least at first, make it easy for the guy. I headed down a leafy path toward the Lowell family plot. The shade was a welcome relief.

The grounds were meticulously clean and well maintained, the hills tastefully landscaped, the ponds clear and sprinkled with lily pads. Marble saints stared heavenward to intercede for the soul of stogie-smoking Amy Lowell. My pursuer was not in sight. Maybe he'd missed the turn. Smelled a trap.

I backtracked.

No one.

I took a new path, wondering whether I should ask the caretaker if he'd seen another tourist abroad. The elderly man slowly raking the immaculate grass looked ready to talk, garrulous. I suppose with such taciturn neighbors, he didn't get much chance to converse.

"Where would I find the Cameron family plot?" I asked as soon as he glanced up and acknowledged my presence. Surely the Camerons would have a tomb here, a palatial monument to illustrious ancestors.

The caretaker gave me detailed directions, past the third elm, a left at the wading pond, down the hill to the right, past the stand of lilacs. Right pretty in spring, he said. White lilacs.

Had he seen a man in a denim jacket? Nope. Hot day.

The Cameron plot was surrounded by a knee-high iron fence, elaborately carved like the metalwork on fancy patio furniture. I don't know one kind of marble from another, but the Camerons favored white with almost invisible pink veins. It made the statues look alive, as if a faint blush warmed their sunlit skin. The oldest grave was dated 1714. Lucinda Eustachia Estes Cameron, wife and mother. Dead at twenty-two. Disease or childbirth.

Franklin Cameron's monument, a tablet between tall fluted columns, was decorated with the veteran's American flag and the motto: He served his country in war and peace. Born 1911, died 1975. Beloved husband and father.

I stared down the path. No blue-jacketed stranger. I searched for the grave I'd come to see, the one that might or might not be there.

It was plain. Almost stark in contrast to the carved seraphim and cherubim of the others. A thin upright marker, with two curved leaves. It took me a moment to realize that the marker was in the shape of a book. Nothing else indicated that the grave belonged to the woman who'd written as Thea Janis.

Dorothy Jade Cameron, said deeply etched letters that would stand the test of time: 1956–1971. Fifteen years old. Younger even than her ancestor, Lucinda Eustachia.

How had they determined year of death? I wondered. If she'd disappeared in '71, she couldn't have been declared legally dead until '78, seven years later.

The caretaker had finished raking his patch. I looked for him outdoors before heading toward the official-looking stone cottage. Cemeteries keep records. If you can't recall the last resting place of some dearly beloved, a cemetery map is generally available.

I wanted more than a map.

He was drinking a can of Coke, his head tipped back, the folds of his chin wiggling as he swallowed. I waited, finally made a deliberate noise, dragging my shoe across the gravel.

"Yep?" he said, slapping the can down on a nearby countertop, looking as guilty as if he'd been caught wielding a bottle of Wild Turkey. "Can I help you?"

"Have you worked here long?" I asked.

"Yep," he said, relaxing. "Best part of thirty-five years."

"Are some of the plots memorial plots?"

"What do you mean?"

"No body buried there, just a stone marker, the way Paul Revere's 'buried' in three, four places," I said.

"We got ashes," he said. "In the crematory."

"No. I'm asking if all the stones, the monuments, are indicators that an actual body was buried here."

"You better get specific with me, miss. Somebody in particular on your mind?"

"Dorothy Cameron. She was a writer, one book in 1970. Her tombstone says she died in '71."

"That's right," he said. "In the big plot. Died and buried in '71. Pitiful thing when parents outlive a child."

"It's not a memorial stone. You're sure? Are there records you can check?"

"I could but I don't need to. I remember that funeral, because she was famous. Fine family. We used to get all the fancy funerals; now we're almost plumb out of space."

"There was a casket," I said.

"Right," he agreed, scratching the back of his neck, shrugging his shoulders like he was loosening them up, getting ready to go back to work with the rake. "I didn't go to the funeral home or nothing, but I do remember it was a white casket, white lilies just mounded all over that grave. Everythin' white, not a speck of color."

"It was a long time ago," I said.

"I been around a long time. But I remember. Maybe not what I ate for breakfast, you know, but a big funeral like that, keeping the press away and all, I surely do remember that."

"Thank you," I said, turning away, feeling the grocery sack hanging from my wrist turn into a heavy weight.

If Thea's new manuscript was genuine, whose body lay under the marble stone? Was that what my client had meant when he said that he was sure someone had made a mistake? A mistake . . .

On the way out of the cemetery, keeping one eye peeled for the blue denim man, I saw it.

Adam Mayhew's tombstone. His monument, rather. The engraving was directly at eye level. Ornate. Large. Anyone visiting the Cameron plot would have been sure to see it, maybe even remark on the detailed border, a ring of carved doves.

I took notes as to the date of birth and the date of death. I'm a detective after all. Then I found a phone booth and dialed the number my client had written down last night.

It was not in service within the 617 area code. I tried 508, the western suburbs, just to make sure. An automated voice told me to check the number and dial again.

7

On the overcrowded, overheated bus, and then on the blissfully air-conditioned Red Line car, possibilities thrummed through my brain, keeping pace with the speeding subway. Number one: My client was a liar and a fraud. Liar and fraud. Liar and fraud. The rhythm fit the rumble of the rail and the sway of the seats.

On the other hand—I tried to convince myself as the train emerged to cross the Charles River at the Longfellow Bridge—Mount Auburn Cemetery's Adam Mayhew didn't have to be my Adam Mayhew. The sun glinted off the golden statehouse dome and I closed my eyes, indifferent to the throng of rowdies boarding at Charles Street Station. Among local Brahmins, name repetition abounds. My blue-eyed bifocaled Adam might be Adam Mayhew, the third, the fourth, the fifth. Not to mention a totally unrelated Adam Mayhew.

Sure. I believe in coincidence. Right up there with the Easter Bunny, astrology, and long-term weather forecasts.

Did I believe in the detailed reminiscences of elderly caretakers? Would he remember a twenty-four-year-old funeral? He hadn't volunteered to check any records. Why should he bother to lie?

I sighed, covering it with a fake cough as I observed my seatmate eyeing me speculatively. He wore a long beard, a skullcap, and a black cassock. A heavy cross on a metallic chain dangled to his knees. He looked as though he might be searching for converts, followers, donations.

Face facts: I have a suspicious nature. I gave it free rein on the T, but at no point did a broad-shouldered male, wearing an unnecessary jacket of any hue or packing a piece in a shoulder holster, make an appearance. The train was so crowded I couldn't be absolutely sure he wasn't on board, so I switched at Park Street, waiting eight minutes for the next jammed southbound cars, maintaining careful surveillance.

If it weren't so damned hot in the tunnels I might join the MBTA police, enjoy the benefits of a regular paycheck.

But would they let me wear bizarre halter tops like Roz's?

Would I wear one given the latitude? Given the body?

Sometimes Roz makes me feel like a gutless wonder; at other times a veritable saint, a reservoir of common sense. No wonder I value her presence in my life.

As I treasure Mooney's.

Mooney's simply one of the best cops around. Hadn't been for him, I'd never have gotten into plain-clothes work, never have earned my detective's tin. Or rather, I'd have *earned* it, I just wouldn't have gotten it, passed over for some guy whose dear old dad and five Irish uncles put in time with the Boston PD.

The trouble with Mooney is he makes me feel guilty, as if I should have stayed a cop no matter what, because he really did climb on to a swaying limb for me. And I paid him back by quitting.

Guilt plays such a major role in my life that my Mooney guilt usually gets shoved to the back of the bus. But today, because I needed a favor, it crept stealthily to the fore, nudging me as I waited on the stoop by the gas pumps for a detective I knew, someone I could tail into the station without causing undue comment. While I climbed the stairs, automatically avoiding the creaky fourth step and the loose rubber runner on the sixth, I ran a mental credit check.

Who owed whom?

I had the uneasy feeling that I was down major points, and about to sink deeper. Maybe I ought to crawl into his office on hands and knees, a true suppli-cant. No. Cops love to gossip. I wouldn't give them the satisfaction.

"What do you want?" Mooney barked as soon as I opened the door. He glanced up warily, peering over tiny rectangular lenses. Noticing me notice them, he quickly lifted them off his nose and stuffed them in a desk drawer, out of sight.

Vanity: not quite one of the seven deadlies, but Mooney was seldom vain.

I merely raised an eyebrow. If I want help I usually

invite him out for doughnuts; I don't drop by unannounced, uninvited.

"Break up with the boyfriend?" he asked.

The best defense is a sneak attack; Mooney knows.

I ignored his question. I wouldn't visit Mooney to discuss my sex life. He's aware of that.

"How's Sam?" he went on, mentioning another former flame since we were on the subject.

The subject of Sam Gianelli is a tender one. We weren't an item when he got injured in an attack on the Green & White garage, but we've been off-again, on-again lovers for years.

"Convalescent center," I said. "Palm Beach. Place looks more like a hotel than a hospital, but Sam's pretty discouraged. They can't seem to get his left leg to match the right one. A quarter inch off here, an eighth off there. Doesn't sound like much, but makes it hell to walk. He'll be pleased you care."

"You've been visiting?"

"Why?"

"Well, actually, I was wondering whether his family's got a contract out on you."

I practically bit the tip off my tongue.

"Why?" I demanded.

"Triola nabbed a punk, thought he could use it to trade down to a misdemeanor."

The guy at the drugstore, the one I'd assumed was DEA. The shoulder-holster man . . .

"I saved Sam's life," I protested.

"A few of the Gianellis might not see it that way," Mooney said.

"Then they're probably seeing about as well as you are. When'd you get the glasses?"

"It's these frigging reports. Play havoc with your

close-up vision. Don't get any ideas. I can still outshoot you."

"At any range," I agreed easily. "You're a great shot, Mooney."

"And you need a favor," he said, nodding his round Irish face, his stubborn chin outthrust.

"How'd you guess?"

"Need it bad," he said. "You compliment me. You smile at me. Not like baring your fangs, either. A real smile."

"Mooney—"

"So tell me I'm wrong. Tell me you've dropped the dork headshrinker and you desperately want me to take you to Mary Chung's tonight for Suan La whatever she calls that stuff."

"Mary's is open?"

"Opened months ago. You haven't been yet?"

"I didn't know." Mary Chung's restaurant in Central Square, Cambridge, has been closed for years, ever since Biogen Labs made her landlord an offer he couldn't refuse. Rumors of reopenings abounded. An entire Internet interest group was devoted to the cult of perpetuating rumors. Mary was in China. Mary had applied for a liquor license, application denied. Mary'd signed the lease on 443 Mass. Ave. No, she hadn't. I'd long since given up, and believe me, my Mary Chung's habit was tough to break. I was a solid twice-a-weeker, a Suan La Chow Show junkie. Mary serves a hot and sour wonton soup—Suan La Chow Show—that defines scrumptious. My grandmother—rest her soul—should forgive me, but it's better than chicken soup for whatever ails you. Guaranteed to clear sinuses, drive away demons, halt meter maids on their appointed rounds. I almost forgot the reason for my visit in my eagerness to get to Central Square.

"I'll take you to lunch," I told Mooney. "My treat."

"Don't get me wrong, I appreciate the offer," he said, "but everything that lady cooks gives me heartburn."

"It's your taste in food that keeps us apart, Moon," I said.

"Nothing wrong with vanilla," he replied stubbornly.

"Yuck," I said. "You probably eat Wonder Bread with mayonnaise, call it a sandwich. I confess: I want a favor. I've got a case that may or may not tie into an old disappearing act. Normally, I wouldn't think the department'd still have paper on anything this old, but it wasn't your run-of-the-mill missing persons."

"We talking Judge Crater or Amelia Earhart?"

I sat on the edge of his desk. His visitor's chair is a joke, designed to torture the fannies of unwary bureaucrats, keep their visits brief.

"Very funny," I said. "I'm mildly amused."

"How old a case?"

I shrugged my shoulders. Might as well get it over with. "Twenty-four years."

Mooney stared at me for a while before shaking his head sadly. "Did you take out an ad in *Soldier of Fortune?* 'Weird clients, weird cases? I specialize.' What you ought to do is get back on the force."

"Like you don't get weirdos? Ten-year-olds killing nine-year-olds over a pair of Nikes?"

"Yeah, we get those," he said. "Too many of them."

"Let me take you away from all this, at least as far as Central Square," I urged.

He shoved his chair away from his desk. Floorboards

creaked. "Twenty-four years? Is my hearing going bad or what?"

"About as bad as your eyesight."

"What do you want from me?"

"Take it easy. I just want to know who handled the investigation. I want to know if it's ongoing or closed."

I want to know why a man claiming to be related to the Camerons told me so many lies. I want to know the origin of the document I'm toting around in a Star Market plastic sack.

"Carlotta, cops here do their twenty, get down on their knees, thank the Lord, and retire full pension."

"Not all of them," I said.

"A few have heart attacks, get shot," he said. "Buried."

"Mooney, come on, some of these guys are married to the badge. Sure, it didn't start out that way—the wife leaves, they never see the kids. What are they gonna do with their retirement? Sit in a motel room till they decide to eat a bullet? Who's been here longest, that's the guy I want you to introduce me to."

"It wasn't run-of-the-mill," he said slowly.

"Right."

"Then before we go any further, you name the case. Some pots we don't stir."

"Judge Crater," I said.

No reaction. No hint of a smile.

"Thea Janis," I said reluctantly, because I've become reluctant to tell a cop anything I don't absolutely have to. I spelled it for him, because of the odd first name and the variety of spellings suggested by the second.

"Thea Janis," Mooney repeated. I let him sit and worry the name for a while, see if it jangled his memory the way it had mine. "Hang on. Let me call Cold Case."

"Cold Case?"

"They're new. One sergeant and two dicks. They sift through unsolved files, revisit scenes, find missing witnesses. Sometimes, after eight, nine years, somebody's willing to talk."

He wedged the receiver between shoulder and ear, dialed.

Mooney's office is one of the few enclosed spaces—other than the rest room—at the old Area D station in Southie, home of the homicide squad. It's more attractive than the bathroom, but not much. It looks like somebody's about to move in or move out, never like a regular place somebody works. There isn't a single poster on the walls. Not a photo on the desk. Maybe I ought to buy the man a plant, watch it wither and die of neglect.

I listened to Mooney chat. Mostly he grunted, "Uh huh, uh huh."

After he hung up he turned to me. "Cold Case is working a nineteen-year-old open murder," he said. "Little boy strangled and dumped behind a liquor store. They've got no file on Thea Janis."

"There ought to be a mountain of paper on this, Mooney."

"Why?"

He was a brick wall. I wouldn't get anything unless I told him. "Under another name," I said. "Dorothy Jade Cameron."

"Cameron," Mooney said, snapping his fingers with satisfaction as the name clicked. "Whoa, have you been blowing smoke at me? Are you looking for whosis? Wonder boy's wife? Marissa Cameron?"

"Is she missing?"

He ignored my question. "You're telling me the

Cameron family wants some old police business rehashed? Now? Bad timing, if you ask me."

It was my turn to ignore his question. "Who'd be able to give me horse's mouth stuff? If the cop in question's retired, I could track him down."

"Carlotta, do you have a legitimate interest here?"

"Not to get unpleasant, but none of your business, Moon."

"Could be my business, Carlotta. The Cameron family's involved in just about every slice of Boston government. Isn't there a Cameron in the DA's office?"

"Scared he'll fire you?"

"Politicians, Carlotta, they can cook you so fast you don't know you're done till they yank the fork out."

"I don't see why any Cameron would object to making sure their sister or cousin or whatever got a decent investigation when she disappeared twenty-odd years ago."

I worried my lower lip with my teeth. I'd almost said "died." "Died" twenty-odd years ago.

"Disappeared," he said, shaking his head. "I don't recall it."

"She was a writer," I said.

"Yeah. Thea Janis. That does ring a bell. But twenty-four years ago I was paying my government's respects to Southeast Asia."

"So that's why you don't have total recall, Moon."

"This has nothing to do with the current hoo-hah," he said. "I've got your word on that."

I looked him straight in the eye and told the truth. "Everything I know about the governor's race I read in the paper."

He stared back, standing, giving himself a slight height advantage. "Woodrow MacAvoy," he said.

I asked him to spell it.

"Surly old cuss," he continued. "That's the main reason I remember him. Retired a sergeant, swore he should have been superintendent. He handled the politicals, the hot seat stuff. Good public speaker. Could really sling the bull with the crime reporters. They'd think they had the whole story, but it was all flim-flam and mirrors."

"If he was that good, I'm surprised he didn't get to be superintendent," I said.

"Does Mary cook anything that won't burn my lips raw?"

His question caught me by surprise.

"You'll go?" I asked.

"She do any food that's not spicy?"

"Sesame lemon chicken. Crab Rangoon. Trust me."

"Always," he said. "That's why I'm driving."

8

We took Moon's battered Pontiac instead of an unmarked unit, which meant I had to enter via the driver's
side and slide across the cracked leather bench. His passenger door is nonoperational, creased and rusted from
an ancient accident. He holds to the Boston school of
thought on auto repair: A perfect car equals a perfect
target, so why bother?

In all other ways, he is atypical.

Mooney will never get a speeding ticket, never earn a
hundred-buck fine for a moving violation. Not because
traffic cops show professional courtesy to homicide
cops. Not because it's tough to get cited in this town of
perpetual scofflaws. The man drives so conservatively I
find it hard to credit his claim of native birth. Boston
drivers are tough and scrappy. They change lanes with-

out signaling; they turn left from the right-hand lane in front of oncoming traffic. Mooney drives like a respectable Midwesterner. Whereas I, born in Detroit, have picked up all the Bostonian tricks of the trade. Take me out of Boston, I can hardly drive. Cops nail me. Citizens honk.

I fidgeted, adjusting the window up a smidgen, down an inch, searching for the perfect blend of pollution and breeze. My hands itched for the steering wheel, my foot for the brake. I actually fastened my seat belt. I was terrified we'd get rear-ended; Moon stops for amber lights.

He remembered that Thea Janis was a writer, but I doubted he'd read *Nightmare's Dawn*—touted as a girls' "coming of age" story—word for word. More likely, he'd been present when a used paperback was passed around, dog-eared to the sexy pages.

Hell, my copy fell open to them automatically.

Moon refused a single taste of Suan La Chow Show, but admitted that Crab Rangoon had its charms. I'd have opted for the train, but he insisted on chauffeuring me to Harvard Square, which was far enough out of his way and so unlike his usual manner that I wondered if he'd joined me for lunch just to see for himself whether or not I was being tailed by a mob hitman.

He dropped me where Mass. Ave. meets Brattle, earning an upraised finger from three drivers.

I jaywalked across the street, spinning a quick three-sixty in front of the international newsstand, gawking like a tourist easily awed by red brick and pricey retail. I didn't spot Mr. Windbreaker. The line at CopyCop *was* half a mile long, as Roz had predicted. Thirty-seven minutes later, I sighed with relief as I tucked two copies of "Thea's" brand-new manuscript into a CopyCop envelope, the original notebook into the original manila envelope, the whole package back into the plastic sack.

A phone booth beckoned. Not exactly a booth, but a machine wall-mounted to a sheltered corner of a bank. I didn't have a pocketful of coins so I tried collect.

It's automated. I did the Miami area code preceded by the operator's 0. Canned accentless voices took charge. I figured Vandenburg wasn't going to accept anything collect from Carlotta, so I murmured "CRG" into the appropriate time lapse on the tape. The sleaze would eat any charges from Carlos Roldan Gonzales.

That call got through immediately.

"No names," I said as a greeting.

"Jeez—"

"Don't hang up. Have you heard from him?"

"No. Stay the hell out of it."

The line went dead. So much for news on the Colombian cartel front.

I watched a guitar picker with a glass eye and shaky fingers try to wheedle quarters for a song. He was too old and too bad to be playing on the street. I put fifty cents in his battered guitar case. He had two missing teeth up top.

I walked along Brattle, aiming for the Avon Hill School. I didn't expect a full complement of teachers and students hanging around in summertime, but I might find someone minding the store. I'd get to view the institution where Thea had spent over a year of her life. If I could see what Thea had seen, maybe it would help me decode a line or two of her prose, her poetry.

I know. If she was dead and buried, what the hell difference did it make? I like to walk; the school wasn't far out of my way. And my "Adam Mayhew" had spoken about Thea's time there as if he'd witnessed it, realized exactly how she'd felt.

Maybe I thought I'd just ring the doorbell and old "Adam Mayhew" would answer the call. He could damn well pay for a day of my time, a day of Roz's time.

The Avon Hill School stared down on the world from a swath of real estate that made local developers drool. Harvard had tried to buy it once. The city had wisely pulled out all the stops, determined to make the college stick its fat checkbook back in its overstuffed pockets. If Avon Hill ever folded, Cambridge was going to make damn sure its land joined the tax rolls. Nonprofits, universities, schools, and churches drive Cambridge taxes so high that regular folks have to move to the suburbs.

The main building was a Georgian mansion, gray with white trim, slate-roofed, and beautifully proportioned, with a pillared center portico. From street level, you could hardly see the dormitories and outbuildings. Even the gymnasium was discreet. Because I'd read Thea's book, the place gave me the shivers. It didn't seem like anywhere children would laugh or play. It looked like the setting of some Gothic horror tale, complete with a wicked governess and a madwoman in the attic.

I climbed the well-kept slate walkway that curved along the hillside, thumped the heavy brass knocker against the oak door. It made a hollow booming sound, but nobody came. I walked around back. There had to be a playground, a soccer field, a summer school class.

Gardeners. Three long-haired males on riding mowers were cutting the grass. The drone grew louder, deafening. I waved and hoped they'd stop. The one riding right-wing waved in acknowledgment. He wore no shirt. Either he hadn't heard that overexposure to the sun could cause skin cancer or he didn't care. Handsome and young could beat the big C any day.

Life had news for him.

He swooped out of line, sped downhill, and halted a few feet from me, standing astride his mower like it was a stallion and he was an old-time outlaw. If there'd been fewer clouds, his gold hair might have shone. He wore dark heavy boots that didn't go with his skimpy cutoffs. Sensible enough to value his toes if not his health.

"Everybody gone for the summer?" I asked.

His face split in a grin.

"Headmaster," he said, wiping sweat from his brow with a muscle-roped forearm.

"Huh?"

"House next door to the biggie. He's the guy pays us."

"You work here all year?"

"Mostly. We cut grass, plow snow. They've got a couple old guys do the roses and shit."

"You work here during the school year?"

"Yep."

I'd located an outspoken informant.

"How old are the kids?"

He shrugged.

"Kindergarten? High school?"

"More like junior high. Older, maybe, I guess."

"They give you a hard time?"

"Not allowed to speak to the snots."

I raised an eyebrow.

"Yeah, and you should see some of 'em, too. Delicious. Wiggle and giggle whenever we buzz by."

One of his mates on the hilltop hollered down at him, made a gesture.

"I gotta be gettin' back to it," he said, staring at his boots. His feet must have been hot.

"Headmaster around?" I asked.

He shook his head no. "Went out. No telling when he'll come back. Walks into the square."

"Old man? Silvery hair? Glasses?"

"Kinda young. New last year."

So much for a heart-to-heart with my lying client.

"Thanks," I said.

"You might try the missis," he said before he gunned the motor and returned to the hilltop.

The house next door was a well-maintained Victorian with a wraparound porch. A box of brochures rested on a rattan table. I grabbed a couple. Educational philosophy, along with a wide variety of classroom offerings, and the option of extensive study abroad. No prices. If you had to ask, you couldn't afford it. I wondered if the brochures on the porch were the gist of the school's advertising. Word of mouth and the old boy network would provide.

I knocked at the headmaster's door. I'd almost given up when it finally opened.

The woman was both young and shy. Her shiny brown hair was twisted severely and coiled on top of her head. If not for her obvious pregnancy, she would have fit the surroundings perfectly. A servant's apron and cap would have looked positively fetching.

Fetching! The otherworldly old-fashioned air of the place was starting to get me. Fetching, my ass.

"Are you selling anything?" she said. No throwback to a gentler age here. Straight to the point.

"No."

"Okay. Um, is it about one of the students, because they're on vacation."

I could simply wait until she hit on the reason for my visit. Or I could supply one.

"Hello," I said, taking the steps quickly, opening the screen door, pressing her hand warmly. "I'm so glad you answered the door. You're Mrs. . . . ?"

"Mrs. Emerson. I'm, uh, the headmaster's wife."

She blushed when she said that, and twisted her wedding ring. She hadn't been the headmaster's wife for long. I wondered if the pregnancy had predated the wedding.

"Is your husband in?"

"No. I'm sorry." She started to close the door.

I wished I'd dressed better. Still, it was hot and old money doesn't flaunt its presence.

I touched my fingertips to my forehead and breathed a deep sigh. "It's only that my sister, Helen, called last night and begged me to take a look around. She's raising two children in Colombia, South America, you know. Political unrest. She hates letting them go, but lately she's been thinking of sending them to school in the States."

"We have quite a few foreign students," the woman said, her eyes brightening as I dangled two hefty tuition fees.

"Helen, my sister, was planning to do the rounds herself. B,B, and N, Southfield, Phillips-Andover, but she had to go in for minor surgery, and the recovery period just stretched and stretched."

"You're not talking about a fall placement?"

"I know it's late. You're probably full." I tried to look apologetic and contrite.

"We do have a waiting list."

"I told my sister it was too late," I said, turning away, accepting defeat graciously.

"We might have an opening or two for *next* September," the woman said.

I paused, feigning reluctance, checking my wrist-watch as though I had a tight schedule.

"Next September," I said, summoning up a sigh of regret. "Those kids need someplace now."

"Since you're already here, it wouldn't do any harm to look around," the headmaster's wife said, as though suddenly remembering her sales pitch. "What age are the children?"

Good thing I'd scanned the brochure.

"Paolina's thirteen," I said without having to lie. I quickly gave my little sister an imaginary sibling and christened her Cecilia. "And Cecilia's fourteen, fourteen and a half."

The woman turned and snagged a set of keys from a nearby hook. Her voice became animated, brisk.

"Let's start with the main building. The school was founded in 1898. We maintain a tradition of excellence."

She'd done this routine before. The mansion door creaked when she put her shoulder to it.

The entry hall was filled with glass cases. Elaborately framed photos hung everywhere, as though someone had banged nails into the molding at random. Classes, sports teams, rowers on the Charles. Shelves and glass cases were devoted to trophies. Silver Paul Revere bowls, some tarnished, some shiny. Aged sepia photographs, lying on their backs. Blue, red, and gold ribbons, some mounted, some piled.

Oil paintings of founders, headmasters, and headmistresses lined the other wall. Talk about gloomy. The entire corridor must have been lit by a sixty-watt bulb.

"Who are some of your famous alumni?" I inquired when she came to a halt. "That's the kind of thing my sister would want to know."

She quickly rattled off a U.S. senator, a popular national news anchor, a rock singer, a woman who'd won the Alaskan Iditarod three years running, an attorney who regularly appeared before the Supreme Court, and several hotshot businessmen, including a software billionaire who could have made all future fund-raising moot with a grant.

"Anyone in the arts? Actors? Writers? My sister's very big on arts education."

She stuck her tongue firmly between her teeth and furrowed her brow. Extreme thought.

"We had a poet, I think," she said.

"Would you mind if I looked at a few of the photos?"

"Not at all. You really ought to come back when my husband's here. He knows so much more about the arts offerings. We do have a cooperative program with the Boston Ballet School."

"Does that mean there's no ballet teacher on campus? What about music? Cecilia plays the cello beautifully."

Damn, I find it so easy to lie to people it scares me sometimes.

She tucked her tongue into the corner of her mouth and furrowed her brow again. "What you need is a faculty list."

"A list would be marvelous," I agreed.

"My husband has them." Her brow stayed wrinkled, her mouth pursed.

"Probably keeps things like that in his office, don't you think?" I suggested offhandedly.

His office. She charged down the hall like a knight in pursuit of the Holy Grail, and I started some serious staring. Class of '73? '74? Which would be Thea's class? No leatherbound edition of *Nightmare's Dawn* graced any trophy case. In light of its content I wasn't surprised.

She came back too quickly, with a flimsy sheet of paper, two large folders, and the flushed face of success. "I've got the faculty list. We have some very prominent professors who give generously of their time."

"Wonderful," I enthused.

"And I brought two applications. Just in case," she said.

I wondered whether they offered a two-for-one deal on application fees. Probably not.

I studied my watch, made a clicking sound with my teeth.

"I really have to be going," I said.

"But you haven't seen the gymnasium—"

"I know, but since there's so little chance of admission—"

"You really ought to hear my husband talk about this place. He's an alumnus."

I did a little rapid arithmetic. He could be ten years older than his wife and still be called "young" by the teenage gardener. He could have been Thea's classmate.

"I'd certainly like to speak to him," I said. "Let me give you my card." I chose a plain one. Address and phone number. Nothing concerning profession.

"A pleasure to meet you, Mrs. Emerson," I said.

She stole a look at my card. "Miss Carlyle."

"Oh, and your husband's first name?"

COLD CASE / 79

"Anthony."

"Tony?"

"He prefers Anthony."

"Thank you so much."

We said our farewells at the door of the Victorian. Once she disappeared inside, I quickly ran my finger down the faculty list. No Adam Mayhew, no teacher with the initials A.M.

I walked back to the mansion and sat on the front porch, not really waiting for the headmaster to return, but trying to put myself in a place Thea might have been. I looked across the grand lawn with the eyes of the young woman who'd written *Nightmare's Dawn*, saw her imaginary snakes and rodents. Moles digging by night, secrets eating at the students by day. Cliques, anorexia nervosa, hazing, bullying, underground societies, exclusion.

I blinked. The sky was azure, furred by high cirrus clouds. The air smelled of fresh-mown grass. To me, it looked like Eden the day before God created apples.

9

It was too hot to rush home. I walked slowly, savoring the colors of late summer blossoms I couldn't name, impressed by the industriousness of bees. No one tailed me. I heard the ragged engine of a motorbike and wondered idly whether any self-respecting mobster would use such primitive transport, but it traveled another street.

Stifling an urge to kick the mail under the rug, I grabbed the envelopes cascading from my door slot. The kind of correspondence I get usually isn't worth bending down for. Circulars from my local hardware and grocery stores, like I have the time or inclination to clip coupons for things I never wanted in the first place. Reminders to visit the dentist who once charged me a bundle to replace a tooth knocked out in the line of duty.

A postcard from Paolina made me smile, her irregular scrawl on one side, a quaint New Hampshire vista—small-town idyll spiked with white church towers—on the other. I inhaled, holding the card close to my face, wishing I could smell the cherry Life Savers aroma of my little sister. She's thirteen now, the single truth in the pack of lies I'd dealt Mrs. Emerson, but I remember her best at seven, bruised, scared, and defiant. Despite her liberal use of trendy free-sample scents, Anais Anais one week, DKNY the next, she'll always be cherry Life Savers to me.

"*Ola,* Carlotta! I'm really having an okay time. Better than okay. Terrific! My cellies are cool even. How's Sam? Kisses and hugs to Gloria and you too. Remember to feed my bird!"

At fourteen, a scant year older, Thea Janis had written:

> perhaps as penance,
>   i must walk,
> barefoot and holy,
>   through snow-wax camellias
>   as bitter as the ichor of
>   the living
>   or fruits of the dead.

If Thea wrote like that at fourteen, why the hell not kill herself at fifteen? What act had she committed that required such penance? What crime, outside her fanciful imagination?

I reread Paolina's card, slightly troubled by her use of "cellies." It's current jail jargon for "roommates."

Did a fellow camper have family in prison? Was I shelling out good money so my little sister could learn to boost cars instead of sailboats? Boosting cars she could learn in her own neighborhood, just by sticking her head out the window.

I hollered upstairs, but it seemed Roz had not returned with information on the Camerons or Adam Mayhew. Damn. I should have trusted her with the notebook and done the research myself.

Most likely, Roz had not trotted directly home from library hour. She'd met a new pal, gone boozing and dancing. She might even be upstairs, awake, alert, and nonresponsive because she and her pal were now between the sheets, except you can't really say "between the sheets" with Roz because she doesn't have sheets. Washing clothes is anathema to her. No sheets; less laundry. Her karate tumbling mats, which double as futons, have started to stink like a used cat box, but I haven't figured out a tactful way to approach the subject, and I probably never will. I keep hoping she'll grow out of it, this constant need to bring home a new boy-toy every afternoon, every night. Maybe she's going for the *Guinness Book of World Records*.

If Roz was home, I'd hear her soon enough. Yowling alley cats have nothing on Roz in heat. I *have* spoken to her about condoms.

Aha! She had left a message. A single page of elegant penmanship, prose marked "B.U. Archives—Acid-free paper. *Do not remove from stacks!*" lay centered on my desk.

A sample of Thea's handwriting. I read it eagerly.

Her matter-of-fact description of sea, shore, and fog made me feel the tickle of tiny fiddler crabs racing over my bare feet, smell the low tide. I removed a magnifying glass from a chamois bag, compared the B.U. Archive's page to one from the notebook given me by Mayhew. My glass does not have the reliability of, say, the renovated and repaired Hubble telescope, but the flowing script seemed remarkably similar in tilt, structure, and style.

I'd be willing to hazard a guess that the notebook was authentic. If that were possible . . .

Damn. I wished Roz had given me more, left detailed information about Adam Mayhew, alive or dead, so I'd know with whom I was dealing. I couldn't pursue the Thea Janis manuscript business, sort out truth from hype, real from counterfeit, unless I could trust my client. Once, I came close to helping an abusive husband locate his fleeing spouse. Nothing like that's going to happen again. Not to me.

Paolina's admonition to feed "her" bird carried me into the kitchen in search of seed. The bird's a touchy issue. I wouldn't own a parakeet by choice; I inherited Fluffy from my aunt Bea, not expecting the pet to long outlive her mistress.

Fluffy's evidently going for the Guinness Book, too. Not under that name. I will not share quarters with anything named Fluffy. She is now Red Emma after Emma Goldman, a hero of mine. Paolina does not approve. She calls the bird Esmeralda, because she is indisputably green, although not in the way any emerald of value is green.

The bird is a nasty lump of feathers no matter what you call her. I filled her seed and water dishes while she tried to peck off my fingers. Feeding her made me recall other responsibilities, such as the cat, T.C., who actually earns his keep by virtue of being listed in the phone book at this address. Thomas C. Carlyle gets fewer harassing phone calls than Carlotta Carlyle would. He gets tons of junk mail, too, but I don't have to read it. If it's addressed to Thomas C., I toss it in the trash.

T.C. deserves better care than I give him. I scratched his ears thoroughly before serving him a can of Fancy Feast Beef & Liver.

Activity agrees with me. Sitting, unless I'm earning money doing surveillance, does not.

I went back to the Avon Hill faculty list. "Adam Mayhew" could have taught there, retired. I opened the desk drawer where I'd stowed Thea's photo. Her knowing eyes stared me down. If I ever got moving on this case, would I start with the presumption that she was dead or alive?

Mayhew had given me the Berlin poem. He'd seemed to believe in Thea's current health. The document Roz had snatched from B.U. looked as though it had been executed by the same person who'd written in the chocolate notebook.

When I was in high school, my favorite teacher stunned us all by running away, deserting a wife and two kids for a student. Sixteen-year-old AnnaBeth O'Reilly with yellow braids and ice-blue eyes. Wonder what happened to her . . .

Her family hadn't held a funeral, that's for sure.

Seventeen names on the faculty list, followed by lots of prestigious initials. How many of them had been teaching at Avon Hill when Thea pulled her vanishing act? Any teacher who'd left Avon Hill the year of Thea's disappearance would be suspect. Thea could have changed her last name to his.

But what about her writing?

Freedom to write, that's what my client had said

Thea valued most of all. Would she run off with a forbidden man if it meant the loss of her freedom to write?

I wanted cold facts. I wanted Roz's report on Mayhew and the Camerons. I wanted a fat file of newspaper clippings detailing the disappearance or death of a prodigy.

I checked my watch. Five thirty-two. Five whole minutes since the last time I'd checked. I wished Gloria was back in business. I have a dozen cards from cab companies on my desk. I could drive a shift for any one of them, but it's not the same. Driving for Green & White was more than a job, it was a second home until the place got torched, with Sam, former lover, and Gloria, dispatcher and friend, inside. Gloria's doing okay, fussing over construction at the new garage, but the company won't be handling business for months.

The phone rang. Roz, I thought. Hallelujah!

Mooney didn't bother to identify himself. He said, "Is it true that the Cameron guy's thinking of quitting the race? Is it some kind of public relations stunt? Does he expect some kind of reaction, a public show of confidence?"

I said, "What are you talking about?"

"Don't you ever listen to the news?"

"No. Run it by me again."

"And here I thought you could give me the lowdown. Garnet La-di-dah Cameron, of the very same family you're so interested in, says he's considering withdrawing his name from the November election. And I was actually gonna vote for the bastard."

"You like him?"

"As much as I like any pol. Every jerk running for office yells about more money for law enforcement. I figured with Hailey, he meant megabucks for jails and prisons, maybe a new electric chair, if he could slip it by the Great and General Court. With Cameron, we'd have a chance for more street cops, more computers. I even sent the bastard money, like he needs it."

When Mooney uses the word "bastard," he's about as upset as he gets.

"Why would he want to quit, Moon? I thought it was in the bag." Democrats outnumber Republicans in this state. Of course our Democrats act like Republicans and vice versa, so it gets tricky.

"I'm not privy to that information," Mooney said, making like a court reporter.

"There's got to be station house gossip."

"You want gossip? What I heard, the sweet young wife plans to divorce him. Extremely bad timing."

I didn't see how the timing would affect me. I hadn't been hired to force Marissa and Garnet Cameron to kiss and make up for an adoring public. That kind of thing turns my stomach.

I hadn't been hired for anything yet. I'd refused Adam Mayhew's money. Face it: My client was a possible forger, maybe entirely off his rocker.

I could hear Mooney breathing on the phone. He's not one for long phone calls. It made me suspicious.

"So you called to thank me for lunch," I said. "Or just to share the speculation?"

"No."

"You found me Woodrow MacAvoy's address?"

"No."

"I give up."

Mooney's voice sounded odd.

"Look, Carlotta, I found the files. Old MacAvoy kept every piece of paper he breathed on, I swear."

"That's great, Moon. I'll be right over."

"No! Carlotta, listen. Seriously. I've got the whole damned case in front of me."

"I heard you the first time."

"Thea Janis . . . your 'missing person'—"

"Yeah?"

"Forget her. She's dead."

The girl in the photo stared up at me from the desk drawer. I smiled at her reassuringly.

I said, "Maybe. Maybe not. Maybe MacAvoy got it wrong. He probably bought suicide. My client said there were clothes found near a beach—"

"No," Mooney said. "No. Forget it. No way." His tone turned rough and gentle, the way it used to when he'd tell parents that their beloved children were gone, dead, shot. "Get this straight. She didn't kill herself. She was murdered. A guy is serving life at Walpole for doing her and two other girls."

I stared at the sheet of archival calligraphy on my desk, at the Avon Hill faculty list.

"But, Mooney—" I began.

"Carlotta, listen! It's not an open case, it's not a cold case. It's a one hundred percent closed case."

I swiveled my chair. My elbow whacked a cup filled with pens, pencils, odds and ends, sent it crashing to the ground. T.C. raced out of the room, startled by noise and debris.

"Carlotta, you okay?"

"Fine. Thanks."

Whose verses, whose prose did I have in my possession?

At first I thought I'd slammed the receiver into the cradle so hard that the phone had clanged in self-defense. Then I realized it was the doorbell. Not Roz. She has her own key. Not someone for Roz. Roz responds to three-buzz salutes.

I was hoping for Adam Mayhew.

Be careful what you wish for, my grandmother used to say.

10

I was ready to chew the man's head off. I expect evasion from clients, but there's a limit. I do not expect earnest requests to find women officially and formally dead. Murdered. The wound felt unexpectedly raw. I probed it gently, the way you'd inspect a canker sore with your tongue, found myself shaken by the depth of my belief in a living, breathing Thea Janis. I'd bought the entire gift-wrapped package. I'd yearned to find the lost prodigy, to be involved, even remembered, as someone who'd played a part in restoring Thea Janis to life and literary fame.

Now I had nothing but a bitter taste in my mouth, and the need to spit it out in words.

Adam Mayhew shuffled through the door like an old man, blinking owlishly. His skin was blotchy, his clothes wrinkled. He looked and smelled like he'd spent time on a park bench sipping a bagged pint of Four Roses. His lips seemed thinner, stretched taut and pressed together as though he were afraid they might blurt sentences he didn't want to say. His blue eyes were cloudy behind smudged lenses.

"Thank you for receiving me without an appointment." Whatever wrenching experience he'd weathered hadn't killed his instinctive politeness. I nodded toward the living room and he followed, sinking with a weary moan into the same chair he'd occupied so jauntily last night.

"What can I do for you?" I asked when the silence turned squirmy and uncomfortable. The man was gazing at the walls, the windows, the fireplace, counting the repetitive motifs in the oriental rug. His right forefinger traced concentric circles on his left palm.

"I'd like the manuscript back." His eyes stayed riveted to the floor.

"Why?"

Sweat beaded his forehead. It was no hotter than yesterday.

He lifted his head and stared at me. If misery were contagious, I'd have caught it. "I'm terribly sorry," he said stiffly. "I've changed my mind. It was nothing—a game, a joke, whatever. A client—er, a student of mine —thought I'd find it amusing. Really, my dear, you were right to be skeptical. 'I'm just a foolish fond old man.' I didn't realize how stupidly foolish I'd become."

His voice shook with suppressed emotion. He seemed close to tears.

"Would you like a cup of coffee? A drink? Whiskey?"

"No. Nothing, thank you. I need the notebook back.

Tonight." He made as if to stand. I wasn't ready to let him go.

"You said you'd changed your mind," I said. "Exactly what do you mean by that? Changed your mind about the authenticity of the new work?"

"I no longer wish to engage your services. Isn't that clear enough?" Misery was changing to anger. An improvement. Angry people talk, occasionally let things slip.

"Have you shown anyone the manuscript?" he demanded intently.

"Not yet," I hedged. I hadn't decided how to play this one.

His shoulders lowered abruptly, as though he were a marionette and his puppeteer had suddenly relaxed the strings. The corners of his mouth drooped and he swallowed hard. Compared to the substantial gentleman I'd met before, this guy was a deflated tire. A different presence altogether. Different mannerisms. Different speech patterns.

Bipolar disease?

I've been seeing, dating—well, truth be told, sleeping with a psychiatrist. Maybe that's why bipolar disease crossed my mind, the mental illness shrinks used to call manic-depression. Was Mayhew off his normal medication? Had he been taking a pill vacation yesterday?

"You don't look well," I said. "A doctor lives two doors away. Would you like me to call him?"

"No! Absolutely not. The notebook . . . Give it to me, and let's finish this sorry business once and for all."

I didn't want to surrender Thea's notebook. I searched for a way to stall, found it in a lie. Lies don't bother me when I'm the one telling them.

"I'm sorry. It's no longer in my possession."

"No longer in—"

"I can get it back. It may take a little while."

"Who has it? What have you done with it?"

"I sent it to a friend at the FBI lab. In Quantico, Virginia. You asked me to authenticate the document. I don't have the necessary equipment. She does."

"Call your friend," he insisted. "Now. Have her return the envelope immediately. She needn't open it."

I studied my watch. The man's panic didn't fit with what he'd been telling me, that he'd made a simple "mistake."

"Consider the time," I said lightly. "She's not at work now. I'll phone her in the morning. Besides, she won't have received it yet."

"You sent it by—"

"Mail. The good old U.S. Postal Service. Don't worry: I insured it."

"You insured it," he repeated incredulously.

"Ought to get there in a couple days," I said, feeling not a tad guilty although the notebook in question was locked in a desk drawer eight inches from his restless fingertips. "Couple days to mail it back—"

"Call her. Have her FedEx it. I'm surprised you'd— didn't you realize what you were dealing with?"

"I thought I was dealing with—how did you put it? —'a game, a joke, nothing—' "

He pressed a hand over his mouth.

"Isn't that what you said?" I asked, feigning sweet innocence.

He moistened his lips with the tip of his tongue. "Yes. Yes. But I'm eager to get it back as soon as possible. No one likes to be, uh, taken in, fooled. As I was."

"Right," I said. "No one likes to be fooled, Mr. Mayhew. That is Adam Mayhew, isn't it?"

"Yes. Adam Mayhew." His stare was venomous.

He was lying. I knew it. Damn Roz for not providing the ammunition to shoot him down.

He noticed the tremble and flutter in his hands, caught them and clasped them tightly in his lap.

"You wanted to believe she was alive," I said gently. "I can understand that. By the way, I enjoyed reading the chapter. And the extra poem. I found my copy of *Nightmare's Dawn*. You were right. Thea was extraordinarily gifted."

"Yes," he murmured.

"One of the new poems, something about a man standing before her in dusty armor, back from the wars. I especially liked that. Do you have any idea who she was talking about?"

"It meant nothing. She didn't write it." He was breathing heavily now, his face red. "You still have the manuscript, don't you? You wouldn't have sent it away. Not so quickly. Show me the receipt. You said you insured it. Where's the receipt?"

See how easy it is to get caught in a lie? I made a display of searching my wallet. While he watched intently, I decided to hit him with Mooney's information.

"It's hard enough to lose someone naturally," I said, "through old age or disease. Her murder must have been horrible. Did you go to the trial?"

He was so rattled he practically fell as he tried to stand. I grabbed his hand to steady him, felt the rough surface of his ring.

"*Veritas,*" I said, reciting the Harvard motto. "Truth."

I lifted his hand toward the light. The print was small, but the year was there. Harvard: class of '54.

"Didn't you know I'd find out she was dead?" I

asked. "A family like the Camerons, it's not like there wouldn't have been press coverage."

He attempted a smile. He tried to speak, shut his mouth and swallowed. Tried again. "I looked at the wrong things," he muttered. "I stared at the surface, but I only saw the reflection. I never tried to break the mirror . . ." He gazed off into space, his eyes unfocused.

I wondered again about drugs.

He spoke quietly. "I made a mistake about the notebook. It's a fraud. I should never have taken it seriously."

"I can have my friend destroy it, save you the bother," I ventured.

"No! Please. Don't torment me. If you have it, give it back. This could be the last chance."

Last chance for what? For whom?

"Does this have anything to do with Garnet Cameron possibly dropping out of the governor's race? Is that why you need the notebook back?"

"No. Absolutely not." He stopped, regained his composure with effort. "You'll want compensation for your work."

"I didn't get a chance to do much."

"I don't leave debts unpaid," he said, counting bills on to a corner of my desk, stuffing them under the blotter. "Thank you. I'm truly sorry to have troubled you."

As he retreated I said, "Mr. Mayhew, if I can help you in any way—"

"Oh, you have, my dear. I'll call in a couple of days, retrieve the manuscript. Just forget about me now. A silly game, an old man's fancy—"

His footsteps echoed as he clattered across the floorboards, changed to a lower note as he pounded down the front steps, stumbled along the walkway. I could barely see his car. I heard a powerful engine rev before he could possibly have gotten behind the wheel.

His traveling companion hadn't come inside.

Dammit. I should have escorted him to his vehicle, brought a flashlight to shine on his back plate.

I sat in my chair, leaned back and propped my feet on the desk, remembered the money. I'd need to pay Roz for a useless day's work.

The putt-putt of an aged motorbike drew me to the front window like a moth to flame. Too late. I couldn't make out anything beyond the noise, the semi-rhythmic sputter. It turned the corner, faded away.

The bills on my desk weren't twenties. Four were hundreds, the rest fifties, which, minus Roz's pay, made it eleven hundred bucks for seventy-two pages of Xeroxing and a Chinese lunch.

Dammit, again. I hate being underpaid. I hate being overpaid. "Overpaid" feels too much like "bought."

11

I sat at my desk and ran both hands through my hair, searching for knots, tangles, split ends. Examining and yanking the offending strands, a few nonoffenders as well. The medical term is "trichotillomania;" that's what doctors call the compulsion to pull hair. In extreme form, it leads to total baldness.

I become a trichotillomaniac when I'm frustrated, when my judgment, which I rely on, has proved utterly false. I'd fallen for Mayhew and his missing author. And now I'd lied, refused to return the suspect manuscript.

Good thing I have an overabundance of hair. Unmanageable bushy red hair. I bisected a strand, wound it around my index finger. Maybe I could tie it there, as a reminder not to believe every nutcase who walked in my door.

When the phone rang I almost let the machine handle it. I practice, but I never quite manage the seemingly simple process of call screening. I think it's because my mom always grabbed the phone first ring, answering in a quavery alto, convinced my cop dad was lying in a gutter bleeding to death. Never happened. He was never injured in the line of duty. Nicotine killed him, not lead.

The hello was pleasant, deep, warm, and female. Gloria's voice is a gospel-tinged marvel, welcome as fresh air. That's why she's the best damn cab dispatcher in Boston. Or was, until they blew the company out from under her.

"Babe," she said, "you givin' my phone number to strangers?"

"How are you, Gloria?"

"Fine. Pretty good for the shape I'm in."

Gloria's shape is round. Rotund. Fat, to put it bluntly. I thought she'd keep off the pounds she'd shed in the hospital. For a while, after her brother Marvin died, she'd refused her favorite junk food delights. Then one day, potato chips, malted balls, M&M's, and Reese's Pieces called to her soul and brought her back to the land of the living. She eats, therefore she is.

She said, "I got a call here from a Mr. Emerson—we're talkin' 'bout a man so stiff he sounds like he wears a coat and tie to bed—inquirin' for a Miss Carlyle. Am I your secretary these days?"

I keep a variety of business cards on my person. Some identify me as a realtor, some an insurance company employee. They're cheap to print and seem to give people confidence. They feature different phone numbers.

"Sorry," I said. "I must have played the wrong card. Did you string him along?"

"Of course, babe."

"What did Mr. Emerson want?"

"Just that you return his call immediately: 555-8330. You got that? Emphasis on fast, as in right now. Hell, I'm scared to keep you on the line."

"Might as well." I'd been fired. I had no further interest in the Avon Hill School and their precious alumnae. That's what half of me was thinking. The other half was busily refusing to accept what Mooney had said, what Mayhew hadn't denied. I wanted to hang on to this case, hang on to Thea.

Thea Janis, murdered, all her promise laid to rest.

"Heard from Sam?" Gloria asked, way too casually.

My antennae tingled. Gloria has a deep-seated interest in keeping Sam and me together. I don't know why, but in the depths of her fantasies, Sam and I are Gloria's dream couple. Maybe it's because she introduced us, watched as we made the too-quick transition from boss and worker to friends and finally lovers, enjoyed each step vicariously. We couldn't be more different, Sam and I, more ill-matched. Mix one former cop with the son of a family of robbers: It's no recipe for bliss.

"Postcard or two," I said tersely.

"Honey, I been meaning to say this for some time—"

Whenever someone says that to you, take my advice, hang up.

Gloria said, "Why the hell don't you drop that shrink? You think you need some kinda analysis, go ahead and pay for it. That man's no good for you."

"Gloria, what makes you think you know what's good for me?"

"If Sam was good for you, that headshrinker can't be. No way."

"I'll tell you a secret, Gloria."

"Yeah."

"Sam wasn't that good."

"Come on."

"Gloria, let's change the subject and stay friends."

"You ain't gonna marry that doc?"

"Marry? Gloria, I tried it once, I'm not going to try it again. If I ever send you a wedding invitation, call Mooney and have him lock me up. I mean it."

Her laugh was a gigantic musical bubble. I gave it the raspberry.

She said, "Paolina call you?"

"No."

"She called me. From a pay phone in town. Paid with her own money." There was immense satisfaction in her voice. For a corresponding moment, I felt deserted and jealous. Why hadn't my little sister phoned me?

"That gal is such a sweetie, wanted to know how I was doin' and all. Maybe being alone up at that camp made her understand a little bit what I been feeling since Marvin died. She's one darlin' child."

I said, "Do you think she's lonely? Is she making any friends?"

I could almost see Gloria shrug her enormous shoulders. She can move her torso. The auto accident that left her paralyzed at nineteen did its damage from the waist down.

"Did she want anything?" I asked.

"Just asked if she could send me some candy."

"Look, Gloria, are you busy?"

"Why?"

"I need information on Paolina's biological father. Do you have access to phones?"

"I'm dispatching for ITOA."

"I wouldn't want to get the indies in trouble," I said. ITOA is the Independent Taxi Owners Association.

"What kind of trouble?"

"The guy with the goods is a nasty Florida drug lawyer. Number one: I'm sure he's got caller ID, and he's not going to respond to any calls from my line. Number two: DEA's got his phone tapped."

"So you want me to dial him? Mess with the DEA? No thanks."

"What I was about to say, Glory, is that the ideal situation would be to place calls from folks we don't particularly like, let the DEA get a fix on them."

Gloria said, "I do enjoy the way your mind works."

"I've got a little list," I said. "Operation Rescue. Citizens for Limited Taxation, Mass. Militia."

Gloria chimed in with, "How 'bout that guy at Harvard, one wrote *The Bell Curve*? Book saying how blacks are generally just stupider than whites? I think the DEA ought to pay him a visit."

"You get his number and figure out how to make the calls from his office, you can dial Thurman W. Vandenburg ten times a day."

"I know somebody who can work pure magic with call forwarding."

"I knew you were the one to handle this."

"I'll need some money for a payoff or two, but I'll do it. It's a deal. What should the message be?"

"Ought to be in my voice."

For a while all I could hear was the whirr of Gloria's

mechanized wheelchair. "I got tape spooling. Go right ahead."

It took a few tries to get it right.

"Thurman, babe," I said, like I'd called the shark "Thurman" all my life. "Urgent I know CRG's status pronto. Call C., in loco parentis."

"Guess that's okay," Gloria said doubtfully. "Can't we add some stuff about wanting that shipment of coke fast? So people get in deep shit?"

"Long as it's not me."

"Trust me, babe. I got contacts everywhere. Phone company practically has to ask my permission before they install a new line."

I believed her. Gloria isn't mobile. She uses phones like weapons. She's the spider at the center of a communications network that puts the Internet to shame.

I tried again. "Thurman, babe, you want those twenty keys, you gotta tell C. about CRG. Pronto." I left out the "parentis" bit. The fewer people who had any idea that Carlos Roldan Gonzales had a kid, the better.

"He might ignore it," Gloria said.

"Not if he gets the call every hour," I said. "Twenty-four hours a day."

"Heavy annoyance," she said.

"That's what I want, Gloria. Heavy annoyance."

"You came to the right place."

"Anybody pisses you off, call from there."

I gave Gloria Thurman W. Vandenburg's private number with confidence. We share the same set of pet peeves: rich folks who resent paying for government services, Bible-thumping folks who want everybody to act the way they do, hypocrites, bedroom peepers, privacy invaders.

"Make me a copy of the tape, okay?" I said. "Any place you can't get access, I'll turn Roz loose."

"Fun, fun, fun at the DEA this week," Gloria said. "Paolina's daddy up to something?"

"I don't know," I said. "I'd like to find out."

Gloria said, "I plan to enjoy this."

"And if I happen to find myself at a creep's house, I'll give Vandenburg a ring," I said.

"You do that, but make sure you use the exact same words as the tape, okay, so we get the DEA going." Gloria's voice got soft and sweet. "You might try calling from your shrink's house."

I hung up, quickly punched the number she'd given me.

Two rings. Pickup.

"Avon Hill School. Emerson speaking."

"Hi," I said. "This is the woman who visited your campus today, Carlotta Carlyle."

"Miss Carlyle, I'm so glad you rang back. My wife was unaware that several of our prospective students have chosen to attend other—"

"It doesn't matter," I said. "I don't have any Colombian nieces who want to go to Avon Hill."

"You're—"

"Not interested. It's okay, Mr. Emerson. I was hired to find a former student. I found her."

"You're some sort of investigator?"

"Private sort."

Silence. He didn't end the call. Neither did I.

"May I ask for whom you were looking?"

Confidentiality didn't seem to matter.

"Thea Janis. Dorothy Cameron. Either name ring a bell? Was she a classmate of yours?"

Silence.

"Would you mind coming over?" he asked very softly.

"Why?"

"It seems odd that Thea should be of such interest after all these years."

"What do you mean?"

"I'd prefer to discuss the matter in person."

"I can be there in ten minutes," I said. Chatting with Anthony Emerson might make me feel as if I'd done something to earn the cash Mayhew'd left behind.

"Come to the school," he said hurriedly. "Not the house."

12

More folks than usual strolled the late night streets, seeking relief from the heat, wearing minimal clothing, several—probably on the way home from Steve's in the Square—licking ice cream cones. Mooney's warning had made me extraordinarily conscious of passersby. I watched. I listened. I cataloged their attire. No footsteps seemed to dog my own. At a quick march, I made it to Avon Hill in seven minutes.

The porch light was off. I didn't get a chance to bang the huge brass knocker. The door opened, eerie creak and all, as soon as I lifted my foot to the first step.

"Miss Carlyle?" He'd been waiting.

"Yes."

"So you have no students to place with us?" he said, his mouth twisting in a rueful grin.

"If I did, they'd need full scholarships."

He shook his head regretfully while I wondered if the school rested on firm financial ground.

"Have you a license?" he asked, still blocking the doorway. "Any document that would assure me that you really are an investigator?"

I gave a sigh. "Look, you invited me over to talk, Mr. Emerson. I had my exercise. I can make it a quick round-trip."

He hesitated only briefly.

"Please," he said. "Come in."

He was a slender man, hiding inside a well-tailored suit too heavy for the heat. His hair, a sleek blond pelt, was so fine that, despite attempts at a ruler-straight part, strands escaped every which way. His long, beaky nose looked like it might twitch at any moment. I'd expected his eyes to be cool blue, but they were brown, dark and deep, nestled in creased pouches that made him older than he appeared.

He'd be thirty-nine if he'd been Thea's classmate.

We walked down the ill-lit trophy corridor toward a room I took to be his office. Large, imposing mahogany desk with matching bookshelves. Persian rugs in reds, oranges, and browns, a leather sofa. Walls hung with gilt-framed diplomas. An airy sanctum in which to greet parents willing to drop large sums in exchange for the cachet of saying, "Yes, our daughter is at Avon Hill. Yours?" Knowing Avon Hill could be equaled but not one-upped.

Perhaps the headmaster kept a more casual work-room elsewhere. This office would do nicely for cadging checks from parents. And for discipline. Scare a kid to death in here. Afraid he'd knock over a vase.

One book sat on the desktop. A yearbook, an elaborate endeavor in a tooled leather binding. A gold satin ribbon marked one of the middle pages.

I showed Emerson my investigator's license. As if offering an even exchange, he asked if I'd like to see Thea's picture.

"Sure."

He waved me toward a plush armchair. "She wasn't the sort who did clubs and sports and rah-rah events. But someone shot a candid. Here. You can see her profile."

The gold ribbon marked the yearbook page. The snap showed little in the way of facial delineation. Thea's breasts jutted assertively. At fourteen, fifteen, she'd had a woman's body, a woman's stance.

"Is this the only photo of her in the whole yearbook?"

"Yes," he said, a bit defensively. "Like I said, she wasn't into clubs, and she never showed for her homeroom picture. It's not as though she were a senior."

Thea'd never made it that far in life, I thought. *Never gotten to be a lousy high school senior.*

"You were her classmate?"

"As much as anyone," he said.

I wished he'd been home earlier in the day. I'd have preferred questioning him while I believed that Thea might be alive.

"We would have graduated the same year," he continued, "if she hadn't—run off."

"Why do you say 'run off'? Why not 'if she hadn't been murdered'?"

His disapproval showed in the tight line of his lips. "I suppose because early speculation centered on with whom she had, uh, eloped."

"Was there a clear favorite?"

Seated in his towering leather chair, behind his wide mahogany desk, he steepled his hands and looked pensive. I wondered if his feet touched the ground. I also wondered how he'd come to rule at his former prep school. Had it been a lifelong ambition?

He said, "At the very beginning, every boy in school probably whispered to his best friend—you know, in complete confidence—that Thea was waiting for him at his parents' summerhouse. That kind of talk stopped quickly."

"What about the teachers?"

"We called them 'masters,' then, because Avon Hill was fighting hard to keep up the old traditions, to ignore the rebellious times. The campus was seething underneath, but on the surface, all was extremely proper."

His pronunciation was faintly British, as though he'd taken classes in the U.K. The accent could have been pure pretension served up for the bill-paying parents, but I didn't think so.

"The 'masters,' then," I said. "Was there talk that Thea'd 'eloped' with one of them?"

He shrugged. "I shared a single class with her. The teacher was a woman."

"Rumors? Speculation?"

"There were rumors about Thea and every man or boy in the entire school."

"Why?"

"She was . . . unusual," he said, fiddling with a shiny fountain pen as he spoke. "For her age. For any age. For this extraordinarily conservative school. My God, the simple fact that her parents sent her here is beyond belief. She was so out of place she could have come from another planet."

"But she managed to communicate with the natives."

"Her disgust, mainly."

"How?"

"By refusing to do whatever anyone in authority told her to do. She was our rebellion poster girl. The rest of us didn't have a clue. We were all so terrified we might be expelled, shame our families forever. And that's what she seemed to want most. She courted expulsion. She was so free . . ."

"Free," I repeated.

"Gloriously free," he said. "In many ways." He fidgeted in his chair and refused to meet my eyes. He seemed caught between wanting to tell me something and wanting to keep it to himself. I wondered how many of his students responded to questioning in the same shifty way, torn between the mingled joys of confession and secret sin.

"Why did you want to talk to me?" I asked, trying to keep anger and impatience out of my voice.

The anger and impatience weren't aimed at him. I was my own target. I shouldn't have come. Why was I there, making inquiries about a dead woman? What did I hope to learn? There was no case, no cause. Just curiosity. Because of a single chapter, some poetry.

"We had rather strange visitors the other day," he said, his manner abruptly casual. The business with the visitors wasn't what he'd been tempted to confess.

"We?" I said.

"I," he said with a smile. "You've caught me in my headmaster 'we.' I'll do my best to avoid it. Promise."

"And the other day was?"

"Wednesday last, the eighth."

"What made the visitors strange?"

Standing, he wasn't more than five-eight, but he cut an elegant figure. He kept his hands clasped behind him as he paced. His stride seemed mannered, studied: This is the way a headmaster walks and talks. Maybe he'd read a book about it, taken a course.

He spoke. "It's summer. Almost everyone's away. If my wife weren't feeling so poorly, we'd be at our cottage in Maine."

I let him take it slowly, ramble on. I had time to kill.

He said, "They were street urchins. Beggars." He pursed his lips around the words, made his visitors sound like characters from a Dickens novel.

"Street kids," I said.

"The boy was older than a kid—a man, I suppose, under all that . . . hair. I'd put him in his early twenties. He had a walk, a strut, an attitude, if you know what I mean, but the girl was very young, twelve, possibly thirteen. She was carrying a blanket, a tablecloth, some piece of fabric. I assumed they were looking for a place to fool around. I went to order them off the property before they went at it underneath the trees or in the shrubbery. None of the gardeners was present and I thought someone ought to remind them that they were trespassing."

I nodded. I'd seen the lush backyard. The gardeners were probably given orders to keep the overhanging foliage to a minimum during the school term.

"They weren't the least bit fazed by my approach. I admit, I'm used to a certain respect from students. I don't know, maybe I've gotten used to cringing cowards. I have power over the teens in my charge. The young man was positively brazen. I couldn't stare him down. I considered calling the police, and believe me, I would not do that lightly. Several parents live close by and I wouldn't like them to think I can't handle any situation that might arise. But I didn't like the way he looked at me. I didn't like his grin. It seemed—predatory. And then, out of the blue, they asked about Thea. Whether this was the school that Thea Janis, the writer, the famous writer, had attended. They wanted to know if there were a memorial dedicated to her, a 'shrine.' They were laughing, stoned or high on something, drunk, but they used the word 'shrine.' And then they asked if I could give them a photograph of Thea. Like Avon Hill was a Grade-B movie studio, and I was some flak who made the rounds to hand out glossies."

He was indignant at such a slight to himself and his school. I moved on, asking, "Can you describe them in greater detail? What were they wearing?"

"The male was slim, almost emaciated. Height, well, he had a couple inches on me. Dirty T-shirt, ripped jeans stuffed into high black boots. His hair was quite dark, slicked into a ponytail, and his beard was straggly, like he hadn't really intended to grow one, just forgotten to shave. Oh, and he wore an earring, a silver dangle. The girl was a wispy blonde, practically a child, like I said, but she was all over the man, rubbing herself against him, touching him.

"I outwaited them, just stood my ground until they took off on one of those horribly loud motorbikes. The seat wasn't really big enough for two, but the girl snuggled up for all she was worth, wrapping her arms around his chest. She was wearing, well, it looked like a man's singlet, cut off so her midriff showed, and cutoff jeans, too. Sliced so high you could see she'd neglected underpants. I mean, her entire 'look' had been manufactured with a scissors!"

"License plate?"

"Didn't think about it."

I'll bet he didn't; too busy thinking about the young blond chick on the back of the cycle, breasts pressed into the young man's back, thighs clutching his butt.

"Color? Make?" I asked to snap him out of his reverie.

"Sorry. Red, maybe."

"Did the engine sound okay?"

"The engine? I'm sorry, I honestly wasn't paying attention."

"Anything else about them. Their names?"

"We didn't introduce ourselves."

"Did they call each other by name?"

"He called her something. Dixie? An odd name."

"Which one brought up Thea Janis?"

"The man."

"Has anyone else come inquiring about Thea Janis?"

"No, and it's not like these two were collecting data for a biography. She's rather gone out of style, I guess, all that rebellion, and inner searching, and early death. I mean, she may be popular at other schools, but we certainly don't teach anything so modern or so . . . sexual at Avon Hill. We're very proper here. The board is quite concerned that my wife remain indoors during the latter part of her pregnancy. That's how advanced we are." One of his eyebrows rose a quarter of an inch. His eyes twinkled to let me know that he found the behavior of the board inexplicable, but somehow amusing. Quaint. Like his British accent.

"I'd like to know why you're interested in Thea," he murmured. "Coincidence, two inquiries in one week."

I ignored his question. Before I left I wanted to know his secret, the one he couldn't quite decide whether to tell.

"How did your classmates react when they found out Thea had written a book?" I asked. He could have tossed me out, but he seemed willing, eager to reminisce.

"Well, at first, we didn't know it was *her* book. It was Thea Janis, not Dorothy Cameron, after all. But we soon found out. It was in the newspapers. We bought every copy in the Square, trying to see if she'd nailed anyone we could identify."

"Had she?"

"Not really. I mean, she used the school cleverly. Her characters had some of the traits of one master or another, but she'd done a good job of changing names and faces. I was just a kid, but I doubt there was talk of legal action. Thea was practically famous. Notorious. And she seemed suddenly different."

"How different? In what way?"

"We stopped calling her Dorothy immediately, called her Thea instead." He stretched out both vowels, gave the name a foreign caress. "It was so romantic. We started watching the way she moved. She *was* different from the other girls. We knew that."

His eyes had taken on their naughty-boy look again.

"By 'different,' do you mean Thea was sexually experienced?" I asked. "Is that what we're dancing around here?"

He sat in his chair. His lips moved as he considered what to say, how best to clothe his thoughts in words.

"She was certainly not a whore," he said finally. " 'Make love, not war,' was the slogan of the times, and free love had obviously found her. She was its exponent. She was—"

"Avon Hill's free-love poster girl."

"That seemed to be one of her ambitions in life, yes."

"You slept with her?"

He lowered his voice as though he expected his words to carry from the great stone house to the smaller Victorian nearby, disturb the dreams of his pregnant wife.

"We were an entire school of virgins waiting to be deflowered," he said, avoiding the singular pronoun.

"And she was the experienced one. At fourteen?"

"Fifteen. She seemed to know what she was doing."

"Who taught her?"

"It seemed to me she had a natural talent for it, as pronounced as her literary talent. A talent for sex."

"Did her teachers grade her highly?"

"There was speculation. I have no idea what was true and what was fantasy, but the gossip didn't seem to hurt her. She was beyond us, older than we were in some fundamental way. None of our lies and exaggerations seemed to touch her. We made up Thea stories. Thea and the aged algebra master. Thea and the gym master. That one was very popular. Thea and the gardener, Thea and the captain of Harvard's football team. She was our group fantasy."

"Was she promiscuous?"

"Not to my knowledge."

"She was fourteen when she wrote the book, fifteen when she died!" I said sharply, wanting to knock the self-satisfied grin off his face.

It only spurred him to self-defense.

"Not like any fifteen-year-old you've ever met, lady. I'm sorry, but you won't make me feel guilty. I slept with her. She seduced me and not the other way around. She abandoned me and not the other way around. I didn't drive her from this school. And none of us had anything to do with her death. That animal who slaughtered her had no idea . . ."

"Had no idea what?"

"He must have thought her an ordinary—"

Words seemed to fail him.

"An ordinary whore," I supplied. "Tart? Wench?"

"Girl," he said softly. "He couldn't have known what a terrible loss, what a terrible thing he did."

"Worse than killing the two other girls?"

"This may sound wrong; it may sound like elitist snobbery, it probably is. But Thea was special. I grieve for Mozart's early death in a way I do not grieve the ordinary peasant's death."

"You were here, at school, when you found out she was dead?"

"It knocked the breath out of me. We had placed her center-stage in so many exotic locales, in so many bizarre fantasies . . ."

"And afterward? After her death?"

"What do you think? Thea became a living lesson to us. Don't take rides from strangers. Don't take walks late at night. Don't. Don't. Don't. In a way, her death marked the end of our innocence."

"I thought she'd already stolen that," I said.

"I never meant to say she corrupted me. She didn't corrupt anyone. She was a wonderful girl. Troubled. Generous. Confused, and confusing."

A helpful assessment, I thought.

I wished I knew more about the circumstances of Thea's death. I should have grilled Mooney. As if he'd have kept his ear glued to the phone just to indulge me.

I said, "I understand Thea called home, said she was spending the night with a friend who lived near school."

"Now that was a giant laugh."

"What do you mean?"

"Said she was staying with Susie Alfred, stuck-up little bitch wouldn't have let Thea in her hallowed home."

"Why not?"

"The prim and proper disapproved of Thea."

"So why the phone call? Was it a hoax?"

He shrugged.

Kids don't usually call home and set things up so they won't be missed. Not kids who get killed.

I pressed harder. "So what did Thea do from the time she left Avon Hill till the time she died? What was it, two, three days? More?"

"No one knows."

"No one knows," I repeated.

I hate answers like that. Solemn, pompous, asinine. Emerson's office seemed to close around me and choke me. I said my farewells as politely as I could. He asked for my phone number and I told him he could reach me at the number he had. Let him filter his salacious fantasies through Gloria.

I felt used, dirty. He'd wanted to tell someone that he'd had a fling with a beautiful girl when he was the same age as his incoming students. His pregnant wife was probably not an appreciative audience.

"Did you read her book?" I asked him as we walked toward the front door.

"Parts of it," he said lightly.

I could bet which parts.

"If you hear from the kids again, the ones who asked about Thea, would you give me a ring?" I asked.

"Sure," he said with an easy grin, opening the door to usher me out.

Lying, ten to one.

13

In my dreams an engine revved, sputtering to a loud and angry whine, close and threatening. The Windbreaker Man rode a red motorbike, perfectly balanced, arms outspread like some gigantic bird of prey. Soundlessly he swooped up girls in his path—teens in pleated navy skirts, crisp white blouses—dropped them at my feet, broken and bleeding, their heads lolling like rag dolls.

I woke up sweating. Heat and light seared my eyelids. Half-waking, half woozy, I panicked, unable to open my eyes, afraid to peer into the fiery abyss. I blinked. Just the sun burning through gauzy curtains, eating the morning haze.

The toothpaste oozed from the tube like a melted

candy cane. I washed my hair, not because it was dirty, but because the cold water felt so good.

I hate the heat.

I hated the fact that Adam Mayhew had chickened out. I hated the glorified guiltlessness of Avon Hill, the easy innocence of its headmaster.

I unlocked my desk drawer and reread Thea's thirty-six pages. A perfect family sits down to a beautifully laid table. Fine china, crystal, and silver gleam in the candlelight. An elaborate multicourse dinner is served, and although insects crawl over their bare feet and snakes twine about their ankles, no one is so gauche as to mention the invasion.

It reminded me of something written by one of the South American magical realists—a Colombian whose books I'd studied in an effort to understand the land of Paolina's heritage.

In Thea's work, the character dubbed "d" was a poet, shunned by the gracious family. "b" spoke in an unheard monotone, telling herself endless repeated stories that made no sense. "b" alone admitted the existence of the reptiles, but seemed unaware of the bugs.

Roz tripped downstairs in a short excuse for a dress, possibly a tunic. Her sandal laces crisscrossed to her knees. She appeared unfazed by the weather. Before I could stop her, she plunked a bulging file folder on my desk, planted her feet in an approximation of ballet's third position, and began her recitation.

"First thing," she said, "I don't have quite as much crap as they wrote about Chuck and Di, but that's probably because most of this stuff is older. I mean, it dates back to when the press was still sharpening its canines."

Maybe if I hadn't just reread "Thea's" chapter, if I

hadn't been buoyed by the magic of her words, I'd have stopped Roz cold. Mesmerized, I let her speak.

"Old man Cameron, that's the Honorable Franklin Cameron, the late U.S. representative from the Fourth Congressional District, was some big deal. Old money, fleets of ships, China trade— You want to know about his mom and dad?"

"Not particularly."

She ignored me, a not unusual state of affairs.

"His dad married money, twice. Had a knack for it. So we got China trade money comingling with Robber Baron money. Nice combo. Enough to get their kid— that's Franklin, father of Garnet—a major league law school education. We're talking Yale here, maybe buy the family a little something, like the presidency. But it seems our Franklin balked at a life of public service. Did a stint in the DA's office, served on the Governor's Council, but couldn't win the big ones. Lost the governorship once, the Senate three times, finally made it to the House of Representatives in 1962. A one-term guy."

"Scandal?" I inquired automatically. Once elected to the House from the Commonwealth of Massachusetts, it's a rare bird who returns north.

"Not a breath," Roz answered. "Not a hint. Not a murmur. The man said he didn't like living in D.C."

I wondered what the real story was. In the early sixties, some matters weren't fit to print in a family newspaper.

"And he never ran for district rep?"

"Nope. Governor or nothing far as local stuff went."

"Kids," I said. "It's the kids I'm mainly interested in."

"No kids from his first marriage. Had it annulled.

Three from his marriage to—get this—the Contessa de la Montefiore, aka Tourmaline Montefiore. *Tourmaline,* right. Family calls her Tessa and I, for one, forgive them. Even if she did give her own kids weirdo names. Beryl's the oldest, born 1950. Then Garnet. Then just plain Dorothy."

Odd. I'd imagined Dorothy—Thea—as the oldest child.

"Which one are you interested in?"

"Dorothy."

"The dead one. Too bad."

"Yeah," I agreed wholeheartedly. "Too bad."

"It was a four-week wonder. A total circus. I don't think I copied all the news articles, but I got most of them."

"Summary?"

"Headlines: 'MISSING!'; 'RUNAWAY WRITER!'; 'SUICIDE?'; 'HEIRESS KIDNAPPED!'; then 'HEIRESS MURDERED!!!' They didn't run with the suicide more than a day, just long enough to mention that there was family precedent. It was big-time stuff. I mean, when they nailed the killer, a couple papers ran her photo with a black border around it, like she was the President or something."

"Go back to the suicide."

She shuffled paper. "Veiled suggestions that someone else named Cameron had given it a try. Then the kidnapping stories swamped it."

Beryl? I wondered. "b" for Beryl, who sat at the perfect table and mumbled under her breath? The one who saw the snakes. Or Tessa. Had she found an effective way to keep her husband from returning to Washington?

I guess I shouldn't have dismissed Garnet or Franklin

Cameron from the suicide sweepstakes, but statistics bear me out. Men succeed at suicide more often, but a greater number of women try it on. The classic "cry for help."

"Family reaction to Dorothy's death?"

Roz frowned, searching for a word. "Muted. I got the feeling the family was holed up, saying 'no comment' for all they were worth, and the journalists were writing whatever the hell they felt like writing. You ought to read the bilge."

She tapped the folder. Maybe I would.

"I got some great stuff on the funeral. It was like a fashion show, swear to God, an all-white funeral. If the family'd wanted to feed the press frenzy they couldn't have done a better job. Here's this kid who's written a scandalous book, and she's getting the 'virgin special' funeral. Not one, but two cardinals presiding."

I glanced at the page of flowing script in my hand, gently closed the calligrapher's notebook. "Adam Mayhew" couldn't have missed such an ostentatious funeral.

"Well, don't get all excited and tell me what a great job I did," Roz said, finally sensing that she wasn't getting the desired reaction. "Just pay me and tell me what else I can do. I bought a videocam. On credit."

"I didn't know you had a credit card."

"I do now. I listed you as a reference. If they call, can you tell them you pay me, like, three hundred a week?"

"In your dreams, Roz."

"Come on. Let me dig more on this totally pseudo Mayhew chump. He's lying like a rug. Thea's mom—La Contessa—she's still alive, and she never had any brothers, step, half, or otherwise. There's no Mayhew comma Adam in any local phone book."

"There's an Adam Mayhew in Mount Auburn Cemetery."

Roz's eyes narrowed. "How do you know?"

"I took a field trip." I bit my lower lip, glanced through Roz's scrawled notes and news clippings. "What can you tell me about Beryl Cameron?"

"Beryl? For the past twenty years, she might as well be dead."

"The brilliant Thea's only sister? She must have done *something* newsworthy. Her marriage would rate a Sunday Magazine special feature."

"Yeah, you'd think. She's in all the press photos, all the late great Franklin Cameron's campaign stuff, throughout the sixties. She's in there stumping with the family, the girls wearing those god-awful matching puffy white dresses and little heels with anklets. I mean the socks are so retro I might give 'em a try. With stiletto heels—"

"Roz."

"Sorry. Then, after Thea's death, there's nothing."

"What do you mean, nothing?"

"Exactly one 'Women's Section' article announcing that Beryl Cameron plans to visit her mother's relatives in Italy. The writer barely mentions the girl's name, uses it as a lead for a piece on what the fashionable young debutante should pack for a trip abroad. Then it turns into a tirade against blue jeans."

"What's the date on it?"

"I think August '71."

After Thea's death. If Thea *had* been kidnapped, then murdered when something went wrong with negotiations for her release, the family might have sent their other daughter away for her safety . . .

No way. Four weeks from disappearance to death.

Hardly long enough for ransom negotiations to go so badly awry.

I doubted a kidnapping. The FBI would have tried to slap a lid on it, but after the murder every detail would have spilled across the front page. And Mooney'd said the man in Walpole had been convicted of killing two other girls besides Thea.

Maybe the family had screamed "kidnapping" to stop the suicide stories.

"So Beryl might live in Italy?" I said to Roz.

"Far as the press is concerned, she never came back. But brother Garnet, he's been busy enough for all three kids. Classic overachiever. Probably can't fit his résumé on a floppy disk, much less a single sheet of paper."

"What's he done?"

"What hasn't he done? Harvard. Yale Law. Law Review. Worked as a public prosecutor, played in a jazz band, married young, divorced young. Ran for state Attorney General, remarried, currently running for governor, as you may have noticed—"

"And his only living sister hasn't been part of his campaign?"

"Hasn't been part of his life, far as I can tell."

"Okay," I said, figuring the eleven hundred bucks could stretch a little farther. "New task: See this photo?"

"Yep. Good work."

"Could you age the subject twenty years?"

"Thea Janis? She's dead. What's the point?"

"The point is I'm willing to pay for it!" I snapped.

"Temper, temper," Roz said. "You want to waste money, I'm your girl."

Until I'd seen Thea's death certificate, held it in my hand, studied the goddamned notary's mark, I intended to believe the phony "Mayhew." I'd believe in his sincerity, if not his name. He'd been on to something. I was presuming a hell of a lot. I knew that. I work in a business where you've got to trust your hunches.

"Can you age her?" I asked Roz.

"She was a looker, huh?"

"If she were alive, would she still be a looker?"

"Bones are bones," Roz said, "but you can do a hell of a lot of damage. I mean, she could weigh four hundred pounds, she could have AIDS."

"Do two or three versions," I said. "No extremes. A little chunky, a little skinny, on target."

"How old is she in the picture?"

"Fourteen."

"So she'd be, what, thirty-four?"

"Thirty-nine."

Roz's eyes lit. "It's gonna cost."

"I know. And you can do one more thing."

"Big bucks in this case."

"Roz, it's practically over. But for the hell of it, find me a 1954 Harvard yearbook."

She opened her mouth, closed it, tried again. "How?"

"I don't care, Roz. Impersonate someone. Walk up and down Brattle Street, bang doors, say you're on a scavenger hunt."

"A 1954 yearbook."

"I want a picture of any graduating senior with the initials A.M."

"Girl or boy?"

"Roz, listen up. You think they let girls into Harvard in 1954?"

It was too hot to contemplate volleyball. I tried to write Paolina a cheery letter, tossed three attempts.

I craved iced coffee, but found myself too lazy to make it. I settled for a breakfast Pepsi accompanied by the world's sourest plum. Roz does the groceries. She has a knack for produce.

I did routine stuff, typing and filing, sending out bills along with one mildly threatening third reminder to pay up or deal with a nonexistent collection agency. Wrote out an account of the Janis/Cameron non-case based on my two encounters with "Adam Mayhew," and my interview with Mr. Anthony Emerson of Avon Hill.

I found myself dawdling over the report. I couldn't help it; I didn't want the case to end. I didn't want Thea dead. My mind kept inventing other scenarios. With Beryl so unsung by the press, I wondered if she could have died, while Thea lived on in obscurity. Writing, but not publishing, perhaps fearful, like other prodigies I'd heard of, that she'd lost her gift along with her youth, afraid she could never live up to such early promise.

Mooney would have laughed at me. When I was a cop he always used to say my imagination would get me in deep trouble. Murderers don't confess for the hell of it, he'd say. And if they do, they don't wind up at Walpole State Prison. A judge and a jury see to that. Still . . .

I found myself in profound sympathy with the man who'd called himself Adam Mayhew. If I, never knowing Thea, wanted so badly to believe her alive, imagine how someone who'd been close to her, who'd cherished her, might feel.

When I started dripping sweat on the pages, I quit and took another shower.

The phone rang while I was in the rinse cycle. I

hopped out, grabbed a towel, and stumbled into my room in time to lift the receiver.

"My house has central air conditioning. The sheets are cool. The wine's on ice."

"And me totally naked. I'll be right over."

"Throw a robe on," Keith Donovan said, ever conservative.

I suppose I've slept with a considerable number of guys, but Keith Donovan's my first psychiatrist, far as I know. Before you label me an indiscriminate tramp, allow me to defend my honor, such as it is, by telling you that I went through a rough time after my first and only husband deserted me for cocaine and the blues circuit. A shrink might say my self-esteem was badly bruised. He might say I needed to prove I was still desirable. I proved it, for a few weeks, with a vengeance. Thank God Cal left me before AIDS became epidemic or I wouldn't be here.

That brief adventure in one-night-stands is why I'm not quite sure whether Donovan's my first psychiatrist. It's not like I cut notches in my belt.

Sex always lands me in trouble. Don't get me wrong. I didn't start out as early as Thea, and I'm not ready or cut out for a life of celibacy. I merely have this unfortunate tendency to get involved with one Mr. Wrong after another. Some last for years, out of inertia, chemistry, whatever.

With Donovan, the sex part's fine. I have the feeling that his profession will turn out to be the fatal flaw. I have no desire to be part of an article in the *American Journal of Psychiatry* entitled "Women and Guns in Bed."

He had a brief affair with Roz before I became interested and available. That alone makes me suspicious of the man's motivation.

Other than that, he's young, handsome, blond, and conveniently located. So much for my motivation.

Keith's house puts mine to shame. The mahogany handrail gleams along the staircase. The polished oak floorboards shine. He makes his bed with matching sheets.

His profession occasionally comes in handy. I can always get a question answered. The man will talk.

"Something to drink?" he said, holding open the door, just in case I hadn't taken time to dress. I had. The neighbors gossip enough.

He ducked into the kitchen to grab a bottle of wine nested in ice cubes, all in a silver bucket. Crystal glasses were poised on his desk, as if they were waiting to have their picture taken for a glossy magazine. Keith uses his entire living room as an office, leaving precious little space for social intercourse. I settled on a square of hunter green carpet.

The Chardonnay was rich and buttery.

"Acacia," he said as he poured, as if it should mean something other to me than expensive, which it obviously was.

I seem to have acquired a penchant for rich lovers. My mother, she should rest in peace, would have found that far more deplorable than promiscuity. Mom was a free spirit. Lovers, yes. Rich, no. Neither she nor my Scots-Irish Catholic father had much use for the Bible, except for the parts castigating the wealthy. I grew up hearing about a steady stream of rich men, camels, and eyes of needles. The message gradually made sense as I grew older.

I took another drink of amber bliss. Keith sank

down beside me. I decided the carpet would be hot, so I stayed upright.

I said, "Talk to me about sexually precocious girls."

"Is this kinky? Do you want to peel your jeans off first?"

"This is business: A fourteen-year-old who seduces prep school boys, possibly teachers as well."

"The five-cent version is: 'Lookin' for love in all the wrong places.' "

"Would she be happy?"

"Miserable. Low self-esteem."

Didn't sound like Thea, polished author, feted poet.

"Would you be surprised if the girl left school, killed herself?" I asked.

"No."

"Why would a young man she seduced say that she was totally into 'free love,' that she initiated everything, controlled everything?"

"Because it lets him off the hook."

"Okay."

"That's all? Okay? Has the girl attempted suicide? Can she get into analysis?"

"Relax. It happened over twenty years ago. You were a baby."

"Was not."

"Were, too."

"I wondered about the 'free love.' You don't hear that much about 'free love' anymore."

" 'Cause there's a price," I said.

We took the wine upstairs and bypassed the day's heat under smooth percale. A restless sleeper at best, I decided to give him a break and venture home around eleven. The night air felt warm and sticky as I scampered across two front yards to my door, holding my sandals, giving the neighbors something to talk about.

The red light on my message machine was going nuts when I came in. Six messages.

Sometimes a week goes by and I don't get six calls.

The phone rang before I had a chance to touch the replay button. Goddamn crazy night. Hot nights are the worst for cops. People go nuts with the heat, attack their best friends, their lovers, with hammers, scissors, anything close to hand.

"You're home. I thought perhaps it is that you un-plug your phone." The voice was heavily accented, fe-male. I like most accented voices, enjoy the lilt, the music.

"Excuse me?" I said.

"Oh, pardon me. I expect a recording device, not a real person . . . I am, perhaps, unprepared."

"Who are you?" I said. It seemed like a good place to start.

"I am Tessa Cameron, Mrs. Franklin Cameron. I be-lieve you know of me."

Tessa. *Thea's mother.* Who had no brother named Adam Mayhew, no brother with the initials A.M.

"Yes," I said. "What can I do for you?"

"It is extremely urgent that I see you as soon as pos-sible. Concerning a personal matter." The voice had the superior tone of one accustomed to name-recognition. She spoke as though she were making a restaurant res-ervation at a dive that had no business expecting any-one of her status to darken their door.

"Not tonight," I said.

She hesitated as if consulting an overcrowded ap-pointment calendar. "At eleven tomorrow morning then."

She seemed certain that my life could be reordered to suit hers. She'd almost hung up before I could assure her that eleven would not be convenient for me. I made it noon, just to let her simmer.

Strictly confidential, she insisted, as though my next logical move would be a phone call to a gossip columnist.

I started revising my positive thoughts concerning accents.

"Please," she said softly, "you will bring my . . . property with you."

"I don't believe I have anything that belongs to you, Mrs. Cameron," I said. Lying is even easier over the phone.

I was ready to say good-bye when she started rattling off directions. The thought that prospective clients might come to me had never occurred to her. I mean, probably her dressmaker, her hairstylist, her personal trainer all attended her at home. Why should I be different?

Why indeed? I took careful notes thinking I'd enjoy seeing the house where Thea Janis grew up. I was glad I'd held out for noon. Maybe I could snag an invitation to lunch, check under the dining table for serpents and scorpions.

I pressed my answering machine's glowing numeral six with trepidation. By the time I'd finished listening to six messages, each from Tessa Cameron, each more demanding than the last, I figured I'd do my damnedest to place a call to Miami Vandenburg from her house.

Let the DEA deal with la Contessa Cameron.

14

At eleven-thirty Wednesday morning, Roz delivered: two yellowed pages, numbers 167 and 168, ripped from an aged yearbook binding.

"I don't suppose you considered making copies," I said.

"Hey, is the guy there or isn't he? I got all the graduating 'M's.' You said you didn't care how I got them."

"Did you kill for them?" I asked, my sarcasm confined to a raised eyebrow.

"No."

"I'm relieved," I said.

She flounced off, forgetting to demand cash on the barrelhead.

She was right; I didn't want to know how she'd gotten them.

No Adam Mayhew had graduated Harvard in 1954. Right. I scanned photos. Eye and hand stopped dead at "Andrew Manley." Same initials. Bingo. You can't visit this detective toting your monogrammed briefcase, wearing your Harvard class ring, and hope to remain incognito. I raised my glance, saw familiar eyes, familiar ears.

Adam/Andrew had aged well. According to a cryptic note underneath his individual black-and-white photo, med school lurked in his future. "Super-surgeon!" it proclaimed. Nickname: "Drew." He'd played clarinet, chess, tennis. His hair was startlingly blond, close cut. At twenty-one he'd appeared hawklike. Now his face had wrinkled and puffed into a kindly ball, the image of gentleness. Which likeness was truer to the man? Do we age into our faces? Create them by will?

My grandmother used to say that up till forty you have the face God gave you. After that, you're responsible for your own wrinkles.

She also used to say, *"In der yugnt a zoyne, oyf der elder a gabete."* Translation: "In youth a whore, in old age a model of propriety."

Hope for me yet.

Armed with proof of Drew Manley's existence, I backed the car down the narrow drive, wishing I'd had the foresight to wash it. A dusty old Toyota always impresses the wealthy clients. Not to mention arriving late for that important first meeting, which I would, unless I used every taxi-driver shortcut and bent the speed limit to boot.

I could have swung out to 128, maybe avoided some lunch hour traffic, but I decided to plow straight through Boston, taking back roads until I could get onto the VFW Parkway, headed south. As I raced along, I found myself glancing at people on the street—grouped at bus stops, sitting on park benches—trying to imagine Thea with twenty-four years of hard living sagging the smooth curve of her cheek. Would I recognize her if I passed her? If she lived next door?

I turned onto Route 109, drove quickly up Summer to Dedham Street. Signs warned of equestrian crossings. Stalls were for rent. No trespassing after dark. I hit Dover Center at six past twelve. It took another five minutes to find the Cameron estate, located off Farm Road, a narrow lane edged with stone fences, another two to navigate the long driveway, majestically lined with tall Dutch elms. Their leaves made a canopy that dappled the sunshine, half blinding me and lowering my speed.

What had "Adam Mayhew," my pseudo-client, said? "The house is big . . . rambling." Had to give the old liar credit for understatement.

I mentally composed a realtor's ad: Magnificent, professionally landscaped Colonial estate. Hilltop retreat with unique architectural details. Three magnificent stone chimneys. Circular drive leading to covered whatchamacallit—I yanked the word "porte cochere" from a deep memory recess. The offering price would be well into seven figures, surely not listed for the vulgar world to see. Like tuition at the Avon Hill School: If you need to inquire, you obviously don't belong.

I liked the porte cochere, probably because I was pleased that I knew what to call it. When the Camerons tossed a small supper party for sixty, their female guests wouldn't risk getting that little black dress drenched by rain, that mink wrap brushed by snow.

The main house was well sited. The additional wings, given the hilltop perch, posed a challenge the architect hadn't met. I couldn't put my finger on it. Maybe the elevation of the left wing didn't quite match the right. Different architects? Warring visions?

Still, the total effect was impressive enough to make me wonder if there were a servants' entrance where I might park my humble vehicle without disgrace.

"Snap out of it!" I scolded myself. I wouldn't get much information out of Tessa Cameron if I let myself be intimidated by her house. I pulled underneath the la-di-da porte cochere, just as if I were piloting a huge black Mercedes S500. Or maybe a Ferrari Testarossa. A red one.

A trim dark-jacketed man raced down five steps and interrupted my fantasies, intent on assisting me from the driver's seat.

"May I take your keys?" he inquired.

"Why?"

"Guests generally park to the left of the big house. I'll be happy to move your car—"

I gunned the engine and drove to the proper area. I don't easily part with my car keys.

So, all in all, I was fifteen minutes late for my session with Tessa Cameron.

She made me wait.

The foyer wasn't bigger than my house, but it was certainly prettier, with a bridal staircase descending to creamy marble tiles. A huge gilt-framed portrait of Franklin Cameron dominated the entryway. Based on photos I'd seen, the artist had been a flatterer, enlarging the man's eyes, strengthening his chin.

I was ushered to the left, into a room with ornate molding. I don't know what the family called it—the drawing room, the withdrawing room. I'd have named it the sunroom because the windows faced south and the plants bristled with glossy leaves. The wallpaper was off-white, with stripes of pale pink and gold, a different texture for each color. A jumble of greenery and rattan gave the place the look of an outdoor garden, but the furniture wasn't casual patio stuff by any stretch of imagination or pocketbook.

The room rated a fat goose egg in snoop-potential. Not a single photograph of the illustrious clan. The only drawers opened to reveal a NYNEX phone book and plain white stationery. Except for the absence of a Gideon Bible, I could have been cooling my heels in a fancy hotel suite. I sensed the decorator's icy hand.

Sharp staccato footsteps sounded first, followed by raised and furious voices. It took me a minute to realize that the argument issued from above. Swiftly I moved toward the window wall. All the better to hear you with, my dears . . .

A woman's voice, high, shrill, demanding. Rapid-fire speech to match the tap-tapping spikes, so angry I couldn't hear sentences because the sounds slid together. I concentrated on isolating words.

"Disgust." Definitely. "You disgust me"? Possibly.

The man replied: baritone, a low rumble of resentment. Threatening?

Other feet approached. I turned in time to see Tessa Cameron enter the doorway as though by divine right, a woman of a certain age. Only her plastic surgeon could tell for sure, but I put her down as the best-maintained sixty-five I'd seen off-screen and unfiltered through flattering light. An oval Madonna face, spoiled by discontented lines edging a pursed mouth. Brilliant amber eyes, all-seeing as an eagle's. Ramrod-straight posture. Once-dark hair gilded the color of money. A faintly foreign air to her gliding walk, as though she belonged in a long gown and lace mantilla.

As she drew close, I couldn't help breathing her scent: Camellias. Her height surprised me. She walked with the calm assurance of a taller person, a *grande dame*. It came as a shock that all her power radiated from a slender five-foot frame.

She wore a simple sleeveless off-white sheath that looked as if it had been cut to her measurements and stitched to her body. Pearls were her only adornment. Made me glad I'd changed out of my jeans. When Filene's Basement, Boston's mecca for the thrifty—not to mention the cheap—holds its annual women's suit sale, I arrive early and take my place among the throng waiting to charge the doors. My sleek blue gabardine has made it through four seasons and, considering how rarely I wear it, I'm hoping for another ten. I'd paired it with a cream silk blouse. My aunt Bea's rose-gold locket dangled in the V-neck. I'd even found a pair of run-free panty hose, which—considering the heat—I regretted.

My hostess looked like she'd been born wearing panty hose and heels. Probably had feet shaped like Barbie's.

"Miss Carlyle?"

"Yes," I admitted, feeling enormous, like Alice after she'd OD'd on Eat Me mushrooms. Size 2 women have that effect on me.

The overhead argument rang out with renewed zeal and increased volume. I wished the combatants would curse each other by name.

"Bastard!" the high voice screeched.

A rumbling burst finished with the word "police," or possibly "please."

"No way did I sign on for this!" Female outrage spewed at broadcast level. "The campaign, yes! But I had no idea what—"

The woman lowered her voice abruptly. I could hardly ask Tessa to clarify.

"Come," she said firmly, her hand clasping her pearls. "Won't you join me in my office?"

Damn, I thought, I'd rather eavesdrop.

15

Tessa led the way, and there was little I could do but follow. Her office, I thought ruefully, was probably soundproofed.

We passed beneath Franklin Cameron's looming portrait. I inquired about it—When had it been painted? Who was the artist?—but she merely shrugged as she executed a quick series of turns, her posture ruler-straight. Each corridor seemed distinguished only by a differently patterned oriental runner. I felt the need to scatter a few Hansel-and-Gretel pebbles. I don't know much about oriental rugs. If someone told me to follow the Isfahan to the Bokhara to the exit, I'd be in trouble.

Tessa's office was a time capsule. Framed posters from her late husband's electoral campaigns covered the walls. Banners swagged the ceiling: *Cameron for Senate! Cameron for House! Cameron! Cameron! Cameron!* All the posters, all the campaign stuff, dated from thirty years ago. My eyes did a quick circuit: No posters from Garnet's current contest.

Had I heard Garnet's voice upstairs? Did he share living space with his mother as well as his wife?

Tessa took a seat behind the tiny desk—I'm sure the decorator'd called it an "escritoire"—Had the decorator determined the nostalgic motif or had Tessa erected this shrine to her late husband?

She gave me an appraising stare.

"You are not exactly what I expected," she said in her heavily accented voice, staring at my bargain basement suit, noting my shoes, my absence of purse, my worn briefcase. I was sure she'd priced my wardrobe to a nickel. Probably knew my left heel wiggled, needed replacement.

"What did you expect?" I asked.

"Sit, please."

I took the visitor's chair, which was too low and cushiony for my taste or comfort.

She shrugged, and her small hands moved expressively. "I don't know. Someone like on television. One of those 'Charlie's Angels,' you know?"

She'd been watching reruns.

"Or maybe a woman like a refrigerator, no?" she continued. "Big, like you, but heavy, like a block." She smiled broadly and I found myself enjoying her animated presence.

"What can I do for you?" I asked.

"It's very little, I'm afraid. Such a small thing."

She faced away from the windows, while I was forced to stare into the sun. Enthroned in her high-backed chair, she appeared tinier, almost childlike. This was a woman who knew how to manipulate her surroundings. She had the best position, the best light.

Some office. The desktop was bare. There wasn't a single bookshelf. What did she do in here?

She smiled charmingly, said, "I can explain perhaps best like this: you have people around you, the people who clean your house, iron your clothes, cook, drive your car—"

Right. A full staff. I keep mine in a kitchen drawer.

"And sometimes these people, they are not as honest as they should be. But you do not wish to call the police because there will be notoriety, and after all Helga is an excellent cook and you would so hate to lose her little pastry treats. But she has taken something and you cannot just ignore this. You would like to handle it within the family, no?"

"What did Helga take?"

"No, no. Not so literal, please. Helga is not my cook. She is a person I make up in my mind to show you—"

"A hypothetical case."

She beamed as if I were her star pupil. "Right. So you say, 'hypothetical.' "

When people start beaming at me and generally behaving like ardent admirers who wish to bask in my wisdom, all my alarm bells go off at once. Either they want me to join a weird cult, I figure, or they're planning a con.

"Tell me a little more about this hypothetical theft," I said.

"It is of no intrinsic value, this thing that was stolen."

"Sentimental value," I suggested.

"Yes. I see you are very perceptive," she said. *"Simpatico."* Her smile was starting to look glazed, frozen, as though it had been pasted on her mouth and was beginning to itch.

"I take it you want my help in recovering this sentimental treasure," I said.

"That is exactly what I want." She seemed relieved. The smile ratcheted up a notch in warmth.

"Can you describe it to me?"

"I believe you already know. It consists of papers, an artist's notebook."

I decided to plant a zinger, see if a woman of such poise could be rattled. "And the hypothetical thief, that would be Drew Manley?"

Her head turned abruptly and she faced me straight on. Till that very moment I hadn't realized that she'd arranged herself at a slight angle, as though she were being photographed, presenting her best side to the camera.

"Andrew Manley," I repeated. "I assume you called me because of Andrew Manley."

Rattled she was. "But he told me he never—"

"He didn't give his true name," I assured her. "He tried an alias. That's one reason I agreed to come to your house. I figured I'd have a better chance of meeting the real Tessa Cameron."

She couldn't decide whether to hit me with indignation or keep her good humor. I could practically see the wheels spin, hear the gears mesh.

"So you know everything?" she said, finally deciding a fishing expedition might be the appropriate response.

"Not everything," I said lightly. "I've seen your photograph, so I do know you are the genuine Mrs. Cameron. But I don't know what you want."

"I only want this thing, this treasure that Dr. Manley took from me." She stared hungrily at my briefcase. "You brought it with you, yes?"

Doctor. He'd made it through med school, just as his yearbook had prophesied.

"You're calling your doctor a thief," I prompted.

"Please, put no such word in my mouth. Thief! Fool, perhaps. He regrets what he did. He said you sent him away, you told him you no longer have this thing, these papers. But also he said you could not show him the postal receipt. He is a man like all men, gullible. He believes you would send this to your FBI. Me, I am not so gullible." She made an elegant exit from the chair, one moment relaxed, the next perfectly upright. "I will see this receipt, or else I will see my stolen property." For a woman five feet tall in heels she was damned impressive.

"I was told the property belonged to your daughter, Thea."

"Dorothea," she corrected, caressing each syllable. Her face changed as she spoke the name. Her mouth relaxed. She looked ten years younger. "My brilliant, my beautiful daughter. She has been dead so long and still they try to use her. Everything they try to steal. Even her true name."

"Dorothy Cameron."

"Doro*thea*. That is where Thea comes from. Franklin, my husband, he will not let me name this daughter after the wishes of my heart. I name Beryl and Garnet, my treasures, and I think this one will be Ivory, Jade, Lapis, a precious thing also. But my husband's mother has money, and for that money, that hope of inheritance, he writes on the birth certificate Dorothy, his mother's ugly name. I spit at him for that. Now, if he still lived, I would spit at him."

Was that why Franklin Cameron's picture hung large in the foyer? So she could practice spitting at a man twenty years dead? Did she use his campaign posters for target practice?

"Dr. Manley told me the manuscript meant your daughter was alive."

She bowed her head, remaining silent for a full minute. Her lips moved as though she were praying.

"Why would he say such a thing, such a lie?" she murmured at last. "You think you know a person, really *know* him, and—"

The knock on the door was strong enough to shake the paneling. It startled both of us.

"Mama, open the door." The voice was deep, baritone, of the same timbre and pitch as one of the upstairs quarrelers.

Tricky Tessa. I hadn't even seen her snick the lock.

"Please," Tessa Cameron whispered to me, "say nothing. Pretend you are not here." Then, loudly, she addressed the door. "Darling, I'm on the phone. Long distance. Very important. It's way past twelve! You'll be late for your meeting."

"Mother, Henry told me you have a guest."

I wondered if Henry was the car-key man.

"Cat's out of the bag," I said to Tessa with a shrug, making my words loud enough to carry. I'd never met a gubernatorial candidate before.

"Ignore, please, this interruption," she said to me, steel in her voice. "I will pay you."

"For what?" I asked.

"Damn him," Tessa muttered under her breath. To

me: "No, I do not curse my son, I curse the chauffeur. Why should I be spied on in my own house?"

I didn't have an answer. The knocking was becoming insistent, taking on a regular rhythm.

She shook her head and her smooth coiffure moved all-of-a-piece. She made a clicking noise with her tongue, an expression of pure irritation, in English or Italian. "Shhhh," she said, moving toward the door. "I'll let you in. A moment, please! Always he must be in charge. Always! His father died when he was young. That is what I say to excuse his behavior. Do not judge him harshly."

Seemed his mother did that already.

Tessa opened the door, and The Man Who Would Be King charged past like she was the housekeeper. He regarded me for a moment, then did a quick reverse, facing her.

"Mama, I thought we'd agreed you'd stay out of this."

"No. No. This is so simple, darling. You watch. You see. Miss Carlyle, this is my son, Garnet. He forgets sometimes the politeness."

Not often, I thought. Not a man with his political savvy and ambition. Garnet resembled his mother, same searching amber eyes, same perfectly oval face. His hair was touched with gray at the temples. No dandruff.

His suit was European-cut, charcoal with a faint stripe. No lint. No creases. He'd teamed it with a pink shirt so subdued it was almost gray, enlivened the ensemble with a hand-painted floral tie that probably cost more than my entire outfit.

All the Dover Camerons, except the elusive Beryl, rated space in *Who's Who*. So I knew Garnet had graduated from Harvard, held a law degree from Yale, was forty-two, and currently married to the much-younger Marissa, with one divorce in his past. No kids. Eighteen when sister Thea had vanished.

For years he'd devoted his considerable energy and influence to politics, on the money side. Fund-raising time, folks heard from Garnet. Folks with money. I bet he rarely forgot his manners then.

He'd racked up favors, bided his time. When the traditional weakness of the Massachusetts Republican Party reasserted itself, he'd picked the perfect moment to switch from money raiser to candidate, fulfill his father's unsated ambitions.

I admit to being politically disaffected, but I vote, even though the things I want to vote for—like giving more money to Paolina's school so they won't have to run an endless stream of bake sales and magazine drives —never end up on the ballot. I was actually looking forward to yanking the lever for this guy. We breed strange candidates in the Commonwealth—rich folks who stand up for the little guy, poor folk who grovel to the rich, longing to be one of their number. The Kennedy model must have rubbed off: Do what's necessary to get rich; once you've got a million bucks to spare, groom your kids for public service.

Garnet Cameron said, "I see you've met my devoted mother, Ms. Carlyle."

Tension there, thick as butter.

She glued a jovial smile on her mouth, said, "You hear, Garnet, what little I say to her. Only that we have lost some pieces of paper from a sketchpad. She has found them. We pay her for them. A check, cash, whatever it is she wishes. It's so simple, you see?"

"You didn't exactly say you lost them," I corrected. "More like Andrew Manley stole them."

Garnet rounded on his mother, but she didn't give him a chance to slip a word into the accusatory silence.

"What? What did I say? *She* tells me his name, not the other way around. Always you belittle me." Tessa had a delightful accent, I decided, like rippling water. I hoped she'd keep talking because Garnet looked as though he desperately wanted her to shut up.

"Listen to me, darling." She addressed me quietly, just woman to woman, as if her son had evaporated from the room. Clients rarely call me darling. "Such hair you have! You need a good haircut, true? I have someone for you, a man who works wonders with such hair! This thing I want you to return . . . The doctor —who is my dear friend—perhaps thought he was doing a good thing, yes, but he didn't realize— 'Stole' is far too strong a word."

"Mama!"

"What? What? All the time, everything I do is wrong, eh? I can see this is a good person, an honest woman—"

"I asked you to let me handle this." Garnet's mouth barely opened; his jaw seemed set, locked.

Tessa said, "I think you should not be late for your meeting."

"Consider it canceled," Garnet returned.

"Dr. Manley wanted the notebook back very much," I said. "*If* I'd had it, I would have given it to him."

Tessa Cameron's eyes flashed. She said, "I don't know why you wish to keep it, but you have no right. This thing we speak of is a—a fraud! It's like with a dead painter, like Picasso, say, a dead master. You think a nobody, a student, perhaps, in an art school, should be able to squiggle lines on a page and then say to me this is a genuine Picasso and you should pay me twenty thousand dollars for this little penciled nothing drawn yesterday? It is an outrage!"

Bingo: Had someone offered to sell her the notebook? For, say, twenty thousand dollars?

"Wait a minute, Mrs. Cameron," I said. "Correct me if I'm wrong, but with art, forgery devalues the true work. If someone finds another thousand 'Picassos,' each genuine Picasso is worth less."

"This would be true, yes," she admitted.

I said, "But if Thea were alive and writing after all these years, a new manuscript would be a gold mine. It would generate tremendous interest in her earlier novel—"

I have rarely been stared down by a woman a foot shorter than me, but Tessa did an admirable job.

"It is not a new manuscript; it is a fake," she said coldly. "My Thea is not alive. You think she would run away and never speak to her mother? She loved me with all her heart. Some son-of-a-bitch, some political enemy of my son's, that is all we'll find at the bottom of this. I will pay you, I tell you, not for the single chapter alone, which I trust you will return, but to make this person—whoever it is—stop what he is doing." She pulled a lacy handkerchief from an invisible pocket, applied it gently to her eyes. "Make him stop writing these hateful forgeries, make him stop breaking my heart."

"Mama," Garnet said, trying to grasp her hands. "Please. I can handle this. There's no reason to tear yourself apart."

"You," Mrs. Cameron murmured spitefully, "you can't even handle your wife. Even now, if she'd stay until the election—"

"Mother, I'm sure Miss Carlyle isn't interested in the election," Garnet said, a smile frozen on his face. If he could have wrapped his hand over his mother's mouth I'm certain he would have.

"You're not the man your father was." Mrs. Cameron hurled the insult like a favorite cudgel.

"Praise the Lord," he answered sarcastically, "and pass the Martini pitcher. Perhaps, Miss Carlyle, you might return some time when my mother is more herself."

I admired the way he'd called her an irresponsible alcoholic without using the words for attribution.

I said, "Look, Mr. Cameron, I have an appointment with your mother, not with you. If she wants to talk, I'm happy to listen."

"She does talk," he said, his teeth clenched.

"And you, you stink of jealousy every time I mention Thea's name." The woman turned on her son. "There's some law, perhaps, that I can't talk about my own child in my own home?"

"What was she like, Mrs. Cameron? I've read her book, but . . ."

"Don't egg her on," Garnet Cameron said. "Please."

She froze him with a glance.

"That was a very naughty book for her to write, no? She was a wild thing, my daughter, like a horse no one could tame. My father owned such a horse once, an Arabian, and only I could ride him. But even I could not tame Thea. She wrote of that stuffy school of hers. She made fun of everything and everyone and some lied and said, of course, they did not recognize themselves at all, and some laughed, but the laughter caught in their throats and choked them." She stifled a noise and I realized she was holding back tears. "Sometimes I think that was why the man killed her, because she spoke to him when she shouldn't have, said something funny and wicked."

"Sit down," I urged, leading her back to her chair. A pitcher of Martinis. If she'd overindulged, the smell of liquor was well camouflaged by her camellia perfume.

"She had no talent for kindness, my daughter," Tessa continued as soon as she sat. "She had a tongue that cut like a blade, so sharp. It was a failing, but I thought to myself, she has plenty of time to grow gentle with the passing of years. In her later life, I thought, she will acquire also this virtue, and become a great lady. And she will be the daughter I will grow old with, the one who will take me to lunch, to tea at the Ritz, because I have already lost my older daughter, and it will be my life to be proud of her and, poof, it is gone, and all I have are memories like a wisp, a puff of smoke."

"Already lost your older daughter? What do you mean, 'lost'?"

Garnet shot me a poisonous glance.

"That's enough, Mama," he said.

She removed a pack of cigarettes from her top drawer, a crystal ashtray.

"Mama, the doctor said."

"What? I do as I please, Garnet. None of you ever understood me. Not even your father. My children only lie to me or preach to me—except for my brilliant girl, my Thea. Truly, she is the only one who listened—"

"Getting yourself killed isn't so brilliant, Mother."

There was a moment of uneasy silence while Mrs. Cameron lit her cigarette with a slim gold lighter. She wasn't a woman accustomed to lighting her own cigarettes. Her fingers shook. Garnet wasn't about to help.

"All pleasures you would deny me," she said bitterly. "Even memory—"

The knock on the door was hesitant this time.

"Contessa? Are you in there?" The voice was high and thin.

Ah, I thought. The arguing soprano.

"Open the door, Garnet," Tessa said.

He didn't like it, but he obeyed. Hell, if she'd ordered me to open the door in a tone like that, I'd have done it too.

16

Marissa Cameron had attempted to repair runny mascara and powder over tear tracks. Neither technique had worked. Her nose was red, her voice shaky. She and husband, Garnet, had been the screaming couple, no doubt about it.

I studied her with interest. The news photo had been a head shot; it hadn't hinted at how truly young Marissa seemed. I mean, there's twenty-three, and then there's twenty-three. Roz is in her early twenties, but Roz looked like a hardened street player in comparison.

Alice-in-Wonderland hair, tied back with a thin blue ribbon, fell almost to the waist of Marissa's yellow dress. In the photo her hair had been pinned and piled, giving her a commanding air. Devoid of curl, her hair hung like cornsilk, emphasizing her narrow shoulders, fragile build. She seemed frail, small, in need of protection.

I sneaked a glance at her feet. High heels accounted for the staccato footsteps, but it was hard to believe she possessed a voice like a diamond-edged cutting tool.

After a brief moment of indecision, a firming of her stance, she ignored Garnet completely. He and I evidently didn't exist. This was between her and her mother-in-law.

"I came to say good-bye, Tessa, and thank you. You've been good to me," she said softly. She sounded brave and stoic and hurt. And somehow wrong, as if she were auditioning for a role she didn't quite understand.

"Darling, please stay." Tessa took her hand, tried to embrace her. With Tessa's cigarette dangling precariously, and only one active participant, the hug was awkward.

"No, Tessa. I can't."

"Is there something you're not telling me? Perhaps you are pregnant, darling? That would explain so much—"

Garnet broke it up with, "There's no reason for Ms. Carlyle to witness this charming domestic scene, ladies."

"Who is she?" Marissa asked.

"Why would you care?" Garnet answered sharply.

A buzzer sounded with sufficient noise to make Marissa jump. Garnet grabbed a slim cell phone from his pocket.

"Yes," he said. "I'm aware of the time. Phone ahead and tell them the traffic's bad on the Pike or something. You know the drill." He flipped the phone shut.

"Garnet, really," his mother said, tapping ashes

carefully into the crystal bowl, "you should go. People hate waiting. Your father never let the voters wait."

"Lot of good it did him," Garnet snapped.

Marissa wavered back and forth, carrying a handbag too large for comfort or style. I peeked around her, through the open door, and noted a pile of luggage in the corridor. A matched set in hunter green. More than she'd need for a campaign jaunt, unless she were planning to campaign out-of-state for, say, six months to a year.

During an awkward silence, I withdrew a standard contract form from my briefcase. Tessa grabbed it, possibly thinking I'd changed my mind and decided to return a scrap of her late daughter's writing.

I said I'd do my best to determine the source of the forgeries.

"What forgeries?" Marissa said. "What are you talking about?"

Her voice had that ingenuous note again. Did she always sound like she was lying?

Tessa ignored her. "I want them to stop immediately!" she said. "And I want to know who is making them up! There is no question of bringing in the police," she added with a quick glance at Garnet.

I wondered if Tessa suspected her older daughter, the "lost" Beryl, of copying her dead sister's substance and style. If Garnet hadn't butted his way into the office I might have found out.

"What's this about, Tessa?" Marissa asked sweetly. "Is there some kind of trouble? Can I help?"

"No, dear," Tessa said. Then, to me, "I'll write you a check, a retainer, yes?"

"Fine," I said.

She kept her checkbook and a gold Cross pen in the

tiny escritoire. A place for everything and everything in its place.

Marissa licked her lips, said, "Well, it's time for me to go. I didn't want to leave without saying—"

"Please," Tessa said, "stay a little longer."

"Mother," Garnet snapped.

Tessa colored, and bowed her head, seemingly reprimanded. She scribbled rapidly, handed me a check and the signed contract. Before I had a chance to say more than a simple good-bye, Garnet seized me by the elbow, not hard enough for me to cry out, just firmly enough to guide me down the halls and out the door without undue fuss. He was extremely efficient. His *Who's Who* write-up hadn't mentioned anything about a stint in the Military Police. He had the moves of a good nightclub bouncer.

Once we were outdoors, he announced, "You can ignore everything that was said in there. My mother will change her mind within forty-eight hours. That's a guarantee. You'll be required by law to return the check. You might as well tear up the contract now. She's under duress. You have no right to take advantage of her."

I shrugged. "She called me," I said. "Not the other way around."

"If you have any writings supposedly penned by my dear departed sister, you'd be wise to get rid of them."

"Your mom wants them; you want to get rid of them. Interesting," I said.

"Good-bye."

A cab pulled up at the porte cochere, honked twice. Henry, the spying chauffeur, was loading Marissa Cameron's luggage into the trunk. Garnet went to supervise —possibly concerned that she might be stealing the family silver—leaving me to walk the last few steps to the Toyota alone.

I usually lock my car doors. In Cambridge or Boston, I practically chain the car to a tree because car theft is so common. In the rarefied Dover air, with the chauffeur on patrol, I'd been careless.

I glanced in the backseat, unconscious cop-rule #27: Never get into your car unless you've checked for unwanted passengers. The humped shape underneath my raincoat moved, and I started to open the back door.

Drew Manley raised his head and looked at me with supplication in his blue eyes. He placed a finger to his lips, then lifted both hands to make driving motions.

I shoved the back door shut, opened the driver's door, got inside, and carefully started the engine.

If I could see both his hands, I figured he probably didn't have a weapon. Still, the driveway seemed especially long and winding.

When we reached the road, I said, "So, Doctor, you want me to turn left or right?"

"Take a left on Farm, bear right at Bridge, keep going straight and it'll get you onto North Street. We can take that into Medfield."

"You comfortable back there?"

"No."

"You might as well sit up on the seat."

"Not yet."

"Is there a coffee shop, a rest area?"

"Drive," he said. "When we get someplace safe, you can help me up."

I tried to miss most of the potholes, but the occasional labored grunt told me I wasn't always successful.

"Don't go so fast," he muttered as we passed a huge red barnlike house on the right.

I slowed and watched the stone fences vary in height and color. Beyond the fences huge lots were heavily wooded, like forests with well-tended lawns; there were mansions back there. I could see the occasional chimney, a slated roof or two. Cars whizzed by, expensive sedans all. I kept to the speed limit; the Dover cops might use any excuse to stop a dirty ten-year-old vehicle.

After four long minutes, we crossed some railroad tracks and I let out a sigh of relief. Intuition—and my surroundings—told me we'd made it to my side of the tracks, the side I felt most comfortable on.

The wrong side.

17

"Where are we heading?" I asked after a while. I find distances amazing in the suburbs. I mean, I like to drive, but miles and miles between corner grocery and gas station would make me nuts in no time. I prefer concrete sidewalks, pedestrians on the march.

His voice was soft, muffled. "Make sure you stay on North. Are we past the Police and Fire?"

"Just passing it. Isn't there any place closer?"

"We could have gone to the Pharmacy, but the whole town hangs out there. Look over on your right. Should be some kind of Chinese restaurant coming up. Big parking lot."

The lot was fairly empty. I pulled into a sheltered spot near the rear. The place was too close to the police station for comfort. I didn't want any sharp-eyed uniform watching me assist an elderly gent off the Toyota's rug.

I half-lifted, half-wrestled him onto the seat. He wore a pale blue knitted sports shirt, dark slacks and shoes. His face was red, his silver hair mussed, his glasses tilted at an odd angle, but he insisted he felt fine. I recommended that he rest a bit before emerging.

"I overheard—" he began immediately. "I needed to tell you—then Garnet came—" He spluttered to a close. "Guess I'd better sit awhile, catch my breath," he admitted grudgingly.

I surveyed the unpromising frontage of the Dragon King. Chinese/American Cuisine, it promised. I've always found "cuisine" riskier than "food." Cocktail Lounge, said another sign, in smaller print than KENO!, which was plastered across the front door in huge yellow letters with a screamer. The establishment sat next to a chiropractor's office and a two-by-four real estate agency.

"You want a drink?" I asked Manley. "Takeout?"

Breathing more easily, he regarded his immediate surroundings with disapproval. "The back of your car's a disgrace," he said huffily. "I must have been lying on shoes, something sharp. Maybe an umbrella. Smelly, too."

"I don't recall inviting you on an inspection tour," I snapped, stung by his accuracy.

"Please," he said humbly, holding out a hand by way of apology, "I could use a chance to stretch my legs."

"Are we going to run into anyone you know?"

He gave the restaurant a dubious glance. "I doubt it."

I helped him out of the car. He staggered once, muttering about pins and needles in his leg.

The interior was generic suburban Chinese place. I could have described the fish tank, the dark carved wood, the vases filled with plastic carnations, the garish dragon paintings without venturing inside.

A sign said "PLEASE SEAT YOURSELF." Evidently business wasn't good enough to keep a lunchtime hostess busy.

We had no trouble finding a small booth. If any cops were drinking in the adjacent red-carpeted lounge, they were plainclothes strangers.

He ordered tea. I ordered hot and sour soup along with hot and spicy green beans, surprised to see both items on the mostly Mandarin menu. He shook his head when the bored young waitress raised questioning eyes in his direction. Maybe she thought I was going to share. I wasn't planning on it; Tessa hadn't invited me to lunch.

The sulky girl made a few scratches on her order pad, and disappeared, taking tiny steps that hardly ruffled her long traditional garb. Daughter or niece of the owner, I decided. Less than fond of her job.

"Would you like to know something I've learned, something I should have learned a long time ago?" my former client asked as soon as the waitress was out of earshot.

I shrugged and kept quiet since I wasn't sure whom I was talking to—the seemingly sincere liar, Adam Mayhew, or the battered bewildered liar of the same pseudonym, the one who'd yanked me off the case. Or the genuine Dr. Drew Manley.

He took my shrug for assent. "Never get involved with a patient. No matter how you feel for her, no matter what your heart says, keep your patients at arm's length."

"If you're trying to tell me you're not Tessa Cameron's half-brother," I ventured, "I already knew."

"I do live there, most of the time. I'm Tessa Cameron's lover—her paramour, she calls me—which is 'lover' in old-fogey talk, or maybe Italian. I have been Tessa's lover since Franklin died. I was in love with her before that, but I never acted on it. For that long, at least, I resisted temptation."

From the way he said it, I got the feeling that Tessa would not have been unwilling before Franklin's demise.

"She won't marry me," he stated simply. "I'm not Catholic."

"What kind of doctor are you?" I asked.

"A good one. Retired."

"Now that I know your name, Dr. Manley, exactly how long do you think it'll take me to find out what medical specialty you practiced?"

He made a face. "I'm a psychiatrist."

"Ah."

"And what's that supposed to mean?"

"Don't you know?" I asked. "It means I'm going to ask whether Tessa is the only one of the Camerons who was—or is—your patient?"

"Ever heard of doctor-patient confidentiality?"

The waitress slopped tea on the table. I wiped it up with a napkin and gave her the eye. I took a sip of hot and sour soup. Disappointingly bland.

"Ever heard of using an alias?" I asked harshly. Doctor-patient confidentiality, indeed!

"About that, um, about the alias. I never intended to defraud."

"What did you intend? More to the point, what *do* you intend?"

He lowered his voice. I had to bend forward to hear him. "I heard what Garnet said. He *will* convince his mother to change her mind. One thing about Tessa, she has intense emotional swings. She loves that boy of hers, beyond moderation, beyond adulation, listens to him like he was Jesus on the Mount."

"So he said."

Dr. Manley took a gulp of tea, eyed the restaurant as though checking for spies. Only two other tables were occupied, and it seemed he found the customers innocuous.

He said, "I want you to . . . continue with this matter, whatever the outcome. The papers are genuine; I guarantee—"

"Whoa," I said. "Stop right there. I'm getting *whiplash,* you know what I mean? Sunday night, it's 'please help me find the missing genius,' then Monday night, it's 'oops, I made a mistake. Forget the whole thing.' " I glared at him. "It's only Wednesday goddam afternoon, and you're flip-flopping again?"

He didn't seem to hear me and I hadn't kept my voice down to any whisper. He stared at the Formica tabletop and spoke slowly, as though he were feeling his way through unfamiliar country. "You know anything about tectonics?" he asked.

"What?"

"Forces, conditions within the crust of the earth, the sort of thing that causes earthquakes." As he spoke he made flat surfaces of his hands, pushed them together with such force that one slid abruptly over the top of the other.

"What about them?"

"There are places where the crust wears thin, and

molten rock and steam break through. Nothing you can do about it. It's a force of nature."

"Hot springs," I said. "Geysers."

"Yes."

"I don't understand what you're trying to say."

"Young woman, there are times when the simple truth bubbles to the surface. Reputation, fame, money —they all have to take second place to a truth when it's spoken and heard and finally recognized for what it is . . ."

If he wasn't deeply moved by the words he'd just spoken, he was among the best actors I'd seen.

I said, "What is it you want me to go on with? So far, I've learned that your 'live' Thea Janis is dead and buried. Murdered. Her mother says so, the newspapers say so—"

"Her mother never saw the Berlin poem, any more than she identified the corpse. It's easy to convince Tessa. I've told you that. She's extremely suggestible."

"Wait a minute. You're basing your theory that Thea's alive on a single poem? One poem? How's this? Thea wrote it a long time ago, thinking about, *imagining* a possible future, a time when walls would be broken, borders eliminated."

" 'Berlin, *now*,' " he quoted.

" 'Now' is relative," I replied.

Damn, his eyes were shining again, so blue and clear behind the silver-rimmed bifocals. He'd regained every pinch of quiet confidence he'd shown at our first meeting.

"She's not dead," he said.

"Tell me another one."

"She phoned me."

"And you recognized her voice after twenty-four years."

"She identified herself. She's coming back. God help her, she's afraid."

"Afraid of what?" I asked.

"She didn't say."

"Of course not," I said disgustedly.

He read the disbelief on my face. I didn't try to hide it.

"Look," I said. "I've read about her big white funeral. Her father and mother went. Her brother."

"She said she needs to talk to me, as a friend, and as a doctor. She says she has to see me face-to-face."

"Well, I'd certainly like to be there," I said, "but I seem to have a problem."

"No! You can't be present. She needs to see me alone. At first."

"No kidding. Well, that's not my problem. My problem is defining my job. You wanted to hire me to find Thea. Now, she's coming for a visit. She's on her way. *She* found *you*. No money for me there. Tessa wants me to prove that the notebook and the poem are forgeries. She donated a good-sized check to the cause."

"Which Garnet will convince her to void."

"Either way, it looks like I'm out of this."

"No," he said. "Please. Work for Tessa till she pulls the plug. Try to prove the documents false. You won't succeed, but I can't pay you the kind of money Tessa can pay. I've left you something in the backseat of your car, if you can find it in that sty."

"I don't need more of your money, not to look for a dead girl."

"Listen to me: Something went wrong, very wrong, a long time ago. I may have been a part of it, unwittingly.

I'm an old man. I don't want to die with this on my conscience."

"With what on your conscience? What changed your mind between the first time you called me and the second? Why have you changed your mind again?"

The waitress interrupted to see if we wanted our empty teapot refilled. I waved her away impatiently.

Manley stared at his empty cup. "The moment Thea gives me permission to tell you, I will."

"In other words, don't hold your breath."

"Go to your car, get what I left there. We can discuss it."

"If it's a check, I'm ripping it up."

"Fine." He flagged the waitress. "I'll have more tea while I wait," he said.

Underneath my raincoat and a lone gym sneaker, I found another manila envelope. I glanced inside just long enough to see that several pages were enclosed, typed this time. Brief statements, underlined, like a bibliography.

In the restaurant, the booth was empty. The waitress told me the old guy had gone to the bathroom. I paid the bill while I waited. After a good twelve minutes, I went to the men's room door and knocked. No response.

I returned to the table. The tiny Chinese girl came to collect her due.

"How much did he give you?" I asked.

"What?"

"To tell me he went to the john?"

She smirked. "Twenty," she said.

I stiffed her on the tip, drove around Medfield Center for another half hour. The good doctor might have strolled over to the police station, but I didn't think so.

I remembered the envelope, pulled onto the shoulder of the road abruptly enough to earn a honk and an upraised finger. The papers were a bibliography, articles culled from psychiatric journals, the occasional book-length treatment. Loftus, E. F.; Terr, L.; Appelbaum, P. S.; Gutheil, T. G. One hardback was titled *Witness for the Defense,* one *Recovered Memory Syndrome.*

Recovered memory syndrome. Was Manley trying to tell me that Thea suffered from amnesia, that staple of forties Hollywood?

I scanned the bibliography. Another text seemed to be a complex psychiatric and legal document discussing crimes remembered years after the fact, usually under psychiatric counseling, and the admissibility of such remembered evidence in a court of law.

My mind was clicking now, and my memory. As I recalled, such "recovered" memories had enjoyed a brief vogue. In 1990, a man had been convicted of murdering his daughter's girlfriend twenty years earlier, on the testimony of the daughter, who claimed she'd been present at the crime scene, but had repressed the memory. The case had been appealed, I thought. Reversed. A recovered memory wasn't something a lawyer would be eager to bring to court . . .

Dammit. Garnet might succeed in convincing his mom to void the contract. I stopped at the bank to deposit Tessa's check as a gesture of good faith, then at home just long enough to rip off the panty hose, change to comfortable clothes. Back in the car, I headed for Area D. Before someone pulled me off this case for good, I was determined to discover exactly what had happened to Dorothy "Thea Janis" Cameron twenty-four years ago. My mind hungered for facts—dates, times, places—clearly written in an orderly form.

I would follow Tessa's mission for the time being. It seemed to me that anyone who knew how to forge Thea's work so well, to imitate her uniquely compelling voice, must have known her, known her intimately, long ago.

I had the feeling I was going to owe Mooney more than lunch before the day was done.

18

Someday police files will exist on-line, uniform print marching across computer screens. No mildewed pages stinking of hamburger grease, blotched with mustard and coffee stains. No stiff brittle paper, no tactile sense of age and wear.

But these are the good old days. Creased yellowing pages rule.

"How'd you find it?" I asked Mooney admiringly.

He wasn't buying my admiration. The expression on his usually mild face was fierce. "Exactly why should I let you see it? Remind me."

I didn't relish outlining my on-again, off-again relationship with either of my "clients." Tessa Cameron might have ripped up her contract by now, and I could imagine Mooney's reaction to my three sessions with

Drew Manley—two conducted under an alias, one terminating in a walkout.

"Mooney," I said, "I've got a major gut feeling: Something isn't kosher. Okay?"

"Not enough."

I breathed in, breathed out. Kept my hands behind my back to keep from snatching the file.

"What's enough?" I asked. "When I worked for you, you trusted my instincts."

"You don't work for me anymore."

"You want me to beg? Get down on my knees? Embarrass you in your own office?"

"I'll think it over," he said like he was truly considering the offer.

My tactics were not having the desired effect.

"Please, Mooney," I said softly, going for basic politeness. Playing for sympathy, too, I admit.

At the same moment he said, "There *is* something you can do for me."

I knew it was going to be bad, because he turned away from me as he spoke.

"What?" I clipped the word, short and precise.

"Hire yourself a bodyguard."

"*What?*" This time I gave the word an elongated vowel and full incredulity.

He faced me. I noticed the skin under his eyes, dark, etched with fine lines. His blue Oxford cloth shirt was starting to fray at the collar. He said, "Did anyone follow you here?"

"Look, Mooney, I don't exactly believe in your Gianelli mob hit fantasy."

"It's no fantasy."

"If you hear it from more than one jail-bound punk, I might start to take it seriously."

"Not good enough," Moon said.

"I'll watch my back, I promise."

I made light of the threat, but that didn't mean my neck hadn't prickled the whole drive from Medfield to Southie, didn't mean I hadn't blasted through ambers, then quickly eyeballed the rearview to see whether any vehicle had followed.

A useless exercise in a city where stopping at reds is considered optional.

"Not good enough," Mooney repeated.

"I'll consider a bodyguard," I said, not meeting his gaze. It was a lie, but I needed to see what the cops had on paper.

I held my breath. Mooney can usually nail me on a lie.

This time he didn't.

The "Dorothy Cameron aka Thea Janis" file was three inches thick, encompassing several smaller files wrapped in rubber bands, the whole thing weighing in at several pounds. The "aka" gave me pause. "Also known as" usually appears on the rap sheets of career felons who go by different versions of their given name for different occasions: Thomas Jackson on a marriage license, Jack Thomson or Thompson or Thomsen when filing a false insurance claim, T.J. or Jeeter on the street.

"No Xeroxing, no stealing," Mooney said, as he handed it over, his lips tight and disapproving. "Not a single sheet of paper leaves the building."

I didn't argue, didn't make a crack about searching me, didn't bother to ask if I could take notes.

At first glance, the file seemed too orderly. Maybe some celebrity bio-hunter had organized it, searching for book fodder. I inquired if that were the case.

"Nope. Woody MacAvoy didn't do much his last

couple years except type and file." Mooney spoke dismissively, if not derisively. "Neatest paperwork around."

A cop who quit caring about the street and surrendered to form-filling and filing is the lowest of the low to Mooney. Pure slime. Mooney has more trouble understanding cops than crooks because he cuts them less slack. To Mooney, a cop is a cross between Superman and God, here to mete out justice on earth.

After the two of us indulged in a brief argument concerning confidentiality and breaches of police security, Mooney locked me in an interrogation room with the file, a Styrofoam coffee cup, and three stale doughnuts for company. So much for trust. The windows didn't open and the last person to use the room had neglected to bathe. I didn't care. Touching the file, I felt close to Thea, the same way I'd felt when I read her manuscript. She was "Thea" to me still, not the late Dorothy Cameron. Manley's doglike devotion—and her own words —had brought her to life.

The file dropped me back to earth with a thud, it being filled with words as far from poetic as language gets. Reports, reports, reports. No better way to organize your thoughts, the instructors at the academy had assured us to universal catcalls. Yeah, sure, if your mind ran to items like height, weight, and date of birth, the cornerstones of all police paper.

I unstrapped my wristwatch, set it in front of me to help keep track of time. I flexed my fingers like a pianist doing warm-up exercises, closed my eyes, and scrunched up my face.

Ready.

From my back pocket, I removed a tiny notebook and pencil. A notebook arrives fresh each August from the Harvard Coop Department Store, which is a co-op pronounced like a chicken roost. It's a calendar, a datebook, has space for phone numbers. Its chief virtue is its size. Teamed with a pencil stolen from a miniature golf course, it hardly makes your pocket bulge.

The initial squeal had gone to the Dover police. Thea's parents had reported her missing on April 9, 1971, at 9:02 P.M., after a gap of thirty-six hours. Thursday morning, the eighth, had passed uneventfully *chez* Cameron. After a rushed breakfast—nothing out of the ordinary—Dorothy had packed a small overnight bag, told her father she'd be spending Thursday night at a girlfriend's house—name: Sue Alfred; address: 48 Brattle Street, Cambridge 02138—studying for a Latin exam. She'd called home to verify. When Dorothy didn't come home Friday evening, Franklin Cameron had phoned the "girlfriend," and learned not only that Thea had never come to visit, she didn't share any of Sue's classes. Sue didn't take Latin.

Franklin Cameron. In my mind, I saw his portrait in the foyer of the Dover house, exerting dominion after all these years. The Dover police hadn't listed his occupation, probably assuming everyone would recognize the name. "Magazine and newspaper magnate," they could have written. "Three-time candidate for U.S. senator, once coming close enough to demand a recount."

I took detailed notes. So far, the case was a simple missing persons, most likely a runaway. Nothing hinted at murder. Victims don't arrange alibis for their killers. Thea had something else on her mind; she'd planned to spend Thursday night somewhere, either alone or accompanied. Query: If she were planning to run away, why hadn't she taken advantage of the weekend, made up some mythical school festival, given herself four days instead of two? Query Two: Why hadn't she used a real friend, someone who'd cover for her? Hadn't she made any friends at Avon Hill?

I wrote, *Where did Thea spend Thursday night? With whom?*

Once alerted, the Dover cops had jumped into action. Every off-duty officer had been notified and brought up to speed. A search of conservation land, property abutting the Camerons' huge estate, was organized with the help of—I read the sentence again—yes, my eyes were not failing me, with the help of the Myopia Polo Club.

I had a brief vision of hounds, horses, and hunters in red velvet trumpeting through the nearby countryside as though Thea were a fox to be brought to bay. Talleyho! Break for tea and crumpets at four.

The thought made me hungry and I bit into a doughnut, gingerly, because it was damn near petrified and I no longer have dental insurance.

The FBI was the next agency on the case, which seemed odd to me. Ah. Someone at Cameron central had called a Yalie pal and the specter of kidnapping had been duly raised. No ransom demands forthcoming. The majority of the FBI material was illegible, heavily crossed out.

I wondered why.

Since Thea had last been seen at the Avon Hill School Thursday afternoon, the Cambridge cops came in swinging. Not a single interview had been conducted by lowly patrolmen. Top brass had handled things from the get-go.

Miss Eva Walters, then headmistress at Avon Hill, had declared Thea an extremely intelligent and gifted girl given to odd behavior. Such as? Well, she smoked cigarettes. Dear God, who didn't, before the Surgeon General's warning? She wore ragged pants and sweat-shirts. Miss Walters thought the young lady actually changed her clothing in the rest room, substituting re-bellious jeans for the ruffles favored by her mother.

Way to go, Thea! I cheered silently.

And then, the *book*. Well, Miss Walters doubted the officer would have read *Nightmare's Dawn,* but the book, "the novelette" as she called it, was extremely vulgar and inappropriate. Really, if the child hadn't been a Cameron, the girl would most likely have been expelled. Miss Walters knew for a fact that other parents were concerned: such a child might infect their own sweet girls with knowledge the headmistress could only term "sexually precocious."

Bet there'd been a run on copies of *Nightmare's Dawn* at the Cambridge cop house.

An entire paragraph of print had been completely covered with thick gobs of wite-out.

A Cambridge officer openly wondered if Thea's dis-appearance was some sort of publicity stunt, arranged by her publisher. He was immediately replaced.

Maybe Miss Walters had done away with Thea, I speculated, afraid she'd smear the school's shining rep-utation with her bad language and active sex life. Miss Walters had not been replaced.

I checked my faculty list. She was no longer on board. Retired? Dead?

Each of Thea's teachers had been interviewed. With-out exception they had declared her "bright," or "clever," damning her with faint praise. Her English teacher, a Mr. Henreid Symmes, seemed particularly defensive, stating that the girl would have been better off with a private tutor. She hardly ever came to class, he said. His age was listed as sixty-four.

Small wonder Henreid Symmes was not among the current faculty.

The search for Thea's school friends, boyfriends, girlfriends, met with denial on all sides. No one admitted to friendship. No one sat with her at lunch. Angrily, I considered Anthony Emerson's belated testimony. Thea had been good enough to bed, but not good enough to share his cafeteria table. Bastard.

Keeping Thea's reputation unbesmirched may have smacked of honor to an Avon Hill boy like Anthony Emerson. Not to mention the fact that he'd have feared repercussions, possibly expulsion.

On the other hand, Thea could have been pure as a vestal virgin. Emerson could have lied. I had only his word for Thea's wanton behavior. And her words, in her novel. Which was a novel, a work of fiction.

Back to the files. The facts.

One Madeleine Pierce, senior student, the same student who'd spotted Thea at the school at ten past two Thursday afternoon, stated that Thea often wandered around the school grounds. She had been observed speaking with the gardeners. One, a casual day laborer no longer at the school, had departed with no forwarding address. The second gardener was a black man named Edgar Barrett Jr.

I'm not saying the cops at the Cambridge PD were more racist than those of other departments at the time, but from the moment they happened on Edgar, it was as if nobody else existed. They extracted such damning evidence as the fact that he'd once told a neighbor that there were some damn fine-looking chicks at that rich folks' school.

Amazing they hadn't lynched the man.

Edgar Barrett Jr. had no criminal record, not even a juvie offense. Fourteen officers had examined him at length. Tape recordings were cross-referenced, but the tapes were not included, nor were any transcripts of his testimony. I wondered why. Maybe because he'd been beaten during interrogation.

I took a sip of tepid coffee that made the bitter taste in my mouth worse. I'd already given up chipping away at the doughnuts. Sucking the sugar coating seemed safer.

Several audiotape cross-references had been inked out, blackened so thoroughly they were unreadable. Had they been effaced by the same hand that had earlier wielded the wite-out?

Back to the FBI. A hot line had been set up, a ten-thousand-dollar reward offered. Thea was swiftly sighted in New York, Las Vegas, and Nashville, as well as every town within fifty miles of Massachusetts. Her home phone had been tapped, but there were no ransom calls. Also no hang-up calls, the kind runaways typically make, just to assure themselves that everything's okay at home, Mom and Dad are in the living room, all's right with the world.

I scribbled down Edgar Barrett's home address and phone number. After twenty-four years, there wasn't much hope he'd still be living in the same place, but I could use his old locale to track him down.

The Cameron family, in stark contrast to poor Edgar, had been granted kid-glove treatment of the type usually reserved for embassy personnel and visiting royalty. Doctors had signed various statements explaining that Mrs. Cameron was too agitated to speak about her beloved daughter's disappearance. Her husband, Franklin, suffered from markedly high blood pressure that had kept him off the campaign trail for six months; questioning might trigger a heart attack. Thea's older sister had been whisked from the house once the kidnapping fear erupted. Beryl also had a doctor's note, explaining that she was "in a highly excitable state, given to hysterical outbursts, and unfit to interview." Several more passages had been thoroughly blacked out. I tried to decipher the doctor's signature, wished I'd smuggled in a magnifying glass. It was one of those infuriating horizontal-line rush jobs that you see so often on prescriptions, but I thought I could make out an initial "A" and a second initial "M." Andrew Manley, psychiatrist, deceiver, and disappearance artist. As far as I could tell, the older sister had never been questioned. Thea's brother, Garnet, had been on campus at the Halloway School in New Hampshire the day Thea disappeared. Several schoolmates could vouch for his whereabouts. Not that there had ever been more than routine disagreements between the two younger siblings. They were close in age and temperament. Garnet led a search of the family's Marblehead summer home, calling his sister's name, investigating their childhood hideaways on the vast estate with its private beach.

A brief note declared that the Marblehead house, while still owned by the Camerons, had been abandoned, uninhabited since the disaster.

A smudge on the side of a sheet of paper caught my eye. A coffee stain? No. An erasure. I turned it upside down and sideways, held it to the light. Nothing. I ran the lead of my pencil softly over the broken fibers: 902869432. I added the numbers to my notes, thinking that I was probably copying part of the long-distance phone number of some retired lieutenant's girlfriend.

On impulse I turned back a few pages. Another erasure. I couldn't get the same fidelity with my lead pencil, but it shared several of the same digits.

A new folder. I tugged at the rubber band, smoothed the curling pages. The Marblehead cops who'd played a role in the summerhouse search entered the fray in earnest two weeks later.

A dog, later identified as a Russian wolfhound named Petrov, had returned home to his family bearing a gift, a lone size six ballet flat, black. The dog's walker —his walker! I thought, give me a break!—had noticed that the hound veered from his usual morning path to dig about in the beach grass. Said walker—an Irish housekeeper named Caren or Karen, Midgeley or Migely, depending on who was filling out the form— had watched idly as Petrov unearthed a frilly white blouse, tearing it with claws which should have been trimmed the previous week except the Doggy Delite van broke down and clipping a dog's nails was beneath the status of a housekeeper, walking the huge animal being penance enough.

The only reason the buried clothes had come to official attention was that Caren-Karen was dating a cop's brother. By the time the actual officer heard about the discovery, dogs and seagulls had reduced the find to cotton and linen rags.

Extensive and expensive lab tests had been done on those rags. Thea's mother bought her daughter only natural-fiber clothing. Only natural fibers were detected. Not a single dead or mauled polyester.

The Marblehead officer plus his chief of police plus a clergyman had ferried the tattered remains and the single ballet shoe to Dover.

They were consistent with Thea's clothing in substance, style, and size, and "could have belonged to the deceased."

I wrote down the date of the report: April 25, 1971. It was the first occasion on which Thea had been referred to as the "deceased." Since there were no blood-stains on the clothing I wondered why. There was no mention of a suicide note, and it seemed a big jump to assume that Thea's clothes on the shore meant Thea's body in the ocean.

I'd been at it for over three hours and papers were spread over two rectangular tables. I'd kept them in chronological order, separated by location.

I was searching for the hard-hitting questions: Did Thea smoke pot, shoot heroin? Drink? Sleep around? Use birth control? Was she pregnant? Either nobody'd asked or nobody'd recorded the answers.

I closed my eyes, checked my watch. Back to work. Abruptly Sergeant Woodrow MacAvoy took control of the presumed Marblehead suicide, gathering all paper-work in Boston. Why? MacAvoy was a homicide dick. Suicide's not even against the law in Massachusetts.

The files were starting to look like documents released under the Federal Freedom of Information Act, words erased, entire paragraphs obliterated. I lifted a heavily blacked-out sheet to my nose, sniffed. No recent smell of ink.

A body—what remained of a female body—was net-ted by an unfortunate Gloucester fisherman ten days after the discovery of the clothing. May 3, 1971. Frank-lin Cameron had quickly identified the remains and ser-vices were already scheduled when a second family requested a dental records check. The Foleys' daughter, Heather, had drowned after falling off a cabin cruiser, too drunk to swim. Prom night.

The coroner's verdict took two full days: Daughter number one, Dorothy Cameron aka Thea Janis. Dorothy, not Heather. I blew out a long breath. What an eternity those forty-eight hours must have lasted for each family. The Foleys issued an apology for causing the Camerons to delay their elaborate funeral. A Cameron family spokesman declared that anyone might have made such a mistake given the condition of the remains, the emotional stress surrounding such a devastating loss. He asked the press to restrict their idle speculation.

The idle speculation—what little of it there was seemed confined to the *Herald,* the *Globe* never touched it—concerned filthy lucre, Thea's will, and who might benefit substantially, and more quickly, by having the girl declared dead.

In my notebook I wrote: What's a fifteen-year-old doing with a will? Underlined it twice.

In a May 14, 1971, report from Beverly—Pride's Crossing actually, the upscale, *upscale* part of Beverly— I first saw the name Albert Ellis Albion.

Albert Ellis Albion. The man now residing at MCI Walpole. Thea's convicted killer.

I took down the killer's vital stats, read his collected confessions, studied his mug shot. Albert, at twenty, had never made it out of high school and not for want of trying. It seemed inconceivable that this was a man Thea would have voluntarily selected as her Thursday night companion. Had she been kidnapped from school? Had she been planning to spend the night at the Marblehead house? Most likely the latter. Albion said he'd picked her up in his van on Route 1A in Swampscott. He said she'd been hitchhiking, carrying a duffle bag. He'd only stopped to help.

His testimony might have been more credible had he not "stopped to help" two other missing teens, Anne Katon, age sixteen, and Eileen Evans, fifteen. Anne lived close to Albert's Lynn apartment, waitressed at a fast-food joint where he breakfasted each morning. He might have known Anne in a casual sort of way, offered her a ride home from work one night. Eileen's bicycle had been abandoned in the woods six weeks before her body was uncovered in scrubby brush near Rocky Ledge Road in Swampscott. There was no evidence he'd ever met Eileen; she hadn't been acquainted with Anne Katon. Neither girl had any tie to Dorothea Cameron. If Albion hadn't confessed to Thea's murder as well, she'd probably have been declared a suicide.

I pored over three forensic studies. Three autopsy reports. Hours Postmortem: unknown for each. Clinical Diagnosis: most of that was beyond me, but I took careful notes nonetheless. Gross Diagnosis: Albion seemed to favor the blunt instrument to stun, a knife for close work. A rock spattered with blood had been found near Eileen Evans's nude corpse. A hammer in the back of his van revealed blood of the same type as Anne Katon's. No knives had been recovered, but a local shopkeeper had sworn to selling Albion at least two instruments that could have inflicted the deadly wounds. Only Thea's body had been found in water. It was more difficult to determine which injuries had been caused before she entered the ocean, which after. Her autopsy report was the only one with paragraphs whited out. Clinical Summary: again beyond my ken. A list of postmortem tests was appended to each girl's report. Each had been sexually violated. Albion was a secreter. His blood type matched the blood secretions in the recovered sperm. No sperm had been recovered from Thea Janis. Floaters—bodies found in water—yield few clues.

I reread his confession concerning Thea, committed it to memory.

I checked the time, raised and lowered my aching shoulders. Rearranged the files carefully, replacing rubber bands, matching the wide bands to the wide indentations, the narrow to the narrow. My goal: to make the stack look as though it had never been touched.

Where in all this sea of forms and files, typed, printed, and scrawled words, was Thea? I no longer felt close to her. There was no sense of her here, of Thea, daughter, sister, child, student, prodigy. I've heard it said that "God is in the details," or maybe it's the devil who's in the details, but Thea surely wasn't. Not in the dates or the names of people interviewed, not in the lists of places searched, not in the language of the autopsy report: dead human female.

I was exhausted, my coffee cup long emptied, my bladder full. I knocked on the door for release, momentarily afraid that everyone had abandoned the patrol room.

Mooney opened the door.

"Are you clean?" he asked.

I sniffed. "Cleaner than the last person you shoved in here."

"Solve the case?"

"I have a few questions," I admitted.

"Such as?"

"Is it too late to get me an address?"

"Is it too late to get coffee?" Mooney asked.

"Are the two related?"

"They might be," Mooney said, softening it with a smile.

"Moon, I'll have coffee with you, street number or no street number."

I hit the bathroom. It took him five minutes to dig up old Woodrow MacAvoy's Marshfield address.

I figured I'd wait till Moon had devoured a couple of doughnuts before I asked him to help me set up a meeting with Albert Ellis Albion, the man who'd murdered Thea.

PART TWO

"I am half sick of shadows," said
The Lady of Shalott.

ALFRED, LORD TENNYSON

*T*he coins felt damp and heavy in his hand. Quarters mostly, a sprinkling of dimes and nickels. Eight bucks' worth, and for that he'd had to stand on line at the bank twenty-two minutes. No Harvard Square clerk at any ritzy store was willing to make change, not even if he bought a pack of cigarettes or chewing gum.

He probably smelled. He couldn't remember the last time he'd showered. Rough paper towels and liquid soap from rest room dispensers didn't seem to do the job.

She answered on the second ring, her voice flat and familiar. Her gray voice, he called it, the one that answered with no enthusiasm, with no hope that the phone might bring good news.

Perversely he chose not to identify himself. If she

couldn't recognize his voice, they had nothing to say to each other.

"Why didn't you tell me?" he asked.

"Where are you?" she responded immediately, even though it must have been two in the morning Seattle time. "I'll come get you. Are you okay?" She knew who it was all right.

"So we're poor folk, are we?" he said, scorn and sarcasm dripping across the miles. "No ready money for even junior college. Work hard, boy, it's the only way you'll get ahead."

"Where are you?" she repeated.

"Massachusetts. 'If you go to Massachusetts, be sure to wear a flower in your hair.' Did you do that? Wear a flower?"

" 'San Francisco,' " she said. "It's 'If you go to San Francisco.' " Her correction infuriated him. He almost broke the connection right then. But the news was really too sweet to keep to himself. And the little blondie didn't seem to understand much.

He said, "He's in your book, huh? The guy running for governor? You were a buddy of the dead sister, right? Did he fuck all her friends and dump 'em? Or maybe you were just one of the servants, huh?"

"Honey, no!" She broke in, interrupting his thoughts.

Dammit, he thought, *didn't she even remember his name?* "Dear, darling, honey," there were times he'd swear she couldn't remember his goddamn name. What did she give him a weirdo name like that for, anyhow?

"Sweetie, you need to listen. I made up all those things. They never happened. Do you understand?"

"Oh, sure. That's why they're willing to pay me the big bucks. They appreciate fiction around here."

"Come home," she said. There was a pleading tone in her entreaty that he found immensely satisfactory. She might as well have told him he was calling the shots, holding the cards, for once in his life. "Come home now. Do you have money for airfare? I can wire it to you. Just tell me where to send it."

"Money," he said. "Now there's an interesting subject. You'll be glad to know I'm getting mine. They're gonna give me a ton of money, you'd better believe it. They owe me big."

"Honey!" Her voice was light and feathery, a panicked whisper he'd never heard before. "Stay away from them, stay away from all of them. Do you hear me?"

"I cut me a deal," he said. "A better deal than you ever got."

"Go to Dr. Manley, Dr. Andrew Manley. Listen, here's the address and phone—12 Standing Brook, Weston . . . 555-8432. I already called him, after you went missing. Wait, please, don't hang up. I'll meet you there as soon as I can. I'll phone him again. Don't trust anybody else, just Dr. Manley. Wait for me there—"

Sure. She always thought she knew best.

He hung up without another word, filial duty accomplished. The phone rang, jarring his ear, immediately. "At the tone please deposit one dollar and seventy-five cents," the mechanized voice squawked.

He thought about walking out, letting the phone ring for all eternity, changed his mind and diligently fed money into the slot. Better not to call attention to himself, not right now. It was chump change, nothing to get bent out of shape about.

The little blonde was exuberant. She whooped and said, right on, or something dumb like that. He wasn't really listening. He'd tuned her out after his visit to the big Dover house.

19

Three phone messages. My popularity was definitely on the upswing. One was a hard-breathing hang-up call, which made me reassess my initial view concerning popularity. One was from Gloria stating that the harassment campaign against Thurman W. Vandenburg had begun. The third was from Paolina, which surprised me because her rustic camp, while it has many charms, has no phones for the campers. She must have walked all the way into town, slid her coins into the pay slot only to hear a recorded message. She sounded okay, said she'd try to call again, didn't give a reason for wanting to talk. Homesick? I wondered.

Insomnia. Blame it on the three cups of coffee I'd inhaled at Dunkin' Donuts, trying to get the stink of the police station out of my nose. Might as well blame it on the phase of the moon. I've got it; I live with it. Gives me extra time for guitar picking. Or if I'm deep in a case, for research.

With little faith, I dialed the twenty-four-year-old phone number for Edgar Barrett Jr., the unfortunate black gardener who'd taken up so much of the Cambridge cops' time during the early days of the Thea Janis disappearance.

The number had been disconnected. No forthcoming information. Thank you very much.

I flipped on my computer, which automatically dialed my on-line service. Icons filled the screen and I double-clicked on Netscape. The Netscape window appeared. I single-clicked on "location": at the top of the screen, quickly typed in http://www.switchboard.com/. "Switchboard" had been on-line for a couple of months now. I got their welcome page, hit the return key. A prompt appeared, asking me to enter information. I typed "Barrett Jr." under last name, "Edgar" under first. "Boston, MA." Pressed the search button.

No hits.

I decided to modify the search. Just Edgar Barrett, leave off the junior part.

Still nobody.

Further modification.

E. Barrett, Boston. Plenty of those. A list of eight, which was all the service would provide at a time, probably not to overwhelm the client. I used paper and pencil to write down those eight—sometimes I'm attracted to ancient technologies—clicked on "next page" for the remainder. Only three more. Of the eleven possibles, five were full names, six were simply E. Barretts, which meant they were probably females hiding behind their first initial. I'd be happy to locate any relative who could tell me about Edgar, so I quickly made up a tale about an old bank deposit I was trying to trace. The tale had its merits: I could be who I was—a private investigator—which would give me credibility since businesses don't do 10 P.M. phone calls. I do, because more folks are home then. The basic answer rate is higher. So are tempers, if you rouse people from sleep.

Money is an interesting topic to most people. Reuniting people with long-lost money is a powerful lure. Even if old Edgar didn't have two dimes to rub together, one could always imply that he'd hit the lottery and kept mum.

None of the E. Barretts panned out, from the worst, who yelled and called me names, to the best, who thought we ought to have dinner together because he liked my phone vibes.

I decided to go with location, mainly because Boston is still a segregated city, and the chances of finding a Barrett who knew Edgar Barrett Jr. were considerably greater in his home community of Roxbury than in primarily white South Boston.

Switchboard allowed me to modify my search to Barrett, *, Roxbury. I worked my way through the alphabet, fortified by a tall glass of orange juice.

Mavis Barrett was cagey, querulous, and opinionated. She didn't think folks ought to use the phone past ten at night, startle people like that. She wasn't eager to hang up. Either she was a lonely woman desperate to talk, or else she knew something about Edgar. She wanted to know how much money was involved.

"A considerable amount," I said. "Otherwise it wouldn't be worth my while to pursue Mr. Barrett Jr."

"That's Edgar Barrett Jr.?" she said.

"Yes," I said. "He's a man of color, could have

called himself 'Ed' or Edgar, might have dropped the 'Junior.' "

"And supposin' he should happen to be dead?" she said accusingly. "His money gonna go to the government?"

"His money would go to his legal heir. If I can locate that person before the statute of limitations runs out." I added that last bit of spurious information because I wanted to prod her a bit. I didn't want our phone call to swallow the whole night.

"He had a boy," she said. "I'm Edgar's sister. Do I stand to get anything? Finder's fee?"

I said, "That would depend on whether your information turned out to be accurate."

I had a strong feeling that if I'd replied in the negative, she'd have hung up and dialed the State Treasurer's Office. Massachusetts publishes a yearly list of unclaimed bank accounts. She was smart enough to figure that if she could cut me out of the picture, she might get Edgar's son to lend her a few bucks.

"What's Edgar's son's name?" I said as though it were a routine inquiry on a list. "Do you know his age? Address? His phone number?" I let my voice take on a weary tone, as if I had little interest in her information, as if I figured it would just turn out to be another false lead.

"Girl," she said, "my brother, Edgar, named his boy Edgar, and young Edgar is living with a woman name of Esther Briony." She spelled out Esther's last name. "They're right up the street from me on Amory Terrace, and they go to bed early 'cause of the children. So don't you go calling them tonight."

"I won't," I promised. "You wouldn't happen to know where your nephew works?"

"And why wouldn't I? He works for the Parks Department. Raises flowers in a city greenhouse long as six, eight fancy cars."

"Thank you very much, Miss Barrett."

I hung up. Would she call her nephew tonight, breaking the rule about late calls? Would it matter if she did? I got the listing for E. Briony on Amory Terrace, Roxbury. Government listings for the City of Boston gave me the location of the city greenhouse. Near Lemuel Shattuck Hospital in Franklin Park.

The doorbell rang. I waited to see if it would chime three times for Roz, who might or might not be at home, alone or otherwise. The bell sounded only once.

Past eleven o'clock, I don't race to the door and fling it ajar. I don't assume that Roz has forgotten her key, which she occasionally does, or that Keith Donovan desires to spend the night, which he occasionally does. Nor do I usually unlock the bottom left-hand drawer of my desk and grab my S&W 40. Maybe Mooney's constant harping on the Gianelli mob threat had gotten to me.

I made sure the safety was set, stuck the automatic in the back of my jeans, and went to peer out the peephole, leaving all the lights exactly as they were.

I keep my porch light on all night. Always have. Helps the burglars ascertain what kind of locks they're up against. And switching on a light to help you squint through the peephole is a dead giveaway that somebody's home. There are evenings when I do not care to be interrupted by Greenpeace or MassPIRG, no matter how noble the cause.

Garnet Cameron shifted from foot to foot on the stoop. I scanned the area. Big car out front.

He was still suited and tied. I was back in jeans and

T-shirt. Sartorial advantage to him, comfort advantage to me.

Had he brought me the tattered contract remnants?

I opened the door. The process takes some time, what with multiple locks and a dead bolt. You can't get into or out of my house without a key.

"I hope I'm not calling too late," he said as soon as he could speak through the screen.

"I was up," I said. "Come in."

"This is a nice place," he said, looking around my foyer, "nice neighborhood."

"You don't have to campaign, Mr. Cameron."

"Garnet. I think you've overheard enough about my life to call me by my first name."

"Would you like some coffee, Garnet?"

"Only if it's already made, Carlotta."

He said my name hesitantly, as though he were tasting it for the first time, savoring it on his tongue.

"It isn't. I've got water, as in non-bottled tap, and orange juice, from the carton."

"Juice," he said, eyeing the wooden coatrack. "Mind if I hang up my jacket? It's warm."

"Go ahead."

When I came back with two glasses of orange juice, he was slumped on the sofa, not seated in the straight-backed chair I keep near my desk, the "client" chair. He looked exhausted.

I sat in my aunt Bea's old rocker.

"I don't suppose you've received that notebook back from your friend?" he asked.

"It should come in a couple of days," I said.

"A couple of days," he echoed as though I'd said a couple of years. "My mother no longer wishes to continue with this investigation. She feels that it will stir up matters better left forgotten. If the press got this between their teeth, they could run with it for three months easily. It could crowd out every legitimate campaign issue, make this a referendum on my family, on part of the past we'd rather forget."

"You don't think there's any chance your sister might have actually written the chapter?"

"Thea? If I did, I'd quit the campaign and help you look for her. God knows I'm tempted to quit already."

"Why?" I ventured. "I thought you were a shoo-in, a sure thing."

"I'm sorry. I shouldn't dump this on you. Sometimes it's hard, that's all. I feel the pressure; it's tough to have a whole family's hopes and dreams rest in one person. I never thought it would come to this."

"Come to what?"

"I wasn't born an only child. Thea's success took a lot of stress off the burden of being the Cameron flag-bearer."

"You still have a sister."

"I have one living sister. If you're treasuring some fantasy that she's the one who wrote the forgery, forget it. Beryl's not capable of writing. Not anything. Not anymore."

The night seemed incredibly quiet. I willed the telephone silent, the doorbell still.

"What happened to Beryl?" I asked softly.

"No one really knows," he answered. "They label it 'schizophrenia,' but that's just a name. It's a neurobiological disorder of unknown origin. There's no cause and no cure. It often hits in the late teens, early twenties. Beryl started hearing voices, making strange sounds, before I went off to prep school, before Thea died. We used to tease her . . ."

"Andrew Manley was her doctor?"

A flicker of distaste crossed his features. "Not the first, nor the last. My mother saw Beryl's disease as an attack on our family, an attack on her as a mother, a visible form of stigmatization. And in some way, I think she was afraid we might all catch it, might all become delusional, scary people talking to ourselves, screaming random words."

"It's not contagious," I said.

"But it does run in families," he said. "I think Thea was especially afraid that she might turn into Beryl some day. They were close, shared the same room, even though we had plenty of bedrooms."

He sat, quiet and composed, on my sofa, so different from the energized dynamo I'd met earlier that day.

"I think my mother is afraid that the truth about Beryl would spoil my chances in this election. People are so uninformed about mental illness. They're so terrified by it. The different are not well tolerated, not here, not anywhere." He gave a short bitter laugh.

"What's funny?"

"Absolutely nothing. My sister, Beryl, is under psychiatric care and, given the success of the drugs they've tried so far, will be forever. My sister, Thea, who'd have been the voice of her generation, is dead. Which leaves me to carry the torch. And the strange thing is that most of the time, I feel up to the task; I feel that I can make a difference, that politically this state is ripe for change—! Forgive me," he said, stopping himself abruptly. "I mistake individuals for audiences. I'll stop the speech."

"It sounded like a good one," I said. "Strong opening."

"Thanks, but no thanks." He stared at the fireplace,

the rug, the mantelpiece. "This is a restful room. I think I could fall asleep here."

"That's because you're exhausted," I said quickly to quash the thought. I did not need a Cameron sleeping on my sofa. "What do you think happened to Thea?"

That woke him. "What do you mean? Everyone knows what happened to her. I remember the whole thing. I wasn't a child. I was eighteen."

"Where was she going that Thursday night? It doesn't make sense. Was she running away? Did she have a lover?"

"Thea," he said, his eyes crinkling at the corners. "Thea was probably off on another 'great adventure.'"

"I don't follow."

"I'm sorry, of course not. My sister saw her life in terms of adventures. If it had been summertime, I'd have been part of the whole thing, which could have involved anything, absolutely anything, from robbing a neighbor's house, leaving the loot on their front doorstep, ringing the bell, and running away, to trying to catch the biggest fish in creation, and then letting him go."

"But it wasn't summer," I said.

"No." He pressed his lips together. "I think she'd decided to spend the night in Marblehead, at our beach house. She could have made it easy on everyone. She could have told Dad. She could have had somebody drive her up. She could have taken a bus, a cab. But no, it had to be secret and mysterious."

"She hitchhiked."

"Yeah, that was Thea—live and learn, life on the road. Maybe she'd find somebody who'd make a good story, a great poem, a character in a play. Instead . . ."

He sat his empty tumbler down on an end table, shook his head sadly.

"I still miss her," he said. "I adored her, worshiped her. Especially as Beryl grew more and more distant. Like I said, I didn't grow up an only child." He swallowed audibly. "I thought I'd always have them, two sisters I could trust with every secret thought—I'm sorry. I'm wandering. I just came to tell you that the investigation is off. My mother's already voided the check—"

He stood, but his exit was spoiled by the insistent ring of the doorbell. It was Henry, the chauffeur, wild-eyed, holding a cellular phone at arm's length like it was a poisonous snake.

20

The chauffeur handed the phone to Garnet as if he couldn't get rid of it fast enough.

"Urgent," he mouthed, then beat a hasty retreat to stand like a sentinel on the stoop.

"What?" Garnet barked into the mouthpiece.

As he listened, his face lost all color, draining from tan to putty. Reaching out blindly, he touched a wall, his fingers barely grazing the surface. Taking two awkward steps forward, he leaned against it. I honest to God thought he might faint.

He said, "Wait. I'll take it in the car."

I said, "Tell whoever it is you'll call back."

"Shut up," he mouthed.

"Is there a scrambler on that phone? Do you want

everyone in the neighborhood eavesdropping?" Dammit, I thought, a politician ought to know better.

"Look," he said firmly into the receiver, "this phone's not secure. Call me at—" He glared at me and I gave my number. He parroted it into the phone. "No, it's not a trick. Immediately."

He stared wildly around the room. I indicated my desk phone.

"Somewhere private," he demanded.

"In the kitchen, or upstairs, first door on the left."

He chose upstairs. My bedroom, with its habitually unmade bed. Took the steps two at a time. The phone shrilled while he was still at the top of the stairs.

I soaked it in: Garnet's pallor, the aura of disaster. The chauffeur was outside, staring at the limo as though someone was apt to steal it, not an unlikely scenario. I sauntered casually to my desk, waited till the phone was between rings, then—oh so gently—lifted the receiver.

If Garnet hadn't been so intent on the call's content, he might have heard the tiny click.

"Please put her back on," he was saying. "My God, don't hurt her. I'm not trying to set you up!"

The other voice was inhuman, metallic, *someone with a digital voice-changer*. "Finger by finger," it said menacingly. "That's how she'll come back to you, Mr. Cameron. It's your choice. Two million bucks or you'll never see more of her than ten broken fingers. Maybe we'll leave the nails on, maybe we won't. You won't even find her body. Understand?"

"Wait!" Garnet insisted. "Let me speak to her again!" The other line disconnected and I pressed the receiver into the cradle as well.

I heard footsteps on the stairs. I didn't have time to analyze my decision.

"We can discuss my ethics later," I said. "I eavesdropped. What are you going to do?"

"You what?" He made his way down the stairs, carefully hanging on to the banister like he needed the support.

"I overheard the phone call."

He sat on the second step from the bottom, sank into it as though all the air had abruptly left his body.

"They've taken her," he whispered. "Oh, my God."

"Who? Who've they taken?"

He looked at me uncomprehendingly, undecided.

"Who?" I demanded, kneeling so our eyes were on a level.

His words came out in a powerful rush. "Marissa. I talked to her. She sounded frightened."

"Wait a minute. Earlier today, she left with a pile of luggage," I said.

"Trial separation," he agreed. "We didn't know how long we could keep it from the press."

"Where was she supposed to go?"

"Her mother's place in Rhode Island. She must be there. This has to be some kind of hoax. Someone who saw her leave—"

"Call Rhode Island. Make sure she got there."

"No! Her mother will be terrified!"

"Let me call. I'll pretend to be a reporter."

"She'll hang up!"

"I'll pretend to be a girlfriend! For chrissakes, what's the number?"

He spoke the digits quickly, but I didn't need to write them down.

"Rosemary," he muttered. "Tell whoever answers you're Rosemary and you need to talk to Missy."

A woman with a twangy Texas drawl answered. I wasn't sure if she was the mother, the secretary, the maid. She said Missy wasn't there in a cheerful voice. Wasn't expected. Did I want her Dover number? I hung up, ruining Rosemary's reputation for politeness.

"Didn't she tell her mother she was coming?" I asked Garnet.

"No. We weren't sure. I hoped she'd hang on till after the campaign. My life isn't always this crazy, this public. Marissa's 'visit,' if it came to that, was going to be a surprise."

Some surprise.

He stood up and started fumbling around the hall, trying to remember where he'd hung his jacket.

"Sit down," I ordered. "Or go in the kitchen and make yourself some toast. We need to call the FBI."

He turned on me, slammed both hands on my shoulders with more power than I expected. "No! He said they'd kill her!"

I pushed him away.

"Of course," I said. "That's what kidnappers do. They terrify you and then they extort money. Unless you believe their threats, they don't get paid. But money is what they really want, not blood. That's your trump card, and the FBI knows how to play it. They don't send guys who come blazing out of cop cars with screaming sirens. Kidnapping is the one thing the FBI handles really well."

Garnet shook his head. "It could be a hoax."

"That's what you said before you found out she wasn't at her mother's."

"She could be somewhere else. Maybe she decided to spend the night with a friend. She's unpredictable."

"Sure," I said. "Pretty soon you'll convince yourself you didn't hear her voice on the phone."

"It could have been a recording—"

"Do you want her dead? Would a dead wife be better, campaign-wise, than a wife who wants a divorce?"

He'd have hit me if I hadn't backed out of range. I'd gotten his attention.

"Look," he said, "I need time to think this over."

"You need to call the FBI. *Now.* Or else I will."

He came close enough to threaten. "If you tell a soul, I'll see you lose your license within the week. Within the week, do you understand?"

"I'm an officer of the court—" I began.

"Don't pull that bullshit on me. You're nothing of the kind."

I should have known better than to try it on a lawyer, but he was distressed. I thought he might fall for it.

"So how long do you have to wait for the first finger?" I asked nastily. If I could provoke him into swinging at me, I decided I'd take the hit. Any reason to call the cops.

"Shut up!" he said. "Just shut up! It's a hoax and that's it. Final!"

He stormed out of the house, ripping his jacket off the coatrack. Henry, the chauffeur, followed like a shadow down the steps and across the lawn. The car doors slammed loudly. Someone gunned the engine. The big Cadillac peeled rubber as it left the curb.

21

I enjoy earning my livelihood as a private investigator. The only other thing I've got going for me is an updated cabbie license. It's not like Karolyn Kirby's itching to call and beg me to try out for the women's Olympic volleyball team.

Practical matters—food and taxes—kept my hand off the phone.

A new thought plunked me down in my desk chair: *If I hadn't answered the door, if I hadn't been home, what would Garnet Cameron have done next?*

Richard Nixon made it lousy for all politicians. Garnet hadn't even muttered, "I am not a crook," and already I suspected him.

I unlocked my desk, removed both copies and the original of Thea's maybe, maybe-not first chapter plus poem, and separated them. I left one copy in my desk drawer, anchored by my S&W 40, which I was glad to remove from the waistband of my jeans.

The original notebook and poem, I moved to my favorite hiding place. It's a good one. Take a plastic litter tray, place your valuables—smothered in Saran Wrap, the flatter the better—inside. Cover with a plastic liner, the same color and cut to the exact dimensions of the litter tray, then pour on the Kleen Kitty, and let the cat, in this case, T.C., my black beauty with the prestigious zip code, go about his business. Few are the burglars who sift the kitty litter.

The second copy I placed in a mailing envelope, which I addressed to myself.

I hit the phone, searching for Mooney. He wasn't in his office, wasn't on call. Which left his home, a place I try not to invade, because his dragon-lady mother, who cordially hates my guts, might be on the prowl.

I had to try.

Mooney answered after five rings and I breathed a sigh of relief.

I didn't identify myself, not wanting to risk my license.

I said, "Have I got a treat for you."

"Really." His voice was dry with disbelief.

"I ought to keep it for myself," I said.

"Maybe you should."

"I mean, I could use the total adoration of an FBI agent. It would be a distinct business advantage."

Mooney kept silent. He's good at that.

"If I give you this, I think it should cancel all outstanding debts," I said. "Plus you'll owe me one tiny favor."

"It would have to be absolutely amazing," Mooney said.

I said, "Don't you want the FBI eating out of your hand?"

"No, I want to be an astronaut when I grow up."

"I'm serious, Moon. If there's any agent whose benevolence would put you in good shape, call him now, and get him over to the Cameron residence. As in Garnet Cameron."

"Why would I drag my weary body to Dover?"

"Kidnapping."

His manner altered completely. It was as if his voice stood at attention, saluted. "Who?" he demanded.

"Marissa Cameron. Help the FBI find her and keep our guy in the governor's race. You can vote for him. I can vote for him."

"That'll make two."

"Moon, I'm serious."

"So am I. If I call my buddy at the Fibbies, what do I tell him? I read it in my tea leaves?"

"Do not, repeat, do *not* use my name. If you do, I'm dead. Tell him a civic-minded citizen picked up a reference to a political kidnapping on her cellular phone. She heard the name 'Marissa.' Got scared and called you. You pieced it together."

"Why'd she call me? I'm not the FBI."

"Mooney, make up your own story, for chrissakes. This is the goods."

"It'd better be. Special Agents in Charge have lost their sense of humor now that everybody knows J. Edgar wore a dress."

"Special Agents never had a sense of humor, Mooney."

"Oh."

"And I want something."

"Besides a cancellation of all debts?"

"I need to meet Albert Ellis Albion. Thea's killer. He's at Walpole, and I'm betting you can get me in to see him."

"Why?"

"Why not?"

"Carlotta—"

"Mooney, people are asking about her. Old manuscripts are popping up. Old manuscripts, and possibly new ones, too."

"Words from the dead?"

"I want to meet the killer."

"And the Camerons? How do they feel about this?"

"Tessa Cameron wrote me a humongous check." This was not a lie. She'd voided it, but I saw no reason to share that information with Mooney.

"And I do the work," Mooney said. "Thanks a heap."

"Don't worry. You'll get the glory."

"Just what I need."

I decided he was not in the mood for questions about Beryl Cameron. " 'Been on the job too long,' Moon," I said, quoting an old blues refrain.

He hung up.

I replaced the receiver in the cradle, idly staring at Paolina's postcard. One year younger than Thea'd been when she wrote *Nightmare's Dawn*. Two years younger than Dorothy Jade Cameron when she died.

Paolina has talent if not genius. No one would call her "my brilliant child," unless they were talking about the sparkle in her eyes or the deep shine of her hair. She has the gift of rhythm. She's the percussionist in her junior high band, swaying to the beat, bringing stick or brush to drumhead, triangle, or bells at the precise moment.

To lose a child, as Tessa had. To lose more than one. To lose "my brilliant child . . ."

The phone rang. I tensed, imagining Garnet at the other end, accusing me of breaking faith, imagining the kidnappers. I'd given them this number!

"Bitch, you'd better stop those calls—"

I recognized Vandenburg from the greeting, halted him with, "Where's Carlos?"

"I don't—"

He was going to say "know." I hung up before he got the chance. I didn't want the DEA tracing him to my phone.

I tried to sleep, but spent most of the night studying Andrew Manley's curious bibliography. If I'd known my computer protocols better, I might have been able to download articles about recovered memory syndrome. But I struck out.

The screen-gazing exhausted my eyes. I could still see the commas and semicolons and prompts after I shut down the machine and turned off the lights. They kept on blipping, humming me to dreamless sleep.

22

I woke secure in the knowledge that I'd forgotten something terribly important. I find the shower an excellent locale for short-term memory retrieval, and it was there, with cold water thundering on my head, that I realized I needed to phone Gloria in order to nail down a piece of this increasingly complex jigsaw puzzle.

Dressed in shorts and T-shirt, I shook excess water from my hair while searching the stoop for the morning *Globe*. No mention of a Cameron kidnapping. Good. I might keep my license.

I dialed ITOA, figuring Gloria'd be dispatching for the Independent Taxi Owners during the morning commute. She zapped me on hold while I burned toast.

She tuned in as soon as my mouth was full. She has food radar.

"Glory," I managed, swallowing quickly, "I need you to locate a cabbie who picked up a fare off Farm Road in Dover, 1:45 P.M. yesterday, possibly heading to the airport. Every detail."

"Do I offer a reward?"

"Twenty bucks."

"That's a reward?"

"It's better than getting hit with a lawsuit."

"Dover," she muttered. "I'll see what I can do. What're you eating?"

"Toast. Burned and plain."

"Why bother?"

"I don't know."

By the time I'd finished my lavish breakfast and headed out toward the car, the heat was shimmering off the pavement. My khaki shorts were the right choice, but the dark upholstery of my Toyota—chosen for durability—was set on "fry." I grabbed a pale towel from my gym bag, smoothed it over the seat. The steering wheel was barely touchable. I cranked the window.

Ought to call the city greenhouses, make sure Barrett was working today. But I wanted to drive, wanted the action, the motion, the illusion of progress. I also didn't want to be home if Mooney gave me away to Cameron and the FBI.

Past Lemuel Shattuck Hospital, there's a road labeled Franklin Park Maintenance Yard. It's a bumpy, narrow track, but if you stay with it to the end, you come out at the city greenhouses.

Six long glassed-in sheds. I don't know what I expected—rose-covered trellises, maybe—but it looked like a strictly utilitarian setup. Screen door on the end of the largest building, an array of sacks and terra cotta pots and tools on display.

When I opened the screen door, a bell sounded. Not as friendly and undefended as I thought.

The man who entered was fat and red-faced. Doughy, not wiry. White. I asked for Ed Barrett, got a quick insulting once-over, a nod toward the far end of the shed.

"He's busy," the guy said, by which I was meant to understand that I was speaking to Edgar's supervisor, who was eager to let me know it.

"I won't take much of his time," I said. "I'm from OSHA, checking employment conditions."

"He make some kinda complaint?"

"No," I said innocently. "Should he?"

The man gave way as I pressed forward. I managed to edge by without getting touched. If I hadn't been from some initialed government agency I doubt I'd have been so lucky.

I passed through a room of cheerful marigolds. The place was hot and humid. The back of my shirt was already sticking to my skin. The man I took to be Edgar Barrett was busily potting chrysanthemums, separating the small stalks, giving them room for their late summer stretch. The greenhouse was a riot of color—apricot, white, pink, flame orange.

"Do you have a few minutes?" I asked, turning to see if the supervisor had followed.

"I doubt it." Barrett was a slim man in his thirties with long agile fingers. He wore an oversized checked shirt, baggy chinos, running shoes. "What you want to talk about? Flowers?"

"Was your father a gardener?"

"Damn good gardener," he said.

"Did he work at the Avon Hill School?"

His fingers kept moving but the rest of him went still.

"You the 'investigator' called my aunt?" he asked scornfully. "Don't waste your time on me. I know that lost money scam is pure con. Mavis can't guard her mouth. Never could."

"I am a private investigator," I said.

"You're a little late. I don't think my daddy needs one now he's dead." Edgar's voice stayed scornful. He kept doing what he was doing with the flowers, untangling clumped roots, setting them in fresh pots, staking the weaker stalks.

"Aren't you curious?" I asked.

"Curious?" he said. "No."

"How about angry?" I said.

He took his time before replying. "Doesn't put bread on the table, that anger shit."

"Your father lost his job."

"My father lost *everything*. Not just that one job, but all the jobs he ever had. He was the estate man for that fancy Brattle street crowd. He went from house to house, and the neighbors all tried to get him to out-do what he'd done for Mr. Polaroid-Company or Mrs. Executive Wife. If he put in a bed of pink tulips at the Armenian church, everybody wanted a bed of pink tulips. Then some white girl goes missing and he can't get work, not even a vegetable patch."

"How old were you?"

"Eight years old, just eight, and I remember it like it happened yesterday. I remember him coming home all beat up and sayin', oh no, nothin' happened to him, *nothin',* he fell down on the street. I remember the way my momma and my aunt Mavis looked at him like he wasn't there anymore. You know, women look at a man long enough like that, he actually disappears, and that's what my daddy did. Disappeared down the neck of a bourbon bottle and that's what he died from. Today, I see a cop on the street—black or white, it don't matter—and I cross over to the other side. Sometimes I spit."

"The police had no evidence against your father."

"Really? You comin' all the way down here to tell me that after twenty-four years . . . Well, I do appreciate it, you understand. I'm sure my daddy would appreciate it."

I didn't apologize. It was too late for that. I don't know—maybe it's never too late. Sometimes I think about traveling to Germany or Poland, countries of my childhood nightmares, places where my mother's relatives disappeared into the camps. I wonder if people will stare at my profile, my unmistakably Jewish nose, and mutter, "I'm sorry."

Would I accept the apology? I don't know.

"I'm sorry," I said.

"What for? Sorry my daddy was uppity? He spoke to a white girl. A rich white girl. Do you understand the gravity, the enormity of his crime?"

I nodded. *As much as I can understand,* I thought.

"They wanted him to give them names," he muttered.

"What names?"

"They wanted my daddy to say he'd brought his buddies along, to ogle little white girls. They wanted to convict a black man. They had a regular hard-on about it, the perp being a black man—my dad, my uncle, some friend of my dad's. Questioned all our neighbors. 'Jimmy Lee, you ever go to Cambridge with Eddie?'

Nobody ever called my dad Eddie. He didn't have a lot of friends before, and he sure didn't have any after."

"The chrysanthemums are beautiful," I said after a while, to break the long silence.

"They're hardy," he said. "They don't break easily. They last a good spell."

I waited a little longer.

"Did your dad ever take you to work with him?"

"Couple times. You figure I hurt that white girl?"

"Just twice?"

"I was eight years old. He must have taken me with him more than twice. Enough so I remember those fancy gardens. He taught me to yank aphids off the leaves, let the ladybugs be. Pull weeds. I learned what good soil smells like when it's wet—"

"Did you meet a man who worked with your dad?"

"Just the Cuban guy."

"Cuban guy have a name?"

"El Producto," he said flatly.

"Like the cigar."

"I'm sorry, lady, I don't remember the guy's name. He was fly-by-night help, somebody didn't know shit about gardening. That's what my dad said. My dad told me stay away from that dude. He's bad business. So I did."

"Why'd your dad think he was 'bad business'?"

"Cause he's always mouthing off about how important he is, and there he's workin' as a gardener, same as my dad. Cause he's some big deal with the CIA, so he says."

The CIA, I thought. Oh, yeah. All this case needed was the CIA.

"The police never found him," I said.

"The police never looked. They didn't hate Cubans

enough to make the effort. Not enough Cubans tryin' to go to South Boston High School. Understand this: If that Albion guy hadn't confessed, my kids would be visitin' their granddaddy in jail."

"When did your father die?"

"Seven years ago. Didn't you read about it in *Time* magazine?"

"He left his son a fine line of sarcasm."

"And not much else."

"I'm authorized to pay you a hundred dollars for your time."

"Oh, yeah? Who from? The Police Benevolent League?"

"Take it as a gift, from your father to his grandchildren."

"They don't need your gift."

"I'm leaving two fifties under this pot of marigolds. Don't disappoint me and let your boss find them."

"Give 'em here," he said. He mumbled his thanks.

I wanted to tell him I didn't need his thanks, but I let him have the last word. He needed it more than I did.

23

I must have driven around the rotary at the entrance to Franklin Park four or five times, brooding at the wheel. When it started to feel like there might be no exit to the merry-go-round, I flashed my turn signal, scaring everyone in sight, and pulled off onto the main track, Jewish War Veterans Drive, although no one seems to call it that anymore. I zipped by the golf course, crowded on a fine morning, past White Stadium, and the zoo's stone lions. Just driving through, I could see that Franklin Park was definitely coming up in the world. Lone joggers paced by. Walkers paraded in multiracial groups. I wondered if the city would ever bring back the stables and the horse trails, made a silent vow to take Paolina to the zoo before she got too "old" and "sophisticated" for such shenanigans. With luck, maybe she never would.

Luck. Edgar Barrett Jr., deceased, hadn't gotten his share of good luck—given that there's a finite amount of luck in the world, an idea open to debate. Even after his death, his unemployment, his alcoholism, had left deep scars in the psyche of his only son, given him a legacy of terrible and justifiable rage.

Would Edgar Barrett, the eight-year-old boy whose universe had shattered, the thirty-two-year-old man I'd just seen, strike back some day? At the police? At the Cameron family? Did reading Garnet Cameron's name in the newspapers make him shudder with revulsion? Did he contrast his father's fate with Garnet's?

Garnet hadn't been abused by the police. He'd barely been questioned. On the other hand, he'd lost a sister he professed to love. Do the privileged classes keep their scars well hidden?

I drove home, hollered for Roz, got the standard response. Nothing.

On-line, "Switchboard" had no listing, professional or personal, for Dr. Andrew Manley. I could have disguised my voice, called the Cameron residence, and asked for him. But the FBI would have a fix on the incoming number before I started to speak, and I wanted to stay out of their way if at all possible.

So I began on Manley's "gift," his bibliography. Most entries were articles from the *American Journal of Psychiatry,* the *British Journal of Psychiatry,* the *Journal of the American Academy of Child and Adolescent Psychiatry,* the *Journal of the American Psychoanalytic Association*—and my personal favorite—the *Journal of Neurology, Neurosurgery, and Psychiatry.* The list included books as well, most of these published by university presses or an outfit called Basic Books.

I could have dialed Keith Donovan; he's a shrink, after all. He'd be able to translate the articles' titles into sensible non-jargon prose. But he might be working. And I felt a strange reluctance to owe Donovan. Mooney and I could deal. I could pay Moon back with information I gleaned on the streets during investigations. Only one way I could pay Donovan back, considering that his domestic skills outshine mine on every level—with sex—and that felt wrong as wrong could be.

I hollered upstairs for Roz again, figuring that she might have been lying doggo the first time. No response, and I never invade her premises because I'm too scared of what I might find there. Roz would have known how to make America Online divulge the location of its psychiatric-journal file and download selected articles. I hadn't a clue. Seems like every time I click on a browser, I'm trapped for hours. There's just so much damned information out there!

Read the manual, Roz repeats like a mantra. I've tried. My manual reads as if it had been translated from Taiwanese to German and then back into English. It could be marketed as a cure for insomnia.

Options loomed. The public library, with its cool high-ceilinged rooms, where I could find a knowledgeable librarian to help me wend my way through the publication stacks. Or a stickler for detail, who'd make me fill out a thousand call slips and wait, wait, wait. A university library, where I could gain admittance by using one of many forged ID's, con a student assistant into getting me hooked into their system.

The Liberty Café. *Yes.*

The Liberty is a downstairs cellar on Mass. Ave., technically in Central Square, but close enough to MIT to practically qualify as a classroom. It offers computer time, doughnuts, strong coffee—and a lone duffer can always count on finding a nerdy show-off, male or female. The exchange rate is fairly even. I'd buy coffee, he or she would preen, find my articles, download them. I'd pay for the time. No one would advise me to read the manual.

And the coffee's really good.

The decor is something else.

As you descend the narrow steps, you might be entering a cavern, or for those in the know, I'm told, a version of Dungeons and Dragons, a role-playing game for grown-ups, or semi-grown-ups.

The low ceiling is lit with stained-glass panels, depicting fantasy and science fiction figures. A graphic detailing the MBTA's Red Line takes up one wall. Tables, chairs, and sofas are arranged in conversational groupings. Rugs cover the uneven floor. It looks like no other coffee shop I've ever seen. And it boasts six computer stations, all equipped with Macs and printers, and just about every server you're likely to need. At four bucks an hour, it's hard to beat.

Two cappuccinos and a "fudgy delite" were the price Stanley—who lived on the fourth floor of East Campus —demanded to put his skills to the test. He used Netscape like he'd designed it. I took notes, and was able to download six articles before my guru had to leave for a summer school class. I got comfy on a sofa, kicked off my shoes, and read, that good old archaic pursuit.

One article was devoted to a discussion of where memory was stored, apparently in all lobes of the cerebral cortex, and other areas, such as the hippocampus and the medial thalamus, that I knew I'd have trouble remembering. A second article dealt with types of memory: immediate, short-term, knowledge-and-skills, priming, associative, and episodic. I learned that "priming" is the kind of memory that makes the transition from roller skates to Rollerblades, from training wheels to a two-wheeler, seem fairly easy, a logical progression. The same article stated that episodic memory is the type involved in so-called recovered memory syndrome, and defined it as "the remembrance of the things that happen in your life—the sad things, the happy things, the scary things." This I thought I could remember. Another article spoke of a specific trial, how recovered memory syndrome had been effectively used to prosecute a man for murder years after the event. The next two addressed rape and abuse prosecutions instituted years after the alleged crimes, and the possible link between recovered memory syndrome and psychiatric prompting or hypnotic suggestion. It seemed that an abnormal number of women remembered childhood abuse after entering therapy.

Whenever someone writes the words "abnormal" and "women" in the same sentence, I'm fairly certain the author is a man. I checked. No surprise.

I shifted on the sofa, sat cross-legged, shrugged, and ran both hands through my hair. My mind was racing in circles.

Memories recovered under hypnosis have been forbidden in Massachusetts courts for years. If the police bring in a hypnotist to try to get an eyewitness to recall the number of a license plate, everything that witness might say on the stand is considered tainted.

I wasn't sure where memories recovered with the aid of psychoanalysis stood in forensic terms.

Recovered memory syndrome was important to my case, unless Andrew Manley was leading me astray for purposes of his own, most likely to protect Tessa Cameron.

Andrew Manley supposedly believed that Thea Janis was alive. I could find absolutely no accounts of individuals who had experienced recovered memory syndrome of their own deaths. Zip.

Most of the deeply hidden—"repressed"—memories involved incest. Okay, I thought, let's suppose the worst. Famous Franklin Cameron raped his brilliant young daughter Thea. She threatened to tell. So he had her killed by a guy he just happened to know, a convenient serial killer on the loose. Sure.

I pressed my hands over my eyes, inhaled and exhaled. I didn't need more coffee. I needed air. A dose of reality.

Outside it was twilight. Amazing the hours a computer can chomp out of your day.

Although I'd parked my car by a meter that had long registered violation, I hadn't gotten a parking ticket. A lucky omen. My gas tank was full. Another omen.

Marshfield, I thought. On the ocean. A cool, starry night. The perfect time to visit a retired cop, ask him why his neatly organized, beautifully typed files sported an overdose of Wite-Out.

24

The Chamber of Commerce defines Cape Cod as comprising fifteen towns divided into countless villages, 365 lakes and ponds, long ribbons of good road, and 399 square miles of land forming a strong flexed arm reaching out to grab a chunk of the North Atlantic.

Nary a word about Marshfield, although when asked to describe the town, most locals hesitate only a moment before responding "down the Cape."

Marshfield, the so-called "Irish Riviera," isn't exactly on Cape Cod, Cape Cod being that land divided from the mainland by the Cape Cod Canal, with Bournedale, Cedarville, and Buzzards Bay tacked on to gain access to lovely Sagamore Beach, and including, of course, those two famous islands, Martha's Vineyard and Nantucket, refuges for artists, rock stars, and presidents.

Marshfield's too far north to qualify. Wrong county. A working-class neighborhood dotted with small, mostly neat, summer cottages a half mile walk from an eroding beachfront.

I am not talking "summer cottages" as in Newport or the Berkshires. I'm talking no foyer, walk smack into the living room, one or two bedrooms max, tiny kitchen, single bath. No insulation, few year-round inhabitants. Often an outdoor shower. Pebbles and sand in the backyard, a few wayward tufts of grass.

Sergeant MacAvoy's place looked winterized, a do-it-yourself job from the way the stovepipe stuck out at an angle through the shake-shingled roof. A lamp burned, which gave me hope as I climbed two steps to a square wooden porch. No doorbell. I knocked, knocked louder. No answer.

Well, it had been a nice drive. Moon ringed with a golden halo, shadowed by scudding clouds. I'd stroll down to the beach, kick off my sandals, wet my feet in the foamy tide, collect seashells for Paolina. Try again, nine-thirty or ten.

I peered in the curtainless front window. A TV the size of a small movie screen occupied most of one wall. A leather chair lay in the reclining position as if its owner had just popped out to go to the bathroom. Maybe he had. I waited five minutes, knocked again. No response. The beach, definitely.

I briefly considered a B&E, just to keep my hand in, see what other goodies Sergeant MacAvoy collected besides giant TV's. I scanned the neighborhood. This was not the big bad city, but Marshfield has a rep: Every other house was probably owned by a retired cop. Even as I stood on the porch orienting myself—ocean to the east; I could hear waves lapping the shore—loaded rifles might be pointed at my head. Former members of the force staying in shape, practicing with newly purchased nightscopes.

I decided on strategic retreat.

I stopped with one hand on the Toyota's door. An aged Buick squatted in MacAvoy's carport. Maybe he hadn't gone far, maybe toddled over to a neighbor's.

I was thinking of doing the same when a porch light snapped on with sufficient glare to blind a burglar. Blinking, I made out a bulky form on the stoop of a nearby bungalow.

"Looking for the old goat?" The voice was a woman's, low and pleasantly rough, trace of an Irish accent.

"Sergeant MacAvoy? Yes, I am. If you know where he is—"

"Where else but the bar?"

"Which bar?"

"You're not from around here." A tinge of accusation there, a bit of suspicion. Foreigner. Beware.

"No."

"Not a troublemaker, are you?"

"No."

"Woody doesn't get so many women coming by. He'd be sad to miss one, I was thinking."

"I'm glad you were thinking that."

"Related to the man?"

"No."

"Doesn't seem to have any family in the world."

A test. If I'd claimed to be his niece, would I have been sent packing, never learning the name of the bar?

"Lucky Horseshoe," said the voice. "Two blocks

south and then cut catty-corner through the lot. If you're walking. You'll see the sign well after you hear the noise."

"Thanks," I said.

"MacAvoy jogs over most nights, so he can stagger back, if you catch my drift."

Another voice, this one male, issued from the house. The woman responded indistinctly and ill-temperedly. Hastily, she banged the door shut. I could hear her husband's "mind yer own business" through the window. "Mind yer own business": the code of the burned-out ex-cop. Why risk your life for twenty-five years and not live to enjoy your pension?

Might as well walk to the bar, I decided, sniffing the salt air, reveling in the breeze. See how my luck was holding out.

25

A rose is a rose is a rose, but a local bar is unique, especially a small-town local. I've learned to do the background fade in Boston's Irish pubs, afterhours cop hangouts, trendy Newbury Street fern-and-pickup bars. I didn't have a clue about Marshfield's Lucky Horseshoe.

On one count, Mrs. Nosy Neighbor was dead on target: I heard it before I saw it. The strains of "Black Velvet Band," belted with more drunken enthusiasm than accuracy, made me feel that my pub savvy might come in handy. A shaky accordion, bad enough to be live, kept a few of the revelers on key. I paused in a narrow, barely lit parking lot and considered my predicament.

I'm no knockout drop-dead beauty, and I've never

regretted it. *Lie. So I regretted it in high school, who the hell didn't?* But I'm basically shaped like a woman —leggy, extremely tall, red-haired—and when I walk into a bar unescorted, men tend to notice, if only to wink, nod, tsk-tsk their disapproval, and speculate about my profession.

Briefly, I wished for camouflage. My khaki shorts, turquoise tank top, and bone sandals were suited to the steamy weather. I hadn't foreseen a bar stop. I could march off to the Toyota, rummage in the backseat, probably locate a disreputable raincoat or roomy sweatshirt, sneakers. Die of heat prostration on the return trip.

I didn't know what MacAvoy looked like. Disadvantage. On the other hand, he didn't know me at all. Advantage.

I could stroll inside, perch at an empty table, order a beer, and keep checking my watch. Pretend my date was late.

I could belly up to the bar, boldly display my credentials to the barkeep, ask him to point out MacAvoy. The barkeep would expect a tip. TV spoils real life. Bartenders think PI's dispense twenty-dollar bills like Kleenex.

A parade of pickup trucks pulled into the lot and broke my reverie. I stepped into the shadows, saw salvation in a mixed crowd of patrons—male and female —going off some factory shift, removing regimental overalls and caps. A group I could enter with, to blend or not to blend as circumstance played the hand.

I walked beneath the horseshoe nailed over the doorway; sure enough, the ends faced up so the luck wouldn't run out.

The money'd run out first. The interior was rustic,

hung with tattered fishermen's nets. The seafaring theme stopped with the nets, as if the owner had discovered them abandoned on the beach, then found other nautical items—shells or boating paraphernalia—too pricey. The accordion player's hat, displayed on a dusty upright piano, had a sign beside it advising that tips were welcome. The piano had so many missing keys it looked like an old crone's grin. The linoleum floor had begun to curl at the edges and the seams. A neon sign flickered "Budweiser" minus the "r." My cover group drew a hopeful glance from the barkeep, then a quick frown. One long-nursed beer apiece, his downcast face seemed to say, not a Chivas-on-the-rocks in the crowd.

The accordion player attacked another tune. A couple of elderly gents applauded and joined in doubtful harmony. I wondered if the accordion player owned the bar, or if he'd married the owner's sister. One thing, he was a drunk, the way his hands skipped over keys and buttons, fumbled the draw.

One of the factory crowd—older teens, younger twenties, wearing cutoff jeans and a rugby shirt—noticed me playing tag-a-long.

"I haven't seen you here before," he said.

Better than some openers I've heard.

"Haven't been here before," I said. "And if the accordion player kills one more song, I'll leave."

"He quits soon," he said with a crooked grin. "What'll you have?"

"I'll buy my own," I said, "but if you're heading to the bar anyway, I'll have whatever's on draft."

"Harp or Bass?"

"Harp," I said. Good choices both; probably what drew the townies. Not the feeble accordion, for sure.

I sat at a tiny unbalanced table till my far-too-young

swain appeared with a generously filled schooner for which he was loath to accept money. Since his buddies were staring speculatively from the bar, I slipped three dollar bills under the table. My new friend and I smiled conspiratorially.

"Jimmy," he said, leaning forward expectantly. He had a good chin, chiseled and dimpled, and he led with it like he knew it was his strong suit. His gray eyes were small, close together under shaggy eyebrows.

"Carlotta," I responded.

"You're not from around here."

Everybody could tell.

"I'm a narc," I whispered, expecting total disbelief. "Working undercover."

The guy stared at me for a split second, burst into laughter. That's exactly what they used to do when I *was* a narc, working undercover.

"You're sure at the wrong place," Jimmy said, " 'less you want to nail a couple underage kids ain't been carded."

"You one of 'em?"

"Hell, no," he said, mixing indignation with pride. "I'm twenty-one."

Well, I was twenty-one once, I felt like telling him, for no other reason than it seemed impossible that I'd ever been as young as he was. Had I ever grinned that own-the-world grin? Had I ever seemed so carefree?

The sickly accordion faded from my mind, replaced by a blues lick: "Been on the job too long," followed by a sweet guitar slide. Dave Van Ronk sings it in a gravelly voice, some old-timey tune about sheriffs and outlaws. The same line I'd quoted Mooney earlier in the day.

The kid asked me something, but I couldn't hear him over the din. I inquired if he was a local.

He nodded, sipping beer from his mug.

"Know a man named MacAvoy, ex-cop hangs around here?"

"Why?"

"Why not?"

"You're not from one of those social service agencies, are you?"

"I don't think they work nights or hang out in bars, unless you're talking about a social service I definitely do not provide."

The kid blushed scarlet, and I couldn't help wondering if he saw me as a possible date, an older sister, or someone who might be his mother's pal.

Hell, how did I see myself?

Not coming on to a twenty-one-year-old. No way.

"Is Sergeant MacAvoy here?" I asked.

His gray eyes searched the room, came to a stop at a table for four, back corner, far as you could get from the accordion. Score one for MacAvoy.

"White hair with glasses?" I asked.

"Next to him, on his right, the heavy old coot, heard he used to be tough."

"Plaid shirt?"

"Yeah."

"Thanks," I said.

"If you mean it, have another beer. On me."

"Blond girl in the denim vest, see her? She's gonna smack me if I don't leave you alone."

"Laurie doesn't own me."

"Is that what we're playing at here? Do I look like the Declaration of Independence? Why not do her a favor? If you don't want her, tell her. Other guys look interested."

"Who?" he snapped.

"Never mind," I said dryly, standing. "Tell her you thought I was your cousin, Elsie. I look a lot like her."

"Well . . . okay, if that's what you want. Nice meetin' you."

"You never met me," I said.

I worked my way past the wounded piano and the small knot of crooners. A sign pointed to the rest rooms. I followed it, hoping the scorned Laurie wouldn't trail me. Girls and Boys, the signs on the doors read, like grade school.

I stared at my face in the ill-lit bathroom mirror. I swear, crow's feet had sprung from the corners of my eyes overnight, like someone had etched fine lines on my twenty-one-year-old face while I was sleeping. Maybe I ought to go back to Jimmy, snatch him away from Laurie, drink him under the table. Take him home as a souvenir.

I ran cold water in the sink, mopped the back of my neck.

The hell with it.

Two things I know about retired cops: they like to reminisce; they like to feel important. I had to hope MacAvoy would be drunk enough to talk, but not too drunk to tell me what I wanted to know.

A delicate balance.

I consulted the mirror as if it were a crystal ball. If I'd carried any powder, I'd have powdered my nose.

I edged out of the girls' room into the narrow corridor, brushed by a leather-jacketed man whose sweaty stink lingered after he passed. I moved a chair into the breach between MacAvoy and his eyeglass-wearing neighbor, sat myself down in suddenly suspicious silence.

"Sergeant," I said, taking a deep breath and placing my ID on the table, "how do you feel about private investigators?"

He took his time studying me, then my photo, passed my license around to his buddies, who nodded and murmured appreciatively.

I spent the time gazing at MacAvoy. Maybe he'd been as young as Jimmy once, almost handsome. Now his face was round and jowly, nose doughy and lined with drinkers' veins. His skin seemed pasty in the fluorescent glare, too pale for a man who lived so close to the sea.

"Well," he announced finally, playing to his cronies, "I think they look a heluva lot better than they used to."

This drew an uproarious laugh that centered attention on our table.

"Can I speak with you alone?" I asked.

"You don't have to ask twice, girlie. Get lost, guys. Find your own fun."

"Outside," I said. "I'll walk you home."

"Haven't had that good an offer in twenty years easy," he said, hauling himself to his feet by putting a lot of his weight on the table. He pulled out his wallet, yanked out a twenty and slapped it down. "Have a round on me, boys." He added another twenty. "Drinks on the house," he announced grandly to the room in general. "I'm feeling lucky tonight."

He tried a little bit of bump and grind and I hoped he'd move it before I decided to hit him in his fat beer gut. I know, I know, I ought to use my feminine wiles to worm information out of old men, but honestly, does that mean I have to put up with crap that was stale before I was born?

I shoved my disgust aside. I'd be truly pissed if the guy was young. Older guys, hell, it was a different world then. Face it. Live with it. Pick your role, I ordered myself. They're limited: mother, daughter, wife, lover.

I'd be the sweet concerned daughter. It comes hard to me, as my late father would attest if he could, but I can pull it off for short blasts at a time.

I linked a filial arm through MacAvoy's and he was wobbly enough that he had no choice but to move, or else look as though I were dragging him unwillingly through the door. A buddy of his hooted as we left, but I had my man in tow and I didn't mind. The old goat slipped an arm around me and tried for a feel, but he was drunk and I was faster.

"Do that again, you'll need to use up some of those Medicare benefits," I cautioned.

He stared at me with hostile drunken eyes. For a brief moment, I wondered if he was carrying his piece. I'd left mine in the car, locked in the glove compartment.

I hoped I wouldn't regret it. Ex-cops, drunk ex-cops, you can never tell.

26

The silence—a mere twenty feet from the bar's entrance—was eerie. The accordion player had called it quits for the night. I regarded the hulking elderly man beside me with misgiving.

"So what's yer problem, girlie?" he said.

"No problem with me," I shot back. "How's your memory?"

"I reckon I remember more than you'll ever know, girl."

"If you want to keep calling me 'girl' and 'girlie,' I guess I could call you 'Daddy.' You like that?"

"Not particularly."

"What do you like to be called?"

He stared up at the single string of wind-whipped red plastic flags that delineated the parking area. Made me think of salvage from a used-car lot, but his face relaxed into a grin, as if he were recalling other decorations, maybe the ceiling of the high school gym. Sock hop, Saturday night.

"Pretty ladies call me Mac," he said.

Sweet daughter that I was, I smiled. "Mac, I'm Carlotta and I used to be a cop, too, but I didn't make my twenty, and I had to go private. I'd appreciate your help."

"Who tol' ya where I live?"

Suspicion wiped the grin off his face.

"Head of Boston homicide."

"An' he'd be named?"

"Mooney. I worked for him. You want to call D street, he'll tell you I'm a straight-shooter."

"Ol' bat across the street tol' ya 'bout the bar, right? Like to use her fat head for target practice. Some con breaks outa the can—some punk I nailed thirty years ago—she'll tell him where to find me, no trouble, day or night. Bitch."

He stumbled and I caught him by the elbow and damned if he didn't try the grab-ass bit again. I stepped on his toe. Hard.

"You really who ya say?" he asked.

"Yep. As I recall, your place is this way." I wasn't relishing the idea of a lengthy stroll with a drunk hanging on my arm, balancing his weight while compensating for pebbles and gravel in my sandals.

"Don't ya have a car?"

"Left it parked near your house."

"Damn, and I thought I'd be gettin' a ride home. Arthritis in my knee, and all."

"I can't carry you," I said. "Sorry."

He didn't take a step. Just stood in shadows smirking, pondering his next move.

"And which a my old triumphs did ya wanna discuss? What's so vital that ya drive out here, track an old booze-hound to his lair?"

I played unconcerned. "Why would you think I'd be interested in your old cases?"

"Ya asked about my memory, girl. I can remember whatcha said not five minutes ago, girl."

The last "girl" came out tough, a hurled insult.

I ignored it. My daughterly role was admiring and respectful. Not confrontational.

"You're sharp," I said.

"You don't know the half of it." He sat on a rough-hewn bench, and patted the seat beside him. I took it, keeping a good five inches between us. The yellowish glow from the bar illuminated the right side of his face. I wondered if his buddies could see us parked on the bench, if I should prepare for some fumbling attempt at romance, something to tell the guys about.

I said, "I can see why you might get stuck with a hot potato like the Cameron girl's disappearance. What I don't understand is why you took over so soon, just weeks into the case. The investigation started in Dover, spread to Cambridge, Marblehead. It would seem that the state police—"

MacAvoy tossed me a disparaging look, then hawked and spat onto the parking lot. "Thea Dorothy fuckin' Janis Almighty Cameron," he said with the careful precision of the drunkard. "Goddamn all Camerons, ya should excuse my French. Don't think I feel much like talkin' about that one, thanks all the same."

"But you're the one who pulled it all together, Mac,"

I said, spreading it on thick. "If it hadn't been for you, Dorothy might never have been connected with Albert Albion. Don't tell me you don't remember him. A cop doesn't get many chances to pin a big-time case on a serial killer. Have you been approached by any Hollywood types? Agents? You know, movie deals? Book offers?"

MacAvoy didn't react to a word of it. Not Albert Albion's name. Not the implicit offer of cash.

"Whole bunch of 'em should rot at the bottom of the sea," he said quietly. "Who the hell do they think they are? They speak and the earth moves, mountains move, cops sure as hell better move. Get outa the way or get the hell steam-rollered."

Seemed like he was talking about the Camerons—not cops, not serial killers.

"Some cases are like that," I said, trying again to remind him that I'd been a cop, too, that we'd played for the same team. "You need to gentle them along, like unexploded landmines."

"Right," he said, giving a single nod, as if the matter were settled, once and for all. I could barely hear him between the flags and the ocean. To my dismay, the accordion started up again.

I said, "I've seen your case file."

"Yeah?" His lack of concern seemed too elaborate, faked.

"It's in great shape," I told him. "What's left of it."

"What do you mean?"

"Crossed-out pages, missing pages, wite-out, erasures—"

"The case is closed," he said, shifting his weight. "What's your beef?"

I thought about the gravel, the stones. I could grab a handful, toss them in his face, run.

"Just a few questions."

"Such as?"

"Why were you put in charge?"

"Musta been my lucky day, girlie. Wanna know how lucky? If it hadn't a been for the Camerons, I'da retired a captain, not a goddamn sergeant. You know the difference that woulda made on my pension?"

I could look it up. Public record.

"Did you ever *see* Beryl Cameron, much less interview her?"

He stared at the bench.

"How about the rest of the family? Franklin, Tessa—"

"The Dover police took statements."

"The Dover police collected excuses, reasons the Camerons couldn't be interviewed—"

"Really now, darlin', does that surprise ya? The rich gettin' treated different from the rest of us? No wonder ya quit. Or did ya get the boot?"

I ignored the scorn in his voice. "Do you recall the date of Albion's confession?"

"No," he said carelessly. "My memory seems to be goin' after all. Ya have a cigarette on ya, darlin'? Smokin' always helps me remember."

"No," I said. "I gave 'em up."

He had a pack, almost full. He leaned against the rickety bench, fired the match on the small stretch of wood separating us. It seemed a deliberately threatening maneuver, a "stay clear" warning. In the flickering light, I caught a glimpse of an irregular five-pointed star tattooed on the back of his hand.

The tobacco smelled better than the stale beer and old vomit of the bench, I'll say that for it.

"Do you recall a Dr. Manley, a psychiatrist who may have said that Beryl Cameron was too ill to testify?"

"Can't say I do."

"Did Beryl Cameron attempt suicide during the investigation?"

"I'm sure I would have noted that in the file," he said. "Darlin'."

"How about this one? Do you think the CIA altered the files?" I asked.

"The what?" he said. "Didja say the blessed initials? Have ya been drinkin', or have I been drinkin', or is it the both of us gone mad?"

I took a deep breath of salt air. "Is there any chance Thea Janis is alive?"

"No," he said. "Not unless you believe in that reincarnation balderdash."

Hell with it, I thought, standing. It had been a nice ride.

"Who're ya workin' for?" MacAvoy asked suddenly. I made like I hadn't heard him, started the trek back to my car.

"Are the Camerons paying you? Or that other guy who's running for governor? If you're trying to shovel up dirt—"

He lurched to his feet. He was awkward, but quick. I didn't waste any time making tracks. I never broke into a run, but I stayed ready, listening, listening for footsteps.

On the drive home, I couldn't shake the feeling that someone was tailing me. Whenever I glanced in the rearview mirror there was nothing, or the usual run of indistinguishable headlamps. Once, the creepy feeling got so bad that I pulled to the side of the road, yanked open the glove compartment, and slapped my S&W 40 on the seat at my side, its metal cold against my thigh. I made sure the safety was on. Waited, humming softly under my breath.

Took me a while to recognize the song.

"Been on the job too long."

Maybe I had.

27

The way I drove I made damn sure nobody followed me. I didn't get a ticket, for speeding or any other violation, but not because I obeyed traffic rules. Past midnight, there's a scarcity of patrol cars on the road.

All that caution wasted. A cop lurked on my doorstep. Mooney. He hasn't written a traffic citation in years.

"Come on," he said.

"I'm tired."

"Gary Reedy's in the car. The FBI wants you."

"You told them about me? You gave up your source?"

"No, Carlotta, that's not the way it went. Garnet Cameron has accused you of bearing false witness."

" 'Bearing false witness'? That might cut the mustard in church, but since when is it a jailable offense?"

"Just talk to Reedy, okay?"

If it had been any cop other than Mooney, I'd have told him to scoot.

Gary Reedy had a FBI man's car, a big Mercury Marquis with a shotgun rack mounted under the roof. He had an FBI man's firm dry handshake, an FBI man's blunt chin and deep gruff voice. I hate to admit it, but I liked the guy. He made me think of the perfect dad, not the perfect J. Edgar Hoover suit-and-tie agent. I'd never even seen him in a white shirt. He wore jeans, as usual. Unfortunately, he tends to label and dismiss me as a gangster's moll because of my involvement with Sam Gianelli.

"Is she game?" he asked Mooney as if I weren't present.

"It's your sell," Mooney said.

"What would I be buying?" I asked Reedy. "This time of night?"

"Where've you been?" Reedy asked. I ignored him. He only does it for practice. He doesn't expect me to answer so I don't.

"Get in," he said, indicating the car.

"No, thanks."

"It would take less time if I drove while I explained."

"On the other hand, if you ask here, I can just say no."

"I need you to confront Garnet Cameron."

"Bull."

Reedy said, "I'm betting he won't call you a liar."

I glared at Mooney, but kept my voice steady as I spoke to Reedy, because Reedy stops listening to women if their voices get high or quavery or possess any quality he might be able to label "hysterical."

"Why on earth not?" I said calmly and reasonably. "Because he went to the right schools? Maybe Garnet won't out-and-out call me a liar. He'll say I was mistaken. That I misunderstood. That Missy—"

"Marissa," Reedy corrected.

"*Marissa* is just playing some little ol' trick on her hubby. Don't expect him to pass out with guilty chills when he sees my face."

"I say give it a try."

I spent a futile five minutes trying to convince the FBI to leave. No dice.

"May I change clothes? I feel a trifle underdressed for Dover."

"Put on a coat," Reedy said. Great sense of humor.

I crawled into the front seat of the car, leaving Mooney the rear, with, I devoutly hoped, no leg room at all.

"Aren't you afraid that allowing me to confront Garnet at this time of night—morning—could constitute harassment?" I asked the FBI man.

"Once a kidnapping's been reported, we assume total jurisdiction. We're in a much more powerful position now that we have the original complainant."

"*Complainant?*" I thought. I love FBI-speak. I didn't bother remarking on the royal "we." The FBI is a unit, a presence, a "we." I hoped Mooney was suffering in the back, getting his legs scrambled on every bump.

I gave my head a toss, both to rearrange my hair and wake my brain. I was no longer Tessa Cameron's employee. I'd gone against her son's wishes and reported a crime. I could expect a lousy greeting at best.

Unless Andrew Manley happened to be present.

"Gary," I said sweetly. "Can I ask you a question?"

"Ask away," he said, while Mooney snorted in the rear seat.

"When did you guys start the profiling business, Teten and Depue and Douglas, and all those guys at Quantico?"

Every FBI agent knows the proud history of the Bureau. They love to expound.

"It was '69 or '70 when Teten started his class in applied criminology," Reedy said. "He asked agents, cops from all over the country, to bring in unsolved cases, you know, the kind that wouldn't let 'em sleep nights. He got a tremendous response."

"Say a girl disappeared in '71, killed by a guy who'd done at least two others—raped and murdered them. Would the FBI lab have paper on that?"

"Only if it was a big-time case, or took years to solve."

"It was big time," I murmured softly, wondering how I could get access to the Fibbie file on the Cameron case.

There was silence in the big car. It moved so differently than my small Toyota that we might have been on a ship at sea.

"Mooney," I said, "did you review the Thea Janis file before you let me see it?"

"You bet," he said. "And after."

"Remember the Albion confessions?"

"I didn't memorize 'em."

I smiled in the dark. I had, and Mooney'd known I had.

I addressed myself to the FBI man. "Gary," I said. "Here's a theoretical: A guy kills a woman he *may* know, then kills another woman, then a third who looks like the first woman. Gets caught standing over the third lady's nude body, knife in hand. No vehicle nearby."

"So?"

"Would you call him an 'organized' or a 'disorganized' killer?"

"You kidding? The guy's 'disorganized.' Miracle he didn't get nabbed after the first killing. No plan of escape on the third murder is enough to indicate 'disorganization.' But 'organized' and 'disorganized' weren't the terms the Bureau used in the early seventies."

"What did the Bureau call them?"

"We had what we called the 'simple schizophrenic,' I think. Poor choice of words, but he sounds like the guy you're talking about. And then we had the 'psychopath.' Your average Ted Bundy."

Albert Ellis Albion hadn't been found standing over Thea Janis's body. According to MacAvoy's reconstruction of the crimes, she'd been the second victim in the series.

"Does an 'organized' killer change?" I asked Reedy. "Become 'disorganized'?"

"Possibly. Over time. Especially if he's starting to lose it psychologically, if he wants to get caught. He could start sending notes to newspapers, bragging to buddies in bars."

I swiveled to face the backseat. "Any progress?" I asked Mooney in a low voice.

"On what?"

"On getting me in to see Albion."

"You do this for Reedy, maybe I'll pull a favor for you."

"I'll expect it," I said.

After fifteen minutes of happy talk about serial killers of the past, present, and future, we left the main road, squeezed between the gateposts, and started up the tree-lined path to the Cameron mansion. The house was ablaze with lights.

More than a single candle in the window to guide Marissa home.

I hadn't noticed any cars on the way up the drive, but the minute we stopped a man stepped out of the shrubbery and reported through the half-opened window that all seemed quiet. He informed Reedy that two agents had heard engine noise from a side road half an hour ago, maybe a motor scooter or a minibike, but it hadn't approached the house and an attempt to pick up the scooter had failed when it turned off into the woods.

A scooter. Like the one at Avon Hill School, driven by Anthony Emerson's "street urchins."

"Did anyone see it?" I asked quickly.

"No. The grounds are heavily wooded," said the agent.

Special Agent Reedy seized control by saying, "I want a full search of the area. Tire tracks. Anything. Have they kept the damned lights on like this all night?"

"No, sir. Place lit up like a Christmas tree about ten minutes—"

The front door opened and Garnet Cameron appeared, elegantly dressed, as if he were expecting the press, not the cops.

"Come in, Agent Reedy. Come in, please."

Agent Reedy seemed puzzled. It was evidently a far warmer welcome than he'd experienced before. "Thank you, sir. Uh, just a few questions."

"We've received another message," Garnet said. "I'm afraid it's more serious than I thought."

"Did you get it on tape?"

"Yes, yes I did. Part of it, anyway. I was rattled. I didn't switch on at the beginning."

"Let's hear it."

We were hastily ushered into a room I'd never seen before, studded with heavy oak furniture. A grand piano guarded one side of a marble fireplace, hardly taking up any space at all. Garnet merely nodded when he saw me.

Reedy moved in and took charge of the machinery.

The same voice I'd heard earlier, the digitized rumble, said, "She's alive. If you mess with us, we'll cut her face."

Garnet's recorded voice shot up an octave. "Let me talk to Marissa! How do I know—?"

There was a loud click. For a moment I thought the kidnappers had hung up, then a new sound began. In a steady voice a woman read aloud. Her tone seemed automated, lifeless.

"That's Marissa," Garnet offered eagerly. "She's reading from the *Times*. Today's—uh, yesterday's—paper."

"It's taped," Reedy said, "but if it is today's news, you know she's alive and relatively unharmed."

"Is she drugged? Why does she sound like that?"

Reedy nodded. "Probably tranquilizers in her food."

The mechanized voice came back. "Mr. Cameron, remember the payoff is two million. Don't bring in the police, or else. Remember her fingers. One at a time. Maybe her pretty little nose first. Or an ear."

"What do you think?" Garnet muttered as the tape came to an end.

"I wish I'd been here. How much of the conversation did you miss? How long before you turned on the recorder?"

"I don't know. Not long. Not more than a sentence, two at the most. Won't you be able to trace the phone number?"

"Yes, but if your perp is sophisticated enough to alter his voice, he's probably calling from a public booth, or he's figured out a way to reroute the call."

I wondered about the voice-changer. Did it mean that Garnet might otherwise recognize the voice?

"Can you raise two million?" Reedy asked.

"No."

"One million, five?"

Garnet took in a deep breath. "Yes. It will take time. You heard them. They'll—"

"No," Reedy said calmly. "Forget the threats. Kidnappers are greedy. They want money. Without your wife, safe and sound, they're not going to get paid. They know that. When they call again, sell them on a new price. Try them out on one million."

"Bargain with them?"

"Think of it from their point of view. One million's a lot better than a dead body to get rid of."

"Mr. Cameron," I asked quickly. "Is this going to have any effect on your gubernatorial run? Do you plan to withdraw from the race?"

Special Agent Reedy was already excusing himself and us, apologizing gruffly for the intrusion. I'm sure he wanted to run the phone number, just in case, but I also got the feeling he didn't like me asking such embarrassing questions.

He glared at me as we descended the steps. He'd have given me hell once we got outdoors. Fortunately one of his men intervened. They'd taken cast impressions of a narrow tire print in muddy ground. Nearby, they'd found a box, addressed in block print to Mr. Garnet Cameron. The box was small, light. The top was loose and no wires or machinery protruded. The exterior surfaces had been fingerprinted. Would the Special Agent in Charge care to open it?

He would. He donned latex gloves.

I was glad I hadn't eaten anything lately. I was geared for a finger.

The box was filled with yellow hair, Marissa Cameron's long flowing hair. The straight shining locks seemed to have been severed with a dull scissors. A block-printed note asked, "Want some more?"

The agent had a message for me, too. Tessa Cameron would like to see me. She was waiting in the gazebo by the lake. The man pointed down a path, said, "About three quarters of a mile."

I shot a brief look at Gary Reedy's taut face, and took off, jogging.

28

As I understand it, a gazebo is an open structure. I spent fifteen minutes searching for something resembling a park bandstand before coming upon a round building made of piled rock, like an old New England stone fence gone berserk. The rocks rose high, into a miniature fairy-tale tower, complete with turret. Huddled by the shore of a dark lake, it looked like an illustration from a children's book. If I waited till sunrise perhaps Rapunzel would cast down hair even longer than Marissa's. The thought made me shiver.

A single round window provided enough light to outline the door. It was surprisingly cool inside. Thick walls. I climbed the winding stair.

Toys of the rich and famous. Maybe Thea and Beryl and Garnet had romped here as kids. And one was dead and one was schizophrenic and one had a kidnapped wife. For a moment I wished I could sweep the cobwebs from the corners, send all the lost children back to an earlier time with a snap of magical fingers.

So they could suffer all that pain again.

The door at the top of the tower was ajar.

Not a single child's plaything. Whatever it had once been, this was Tessa's hideaway now, with creamy sofas and thick rugs. The portrait on the far wall had to be Tessa when young. She'd been exquisite. More conventional than Thea, but those were more conventional times.

My eyes automatically searched tabletops, bureaus. No photos or portraits of the late Franklin Cameron. No family memorabilia at all.

"Mrs. Cameron?"

"Thank you for coming."

She seemed to have nothing more to say. She just sat on a sofa, staring into nothing, playing with her jeweled hands.

"Was there something you wanted?" I asked.

"Merely a progress report. Have you an idea now who could have faked my daughter's writing?"

"Excuse me, Mrs. Cameron. Your son told me you no longer wished to pursue the matter. He brought me the contract you'd signed, torn to pieces. He said you'd voided the check."

She seemed stunned, said, "It's a lie. All lies. Why should I change my mind? Of course, I want to know who did this. Why would I not want to know?"

I shrugged. "Then I'll assume you're still paying me."

"Certainly! I am, perhaps, sorry you called in the authorities about this latest . . . misadventure. Oh, I realize you feel you had to do it, but now I think, yes, I worry that we may all be playing into Marissa's greedy hands."

I said, "Wait a minute. You think the manuscript is fake—and now you think the kidnapping's fake? Why would Marissa throw in her lot with kidnappers? She could just divorce your son. Take him for alimony."

"She needs no money. Her family has considerable assets."

"Do you think it's personal? Does she hate your son that much?"

"It's political."

"What does that mean?"

"It's a diversion, to take my son's mind off the election at a critical stage."

I hesitated, sniffed the air. I couldn't smell her camellias. Could this be the house she shared with Dr. Manley?

"What is it?" she asked.

"Does this remind you at all of the other time," I asked, snatching at straws, "when Thea disappeared?"

Her chin came up. "How could it?"

"I've read the police files. The FBI thought Thea might have been kidnapped. Your phone was tapped then; it's tapped now—"

"*Then* I was out of my mind with worry. *Then* I couldn't eat. *Then* I couldn't walk or talk."

"Did Thea disappear during a political campaign?"

She ignored the question. "Have you made any progress?"

"I'm not sure. I did speak to Andrew Manley again. I'd like to question him, but I haven't been able to locate him."

She shifted position on the sofa, crossed her elegant legs. "Would you care for a drink?"

The fairy-tale castle had been furnished with a wet-bar. On it stood a frosty pitcher, an assortment of dark-tinted bottles. Only one Martini glass had been used, I noted.

"No, thanks," I said.

She bit her lip. "Please then, won't you sit down?"

Velvet upholstery tickled the backs of my thighs. I waited.

She said, "Dr. Manley decided I might wish to explain further . . . concerning the notebook, the manuscript."

"I would be interested in interviewing the doctor," I said.

"Dr. Manley is out of town," she said firmly. "He thought I might tell you how we came by the first chapter. Why we're so anxious to recover it."

Talk, I urged her silently.

"We'd been out—a restaurant, dancing. Drew and I have been close friends for years now. We knew my son was away at a fund-raiser. Marissa rarely entertains. We were puzzled to see so many lights in the living room, even a fire in the fireplace. On a steamy night, hot like this one."

"When was this?"

"Last Saturday night, the night before Drew came to see you."

"Go on."

"We assumed Garnet had come home early, so we went to join him for a drink."

She hesitated so long that I had to prompt her.

"Yes?"

"No one was in the room. A notebook lay on the

floor, a notebook so like Thea's that when I saw it I couldn't breathe. I thought I might have a stroke, a heart attack. Drew made me sit on the sofa, take deep breaths. I saw a few scattered pages as well. Drew gathered them all. He was breathing so quickly, I became worried about him as well. He brought me the notebook. He asked if it looked like Thea's beautiful script, and it did! I thought my heart would burst! But he insisted it was forgery, and for proof, he showed me the note."

"What note?" I asked, my voice barely a breath, a whisper.

"The note that demanded money."

"Where is this note?"

"We burned it."

"You *what?*"

"In the fireplace. Really. Drew said I shouldn't have, but I don't know . . . It was so hot, so stuffy . . . And Thea is dead. She would never beg for money. And so we knew that the rest of the manuscript—"

"Whoa. What 'rest of the manuscript'?"

"The note said we would have to pay more and more for each notebook, for each chapter, that it was vile, obscene, that it would ruin the whole family forever. Politically. That it was Thea's confessional—written long ago—given to a friend before she died."

I waited a moment, thinking. *Berlin, now.*

I asked, "Why believe the note if you disbelieved the manuscript?"

She shrugged helplessly. "Drew said that he would handle everything."

Her precious Drew had insisted the manuscript was genuine. Then he'd veered off the track, changed his

*mind utterly and completely. Disappeared. Come back.
Done the vanishing act again.*

I licked my dry lips. I said, "Your son is involved in a
political race and his wife disappears. Was your husband campaigning when Thea disappeared?"

She placed her fingertips on her temples, rubbed
them in delicate circles. "It was so long ago. If he was—
and I doubt it—he lost or gave up. Franklin was never a
successful man. Nothing he ventured went well. Why
do you ask?"

"I'm looking for parallels," I said. "Your husband.
Your son. Then. Now. Thea. Marissa."

"There are none," she said. "None."

Okay, I thought. Let's switch the subject.

I said, "Your daughter Thea left a will."

"Her agent advised it. 'A literary heir,' he said, 'for a
literary legacy.' "

"Did Thea leave much money?"

"No. A trifle."

"Who gets her royalties?"

"I don't remember."

"Don't or won't?"

"Please," she said. "Stop."

"Mrs. Cameron," I said.

"What?"

"Someone other than one of your son's political op-
ponents could be imitating Thea's work."

"What do you mean?"

"Let's talk about your other daughter. Let's talk
about Beryl."

She stiffened and drew her shoulders back as though
I'd tried to hit her.

"I would prefer not to."

"I'll be leaving, then."

She waited until I stood and took two steps across the room.

"You are right," she said. "All Thea's money goes to Beryl. It is not legal, not by law—because of Thea's age, so young when she died—but I honor Thea's wish. Beryl collects all Thea's royalties."

"Where?" I asked.

"No parent should outlive her children," she murmured softly.

"Excuse me, but does that mean you want me to think Beryl is dead? Instead of mentally ill? In a cemetery instead of an institution?"

"I didn't think you so cruel, Ms. Carlyle."

"When a person's left in the dark, Mrs. Cameron, sometimes she can be unintentionally cruel."

Tessa turned her back, staring out a window overlooking the dark lake. I tried a few other questions, concerning Beryl's current whereabouts, whether Dr. Manley might be considered an expert in recovered memory syndrome.

Through it all, Tessa Cameron sat as though caught in some fairy-tale spell, speechless, motionless. She didn't react when I left. I stood silently near the bottom of the winding stair for five minutes, but heard no noise, not a single footfall.

Mooney drove me home. There was a single message on my phone. The Dover cab had taken Marissa Cameron directly to the United Airlines terminal, dropping her at 2:18 P.M. Wednesday, August 16. Yesterday—no, two days ago now. No one using that name had departed Boston on a United Flight Wednesday afternoon, evening, or Thursday morning. Gloria was checking other airlines. She'd put the word out to all Logan cabs: If a cabbie had picked up Marissa and her hunter green luggage at the airport and driven her anywhere in Metro Boston, Gloria would find out.

I managed to brush my teeth, but dropped into bed with my clothes on. Sometime during the night I must have unbuttoned my shorts and tossed them on the floor.

29

While fighting my way south the next morning on Route 95, America's "technology highway," a semicircular marvel snarled with perpetual traffic jams, I pondered Drew Manley, once and future client, Harvard, Class of '54, Beryl's psychiatrist, and Tessa's lover. His phone number was not only unlisted, but unavailable through my usual sources. A bottle of Wild Turkey at Christmas used to buy better service at the phone company. Doctors normally have listed numbers. Highlighted in red. How the hell did Drew's clients reach the man?

Was he truly "out of town" as Tessa had insisted? Something about her manner had been odd when she spoke the words, but considering the strain she'd been under, I couldn't tell if she was lying. Maybe she didn't know. Maybe she suspected her lover had lied to her.

I could phone every psychiatric institute in the commonwealth, ask to speak with Manley concerning an urgent matter. Oops. Hadn't he described himself as retired? Damn, that would make it harder. And what about Beryl? Psychiatric hospitals are even less eager to name their patients than their staff. Let's see . . . I could send a single rose to Beryl Cameron at ten, twenty different hospitals. I could learn that Beryl lived out of state, existed under an alias. Beryl Jade? Beryl Ivory? Beryl Franklin?

Had Manley ever seen Thea as a patient? How had he come to know her, to care about her so passionately?

Around eleven, Route 95—formerly and still referred to as Route 128 just to mess with tourists' minds—takes an uneasy breather for less than an hour and then swamps with lunchtime travelers and mall-crawlers till the evening rush begins at three. Some technology. Four stalled lanes to choose from—five, counting the highly traveled breakdown-lane—each filled with cars inching along, exhaust pipe to front bumper, spewing environmental poison, each bearing a lone commuter inmate waiting for the wail of sirens, the cherry flashers of an ambulance, some clue as to why and when standstill became the norm.

I molded my backbone to the Toyota's cushy seat, closed my eyes, and listened to strains of "Up on the Lowdown," picturing Chris Smither onstage at Johnny D's, playing that shiny blue Alvarez guitar. I've driven a cab on and off since college, don't need my vision to tell me when traffic's on the move. I tapped my foot to the rhythm and ticked off items on a mental checklist.

Number One: Find Manley. Number Two: Find Beryl. Number Three: Locate Marissa Cameron. Of course the FBI would be on top of her disappearance, but I had an angle they lacked, *if* the motorbike mentioned by Emerson at Avon Hill was the same as the "scooter" the FBI honcho had heard in the woods near the spot where a box of Marissa's severed tresses had mysteriously appeared.

And I had Gloria, always an ace in the hole.

I zipped into the passing lane ahead of a too-slow Ford Bronco whose owner thought size alone could intimidate. Frustrated, he sounded a derisive bellow on his horn. I ignored him. Give a driver the finger these days, and it might turn out to be your last act. I recalled the Cameron family plot set on its graceful hillside, the Mayhew statue next door. The fickle finger is not what I want engraved on my tombstone.

A partial manuscript seems important, then unimportant, but Mrs. Cameron can't wait to throw money at me to take possession. No wonder, if the complete manuscript were as scurrilous as the accompanying note had painted it. The note that Tessa and Manley had burned.

I stifled the impulse to yell obscenities at erratic tailgaters until I reached the Walpole exit. With a nod to Mooney's Gianelli-connected hitman, I scooted over three lanes within a scant quarter mile, used the breakdown lane, and made a two-wheeled screeching departure.

If anybody was tailing me, I'd know.

It's illegal to change lanes without signaling in Massachusetts. It's illegal to pass on the right. Not illegal enough to wind up where I was headed. Not by a long shot.

In the great Commonwealth of Massachusetts criminal sentencing is not so much a matter of time as it is a matter of place. In other words: A Concord sentence is not a Walpole sentence. The Concord Reformatory is such a relatively mild-mannered pen that it easily coexists with the venerable and wealthy town of Concord. In stark contrast, Walpole residents have finally gotten their penultimate wish: Walpole State Prison is now called Cedar Junction to differentiate it from the town proper in the hope that the value of Walpole's real estate will rise as quickly as that of communities that boast malls and Main Streets instead of watchtowers and barbed-wire fences.

Most Walpole townies wish the prison would burn to the ground with all inmates present and accounted for while all guards, cooks, and personnel who earned a living off the prison but actually lived in town were mysteriously off-site.

Extremely violent offenders wind up at Walpole. The major leaguers of the crime world. When a judge gives "Concord time," it usually means an automatic two-thirds off for good behavior. "Walpole time" ticks slowly.

The road cleared once I abandoned 95. I cranked down the window, enjoyed the hot breeze. The closer I got to the prison grounds, the emptier the road became.

Approaching the first guardhouse, I slowed to a crawl to give the uniformed watchman plenty of time to record my Mass. license plate and get a fix from the Registry of Motor Vehicles. Why make armed men nervous, I always say.

The guard checked my ID and made a phone call. Mentally, I prepared myself for a body search. I didn't know if they had any female personnel available for a pat-down, although they certainly would if it were visitor's day, which I sincerely hoped it was. My body may not be a holy temple, but I do what I please with it, and only what I please.

Considering bodies as temples led me straight to thoughts of Roz. How was she progressing with the artful aging of Thea's photograph? How had she gotten hold of those pages from a vintage Harvard yearbook? Had she actually gained entry to Harvard's Alumni Office, its Holy of Holies, where guardian gargoyles keep track of who's donated sufficient dough to guarantee the admission of feeble-minded grandsons? Back in '54, they wouldn't have needed to worry about dumb granddaughters, never imagining that Harvard would cease to be an all-guy preserve.

Guys. There were 834 of them where I was headed down a rutted road, 834 in space originally built to incarcerate 633.

All I cared about was one prisoner. Albert Ellis Albion, #72786537. Al-Al, they called him when they called him anything, Mooney had told me bright and early. Said the word was that Albert belonged at Bridgewater, the prison for the criminally insane. Overcrowding kept him at Walpole where he wasn't much bother to the general population.

The guard nodded me down the road and I pulled into the pocket-sized paved lot, avoiding the space reserved for the warden. I'd dressed for the occasion. My goal would have been easier in wintertime: layers from L. L. Bean. The weather being hot enough to boil eggs, I exited the car wearing loose khakis and a shapeless oversized T-shirt, my hair tucked under a cap that was already making my scalp sweat. My "look," if you could call it that, was deliberately asexual. Eight hundred thirty-four guys cooped up without conjugals is a lot of guys.

Al-Al hadn't had a visitor, other than his court-appointed attorney, in eight years.

30

The yard was concrete—walled on two sides, barred on the third and fourth. Barbed wire topped the square like a misguided attempt at Christmas decoration. Forty men were out for morning exercise, most of them stripped to the waist, prison-blue shirts slung low around their hips, sleeves wrapped and knotted below their navels. They'd segregated themselves, whites to the left, dark-skinned blacks to the right, shades of coffee and cream in-between. Thanks to mirrored sunglasses, I could stare without fear of repercussion at some of the best pecs, abs, and biceps I'd ever seen.

What a country, huh? Nobody's fit except the very rich and the hard-timers, sharing the twin luxuries of time and easy gym access. No swimming pools, saunas, personal trainers, or health spa extras for these guys,

though—unless you counted the morning's humidity as
a steam bath. But their gym had to be stocked with
serious machinery. Nautilus, I diagnosed by muscle def-
inition.

In my sexless attire, I drew minimal attention. A
black man wearing a kerchief headband dropped to the
sweltering pavement and did five quick one-handed
pushups for my benefit.

I walked briskly down the pathway indicated by the
guard. Eyes seemed to pierce my skin.

Every doorway was a challenge, an airlock-type arrangement called a sally port. Into a tiny room, door
clanging shut behind me, locking automatically. Questioning and identification procedures before the next
barred door opened. Security cameras monitoring the
entire business.

Concrete and steel. The sound of chains dragging
along the floor, a man's abruptly shouted command.
My hands felt clammy. I tried not to think of prison
riots, news articles naming the hostages.

I was treated well. No strip search. I was asked to
sign a book, list my address, phone number, Social Security number, and the name of the prisoner I wished to
visit. I had to formally declare that I carried no weapons. A metal detector backed my word. I wondered exactly who Mooney had called. Possibly, Albert's public
defender was held in high esteem. Maybe the guards
were so surprised that somebody'd come to visit Al-Al
after all these years, they were cutting me a little lee-
way, hoping for some action.

I fell into step behind two visitors, women dressed to
display it, bright flowers in a sea of drab, a treat and a
temptation to their men. Husbands, boyfriends, lovers?
Fathers of their children? I couldn't overhear more than

a brief snatch of their conversation from the enclosed carrel to which I was led. A flat-voiced guard explained that my prisoner would be escorted to a corresponding carrel on the opposite side of the glass partition. We could speak via telephone hookup. No one would eavesdrop on our talk. We were not allowed to touch the glass.

A second guard with a bumpy boxer's nose and wire-rimmed glasses steadied Al-Al with a two-fisted grip, one hand on each shoulder. Without help, Al would have toppled from the chair. I have seldom seen a sorrier specimen. He looked dried up, wrinkled as an old man. Mooney'd said his public defender had given his age as forty-two.

What had he looked like as a teenage killer?

At first I assumed he was drugged to the eyeballs. Thorazine, something that in large doses turned humans into extras from *Night of the Living Dead*. In a whispered throaty response, our first communication, he assured me he wasn't taking anything. Unless it was in the food, he murmured conspiratorially.

"I want to talk to you about some things that happened a long time ago, Al," I began. "Would you like me to call you Mr. Albion? Al? Albert?"

"Who told ya my name?"

"Your lawyer," I lied. "Harve Kelton. The man who defended you at your trial. Remember him? He sometimes writes to you. He told me he represented you at a parole hearing this year."

"Yeah?"

"Can you talk about your hat?" It wasn't what I'd planned to discuss. I didn't really want to know, to tell the truth, but the fact remained that I was chatting with a convict wearing headgear constructed of patchwork

aluminum foil, possibly remnants from assorted chocolate bars, twisted and folded together to form a crude
knight's helmet.

"Pretty smart," he said with a chuckle I can only
describe as weird. It held no hint of humor.

"Your hat?"

"The rays," he said. "Keeps out the rays."

"They shoot X rays at you?"

"Particle rays," he said. "They haven't used that
X-ray shit since the Aryan Brotherhood stole the ma-
chines."

"Particle rays," I agreed.

"Zap 'em. Particle-beam radiation fields. You can
never tell when you'll get zapped." He nodded solemnly
and his makeshift headgear took a dive, almost covering his nose. He hastened to right it.

I had to assume the headgear postdated the crimes or
he'd be in Bridgewater no matter if they had to wedge
him in with a shoehorn. Unless the guards believed he
was feigning his mania, wearing the helmet as a gag,
searching for a Catch-22 release to a better environ-
ment.

If Al-Al thought Bridgewater was better than this,
given the latest round of budget cuts, he was crazy
enough to belong there.

"I'm Carlotta, Al," I said. "That's my name."

"Lawyer?"

"Investigator."

"Like cop?"

"Something like a cop."

"I ain't done nothin'. I been here 'most forever."

"I know, Al. You've been here a long time. Have
they been shooting rays at you a long time?"

"Yeah, long time. Long time. Long time." His voice

turned singsong and his eyelids fluttered. Nap time. Great. I took advantage of the break to fish my tiny notebook out of my pocket. I'd recorded the names of Al-Al's victims, the particulars of his confessions.

"Al," I said loudly. His head jerked, knocking the headgear further askew. "Do you remember Anne Katon? The waitress? The woman you killed?"

"Oh, jeez. Oh, jeez," he whispered. "I don't wanna talk about her. She's not mad with me or nothin'. I love her. I love her."

"Anne?"

"Yeah, man, why you gotta say her name?"

"Did you know her?"

"Sure, I know her always. She was my girl. I watch her grow up. Are you protected from the rays? Your hat lined with foil or something?"

"Do you remember Thea Janis?"

"Is your hat lined?"

"Yeah. I'm safe. What about Thea?"

"What kinda name is that, Thea? Tay-ah. Tay-ah. Tay-yah."

"How about Dorothy Cameron? Thea Janis. Dorothy Cameron. Do either of those names ring a bell?"

"Bells, bells, bells," he chanted. "I like bells, bells in hell." He giggled, muttered, " 'S'cuse me very much."

"Anne Katon," I repeated.

"I'm sorry, Annie," he keened. "I didn't mean to hurt you. Your mouth wouldn't stop talking, wouldn't stop talking, wouldn't stop talking, wouldn't stop, wouldn't stop."

"Did Annie have yellow hair?"

"Brown hair, long hair, sometimes she let me touch it. Long braid. Let it loose, Annie, let your hair hang loose and soft."

I consulted my notebook. Eileen Evans had been the third victim. Thea, the second. I'd try them out of order.

"Did Eileen have brown hair like Annie's?" I asked.

"Eileen?"

"Eileen Evans?"

"Is that your name? You have nice red hair, Eileen. I'd like to touch your hair, but don't you dare take off that hat. They'll zap you for sure."

"Did you go out with Eileen?"

"With Annie, Annie, Annie. Her name was Annie, not Anne, not Anne, Eileen."

" 'Thea was small, just five feet tall, with brown hair in a long braid, and bare feet. She was waiting for me by the side of the road. She'd taken off her sandals.' " I was reciting from the man's own confession, a document suspect if only for its perfect grammar. But you can never tell. Confessions are usually taped, and sometimes transcribers decide to pretty them up.

He didn't react in any way.

"Did Thea have long brown hair?" I asked. "Did she look like Annie?"

He scrunched up his face. I stared at him for a good five minutes before he opened his eyes. I wondered if he thought he was under ray bombardment. Maybe I ought to scrunch my face too.

"Her," he said abruptly.

"Thea," I prompted. "Dorothy."

Al gazed at me for a long time, adjusted his aluminum helmet. It looked a little like the Tin Man's headgear in *The Wizard of Oz*.

After running his fingers over each wall and banging the telephone rhythmically on the ledge of the carrel, he said, "You won't tell anyone?"

I said, "My hat lets me listen. It won't let me tell."

"Ah," he said, nodding slowly.

"Ah," I repeated, mimicking his nod.

"The five o'starfish was walking by the sand-oh. The five o'starfish was walking by the sand-oh. The five o'starfish was walking . . ."

His voice trailed off. Half the time when he spoke it didn't sound like conversation, more like recitation. It reminded me of something.

Of course: "The Walrus and the Carpenter were walking close at hand . . ."

"The starfish said Thea belongs in the sea," he continued singsong, staring into my eyes. "She belongs in the sea, the sea star said, in the sea, in the sea, in the sea, in the sea, in the sea, in the sea, in the sea, sea, sea, sea, sea, sea, sea . . ."

"Al—"

"In the sea, in the sea, in the sea—"

His voice rose and the guard materialized from another section of the room. He took the phone from Al's unresisting hand.

"You want to listen to him chant?" the guard asked, bored as bored could be. " 'Cause the guy goes on for hours."

"No. It's okay."

He hung up and started Al-Al back on the journey to his cell without another glance in my direction.

Confessors. They come out of the woodwork on serial killer cases. For the Boston Strangler, they'd had thousands. Of course this man had actually been convicted, had actually killed. That gave him a certain credibility.

Still, if I'd asked him whether he'd killed Amelia Earhart, I could guess the response: A star told him she belonged in the sky, in the sky, in the sky . . .

Traffic was better on the drive home. I rolled down the window and sang low-down dirty blues to a wind accompaniment, every tune I could think of that had to do with jail, from "Ain't No More Cane on the Brazos" to "Hard-Time Blues."

Where did Al get the money for all those chocolate bars? Did other cons contribute Hershey wrappers? How much money was in his prison account, if any? What sort of work did he do at the prison, if any? Did his attorney bring him aluminum foil, smuggling in Reynolds Wrap boxes with the serrated edging removed?

One thing: Al-Al had *known* Anne Katon. He'd remembered the color of her hair, remembered that he'd done something bad to Annie. His last victim, Eileen Evans, drew a blank.

And Thea belonged in the sea. Maybe she'd looked like a starfish. Which—to a man as disturbed as Albert Ellis Albion—she may very well have done.

I pulled right, stopped abruptly on the grassy verge as several cars honked their disapproval.

I'd gotten it wrong.

Not the five o'starfish. The five-oh starfish. Five-oh's been slang for cop as long as I can remember. An old TV series, set in Hawaii and probably still in syndication in Albania, had started it, and the practice clung. I could see the wriggly lines on the back of MacAvoy's hand. Not an odd five-pointed star. A starfish.

The five-oh starfish said that Thea belonged in the sea.

31

What with musing about starfish and cops, I manipulated my various front door locks on automatic pilot, likewise descending the single step into my living room. I didn't notice Roz behind my desk until I practically sat in her lap. She, busily pushing buttons on a portable tape recorder, ignored me as well.

I cleared my throat and did not get the desired effect. When people do that in the movies, assistants bail out of desk chairs like they've been stung by killer bees.

Roz glanced up and kept her fanny firmly in place.

"Nice tape recorder," I said. It was. A tiny Nakamichi, studded with red, green, and yellow buttons.

"Gloria's got me playing it from some extremely weird places. See, I sneak in, call a number, hit this button, and your voice zips over the fiber optics. I figure I've visited every ultra-right looney who can afford a telephone."

"Is Gloria paying you?"

"Sure."

Great. I pay Gloria. She pays Roz. One big circle, with me supporting the globe.

"This guy called," Roz said.

"Name?"

"Wouldn't give it."

"You'll make a fine secretary one day."

That got her out of the chair. I eased myself into it. There were no notes on my desk, even though I keep a pad of pale blue "While you were out" slips in plain sight.

"What did this 'guy' have to say for himself?"

"Asked when you'd be back. I said I didn't know. He called twice."

"Old? Young? Foreign?"

"Kinda old, I think."

"Not Mooney?"

"Not Mooney."

"You watch TV while I was out?"

"Some."

"Any local kidnappings?"

"Not on MTV."

I glanced at the front page of the *Globe*. If news had leaked, the local rags ought to have picked up on it first. If the kidnapping were genuine, I wouldn't expect any leaks. Gary Reedy and the FBI would prevent that.

"I take it Gloria hasn't called."

"I woulda said."

Damn. There was no point in calling her. As soon as she knew anything about Marissa's departure from Logan, by air, sea, or cab, she'd get back to me. Gloria is reliable. You don't have to tell her twice.

Had Marissa been nabbed at the airport? Was she somehow involved, even cooperating, with the kidnappers? Would a kidnap scam play as a vote-earner for Cameron? Poor little rich boy, victim of fiendish plot?

If the Cameron campaign organization thought they could fool the FBI, I hoped they were up to speed on DNA testing and all the rest of the modern investigative hoopla.

Roz looked comfy, wearing either a short dress or a long tank top. The garment had been crocheted on large hooks for good ventilation.

She said, "Any work for me?"

I said, "I want a financial report on a retired cop. Woodrow MacAvoy."

"SSN? DOB?"

"I have neither his Social Security number nor his date of birth. I've got last known address—31 Monroe, Marshfield."

"That ought to do it." Roz waltzed to the side table, flicked on my computer—a gift from Sam Gianelli—waited while it whirred and flashed, then busily entered strings of numbers and letters, her long varnished nails flying over the keyboard. Roz learned some unsavory gimmicks and passwords from a master hacker not long ago. Since I was paying her salary while she attended dubious computer practices school, I take advantage of her techniques whenever possible. I don't try to defend the ethics of computer snooping. If information's out there, somebody's going to get it. Might as well be me.

"TRW and Equifax are backed up," Roz said. "One third of the country is running a credit check on another third."

The rest want to know if their boyfriend or girlfriend has AIDS, I thought.

"What about your artwork?" I asked.

"The hanging?"

"The stuff you're doing for me. Aging the girl in the photo."

"It's hard."

"Does that mean it's not done?"

"It's easier to work from life, Carlotta. You see that little line you have? To the right, near the bridge of your nose? That's gonna turn into a lulu because you crinkle up your face when you're staring at the computer screen. The photo, shit, I can't tell how she moved her face. I can do some basic stuff—you know—Anatomy 101. The jaw separates, the skin loosens under the eyes, under the chin. But if there were a videotape, a series of photos, I could do a lot more."

I said, "Keep working on it."

I dialed Mooney. He picked up on the first ring.

"You're not at the Camerons," I said.

"I have a job. Where are you?"

"Home. Any progress?"

"Reedy shut me out. Says it's Cameron's idea, but I don't know."

"What's Reedy's game plan?"

"Get the kidnappers down to a million, a half a million, whatever, mark the bills so nobody can tell, observe the drop, get the woman back, then arrest the crooks."

"You make it sound so simple."

"Christ, if Reedy wanted a Stealth bomber to observe the rendezvous point, he could have it."

"Does he want a Stealth bomber?"

"He wants us off his audio frequencies. He wants all

local police to close their eyes and take a giant step into the ocean."

"Good old Gary," I said. "So he buys the whole scene?"

"He's playing it by the book. I guess he has to."

"And the FBI doesn't even have a post in Butte, Montana, anymore," I said.

"Yeah," Mooney said. "But if Gary Reedy screws this up, they'll reopen it just for him."

"Serve him right, keeping you in the dark."

"What do you want, Carlotta?"

"To soothe your ruffled feathers, Moon."

"Bull."

"Well, I'd be interested in any rumors about the quality of Woodrow MacAvoy's retirement."

"If I hear anything I'll let you know."

"Mooney—"

He hung up. Dead end on that front. If Gary Reedy'd been nicer to Moon, he'd have been nicer to me. What goes around, comes around.

I took it out on Roz.

"For chrissake," I said. "Haven't you found me anything on Heather Foley's family yet?"

"Who?"

"Heather Foley. Girl from Swampscott. Fell off a boat and drowned twenty-four years ago. Same time Thea disappeared."

"You didn't ask," Roz said.

"I'm asking now."

32

Roz, cowed by my vengeful mood, decided that research at the Liberty might be more fun. I can't say I was sorry to see her go. I needed to concentrate.

First, I attempted and finally produced a brief and cheerful postcard to Paolina, informing her that the bird, cat, Gloria, and myself were all well and looking forward to her return. I walked four blocks to stick it in a mailbox. Just to use up nervous energy, I told myself. Not to look for an armed man wearing an unseasonably hot windbreaker. Not to listen for the sound of a distant motorbike.

As soon as I got back to the house, I had another thought about Andrew Manley and phoned the AMA. I got a recorded message with a classical music background for my trouble. Honestly, when the American

Medical Association can't afford full-time secretarial help, you've got a crisis on your hands.

What kind of crisis? What did I have? What did I know? I twisted a strand of hair around my index finger and yanked till it hurt.

It was after 3 P.M. I tried to recall when I'd last eaten. What. Some folks wouldn't call peanut butter on a stale bagel breakfast, but when that's all the stuff in the fridge that isn't sprouting mold, it's breakfast.

I rummaged till I found an apple in the fruit bin, cut off the bruised hunk. Lunch. Yum.

I sat at my desk, fidgeting till I got comfy.

It looked like extortion; it smelled like extortion. Someone—besides Roz—coveted a considerable chunk of Garnet Cameron's wealth. Now a lot of people on planet Earth want money, so that didn't narrow the field much, but in this case it would have to be someone who knew something that would make Garnet fork over wads of cash. He or she couldn't march up to Garnet and demand the dough for reasons unknown.

I'll make Tessa tell me how to find Manley. I gritted my teeth while I punched phone buttons. Mrs. Cameron was unavailable.

Manley and Tessa burn the extortion note. No sale. Next step: Kidnap Marissa.

I finished the apple, returned to the kitchen to seek other edibles. A package of cellophane-wrapped bread sticks was stuck at the back of the silverware drawer. I dunked them in peanut butter. One cracked, one held.

Maybe the beautiful and argumentative Marissa was behind it all, I thought. Maybe she'd signed a prenuptial agreement she now regretted. She'd know to a penny how much cash Garnet had raised for the election. Maybe she was desperate to leave him, but felt some of his wealth should accompany her . . .

Wouldn't she need an accomplice? The digitized voice had sounded deep—definitely male—but couldn't gadgetry account for the bass notes?

Why hadn't I heard from Gloria?

I tugged at my hair and chewed stale bread. I was forgetting Thea. Thea was at the heart of everything, at the heart of the maze.

And who was Thea?

Her mother's perfect daughter? A hellion bent on seducing every male at Avon Hill? Manley's young woman of piercing intellect and prodigal prose? A suicide? A homicide? A victim, yes. A victimizer as well?

I unlocked my desk, removed the manuscript copy from the self-addressed envelope. Genuine? Fake? Old? New? I flipped through it, read:

> perhaps a word shall fall
> and then another
> (silent as heat strangling
> a cry
> dark as a panther
> whispering lullabies
> to jungled dreams)

It seemed to me most likely that the extortionist would be a figure from the past, someone who knew that Thea Janis hadn't died at the hands of Albert Albion.

Woodrow MacAvoy?

I considered Al-Al's simple words: The five-oh starfish said Thea belongs in the sea. I pondered three scenarios.

One: Woodrow MacAvoy coaching Albert Ellis Albion to commit murder. I discarded it. Unlikely in the extreme.

Two: Woodrow MacAvoy, finding Thea's body— dead of a drug overdose, possibly with slit wrists—suborned by the Camerons into forcing a murderer to knife the already dead girl, dump her remains in the ocean. Why? So her death wouldn't be labeled "suicide"? Because some insurance policy might be invalidated by suicide? So she could be buried in holy ground?

Number Three: With no body on hand and no likelihood of ever finding Thea, Woodrow MacAvoy, given complete control of the Cameron case, convinces Albert Ellis Albion to confess to another murder. Why? So someone wouldn't have to wait the required seven years for her death to become official?

But there was a body in Thea's grave . . .

If MacAvoy had gone out on a limb for the Camerons, had they sawed it off? Or were his angry accusations a front? Had the Camerons made it worth his while to cooperate? If so, why the crummy cottage?

With the giant-sized TV.

MacAvoy had laid down two twenties in the bar. Forty bucks might represent a sizable chunk of his monthly pension.

Dammit. I felt tugged in all directions. I had to get back to MacAvoy, find out what the five-oh starfish had really said to Albert Albion, why, and when. I needed to dig up enough dirt on MacAvoy to get him to talk to me. I needed to locate Drew Manley, to find sister Beryl. I wanted to know if Heather Foley's body had ever been found. I had the feeling that pieces of the puzzle were slipping through my fingers, plunging into my dream abyss.

My sleeping hours had been erratic of late, not to mention my meal intake. I rested my head on the blotter, just for an instant, because my hair seemed so inexplicably heavy.

The phone jangled. I opened my eyes into darkness. The street lamp down the block glowed yellow.

"Señorita, por favor, sin nombres."

I'd heard the voice before. Once. Deep, drop-dead sexy, from far, far away. This time it sounded as if Carlos Roldan Gonzales, Paolina's biological father, were in the next room.

"Hello," I managed.

"It is a good trick you play with Señor Miami, but muy peligroso."

"I needed to know—"

"Now you know."

"Señor—"

"Adios, señorita."

The line clicked. Paolina's father was alive. Alive where? Alive how? Alive for how long?

I stared at my watch, flicked on the desk lamp. It couldn't be, but it was past ten o'clock. I'd slept a full night's worth.

The phone rang underneath my hand, startling me. Maybe I'd get to hear the voice again. I inhaled, sucked in a good deep breath. I don't know why, but certain voices affect me in ways I can never understand.

"Miss Carlyle." It was certainly not Carlos Roldan Gonzales. "This is Drew Manley."

All the questions I had to throw at him, and he hardly gave me a chance.

"Listen, carefully," he said. "I've found her." His voice wavered, but a touch of the playful puppy quality was back.

"Where are you?" I asked quickly.

"The summer house. Marblehead. Can you come, please?"

"Why? Why not go to Dover, tell Tessa. If you've found Thea Janis, alive, they'll kill the fatted calf, the whole bit."

"It—the situation—is not uncomplicated."

"Call the police."

"Please, Miss Carlyle. Help us."

"Help me. Where is Beryl Cameron?"

"We'll discuss that when you get here. Please come."

"Thea's really there?"

"Yes."

"You've lied to me before."

"I've lied," he said. "I've been misled."

"Are you lying now?"

"No. I need you. Thea needs you."

It's easy to dissemble on the telephone.

He gave directions so clearly he must have read them off a printed card.

"There's a shack, a small shed, on the beach. Let's meet there," he said.

"Why? Why not the big house?"

"No key," he said easily. "Please hurry."

"A public place," I said. "A doughnut shop—"

He'd hung up. I was talking to myself.

"Roz," I shouted up the stairs.

Nothing. Ten's too early for her to come home. She'd still be at the Liberty, if she hadn't already picked up a mate for the night.

I should have waited for morning. I considered writing down everything I knew about the case, locking my scribbled thoughts away as a life insurance policy. They do that on TV. I knew so many oddly assorted facts; I'd guessed at so many others. For all I *understood*, I might as well write my journal on toilet paper, flush it.

Before I left the house I loaded the S&W 40, checked the safety and the extra magazine, stuck them in a paper bag along with my waist clip. I wasn't planning to sit on hard metal all the way out to Marblehead.

At the last minute I grabbed the phone and dialed Gloria.

"ITOA," she answered. "Where are you, and where can I take you?"

"It's me," I said, because she can identify any voice she's heard before. "Who runs cabs in Marblehead?"

"North shore, north shore. Outfit called Clancy's. There's no Clancy to speak of."

"Can you give me the garage address, call and tell them I might want to borrow a cab for a couple hours?"

"I know a few drivers there. Maybe I could work something out."

"I'll pay double rates."

"Don't tell 'em that; it'll just make 'em think you're planning to bust up their cab."

"Fix it for me, Gloria."

"Consider it done."

"Nothing on Marissa Cameron?"

"Not yet. Lots of cabbies at Logan. You take care now."

Take care. I glanced at my desktop, grabbed Paolina's postcard, rubbed it against my cheek, and stuck it in my pocket. A talisman, a warning.

If I get hurt, who'll care for Paolina?

The sky was hazy, the air still. I started the engine.

Off to Marblehead, where remnants of cotton and linen clothing had been discovered twenty-four years ago.

33

I took narrow back streets to Kirkland, crossed the Charles on the McGrath and O'Brien Highway, swung unimpeded around Leverett Circle, an exhilarating feat. If I hadn't promised Manley I'd hurry, I'd have done the rotary twice, for the sheer bliss of circling at a speed never allowed by daytime traffic jams.

Late night is the only time to drive Boston. Long-haul truckers and cabbies frequent the roads, professionals, extending each other professional courtesy. I hit the left-hand lane and floored it. The new Fleet Center loomed to the right, never to replace the Boston Garden with its obstructed views, knee-squeezing seats, and hardworking basketball teams. Route 3 heading to 93, cutting over to take the Tobin Bridge, craning my neck to catch the outline of *Old Ironsides*. On to Route 1, following a red river of taillights.

Marblehead's as far north of Boston as Marshfield is south. Past Revere, Lynn, Swampscott, where Heather Foley had lived and died. Near Salem, where nineteen witches were hanged, one "pressed" to death with heavy weights. Sandy beaches, icy water, grand seaside estates, fewer summer people.

I studied headlamps in my rearview mirror. Nothing out of the ordinary, except the pounding in my chest. I piloted the car Boston-style, weaving lanes and signaling false exits to lose any followers.

I listen to old blues tapes when I drive, anything from Muddy Waters to Mississippi John Hurt. I riffled through my tape collection while stretching the speed limit.

I stuck a Rory Block tape into my boom box and drummed my fingers on the steering wheel to "Terraplane Blues." What if the whole setup was politically orchestrated? First, "Mayhew" coming to see me, stirring up interest in Thea's disappearance. Then Marissa's kidnapping.

Was Tessa in command? Had she taken her late husband's campaign losses to heart, determined the same fate would never conquer her son? When the Thea gambit didn't pan out as planned, had Marissa been pressed into duty for the next publicity stunt?

If so, where was the publicity? Mama hadn't gone public with Marissa's kidnapping. No tearful interviews with the family. No televised appeals to the villains.

Every thread I yanked unraveled in my hand. I gave it up and drove.

My shadowy mob pursuer seemed nothing more

than a remote possibility. I felt fine sitting in the driver's seat with the window wide and the breeze blowing my hair, whispering a destination.

The beach shack at the Camerons' summer place.

Once I left the main drag, scooting off 1A to 114, I drove cautiously, stopping at each amber light. Small-town cops have little to do late at night but watch for unknown vehicles behaving strangely in good neighborhoods. How would I explain my presence to a cop?

I smiled. Tell him I was on a pilgrimage of sorts, that I wanted to see the house where Thea Janis had spent her few summers, the beach from which she might have taken leave of this world. Better than saying I wanted to check the place for lights, cars. For Drew Manley, former shrink who'd supposedly found a phantom.

I went back over the phone call, trying to recall every word, each shift in vocal tone. Did I believe Manley?

It had been his voice. Definitely his. Breathless, a little wavery at times. Odd. But if he'd actually seen Thea after twenty-four years, he certainly had a right to a quaver in his voice.

Did it matter whether or not I believed he'd found Thea? I needed to talk to him, needed to understand where he was pointing me with his references to recovered memory syndrome.

Did I believe he was at the beach house with a living breathing Thea Janis at his side?

Wanting to believe is not the same as belief. Not the same at all . . .

Maybe Beryl was with him, I thought. Could the older sister, Beryl, have written *Nightmare's Dawn?*

I pulled over near a Texaco station, flipped through my Arrow street map. Page fourteen. I wanted to locate various approaches to Marblehead Neck, a posh section of real estate. It seemed to me that varying Manley's directions might be a good idea, considering the elusive motorbike.

I found exactly one road to Marblehead Neck. *One.* If the cops didn't have it staked, they wouldn't be much of a force. There's always a cop car close to the richest part of town. Just in case.

Time to stop at the garage.

I turned on 129, driving away from the ocean. The streets and houses grew closer together. Smaller. The cab company was near the hospital. Good location.

I parked on the street two blocks away. No need to advertise. I transferred my 40 into my waist clip, slipped it in the back of my jeans, pulled my short-sleeved T-shirt over the bulge. I stuck a flashlight in my back pocket. Useful, and a decoy as well. Somebody asked me what I had back there, I'd show them the flash. First.

The dispatcher had a cab waiting. He'd talked to Gloria. He spoke cash.

Since I had no passenger to ferry out to the Neck, I got the next best thing. I stopped at an all-night convenience store, bought a bottle of Tylenol, the liquid stuff you give to squalling feverish babies. I'd have bought booze if I'd found an all-night liquor mart. Liquor and medicine make up eighty percent of cab deliveries.

Maybe no one would challenge my approach. I kept the white paper sack in full view on the passenger seat. Be prepared.

A causeway separated the Neck from Devereux Beach to the south and Marblehead harbor to the north. Once home to a sturdy fishing fleet, the well-lit harbor seemed moored with pleasure craft. Silvery lights studded a sailboat's mast.

I wondered which end of the causeway the cops routinely watched. Maybe they switched off. That would be smart.

The coastline of Massachusetts is a precious resource. What makes people flock to live near large bodies of water? I don't know, but whatever it is, I've got it bad. The Charles River's okay, but I'd trade it for an ocean view in a second. By law, the beaches of Massachusetts are open to all. So why do real estate ads tout deeded rights to two miles of sandy beach? Because, technically, the public area "open to all" equals only that part of the shoreline betwixt and between high water and low water marks. In other words, the peons get to wade. I hoped it wasn't high tide.

If a cop stopped me, I'd ask.

None did. There could have been unmarked units in the thick dry brush, but I didn't see a single one. Couldn't hear much because of the rhythmic ocean roar.

Ocean Avenue's a big deal, skirting massive dwellings, each no doubt alarmed to the hilt. Schools of architecture waged a silent war on Ocean Avenue. I passed a Norman castle, a futuristic domed dwelling, a Georgian manse. Did the rich folks who lived in these artifacts speak to each other? Condemn each other's taste? Fifty-six was the number of the Cameron place. Fifty-six Ocean. There. A timbered English country house that stretched to fill an enormous hunk of land. The little house that grew.

Pitch dark. Unlike its neighbors to either side, I inspected further, shining my flash at the ground.

Just as Manley had said, a narrow unmarked lane ran down one side of the property. I didn't like the look of it. I drove a couple houses down, passing a French château and a haphazard brick pile with ornate windows. Each dwelling extended approximately the length of a city block. I stopped and got out of the cab near a signpost that read "DESMOULIN LANE." It didn't seem much of a lane, more like rough steps hacked into a bluff, but it traveled in the right direction. I decided to follow it, walk along the shore, observe the back of the Cameron estate before declaring my presence. As long as I stayed on the shoreline, I wouldn't even be trespassing.

It seemed safer than the direct approach to the low-lying shack that Manley had described.

As I descended, the surrounding area seemed to fade, its rocky outcroppings blurring into hazy outlines. Damp air floated off the water, changing into a low cloudy mist that shrouded everything in its path.

Fog. Sudden whiteout fog. How frequently did it visit this shore? I walked a hesitant ten paces and could no longer see the bluff, the steps. A distant foghorn keened. Had it called to Thea? Did she step into the mist once too often, hear the ocean sing her name? Had sirens sent fog to envelop her, extending soft welcoming arms to lead her to the waves?

Behind me, an irregular tapping. Hard-soled shoes clambering down the same steps I'd taken? The noise raised hairs at the base of my neck.

The soft sand above the surf line shifted under my sneakers, slowing me, dragging me down. I ran toward the Cameron house. A pinpoint of light shone to one side, partly shaded by an overhanging branch.

Some ramshackle outbuilding. A changing house for midnight bathers? The shack where Manley waited to tell me the truth at last.

A light glimmered at the back of the small wooden hut, none at the front.

Manley?

I listened for a follower. I couldn't hear anything, but I wasn't sure of my senses, didn't trust them with the rhythmic surf and the silence of sand.

Should I call his name? A part of me felt that a cry for Thea, long dead, would be more appropriate. Maybe as likely to be answered.

Stop it, I scolded myself. The misty seascape and eerie foghorn were filling my head with every ghost story I'd ever heard or read.

I imagined my voice ringing out of the fog, telling everyone, anyone, where I was.

No way.

I took stock, breathing deeply, slowing my heart rate, pretending calm to regain calm. Why would Manley lurk in a shack by the water's edge, exposed to cold and rough weather? Why not wait in comfort in the big house? No key, he'd said. If "Thea" were with him, if she'd spent her childhood summers here, surely she'd recall a secret way to enter, an unbarred window, a hidden key.

Things change in twenty-four years.

Thea's dead, the fog whispered. I tried to remember her words: "the mind remembers lonely long after in dark places . . ."

I crept toward the shack. My nose twitched at the smell.

The interior was brightly lit by a kerosene lantern positioned behind a red motorbike. An aged Honda, its engine cool, leaking oil like life's blood onto sandy floorboards.

34

Wood shavings had been swept into a pile in the corner. Dented, as though someone had slept there. A tramp? A squatter?

With a red motorbike.

Why the lamp? Why advertise someone's presence? I shoved my flashlight in my back pocket, removed a Kleenex which I used to cover my hand before grabbing the metal hoop over the burning kerosene lantern.

One if by land, two if by sea. The jingle every Massachusetts schoolchild learns came to mind. Was the lantern intended as a signal to someone on the water? Manley?

I edged outside and saw what I should have noticed first, before kerosene and motor oil had taken out my sense of smell. The lamp had misdirected me, urged me inside, not out.

The shape in the sand could be a sleeping tramp, I told myself. The dark stain beneath the shape wasn't the right contour for a shadow.

If I'd been a cop I'd have stopped right there, called for backup.

Any move I made might disturb a crime scene. Sand would hold footprints. For how long? Was the sleeper, as I'd dubbed him in my mind, even though I suspected he was dead, lying above the high water mark? Would the sea claim the body if I didn't act?

My foot hit something that snapped with a thunderous report on the silent beach. I bent, knelt in the sand. My hand reached for them, but I stopped in time, examined the object in situ.

Bifocals. Intact except for the earpiece my sneaker had smashed. *Adam*—no Andrew—Drew Manley's glasses, frames I'd last seen sliding down my former client's nose.

Manley, with his merry blue eyes.

I lifted the lantern high.

He was dead. Lying on Cameron-owned beachfront. The visible side of his face was smashed, dark with coagulated blood. Blood had soaked into the sand, but it no longer seemed to run freely. How long after he'd made his phone call had he died?

If I got close enough to touch him, assure myself of his identity and fate, would I risk obscuring the reason for his death? As a cop, how I'd cursed civilians who'd messed with crime scenes.

Approaching footsteps. Definite this time. The matter-of-fact slap of leather on sand. With nowhere to hide, I slid to the sand, a second sleeper.

"Alonso? You okay?" The voice was childish, high, giggly. "Like what you been using, man? You save some?"

She went to the other sleeper first. I heard her sharp intake of breath. "Oh, man," she muttered. "Alonso, man, how'd you mess up on me like this? Shit. Alonso? You do this guy or what?" There was fear in her voice. Then she was squatting on the sand, snatching at things, shoving them in her backpack, rifling Manley's pockets unless I missed my guess.

I lifted my weight into a crouch as noiselessly as I could. My knee cracked, gave me away.

She turned immediately. Instinctively let out a yell. I wasn't Alonso, who'd messed up so badly. I'd spooked her.

She ran.

I ran.

She was young, wiry, and scared. I was taller. The length of my stride was almost twice hers. Every time her feet landed in the soft sand, she lost ground. I didn't bother yelling. Waste of breath. I ran till I could launch myself with certainty. My arms circled her legs, yanked them out from under her.

She fell without noise, rolled over. Instead of striking out, she tried to use her hands to protect herself. I grabbed her by both wrists and flipped her. A knee in the small of her back pressed her to the ground.

"I'm not going to hurt you," I said. "Are you okay?"

"Yeah," she said shakily. "I guess."

"Who's Alonso?"

"A guy. You're hurting me. Fuckin' said you wouldn't, but you are."

"If I let you up, you have to promise not to run."

She squirmed vigorously. I kneed her harder. Tough kid. I'd seen tougher. Me at her age, for instance.

"Okay, we'll talk down here," I said.

"I won't run."

"How can I trust you?"

"Take my word for it."

"How about if I take your backpack instead? Looks like you lifted a few things off the corpse, huh?"

No response. No movement.

"You know him?" I asked.

"Some guy I never saw before. Honest. Some old guy."

A Harvard ring, a medical degree, a presumably distinguished career . . . Manley's death turned him into "some old guy," muttered by a dirty kid with a mouthful of sand.

I yanked at her backpack and she put up a struggle.

"Dammit," I said. "Quit wiggling. What the hell did you take from him? A million bucks?"

I decided to concentrate on the pack. If she fought like a demon for it, she wasn't about to leave it. I pinched the clasps and emptied it onto the sand. A hail of bananas, apples, oranges, fruit of every description.

"What the hell?"

She scrambled for the produce. "Why don't you just leave me the fuck alone?"

"Did Alonso kill the old man?"

Falling hard in the sand hadn't made her cry. Fear hadn't made her cry. Alonso's name, linked with a killing, did. She bent her head and howled, sobbed till I thought someone would surely hear us, call the cops.

"Who's Alonso?" I asked again.

"I met him on the road. He's got a bike. He picked

me up, like, almost a week ago. He's really nice. He's cool, like, an artist, and stuff."

"He's been living in the shed?"

"Not for the past couple days. Not since Wednesday. He had stuff to do. He took off, but, like, I thought maybe he'd come back."

"His bike's there."

While we spoke my fingers continued to search her pack. What had she stolen? Wallet? That would be most likely. But her hands had darted into the pockets several times. A notebook?

"Does Alonso have a last name?" I asked.

"Forget it. He is, like, totally cool. He calls himself Alonso the Alien sometimes. Guys like him don't need a name."

My fingers closed on a small Coop book, like my own. My sandy friend probably hadn't attended Harvard.

Manley's appointment book.

What a mess.

I had an obligation to report a crime.

I had a small girl crying her eyes out in the sand over one Alonso. If Alonso were alive, he probably had sufficient street smarts not to come back for his bike.

If he hadn't stayed here the past couple nights, why had he left his bike?

I remembered the pooling oil.

Had someone disabled it?

Why?

For the same reason someone had left the lamp lit? To attract attention to a crime scene? It was only a matter of time before someone called the police.

Hurriedly I opened the notebook, flicked on my flashlight.

Today's page, Friday, the seventeenth, was marked "see A. at C's." A. for Alonso the Alien? Other dates were sprinkled with initials and shorthand scribbles.

"Come on." I tugged at the bawling child. She couldn't have been more than twelve.

"I won't go to the cops," she wailed. "They'll send me home."

I wanted to reassure her. Tell her there were worse places than home, but in this business I've learned that sometimes there aren't.

"We're not going to the cops."

"You promise?"

"We'll look for Alonso."

"Yeah," she said enthusiastically.

It got her up and moving. If I found this Alonso on the way to the cab so much the better.

I wanted off Marblehead Neck before the cops came.

35

Close up, I thought she might be even younger. Eleven. Scrawny. She didn't question me when I had her lie on the floor of the cab while we made our way back over the causeway.

We hadn't found Alonso.

He had no last name. Neither had "Pix"—a street name if I'd ever heard one. Short for Pixie, which would be an offhand reference to angel dust, or maybe she did pics, as in child porn, to earn her bread. She wasn't parting with her straight name. I'd go through her backpack more carefully when I had time.

I parked the cab near my car, left the keys under the floor mat. I'd call the dispatcher later and apologize for the irregularity, but I couldn't leave Pix alone and I didn't want anyone to see her.

For now the stuff I wanted was spread on my dashboard. Manley's wallet, loaded with cash and credit cards, removing casual robbery as a motive. Manley's Coop book. Manley's watch.

"You gonna call the cops?"

"I am the cops. Private."

"Shit." She made a move to unlock her door. I slammed one arm across her.

"No more running," I said.

"Whatcha gonna do with me?"

"Good question." It was one of a hundred rolling through my head.

"This is complicated," I said. "I need to hear about you and Alonso. Like did he send you away tonight because he had to meet a guy?"

"I haven't seen Alonso since Wednesday—"

"Sure."

"You're thinking drug deal?" she asked. "Forget it."

"I'm just asking questions. I don't have answers."

She took her time thinking that over. "Alonso was takin' care of me, like I said, up till a couple nights ago." Her voice faltered.

"Something go wrong?" I asked.

"None of your fuckin' business."

"I can make it my business, Pix."

She swallowed. "Look, he found another girl. 'A real woman,' is what he said, which, like, means she's older than me. He was always on me about how young I am."

"And how young is that?"

"None of your— Anyhow, before, when he was with me, I used up a lot of his bread, you know. So I thought I'd go out and earn a little back. Not trickin'. Boosting groceries and shit. I didn't know where to find him so I thought I'd leave the stuff at the shack. I mean, I pay my fuckin' debts, you know?"

I like stories backed by facts. The bananas on the beach were accounted for. Crime scene with bananas. It sounded like one of Roz's paintings. What a mess for the local cops.

"Where did you meet Alonso? Did you go to school with him?"

"Harvard Square," she said, drop dead cool. "School is for fish."

"You know your way around Marblehead?"

"Nah. Alonso never was here before either, but like, he had friends."

"Friends tell him about the shack?"

"I guess. He knew it was there. It was like a really neat squat. I mean, some cities have good squats, and I was in this decent place in Cambridge, but the landlord found out, and then it was DSS, and they totally stink, you know?"

Department of Social Services, and sad to say, they do stink. Underfunded. Overworked.

"Alonso didn't tell you he had a meet with anyone?"

"Nope." She squared her jaw and shut up. Like nobody ever believed her anyway.

I turned on the engine.

"Hey, where we goin'? I gotta find Alonso."

"Things have taken a turn for the worse," I said. "I think you'd better stick with me."

"Oh no."

"Pix, or whatever the hell your name is, you've got two choices. Me, or the cops. And DSS is better than the place they stick kids involved with murderers."

"That guy was killed?"

Did she think Manley'd fallen on his head? In the sand?

"And your Alonso is prime suspect," I said.

"No way." Pure hollow braggadocio. True as a tin whistle.

"And you stole from a corpse. Not cool," I said. It made me feel great to terrify an already terrified little girl.

"What are you going to do?"

I said, "Look for a gas station that's closed. That's our best bet."

"Our best bet," she echoed, looking at me for the first time like we might be a team, like I might be her guardian angel in disguise, her rescuer.

God, I try not to think about it: Where do all these throwaway kids come from with their made-up names and their made-up minds? Nothing's going to get better. Live hard, die young. School is for fish.

"There," she said. "Arco on the left."

She had good eyes. I yanked the wheel. A phone. The number of pay phones I'd been using lately, I ought to get an award from NYNEX. I thought of dialing Vandenburg in Miami just for the hell of it. Instead I did the old 911, using a fold of my shirt to hold the receiver and my knuckles to punch buttons. Probably should have covered my knuckles. This DNA business is getting ridiculous, and I'm not in the forefront of forensic technology. Eventually the cops might trace the call to this phone. Somebody might say they saw us stop.

I glanced over to make sure that Pix was in the car, eating the sandwich I'd bought from the vending machine. She was. Feed her, she's yours. Like a dog.

The phone rang and I thought of all the things I might tell the police. Body on Marblehead Neck behind

56 Ocean Avenue, the Cameron estate, is that of a white male, in his sixties. Name: Andrew Manley. Psychiatrist. Escort to Mrs. Tessa Cameron. Tessa's lover.

Instead I tightened every muscle in my throat, muttered in a cranky crone's voice, "Just 'cause them brats live on Ocean Ave., you never send anybody to shut 'em up! Noise! Drugs, I wouldn't be surprised. You go on and get somebody down there or I'll be writing to the papers, you see if I don't!"

I didn't wait for a reply.

It wouldn't get the quick response a homicide report would bring. Give me a chance to get Pix out of town, talk to a cop who might know how to help.

I started driving too quickly, stomped the brake, cruising slowly and gulping air. In, out, in out. Count to ten. Count to twenty. What the hell did it help? What had I done since Andrew Manley had first stumbled into my life with his precious manuscript in his monogrammed briefcase? What was my role in this mess? Reporting kidnappings? Reporting murders?

If Pix hadn't been watching, I might have tried to punch the safety glass out of the side window. I might have rested my head on the steering wheel and cried. *I hadn't found Thea, I hadn't saved Manley.*

At the end of the rainbow, a dead man with shattered bifocals. Not an ounce, not a speck of gold.

36

Pix was a talker. I could have her opinion of the goddamn government—thank you very much—the last fifteen terrific movies she'd seen, the last four guys she'd
screwed, the AIDS epidemic, which she personally considered a scare tactic to keep kids off the street. She was
getting on my nerves. I'd have knocked her clear into
the backseat, except that her chatter was studded with
useful gems.

Alonso had deep brown "bedroom" eyes, and she
thought he was, like, different than anybody she'd ever
known in her whole entire life. He had a killer tan or
maybe he was Hispanic, but he didn't speak Spanish so
maybe he wasn't, and his eyes were so terrific anyway,
and she had no idea why he called himself the Alien,
which was cool. Yeah, and he was really thin, but not

like the sick kind of thin you get when you have AIDS. Pix could tell. He had muscles, not like some stupid beach bum prick, regular-guy muscles, and that way cool Honda motorbike and she was pretty sure it wasn't stolen, but he had trouble getting enough bread to keep gas in the tank. He was totally uptight about money.

When I asked if the motorbike had a Mass. license, Miss Chatterbox looked at me as if I were crazy. She wasn't about to betray Alonso to an almost-cop. Took her almost two minutes to start blabbling again.

Yeah, and did I know Alonso was like an artist? Yeah, I said, she'd mentioned that. Well, not really an artist, she said, but a writer.

I kept silent. It's the best way to question a talky witness.

See, she knew because, well, first she thought he was an *artist* artist, like a painter, because he had these artist's, like, pads of paper—whatcha-callems?—sketchbooks and stuff. But when she took one, and she wasn't like gonna steal it or anything, she was just interested, it was full of pretty weird writing, not pictures like she thought. And did he get pissed when he found her reading it. Wow, talk about ballistic! Talk about postal! He said the stuff was worth money, and she thought he was, like, pretty full of himself 'cause she could write big words, too, but nobody was gonna pay her diddly for it. And she didn't know who'd pay for shit with one word here and another there and some of it not even like real sentences with verbs and stuff.

" 'I have been here for an hour,' " she said, " 'watching rain beat melancholy, on panes and regrets, I can neither conquer nor break—' "

"What?"

"It's Alonso's. Would you pay for it?"

It hadn't been part of the chapter I'd read. I was certain of that.

"Do you have it?" I asked.

"Maybe. Depends."

"How many sketchbooks did Alonso have?"

"Tons of 'em," she said. "I don't think he should of gotten pissed when I just read one."

For "read" one I substituted "took" one. Where was it? Did her knapsack have a hidey-hole, a zippered compartment I hadn't searched?

I took a good look at Pix, bottle-blond, short boy-cut hair. Sturdy kid's body. Thin gawky legs.

"You and Alonso went to visit a school." A young man and a girl, Emerson had said. Street urchins.

"So what?"

"So *why?*"

"Is my mom paying you to find me, or some kinda shit?"

It wasn't much as cries for help go, but Pix had imagined it, that her mother would try to get her back. I wished the damned woman *had* hired me.

"Why did you go to the school?" I asked.

"Alonso said he wanted to visit his alma mater. That's like old school, right, like he went there, with uniforms and shit. This old fart almost threw us out. Alonso just laughed."

"He asked about a woman named Thea Janis."

"Yeah. Like he always talked about her. He was pissed the old fart didn't have her picture. You know about her? 'Cause I don't, and the way Alonso talked, it's like she's some movie star, somebody I oughta know, and, like, I'm not ignorant."

What the hell would I do with her? Lock her in a closet? Keep her on a leash?

Roz. I could stick her with Roz. Or vice versa.

Like Alonso was maybe not exactly right in the head, Pix was saying. Not wrapped real tight, maybe.

I tuned back in. Fast.

"What makes you say that?" I asked.

"He was lookin' for a shrink. Is that such a big deal?"

Seemed like he'd found one. On the beach.

"Was he looking for a particular shrink?" I asked. "Or just somebody to talk to?"

"Guy who worked at that place for wacko rich kids."

"What place?" I asked.

"Like, you know, rich suckers send their kids, the kids who aren't quite right? You have to know it, it's like famous, for chrissakes. It's like Harvard for the messed-up, you know. Celebrity kids go there when they totally fuck up."

"In Weston?" I asked almost afraid to break the flow.

"Yeah, right, Weston. Rich people live *there*, all right." She couldn't exactly remember, but the shrink had something to do with the place in Weston where all the bratty kids who couldn't cut it go, you know, the ones fried their brains and took dope and didn't want an Ivy League diploma.

I was stopped at a red light. If I hadn't been I'd have pulled off the road.

Weston Psychiatric Institute. WPI had been initialed on Drew Manley's calendar. Every single week, once or twice. WPI. WPI.

My house is close to Harvard Square. Pix shut off

the conversational flow and started to pay attention to her surroundings as soon as she clicked on the fact that we were now in friendly Cambridge, miles from the corpse on the beach, close to places she could negotiate, squats where she could disappear into the anonymity of street life.

"Stay put," I warned, draping my arm across the back of the seat, leaning to reach the passenger side door lock, keep it locked. And I could have held her, stopped her, if it hadn't been for the three cop cars parked outside my house, flashing their cherry lamps. One look at them and she was in the backseat, out the door, and gone.

My hand moved automatically to the dashboard, swept Manley's belongings to the floor. I didn't have time to stash them in the knapsack, and I sure wasn't taking it out of the car for the police to admire. In the dark, I shoved it firmly under the passenger seat.

By the time I exited, Pix was halfway down the block, a fleeing shadow. I was tempted to pursue, but curiosity dragged me home like a cat.

37

I admit my heart was pounding double-time. I know cops don't deal in miracles. These couldn't possibly have made a connection between the cab that left Marblehead Neck and my Toyota, couldn't have known about my anonymous phone call or the corpse on the beach, much less the stash in my car. Still, I was vastly relieved when they didn't take off after Pix. God knows what tale she'd have concocted.

I was further reassured to find that all the troops were Cambridge cops, nothing fancy like FBI agents. Marissa Cameron's kidnapping was not on the immediate agenda.

The police made me flash my driver's license and formally identify myself as the owner of the house.

Attempted break-in, they said, reported by a neighbor.

"Would the neighbor happen to be a doctor two doors down named Donovan?" I asked.

"We don't have that information, lady."

I viewed the damage to my back door, which was practically hanging off the hinges. Who? Mooney's hot favorite—the contract killer hired by the Gianellis? Not poor Drew Manley, no matter how much he'd wanted "Thea's" notebook back. Not the motorbiker, what with his aged Honda leaking oil in the Marblehead shack.

Yanking doors off hinges didn't seem like Tessa Cameron's style.

I wondered if Dr. Manley had deliberately lured me from home by invoking Thea's name. For the first time, it occurred to me that he might have been speaking under duress, perhaps with a gun pointed at his head. What I'd taken for breathless excitement could have been barely controlled panic.

The cops seemed to think I should be thankful they'd had patrol cars in the area, maybe grateful enough to invite them all in for a drink. Must have been a slow crime night. They had no physical description of the burglar or burglars. They were sure the perps were no longer on site.

"Did you come in with sirens wailing?"

No one answered, so I figured they had, giving the suspects plenty of time to run. It's easier that way. Safer.

Would I care to fill out a report?

"Did they get in?" I asked.

"Nope," one of the boys in blue said. "I had to

squeeze through the back door to check the premises.
Do you live alone?"

Since I didn't recognize any of the cops, I told them
my husband was out of town and the two rottweilers
were at the vet. Alas, one of the guys knew me, so the
gag didn't play. Detective Hummel had been fully
briefed about the supposed mob contract. I suspected
he knew Mooney, hoped he did. If he didn't know
Moon, then the story was general cop house gossip:
Carlotta Carlyle has been elected body most likely to
get splattered across town.

Maybe the guy on my tail was a policeman, not a
DEA agent or a crazed mobster.

I asked Hummel point-blank: Did he have anybody
shadowing me? He gave me the weary once-over, the
glance of a cop who's seen too much in one day.
"Nope."

"Not enough manpower," I said. "Right?" It's pure
bull. Threat on some Harvard-connected high life,
they'd locate the essential personnel, and fast.

"You got it," Hummel said.

I dealt with the front door locks, glanced around the
foyer and down the single step into the living room.
Nothing seemed out of place.

"You want us to check inside again?" Hummel
asked.

"Nope."

"Maybe you could spend the night with a friend," he
suggested. "Or call somebody to spend the night with
you."

"You think my burglars are gonna come back?"

"If they do, two's better than one."

"You got any stats on that? Burglars preferring sin-
gles?"

One of the other cops touched him on the shoulder. "I gotta go," Hummel said.

"Thanks for getting here so quickly," I said. Then I did a thorough room-to-room, gun drawn. Nobody home but a hungry cat and a terrorized bird. Roz's bedroom was a wreck, but that was normal. Mine wasn't much better.

I was checking to see that the manuscripts were in place, both the original—which meant digging through the kitty litter—and the copy, when the bell rang, once, sharply. I patted the small of my back to make sure I'd shoved the 40 in my waist clip, approached the door slowly.

Keith Donovan stood on the front stoop, the porch light haloing his fair hair. I wouldn't have to call a pal to spend the night.

I yanked the door open.

"Hi. Are you okay? You look—"

"Rumpled, hot, disgusted. Take your pick."

"I saw the cop cars."

"Just your everyday break-in attempt."

"Attempt?"

"They didn't get in. An 0511 in cop talk. Nighttime attempt with forcible entry. Did you call 911?"

"No."

"A guardian angel must be watching my house."

"Not necessarily," Donovan said. "Why not spend the night at my place?"

He wriggled his eyebrows playfully and I had to wrestle my thoughts out of his air-conditioned bedroom. Quit kidding yourself, a voice hollered in my head: You don't want to question him about fellow-psychiatrist Drew Manley, dead on the Marblehead sand. You want to rip off your clothes and fool around.

It's happened before in the aftermath of a messy death. Nothing so life-affirming as sex.

I swallowed and said, "Let's stay put."

"Nervous?"

"Not nervous, but if anybody does decide to break in later, I'd like to be the welcoming committee."

"May I join you?"

"The sheets aren't clean."

"I don't mind that so much as the gun on the night-stand."

"Better than under the pillow," I said.

"Long as the safety stays on, I'll risk it."

I took in a deep breath. "Do you know a shrink named Manley? Andrew Manley?"

"Excuse me, but this doesn't sound like on-the-way-to-the-bedroom chat. I came over to soothe and relax you—"

"And help fix my goddamn back door."

"Not exactly. I'll admire you while you do it, Carlotta. I'll pour you a drink if you've got anything drinkable."

My dad taught me the basic use of the hammer and screwdriver. Why so many fathers failed to pass this information on to their sons, I have no idea.

Donovan inspected my refrigerator, no doubt wondering why my mother had failed to pass on any culinary expertise.

"I'll bring something from my place," Keith said.

"By the time you return I'll have this sucker nailed," I said.

I didn't do the repairs with finesse. I'd have to get a locksmith on it in the morning. My objective was one night's safety. I used a lot of ten-penny nails, curses, and hammer strokes.

Sweating, I wandered into the living room. My message machine blinked. I checked, and all the messages were from Vandenburg, demanding I dial back at once!

Hah! He must have heard that Carlos had been in touch with me. He could wait till snow covered Miami for me to return his calls.

Keith Donovan brought Sauvignon Blanc and a pricey-looking jar of blue massage gel.

"Patient give you that for a present?" I asked sweetly.

"You don't want to know."

"Is it good for massaging feet?" I asked.

"What is it with you and feet?"

What it is with me is that feet are a major erogenous zone. Rub my instep firmly using a circular motion of the thumb, and I make low guttural noises, and forget to ask questions—

"Dammit," I said. "I need to know about Manley."

Donovan made tracks for the kitchen. If it had been his kitchen he'd have returned with proper stemware, the wine ensconced in a silver bucket. Since it was my kitchen he'd grabbed a couple of water glasses and a bowl into which he'd chipped ice from the side of the freezer. I grabbed one of the larger chunks, ran it over my forehead, and held it at the pulse point in my neck before popping it, dripping, into my mouth.

"Manley," I stated firmly as we settled on the rickety sofa. I'd kicked off my sandy sneakers, removed my khaki jacket, unbuttoned the two top buttons of my blouse. Donovan smiled encouragingly, like he hoped I'd keep unbuttoning. I wanted to. It felt as though I had sand in my armpits, sand in my bra.

Donovan handed me a glass of wine. I noticed he was staring out the window.

"See anybody?"

"No."

"You seem jumpy."

"Your house was almost burglarized!"

"Tell me about Manley."

"What do you want to know?"

"Basically, everything you know."

"Nice guy. Good shrink. Drink up. Let's go to bed."

It sounded as if the two men had more than a nodding acquaintanceship.

"He ever ask you about me?"

"I don't remember. I may have mentioned you."

"Does he do much work at Weston Psychiatric?" I kept my verbs present tense. I wanted to hear what Donovan thought of the man before he knew his fate. Death tends to freeze opinions, turn them into eulogies and summations rather than day-to-day observations.

"I think he's semiretired. He doesn't accept new patients, I know that. He specializes in long-term analysis, the kind fewer and fewer medical plans pay for."

Beryl Cameron, her sister's literary heir, wouldn't need medical insurance to afford Drew Manley's continuing care.

"Is he a specialist in recovered memory syndrome?"

"No. Why?"

"It's a topic I keep running across," I said.

"My advice is keep running. RMS is fraught with incredible problems. Judges and juries don't seem to understand that it's a case by case process. That some alleged victims show actual signs and symptoms of abuse, while others may have been prompted or misled—"

"You seem to know quite a bit about it," I said.

"It's a psychiatric hot button right now. If it comes

to a trial, you can hire a top gun, a forensic shrink who'll quote you chapter and verse on why all alleged abuse victims must be believed absolutely. And the other side can hire their own gun, another highly credentialed forensic shrink, who'll quote you chapter and verse on why no alleged abuse victims who delay coming forward can be believed for one instant. In Boston, a federal judge just ruled that repressed memories have sufficient scientific validity that a jury may be allowed to hear them. Whole business could change tomorrow."

"Which side are you on?"

"Right in the middle. With the yellow lines and the dead armadillos."

"Here's to the middle," I said. We clinked glasses. Mine was almost empty, and I thought about pitching it in the fireplace. More debris to clean up from one hell of a night.

"So did you ever work at Weston?" I asked Donovan, blinking my eyes. The wine and the long drive and the sheer physical exertion were starting to catch up with me.

"I've been there. When I was a student."

"Long ago and far away, huh, old man?"

"Undo one more button and call me an old man. Dare you."

"Work first," I said, draining the last sips of wine. I grabbed another ice cube and ran it over my face. If I closed my eyes I could still see headlights, taillights. I felt disoriented. Maybe I should phone Tessa Cameron, tell her the latest developments.

Donovan leaned over and gave me the kind of kiss that makes it hard to concentrate.

"Whoa," I said. "Could you get me into Weston Psych?"

"As a patient, maybe. As an investigator, no."

"If I entered as a patient, could I get out again?" I asked. Just a few more questions and I'd give it up, let go, return his kisses, unbutton his shirt. Wipe away the memory of Manley's still body abandoned on the beach.

"Depends on who commits you."

"Ah," I said.

"Ah?"

"It's August, Keith. Aren't most shrinks out of town?"

"Yeah."

"Could you make a phone call for me, just to find out if someone is a patient at Weston Psych?"

"Carlotta—"

"It's not like you haven't done it before, Keith."

"I know. But Weston Psych is a different animal. They're extremely . . . cautious."

"So be extremely sneaky, Keith. I have confidence in you."

He took another sip of wine, glanced at his watch, said speculatively, "It might be easier to put one over on the night staff. Patient's name?"

"Beryl Cameron. Long-term care. If they say they have no Beryl Cameron, try Beryl Franklin."

I listened on the extension while he jumped through hoops, listing his credentials, linking his name with Manley, inquiring not whether Miss Beryl Cameron was a patient, but instead whether she was receiving more or less than 600 milligrams of Clozaril per day.

"Six hundred and fifty," came the reply.

"Very good," I said admiringly, after we'd both hung up. "What's Clozaril?"

"Brand name for clozapine."

"Which is?"

"An extremely powerful antipsychotic drug used to manage patients with severe schizophrenia."

"Why did you choose it?"

"Manley. WPI. Long-term patient. Call it an educated guess."

"I want to visit Beryl Cameron. I want to know who committed Beryl Cameron."

"Good luck," he said.

"Donovan."

"Don't look at me like that. I can't help you get into WPI."

"You're staring down my blouse," I said.

"You finally noticed."

"It's been a long hot day. I could use a shower."

"After," he said.

"After what?"

His index finger traced my neckline, lingering at the third button.

He rubbed his fingers together. "Sand."

"Possibly kitty litter," I warned.

"Shower first," he said. "Take your clothes off down here, so we don't mess up the house."

"Is that what your mommy used to make you do?"

" 'Mommy'? Is that shrink talk?" he said, undoing the three remaining buttons on my shirt. "I thought shrink talk was forbidden."

A fine sprinkling of sand fell on the floorboards along with my shirt and bra.

"Hey," I protested. "You take off some clothes, too. This is getting one-sided."

"I'll join you in the shower once the first layer of grit goes down the drain."

I made for the stairs.

I was washing my hair, eyes closed, when I heard the shower curtain move. I felt him behind me, his breath on my neck. He worked the shampoo into my hair, strong fingers building up lather, massaging my scalp, twisting my curls into a ridiculous upswept mass. His soapy hands slid to my breasts and belly and thighs. I snuggled back against him, one hand massaging his erection. When I turned to rinse the shampoo from my hair we met face to face, hands and lips working. Miracle we didn't fall and maim ourselves in the shower stall. We never got around to the massage gel.

Sometimes after we make love, I catch Donovan watching me in a particular way, his eyes slightly narrowed, his forehead furrowed. And I wonder if he's thinking about Sam Gianelli, my former lover, my former boss at the now defunct G&W cab company. It's not like I deflowered a virgin when Donovan and I went to bed. And I know all about Roz. It's very involved, and when I see that look cross Donovan's face I'm tempted to ask what he's thinking.

Then I remember he's a shrink, and I keep silent.

Last thing I want is long-term analysis. Short-term sex does fine.

Except, of course, that I couldn't sleep. With the heat of the moment past, memories flooded back. And guilt. And trepidation. If someone had tried to break into my house, why wouldn't he tackle the car, an easier target? The car with Manley's credentials, with Pix's knapsack . . .

I slipped on shorts and a T-shirt, crept out of the

room, and down the stairs. Donovan shifted in his sleep, but didn't wake.

I couldn't use the back door. On my way through the living room, I stopped at my desk, worked latex gloves onto my hands. I hesitated at the front door, wondering whether to shut the porch light. The light would outline my silhouette. Turning it off might clue in an observer, announce the action about to take place. I turned off the light, waited five minutes.

The cement stoop felt cold on my bare feet. I walked in the damp grass, used my key quietly, wishing I'd flipped off the car's dome light.

I stood, the passenger door ajar, waiting. Nothing moved for two long minutes. I counted one hundred and twenty beats silently—one, one-thousand, two, one-thousand—then bent and fumbled all of Manley's effects into Pix's knapsack.

Inside, I shook the contents onto my desk. Remembering Pix's comment, her quoted verse, I kneaded the knapsack, squeezed it. No hard cardboard backing, no place to hide a calligrapher's notebook. A crumpling sound. Paper. A single sheet folded into an inner zipped compartment. Cream-colored with wavy lines.

Words heavily crossed out, rewritten, altered. This was a working draft, prose, almost poetry. I recognized the elegant hand, the elaborate script I'd come to associate with Thea.

"for b," it said.

"call her precious, call her jade, call her gemstone, loadstone of loathing. always she kept her self to herself. call her secret, silent, sleeping. arms above my head, twined together with white ribbon, twirling ribbon from birthday gifts, carefully saved in a scented drawer, she feels nothing. sensation flees, gone before it should begin. whisper her name when you come she is not here she cannot hear there is no here"

It stopped abruptly. No punctuation, in the middle of the page. I read it again, smoothed the crinkles, turned it over.

On the back, a childish hand, barely legible, had scrawled: "once upon a time Alonso told me he was an FBI guy"

I reread it twice, locked everything in a drawer, threw away the latex gloves. I took another shower before returning to bed.

38

I have no idea how late we'd have slept if Roz hadn't burst into the bedroom, brimming with news.

What with the heat, we'd dumped the sheet during the night. Donovan made a sleepy attempt to grab it off the floor. Roz assisted, giggling like a madwoman.

"It's not like I'm seeing anything new, honey," she informed him dryly.

I, on the other hand, *was* seeing something new: Roz's hair. Roz's bizarre hair, differently cut and colored weekly, has become such a given that I hardly notice it anymore. Cornrows, Mohawks, it's the same to me. Last night, while my back door was getting wrenched off its hinges, she'd evidently crossed a new threshold.

I can only describe it in terms of a monk's tonsure.

The top of her head was clean-shaven, shiny, an area the diameter of an orange. The surrounding fringe, four to five inches long, stood out in a spiky halo of neon purple and Day-Glo pink.

Donovan smothered his face in the pillow.

"Are you laughing at my hair?" Roz asked.

Donovan, immediately serious, lifted his head. "Why would anyone laugh at your hair?" he said.

"Roz," I said. "Is this urgent?"

She said, "It's past ten o'clock."

"So what?"

"So Woodrow MacAvoy has hidden assets."

"Give me the bottom line."

"It took me hours. I expect money."

"Understood. If you want hours to explain your cleverness, you wait for me to get dressed. Urgent, I can handle in bed."

"Bottom line: Remember the T&C's?"

"Turks and Caicos Islands."

"This is the good part," Roz chortled. She was talking to me, but she was watching Donovan like he was an artist's model. Maybe she'd paint him in the nude for some new display. Bet he'd love that. "I'm not sure I could have gotten it alone, on our computer, but I found this guy who used to do a lot of work in banking security."

"At the Liberty?" I asked.

"Right. I bought him major hours of on-line access for which I expect to be paid."

"You haven't told me anything yet."

"Your Sergeant MacAvoy may live like a poor man," Roz said, "but he's got bucks in offshore tax havens."

I said, "As in how much?"

"I found at least six hundred fifty K, which oughta

dwarf my request for a mere three hundred bucks, Carlotta. I kept track of expenses and everything."

"I'm not paying for the haircut."

"You don't like it?"

"It's fine."

"And I finished the drawings you wanted. Another hundred."

"Where'd you sleep?" I asked.

"What business is it—"

"Let me rephrase that. Why weren't you home when the house nearly got torn apart?"

"The back door, huh? I noticed. I slept with a friend. Kinda like you. How you doin', Keith?"

He'd long since removed his face from the pillow. "Fine, thanks."

I said, "Roz, on your way out, one thing."

"Money," she said.

"I don't keep it under the mattress. Something's bothering me. You know how when you wake up suddenly—"

"Yeah," Roz said bluntly, "all your brain waves and shit are screaming at you. It's creative time."

"There's a number," I said. "A number . . . It was erased from Thea's file every time it appeared. Nine digits. It's on my desk, under the blotter. It could be a Social Security number. Pop it in the computer and see what comes out."

"Probably nothing."

"Probably."

"Oh, and Gloria called. She says call her at ITOA."

"As soon as I'm awake."

If Roz had left right then it might have been okay. Instead she said, "Did you see the morning news?"

"No."

"Here's the paper. You owe me fifty cents. That guy Manley, the one in the Harvard photos, he's dead." With that, she bowed out. Didn't even close the door.

"Goddammit," Donovan said. "You knew last night."

How had they identified the body so quickly? I had Manley's wallet, his appointment book. It wasn't like some cop could have reached in the victim's pocket, yanked them out: Exhibit A.

Donovan repeated, "You knew."

I went defensive. "It's not like he was your best friend."

"He was a human being. So am I. You could have told me."

"I'm getting dressed," I said.

Donovan stayed in bed till I left the room. Not even a morning kiss.

39

I dressed in white, for steamy weather, and in case I had to infiltrate Weston Psych without Cameron family permission. Sneakers, especially with leather tops, look like nurses' shoes these days. And nurses don't look a thing like they used to when I was a kid, all starch and frilly caps and dresses. Anything white seems to do the trick today. I rummaged through my dresser, found painter's pants and a snowy T-shirt.

Roz gave me the eye and a sheet of printout on Woodrow MacAvoy. I read it while I downed orange juice.

Roz said, "You think Donovan's waiting for me to bring him breakfast in bed?"

"Not funny," I said.

"Did you see his face?"

"Anything on that SSN?" I asked.

"Nope. It doesn't appear to be a Social Security."

I dialed Gloria.

"What have you got for me?" I asked.

"Good morning to you, too, sweetheart," she said, her deep voice liquid music. "Took me a while to get your Logan cabbie 'cause he snatched the fare."

"Shame, shame," I said.

Logan International's got a cab shortage. Boston's got a cab shortage. They handle it like any crazed bureaucracy, with rules and regulations that make no sense, and fines to back up their foolishness. If you drop off a fare at Logan, you can't pick up a fare at Logan until you first circle the entire airport, register at the taxi pool, and pay for the privilege. Unless you're a bona-fide Boston cab, not a Cambridge cab or a Chelsea cab or a Somerville cab, forget it. I mean, we have a cab shortage around here, you know?

"Guy's a Brookline Red Cab jock, doesn't want trouble," Gloria said.

"I'm not trouble," I said.

"Oh, yeah, sing it, honey. I know exactly what he knows, so you're gonna leave him be."

"Provided you tell all."

"Picked up the blonde two forty-five Wednesday P.M., International Terminal, dropped her at the corner of Marlborough and Newbury. No address."

"What about luggage? She had a ton of luggage."

"One small rollaway bag, that's it."

She could have stashed the rest of her luggage at the airport. No lockers anymore, not with terrorist threats, but she could have abandoned it near a claim-your-luggage roundabout. Without tags, it could still be there. If it hadn't been stolen.

"Anything else? Anything she said, anywhere she stopped?"

"That's all she wrote," Gloria said. "This is the part where you say 'thanks.' "

I did. Then, without cradling the receiver, I phoned Mooney.

"You checking in for the daily kidnap report?" he asked.

"Where else am I gonna get it?"

Mooney said, "You know, at first, I figured they were gonna do a total media rush, tearful Mama, noble suffering husband, the whole nine yards."

"So you think the kidnapping's genuine," I murmured.

"Don't you?" he said guardedly.

I hesitated. "I'm not sure anymore."

"That's what you called to tell me. I should dial Gary Reedy and say, hey, the woman who brought me on board this thing, now she thinks maybe it's a put-up job."

"That's not why I called. Mooney, I need help. Please. This is haunting me."

"The FBI is haunting me. You know, the drop was set for last night, and then nobody showed."

"Where was it supposed to go down?" Please, not Marblehead, I thought. No. If it had been Marblehead I'd have been in federal custody.

"Sorry, that's privileged information, which means I don't have a clue."

"Mooney, look, there's this number on Thea's file, on the Cameron-Janis file."

"So what?"

"It's erased. Over and over again."

"I thought you said there was a number."

"It wasn't that thoroughly erased." I read it to him. "It's nine numerals so I thought it might be a Social Security but I can't get anything on it."

"So?" His tone was dead, indifferent.

"Could it be a cross-reference to another police file?"

"Could be."

"But you won't check it out?"

"Carlotta, if and only if I get everything cleared off my desk today, which will be damned near impossible, I might be able to look it up, as a favor."

"Which I will repay. Up front. Now."

I gave him everything I knew about Marissa Cameron's departure from home Wednesday afternoon, including the argument I'd overheard. I gave him the Dover cab. The Red Cab.

"You got this from Gloria," he said.

"Maybe."

"I don't get it," he said. "Sounds crazy. Marlborough and Newbury. Why's a woman do something like that?"

"See if her family owns anything in the area."

"I intend to. But why?"

"Here's one possibility," I said. "I'm not saying it's the goods, but suppose she cooked this up with Garnet, okay?"

"One good reason?"

"To transfer money from Garnet's campaign fund to a more personal account. How's that?"

"I'll call Reedy."

"Don't forget to run my number!"

He was already hanging up the phone.

"Roz," I said, "talk to me about Heather Foley."

"You'd have been proud of me," she said.

I had the feeling this was gonna cost big.

"Why?"

"I phone-scammed the Swampscott PD," she said smugly.

"Sounds promising. How?"

"Meet Alberta Stoneham, earnest girl reporter for the weekly *Tab*."

"*Tab*'s okay," I said. "They use a lot of freelancers."

"See, there were a ton of Foleys in the Swampscott book, so I buzzed the police department's community relations officer. Gave him polite. Gave him sweet young thing. Told him I'm doing a story on water danger, alert the teens to beach and boating hazards. Do you love it?"

"I like it. I'm lukewarm."

"I worked him back year by year, and man, I had to listen to a lot of really pathetic shit. Once I got him on to boats, it didn't take long to shift to alcohol and boats, and bingo, we finally hit Heather Foley."

"And?" I was on my third glass of orange juice by now, wondering if Keith was ever going to join us.

"Body never recovered. Sad tale. Cop runs at the mouth a little, says she was the only good kid in the whole damned family. So I tell him I'd like to do some follow-up, and right off, he gives me the address like he's got it memorized, and I write it down, and it's yours. Impressed?"

"Yeah," I said. "Now, want to watch an expert?"

"Always eager," she said.

I hit information for the 212 area code, got a listing for Knopf, publisher of *Nightmare's Dawn*.

"Rights and permissions," I said to the young woman who answered the phone.

I got to listen to a string quartet play slowed-down warmed-over Beatles' tunes. After four minutes of that,

I was relieved to hear a human voice, even a nasal monotone.

"Subsidiary rights. Olive Anders speaking."

I wrote "Olive Anders" on a sheet of paper. Also "subsidiary rights." If you're going to scam somebody you have to use their language.

"Yes," I said, giving Roz a glance. "My name's Alberta Stoneham." I'd already written the alias at the top of the page. "I'm doing a book on modern women writers, and I'd like to quote *Nightmare's Dawn*, by Thea Janis. You published it in 1970. Since the author's dead, Miss Anders, do you think I'd get into any trouble, any legal difficulties if I were to use, say, an entire paragraph or a complete poem?"

Always use the person's name when playing phone games. Be extra polite. Assume that she can and will help you.

I gave a small inaudible sigh for the naiveté of sweet young Alberta Stoneham. If she were real, she'd soon learn what I'd learned: There's always someone to pay, somebody sticking their hand out for a little commercial grease.

"Hold on, please."

I got to hear more tortured Beatles. The glorious irony of "What would you do if I sang out of key?" played out of key courtesy of a low-battery tape recorder.

"The Alicia Worth Agency handles that account."

"Thanks you so much, Miss Anders. Could I trouble you for the phone number? I'm not in Manhattan, and I'm working on a very tight budget. Every call to information . . ."

The Alicia Worth Agency also had a 212 area code.

"Who are you gonna be now?" Roz asked.

"The IRS. See where the 1099-Miscellaneous forms wind up."

Roz raised an eyebrow. I'd impressed her. A command of IRS form language is impressive, I think.

Alicia Worth agreed. She affirmed that Miss Beryl Cameron received regular royalty statements. No, they were not sent in care of the Weston Institute. They were directed to Mr. Garnet Cameron, 87 Farm Road, Dover. I assured Miss Worth that her cooperation would clear the matter completely. No need for an audit now.

Roz said, "Neat." Flounced upstairs.

While the phone was still hot, I dialed Garnet Cameron.

"Disconnect the tape, Garnet," I said. "The FBI doesn't need to know where your sister, Beryl, lives. The family seems somewhat reluctant to divulge her whereabouts."

"Miss Carlyle, Beryl is none of your business."

"Garnet," I said. "I'm claiming a favor. I think you owe me one."

"I don't owe you a thing, except the FBI on my doorstep. If it weren't for them, I'd have Marissa back by now. I should have paid the damn kidnappers whatever the hell they wanted."

"Any news? About Marissa?"

"No. The FBI's handling everything. They screwed up last night. She could be dead for all I know."

For a moment he sounded so human, so wounded, I could barely bring myself to renew my demand.

"What do you want," he snapped, ending the spell, turning from sympathetic frog to arrogant prince in no time flat.

"You owe me a call to the Weston Psychiatric Institute. Tell whoever's in charge that I'm on my way right now, and I'll be visiting your sister on behalf of the family. I'll expect them to welcome me with open arms."

"You have a lot of nerve."

"I've got the goods to back it up. You want to hear the 'or else' part?"

"Why not?"

"Or else I release selected paragraphs of writing attributed to 'Thea Janis' to every trash tabloid in the U.S."

"You've got the notebook back! It belongs to me, to my mother."

"Wrong. It belongs to Beryl."

The phone went dead.

I listened, but heard no footsteps on the stairs. Hurriedly, I donned gloves, removed all Manley's possessions from my locked desk drawer, shoving them into an envelope. I folded the single sheet of paper, tucked it in my back pocket.

If Manley kept an office at WPI, I intended to dump his stuff there.

I checked the location of the Weston Psychiatric Hospital in the phone book, on a map. Almost as an afterthought, I phoned the city greenhouse, asked for Edgar Barrett. I hummed to myself while I waited, appreciating the lack of piped-in melodies.

"You said the Cuban gardener, the one who worked with your father, told you he was with the CIA," I said once our respective identities had been established.

"So?"

"Could it have been the FBI?"

"Lady, I was eight years old. He could have been the Man from U.N.C.L.E. He could have said NASA, if they were around then."

"Could his name have been Alonso?"

"If that's a Cuban name."

"Thanks for your help."

"And yours." He slammed the receiver down.

Before I got out the door, Sleazebag Vandenburg called, demanding to know whether I had a location on our mutual friend. I hung up. So many people had been hanging up on me lately that it felt good to be in the power position.

I should have listened to him more closely, but I was revved for my visit to Weston Psych.

Roz shoved an envelope into my hands as I walked out the door. I assumed it was an itemized bill. Assumptions, they get you every time.

PART THREE

Out flew the web and floated wide;
The mirror cracked from side to side;
"The curse is come upon me," cried
The Lady of Shalott.

ALFRED, LORD TENNYSON

*M*an, why the hell didn't she answer the phone? He'd tried five, no six times, and, for sure, she had to be home. Where the hell else would she go? He'd even had the stupid operator check the line.

Everything had taken a crazy swing and now the motorbike was history. Cops could be after his ass, watching him punch numbers on the stupid pay phone, for all he knew.

Didn't she say she'd always take care of him? That he could always come home? That he could always call if he was in trouble? That she could handle everything?

His hand rummaged through his jeans pocket. He still had the house key. He could go home. He could start thumbing now.

Hell, how far would he get? It wasn't the great wide-open road, like it used to be, not like it had been for her, thumb out, thigh out, everybody ready to stop and give you a lift, have a little party. Get high.

No way.

He hung up the phone, drew deep breaths into his lungs.

Stop it, he scolded himself. Panic he didn't need.

It wasn't like he was alone. And there was the money, that was sure to come through. He had a place to stay. He had a lady. No use making a big deal over the bike.

He didn't need Seattle, not when he had Boston, a fine lady to care for him.

It would turn out okay.

Dumb move, trying to call.

Dumb move, panicking.

40

In the parking lot, removed from traffic by distance and high sculpted hedges, it occurred to me that Roz's envelope seemed more stylish, more the thing to carry, than the one into which I'd hastily shoved Manley's wallet and appointment book.

I unfastened its string closing to expose not a bill, but two charcoal drawings, separated by a sheet of tracing paper. *Thea Janis, as she might be, were she not dead.*

Roz is given to extremism, to caricature. She does not consider kindness a virtue in art. The two sketches, the two Theas, if you will, had been executed without romantic illusion. Fifteen plus twenty-four equals thirty-nine, any way you spin it, but I found Roz's efforts almost cruel. Maybe it's our relative ages. From her comfortably twentyish perch, she sees almost-forty as older, harsher, than reality. Approaching thirty-five, I perceive the same age as youthful, vigorous.

I fixed the images in my mind, one heavy-set, one thin, both with small chins, generous mouths, wide eyes. The plump version had short curls; the thin version, long straight hair. One wore glasses. One didn't.

On the back of the thin woman, Roz had scrawled: "Sorry. Consider these freebies. I can't do 'em justice. Too many variables. What if she had her teeth fixed? Bonded? Hair permed? Eyebrows plucked? Everything changes, you know?"

The note echoed my police academy training. Ears and fingers. Ears and fingers stay the same. I transferred Manley's wallet, added the sketches, sucked in a deep breath.

Everything changes.

The Weston Psychiatric Institute could have held instructional seminars on security. They handled it with greater finesse than Walpole, with the thoroughness and precision of machine tools. A cordial man in suit and tie vetted my driver's license, phoned Garnet Cameron and spoke to him personally, guaranteeing that he'd okayed my visit even though three attendants had talked with Garnet concerning my imminent arrival barely half an hour earlier and the shift hadn't changed.

My whites wouldn't have passed muster. My threat evidently had.

I was required to sign a form declaring that I would visit Miss Beryl Cameron and only Miss Beryl Cameron and would comply with physician's orders. Since I didn't see any physicians, just security guys, I signed, deliberately scrawling my signature as illegibly as possible.

I found myself wondering what type of force the guards preferred. No trace of a holster marred my companion's admirably cut jacket. The Windbreaker Man could have picked up a few sartorial pointers. Syringe in the pocket? Taser? Mace or pepper spray?

The institute consisted of three large red-brick buildings and a couple of smaller dwellings. A gymnasium and a swimming pool, enclosed for year-round use, added to the campus illusion. Each major building or "dormitory" seemed to house a different level of illness, a single stratum of madness or aberration. Each had its own dining hall so the categories never mixed. I wondered if one could graduate from dorm to dorm, climbing the invisible ladder, until someone labeled you sane enough for this world.

All residents were housed in splendor; the armor barely showed, like bones under translucent skin.

I was to be accompanied at all times, not by the suit, but by a wardress. She would promptly escort me from the grounds if I upset Miss Beryl or any other "client," a term all seemed to prefer to patient or inmate. My assigned companion clanked as she walked and it took me a moment to find the reason—keys at her belt, obscured by a white apron and ample stomach.

She had a badge on her chest that said "Jannie." Nothing that implied credentials. At first, I figured that meant she had none, wasn't even an LPN. When I continued to see people labeled only with first names, I decided they were attempting the illusion of chumminess. All pals together at WPI. Some could leave at the end of the day and some couldn't, that's all.

I've visited state institutions in my work, and this was so far above the best of them it could have existed on a different planet. Fresh flowers were arranged in cut-glass bowls the size of beachballs. The atmosphere and smell sang first-class hotel not medical supervision. Nor did the visible "clientele," dressed in casual jeans and shirts, look like they were incarcerated for anything more serious than a rest.

I should've taken Donovan's advice, checked in.

If not for the chaos caused by Manley's death, I doubt I'd have caught a glimpse of the wood-paneled records room, disguised to look like a library. Surely I'd never have had the opportunity to glance at Beryl's chart long enough to determine that she'd been a "client" for twenty-seven years. Three years outpatient. Twenty-four residential. A very long interval of rest had carried her through her teens, dumped her at the door to middle age.

"Put that down," Jannie said. "Follow me."

Twenty-four years rang the coincidence bell too loudly . . . Had the already disturbed older sister, jealous of the younger Thea's success, killed her? Had MacAvoy been paid for a cover-up, with the Camerons agreeing to Beryl's perpetual incarceration as part of the price for his silence?

A college-like quadrangle separated the buildings. A pickup volleyball game was in progress.

Inside Hydrangea Court the quiet was broken only by the soothing sounds of classical piano, so acoustically true it could have been live. By this time, a Steinway in each building, equipped with a concert pianist, wouldn't have surprised me. I wanted to see the glossy brochures this place sent out. I wanted to see a "client" 's monthly bill!

An image of Pix, so desperate, so full of life, invaded my skull. Would she wind up in an institution, not an eighth so well run as this one?

The ground-floor rooms were grand, but perhaps the upstairs accommodations were spartan. I'd declined to meet Miss Beryl in the sunroom, insisting that her room would be the only acceptable locale. Garnet Cameron must have okayed it because Jannie unlocked and relocked a door, led me silently to a staircase.

I felt a slight tickle at my back and wondered if I could overpower the robust Jannie in a pinch and run for the gates, scale them. Just a reaction to locked doors. I'd felt it at the prison, too.

Jannie guided me down a wide plushly carpeted corridor. Doors to either side were numbered. Fancy hotel with double-keyed RABB locks.

She stopped at the end of the hallway, clanked her key ring, and entered a corner suite. At first, I thought it was empty. Then I noticed Jannie staring at the bed.

Beryl's hair was pulled back from her face, combed and rolled into a chignon. White as snow. She was slack and plump, with pimpled pallid skin. Her eyes had no sparkle, no light.

Lost, I thought. Her mother said she was lost.

Beryl didn't look like either aged portrait of "Thea." Both of Roz's efforts glimmered with intelligence, showed liveliness in their widely spaced eyes. I knew that drugs, especially strong antipsychotics, could dramatically change a person's appearance, adding pounds, puffing features. I tried to see beyond the bloated outline, to find the girl of the early news photos, the one who resembled Franklin more than Tessa. I gave it up.

She had brown staring eyes, shadows beneath them. Darker than Tessa's.

"Hi, Beryl," I said. "Mind if I sit down?"

Nothing.

Jannie made a noise, a polite snort.

I pulled a chair closer to the bed. Not an institutional chair. Beryl's sunny room was filled with polished mahogany. Her bed had a flowered canopy. There was nothing remotely institutional in the graceful lines of the furniture. Her own? The chair I sat in was deeply cushioned, slightly worn, comfortable.

"Have you seen Garnet lately?" I asked, as though we were continuing a friendly conversation.

Nothing.

"What about Marissa? His wife."

Nothing.

I gave Jannie a look. If she snorted again, I'd smack her.

"Do you remember your sister, Thea?"

Beryl hummed a little tune. Her voice sounded oddly unused, like a kid's music box opened after years of dusty silence.

"Is she medicated?" I asked.

"Of course," Jannie responded.

"Sedated?"

"Mildly."

"Is she always like this? Did Garnet Cameron order extra medication for her today?"

"Mr. Cameron is not a doctor."

"And she hasn't seen her doctor today."

Jannie bit her lip. "No."

"Because her doctor is Andrew Manley."

I used present tense. I wasn't sure what Beryl absorbed, but I didn't want to be the one to bring her bad news.

What had Andrew Manley said about writing, that writing was the way Thea experienced the world, communicated with it?

Had the two sisters always been so different?

What had happened to Beryl?

I should have begged Donovan to come with me. He'd have known what to ask, where to look. Did reputable psychiatrists condone lobotomies? Had they in the early seventies?

"Has Beryl ever had electroconvulsive therapy?" I asked.

Jannie shrugged. I was getting extremely tired of her matter-of-fact shrug.

If this was Beryl—Beryl as she normally existed—she couldn't have written the new manuscript. Not this colorless woman with dead eyes.

Could she have written the first manuscript? Had Thea taken credit for it? Why? The girl who'd written *Nightmare's Dawn* was sexually precocious. Maybe in another age, in Victorian times, such a child might have been shut away, punished.

I stared down at Beryl. She hadn't acknowledged my presense in any way. She hummed tunelessly, moved her fingers rhythmically, in a way that seemed more indicative of autism than schizophrenia to me, but what did I know about such complex labels?

All I knew was that my questions would go unanswered. Where was she when her sister died? Did she see her die, perhaps help her along in her journey out to sea?

"Were you jealous of Thea?" I asked sharply.

No reaction. Nothing. I didn't look at Jannie.

Instead I stared at the furnishings. From home. If Beryl could tell me nothing of her earlier life, maybe her possessions would. Surely she'd collected things, written things. A sample of her handwriting might prove interesting.

I expected Jannie to jump down my throat when I opened a drawer. She didn't, just stared listlessly out the window. If she'd cracked it an inch, Beryl could have heard the noise from the volleyball game.

Beryl watched, devoid of curiosity, as if her personal privacy had been violated so often she no longer had the right to any secrets.

Maybe she had no secrets. Just neatly folded cotton underwear and uniformly pink nightgowns, smelling faintly of camellias, as though Tessa had folded them, or selected the sachet bags. A collection of stuffed bears peeked from one drawer; dolls, some with broken arms, twisted legs, filled another. I kept looking, methodically searching for a diary, a notebook, until I came upon unexpected treasure: a scented wooden box. Large, made of sandalwood, filled with family photos, neatly inscribed on the back. If Beryl had printed the captions, the ink light and feathery, bearing no resemblance to the heavy definite strokes with which Thea had penned her prose and verse, I'd have the answer to one question.

I lifted the heavy box out of the drawer, arranged it at Beryl's side.

"What are you doing?" Jannie asked.

"Refreshing her memory."

"Good luck."

"This could take time. No reason for you to stay. Want a cigarette break?" I was sure I'd smelled tobacco in her hair.

She gazed longingly toward the window.

"I won't tell," I said. "I mean, what's the big deal?"

"Five minutes," whispered Jannie, her hands already patting her pocket. Addiction, what're you gonna do about it?

As soon as she left the room, the desire, the compulsion to rid myself of all Manley's stuff, to dump it in Beryl's bureau, was almost overwhelming. No. It would be too easy to prove I'd been here, too easy to backtrack his wallet to me. I had to find out if Manley'd kept an office here, better yet a room, a place to stay when he and Tessa were on the outs or playing it cool.

I took the two sketches of "Thea," and the written document I'd stolen from Pix, blended them into the photos.

"Let's look at these, Beryl," I said. "Is this your mom?"

It was labeled Tourmaline Cameron. I'd almost forgotten Tessa's given name.

Beryl didn't seem unhappy or distressed. She hardly seemed there at all.

"Did you write this?" I pointed at the caption.

Her whispered "yes" caught me off guard.

We went through the photo box together, item by item. Garnet and Thea and Beryl as children. "Father, 1962" showed Franklin Cameron as a huge hulking man. Garnet had always looked like his mother. Once, when the kids had been very young, they'd had a spaniel named Beanie.

I tried out the thin version of "Thea" first.

"Have you seen this lady, Beryl?"

She put her hand to her throat, pointed at herself. I wondered if she'd looked like her sister once, before the medication had altered her shape.

The heavy-set "Thea" got no reaction.

"Can you read this?"

I gave her the page I'd taken from Pix, the page "for b." She read it once, read it again, folded it, and pressed it against her breast. "Mine," she whispered. "My white ribbons."

Jannie entered and with the uncanny skill of prisoners everywhere, Beryl secreted the paper beneath her nightgown, more quickly than I could have done.

"Getting anywhere?" Jannie asked derisively.

"There sure are a lot of photos," I said with a sigh, wanting her to know she was in for an extraordinarily boring time if she stayed.

"Yeah," she said. "Guess so." She watched the volleyball game, staring out the window. I got the feeling that the window was as far as she planned to go now that her nicotine demon slept.

I went back to the photos.

They seemed curiously impersonal. I could find no family member missing from the shots. Were they works done on commission? Had a servant taken them, perhaps the chauffeur? Had they been used as campaign fodder, stylishly shot by some public relations maven? "The perfect family picnics in style." "The perfect family poses at the beach." "The perfect children play leapfrog on the lawn."

Beryl patted her breast. One tear rolled slowly down her cheek.

"Are you a therapist?" I asked Jannie.

"No."

"A nurse?"

"No."

"Who'll be her—"

She cut me off. "That decision hasn't been made yet. You'd better leave. You seem to be upsetting her."

Beryl caught me by the hand, hung on tight.

Jannie shrugged. "Stay," she said.

I righted a photo facedown in the box. A handsome

man with laughing foreign eyes, dark complexion. It was a snapshot, but it wasn't like the others. It lacked their curious formality, looked like it had been held, handled. Its edges had been bent and straightened.

There was no caption.

"Who's this?"

No answer. What did I expect?

"Have you seen this man?" I asked Jannie, walking to the window, lowering my voice.

Beryl followed me with her eyes. Her hands plucked at the sheet.

"No," Jannie said. There was some secret satisfaction behind her complacency. She was telling the technical truth, but she knew something.

"How long have you worked here?" I asked.

"Eleven years next March the first," she said as if she'd been counting every day.

"Who's worked here the longest?" I asked. "I need to see that person."

"You can only visit with Miss Beryl," Jannie said stubbornly.

"Don't give me any crap," I said.

"How dare you?"

"Just get me the right person."

"I take it you want to know who's in the picture."

"Yes."

"Well, I could tell you, if you weren't so rude."

"I'm sorry," I said. "It's been a long week. I would really appreciate it if you'd tell me."

Her tongue peeked out of the corner of her mouth. She was making up her mind.

"I won't tell anyone that you told me," I said encouragingly. "If anyone asks, I'll say Beryl let it slip. She does speak occasionally."

Jannie drew closer, ready to gossip. "He was a gardener here." Her eyes were amused, above it all. "The clients often, well, they don't see men of their own, um, social class, and they get crushes, especially the younger ones."

"It's an old photo," I remarked.

"She's always had it. Since I came. Some days it's faceup, some days facedown. Sometimes it's on top of the box. Once I found it in the trash, but I didn't throw it away. Means something to her," Jannie said with an elaborate shrug. "I guess."

She's always had it.

Always dating back eleven years next March first.

"Does the man still work here?"

"No."

"Did he work here when you started."

"No."

"How long ago did he leave?"

She shrugged again. "He was just day labor, I think."

"Are there records?"

"There are rumors."

"Yes?"

"You can see how he's so good-looking . . ."

"I see."

"One day he was gone. And the rumor was his past had caught up with him. Can't have men working around the place with that kind of reputation."

"What kind? Was he a thief?"

"Nothing like that." She smiled; she was enjoying this, drawing it out. "In his previous position he'd fooled around with one of the lady clients."

"Do you think he fooled with Beryl?"

"Can't say."

"Won't or can't?"

"Unconfirmed rumor," Jannie said. "What's that worth in a place where half the people talk crazy— excuse me, I'm not supposed to use that word."

She stroked the picture. "Looking like he did," she went on with a giggle, "kind of like that movie star, you know, Omar Sharif, I always thought he coulda messed with at least half the clients. Don't I wish he was still here when I came. Coulda maybe messed with me, too."

Beryl said, "Come here," not clear as a bell, but a definite summons.

Jannie was all over her in an instant. Did she want her pillows plumped? Did she want a glass of water? A doctor to talk to?

With a curt nod, Beryl indicated me.

"Give me," she mouthed, "Alonso's picture."

"Alonso," I repeated.

Another tear fell, beading for an instant on her cheek, rolling toward the pillow.

Jannie, rebuffed, stalked back to the window.

I whispered, "Trade with me, Beryl, for a little while. Let me keep Alonso's photo. It's very important. And you can keep what you have."

"Always," she said.

"Yes. You can keep the paper always. And I'll bring Alonso's picture back to you."

"Promise."

I promised.

"Cross your heart and hope to die." Her voice was like a memory, a ghost of a voice. As I promised, I thought about all the things she'd lost in her life, lost to illness, lost to fate.

"I'll bring it back," I said, making a child's-promise

cross above my heart, sliding the snapshot into my back pocket with my other hand.

We kept sifting through the photo box; several times I asked Jannie to identify Garnet or Franklin as a young man, so that she wouldn't fix on the photo of Alonso as the sole item that had caught my interest.

It was the only photo of a nonfamily member. A gardener who'd been fired from a previous gardening job. Alonso.

At last I thought the time was right to replace the sandalwood box in the drawer. Beryl had long since released her hold on me. She seemed to be sleeping, but her eyes were wide and staring.

"Good-bye, Beryl," I said. "I'll visit you again soon."

She didn't react, but Jannie did, with a deep sigh of relief, as though I'd been keeping her from her favorite TV show of the decade.

Quickly I made a decision. The complex was too vast to search. If it came to court, it would be Jannie's word against mine. She wasn't a therapist; she wasn't a nurse; she'd already taken an illegal cigarette break. I'd take my word over hers any day.

Bet I lie better than she does.

"I'd like to see Dr. Manley's office," I said, once we were in the hallway, ears buffeted by piano concertos.

"Wouldn't you? Well, I could have bounced you half an hour ago. The minute a tear fell down her cheek—"

"But you didn't bounce me, Jannie. You like Beryl. You'd like her to get better, wouldn't you?"

"Course I would. Who'd like to be shut up for life, even here?"

"What's the harm in letting me into the doctor's office, for two minutes, while you have another cigarette?"

"You'd take something."

"I wouldn't. On my honor."

"Not good enough."

"Is fifty dollars good enough?"

"Let's see it."

I had two twenties and a ten ready in my pocket.

She could have turned me over to security. I wouldn't have tried it if she hadn't taken her ciggie break, if she hadn't been so gossipy about Alonso's photo.

She wasn't going to risk going over to another building. She could get caught, fired. But she'd give me directions, a key. I should leave the key in the lock, and she'd get it back in ten minutes. Ten minutes. No more than that. Did I understand?

I did. After placing the good doctor's wallet and appointment book at the back of his desk drawer, where they could have easily been overlooked, I wiped my prints off every surface I'd touched, and then some.

Outside I started shaking. That place scared me more than any prison I've ever entered.

41

I spent too much time trying to locate Mooney, to see if he'd traced the number erased from Thea's file. No luck at one o'clock, at two, at three. Yes, I was snatching at straws, but why those careful erasures in a file covered with wite-out and scrawling black marker? Had someone wanted to be able to find that number again? Why?

I left a message asking Mooney to call me; I don't usually do that.

I bought both the *Globe* and the *Herald,* sat on the stoop, and studied each account of Manley's death. Dr. Andrew Edgar Manley had been found bludgeoned to death near a burning shack close to the ocean's edge. Flames had attracted the neighbors' notice. Mr. Hector

Davies of 46 Ocean Avenue had promptly phoned the fire department.

I swallowed. My throat felt tight and raspy. The murderer had returned. Had he tried to obliterate his crime through arson, or call attention to it with flame? Call attention to it. Otherwise he'd have moved the body into the shed. Or had the police department merely responded to my anonymous tip? You can't believe everything you read.

The murderer could have been there, watching Pix and me fighting in the sand, blotting his footprints with ours.

Manley had last been seen at an eight-thirty dinner party. Guests and location were not named. The Marblehead police promised an early arrest. A tramp, a young man in his early twenties, seen loitering near the shed, was urged to contact the police immediately. The burned hulk of a motorbike would be inspected by forensic specialists at the police garage.

Manley's obituary consisted of a string of honors and degrees, publications heralded for their clarity and brilliance. One of the primary founders of the Weston Psychiatric Institute, he'd given up private practice to concentrate on a passion for travel and rare manuscripts. At the time of his death, he remained an active member of Weston Psych's Board of Directors. He was survived by a sister, two nieces, one nephew.

I wondered whether the police had discovered that Manley'd made a phone call an hour before his death. Whether they were searching for Pix and me, or just the man, Pix's friend, Alonso. The "tramp."

Roz, sporting a lime T-shirt declaring "Born-again Pagan," approached.

"What?" I demanded.

"Grouchy," she observed.

"You'll get your money."

"I thought you might like a few more tidbits on MacAvoy."

"Such as where he was last night?"

"That, I don't know. The man plays it close to the vest, but the man is loaded."

"More than the offshore accounts?"

"He owns excellent real estate all over the Cape, Wellfleet, Yarmouth, Hyannis. A thirty-foot yacht. Part-interest in a Sanibel Island marina. That's in Florida."

"I know." No problem waving two twenties in a bar when you own a boat and a marina.

"That'll be an additional hundred bucks," Roz said.

"Add it to your tab."

She padded happily away. Lime green bike shorts matched the T-shirt. I think they had a slogan on the ass, but I couldn't read it. Maybe "Following too Close."

I grabbed a tendril of hair, twisted. According to Albert Ellis Albion's confession, Thea belonged in the sea, the sea. Near the same stretch of sand on which Manley had died so horribly last night? What was the link between the deaths, one so long ago, one so recent?

Who could I ask?

Tessa wouldn't give me the doctor's location when he was alive. I doubted she'd be more cooperative today. I'd already played my ace with Garnet. The threat of divulging Thea's writings had been good enough to get me in to see Beryl.

Beryl. Damn the toll disease and medication had taken. She must have been so different when Thea first disappeared. Or had she? Manley could have told me. He was dead.

MacAvoy, however, confronted with his unexpected, unaccounted-for wealth, might be eager to talk about sister Beryl. About a lot of things . . . Might prefer it to a chat with the IRS.

He was an old man. Surely, he'd rather spend the rest of his days in the Lucky Horseshoe, downing beers with his buddies, than delivering endless receipts to an IRS agent in a windowless Boston office.

Confrontation time. It couldn't wait.

I couldn't wait.

42

I'd lived with the prickle at the back of my neck so long, I was starting to ignore it. As I drove, I took simple evasive actions, but the "mob hit man" existed only in a remote recess of my mind.

The number on Thea's file, the carefully erased number, was at the forefront. Roz couldn't relate it to any number that would open a computer file. Mooney, I couldn't reach, but maybe MacAvoy might be persuaded to explain it. Patting my pockets, searching for a stick of gum, a mint, I touched Paolina's postcard, murmured a silent "I'm sorry."

Paolina and I have a deal. I don't do dangerous places without backup.

MacAvoy's an old man, I told myself.

Still, I'd packed my gun. Once a cop, always a cop. That held for me as well as MacAvoy.

I stopped for a burger and fries at a dive near the South Shore Plaza. I'd had a beer at the Lucky Horseshoe; I wasn't about to trust its food, nor did I cherish the idea of dining with MacAvoy. I took my time, dunking each fry in ketchup, chewing slowly, brooding. I sipped my coffee slowly. I found a pay phone, collected appropriate change, and tried Mooney twice, once at the office, once at home. No luck.

The last light left the blue-black sky as I parked near MacAvoy's driveway.

Nobody home.

Mrs. Nosy Neighbor recognized me as soon as I showed up on her well-lit porch. Mac wasn't at the bar tonight. Good thing I'd stopped by. He was drinking, yes, but down the beach. Sat like that a lot of nights, beer cooling in the tide. When he set off east with a six-pack in hand she knew where he'd be, perched on a chunk of old seawall.

She gave excellent directions. I hoped my neighbors didn't keep such good track of me.

I walked back to the car. It was a coin flip, drive or walk. It was hot. I drove. After five minutes, the road narrowed into a path. I parked in the shelter of a wind-twisted tree.

I carry a miniature tape recorder in my glove compartment, along with a Polaroid camera, two shades of lipstick, a few other odds and ends. I made sure the recorder's batteries were working and tucked it into my cleavage, fixing the whole shebang into place with cloth tape stretched from cup to cup. It was less than comfortable, but whatever MacAvoy said, I wanted. The money, he could lie about. The Camerons wouldn't have been foolish enough to wire it from one of their accounts straight to his.

A man's lies often tell more than the truth.

My sandals slid in gravel as I inched downhill. I wondered how many beers the old sergeant had drunk. I hoped he hadn't taken his pistol along to plink cans as he tossed them in the ocean. The local constabulary wouldn't take kindly to that, not even in an old cop. Kill off too many tourists on the pale crescent of beach.

The ocean, suddenly. Endless dark and a sky pierced by stars. He sat motionless on an algae-stained stone wall that appeared cool and damp from the last high tide. The breeze and the smell hit me like a tonic. I inhaled tangy salt marsh, felt my dry skin moisten, my shoulders relax. A retirement home near the ocean, even a tiny one . . . Way to go, MacAvoy.

If he'd always wanted to live so simply, why bleed the Camerons? Since he'd blackmailed them so successfully, why had he chosen to subsist within the means of a retired cop? Maybe he had big plans for the future, maybe he got immense satisfaction just knowing his investments were out there, gathering interest, knowing he was different than the average fixed-income retiree.

I cleared my throat. Either he hadn't heard my scuffling approach, or he was pretending deafness. After a bit, he turned his head and grunted. The moon was full. I hoped the grunt meant recognition.

"What brings you back, girlie?" Recognition, all right.

"Don't you mean, what took me so long?"

"Nope," he said curtly, turning his eyes from the shoreline, staring at me. "Got a cigarette?"

"Nope."

He took out a pack and lit up, scraping the match

head along the stone wall, expertly cupping the flame from the breeze. Dark wiggly lines flickered on the back of his left hand.

"I don't use my own if I can bum," he said. "Learned that as a cop."

I inhaled secondhand smoke, thought about how easy it would be to join him, to share secrets over a filter tip. Once a smoker, always.

"You want one?"

"Yeah, but don't give it to me," I said.

"And why would you be interested in talking to me again?" I suspected the whole cigarette ritual was a ploy to stretch time, to search for the right opener. I wondered just how drunk the man was.

"Tessa Cameron," I said.

"The old lady?"

"I wouldn't call her that. Not to her face."

"Better not to," he agreed.

Surely he wouldn't have thought of her as the old lady twenty years ago. Had he seen her more recently?

"She hired me," I said.

"Why?"

I avoided the direct answer. "Case sure moved fast once you came along, Mac. Before you took charge, it was all over the map, a file in Dover, a file in Cambridge, another in Marblehead . . ."

"Yeah," he agreed, nodding and puffing, one hand on the cigarette, the other massaging his arthritic knee. "And the FBI thinking it was a kidnapping. Once the feds and the staties get into the act, they hate to move out."

He'd wolfed his cigarette. Now he began the ritual again, the scrape of a match, flickering light teasing my eyes with a partial view of the crisscross lines on his hand. I made a quick diving grab. He was drunk enough to misunderstand my motive. In the best interest of my client, to further scientific research, I took a long drag of the newly lit coffin nail. In the reddish glow the tattoo stood out clearly.

The five-oh starfish said Thea belonged in the sea-oh. I could almost hear Al-Al's singsong voice on the breeze.

Returning the cigarette, I dropped Mac's gnarled hand, which he immediately maneuvered to fasten on my thigh. I slapped it off lightly.

"Mrs. Cameron have a problem?" he asked encouragingly.

"Someone seems to be writing a new novel," I said. "Supposedly Thea. But she's dead."

"People," he said disgustedly, shaking his head so hard that his jowls vibrated. "Sometimes you wonder why God let 'em loose on the planet. Place woulda been better off with dinosaurs."

"So what do you think?" I asked.

"First off, I wouldn't believe Mrs. Tessa Cameron if she was swearing on a Bible."

"You think she made the story up?"

"If she could use it to get her photo in the paper, sure. Hell, she'd make it up if she were having a dull day, nothing better to do."

"Mac." I kept my voice low and soft, a whisper meant to blend with the rushing tide. No accusation. "You sure there's no possibility that Thea Janis could be alive?"

"Not a chance in heaven or hell," he said. "Some things even the rich can't buy. Not much, mind you."

"I visited Albert Albion at Walpole."

"Did you now?"

"He talked about you, Sergeant."

He puffed on his cigarette. I helped him inhale.

"So you saw Al-Al. That must have made his year."

"I'm not sure he'd remember, Sergeant."

"Are you trying to say something, girl?"

He didn't seem to like being reminded of his rank.

"Aside from his confession, which sounded pretty bogus by the way, was there anything, any hard evidence, that made you fasten on him as Thea's killer?" I asked.

"You're talking a long time ago," he said.

"But you've got a hell of a memory, Mac."

The ex-sergeant mashed his half-smoked cigarette out on the stone wall, hurled the stub angrily at the sand. "Tell me, what's-yer-name, Carlotta, the ex-cop. Albert. Al-Al. Did he look all there to you? Hundred percent?"

"Not even fifty," I said. "Man wears tinfoil on his head."

His hand edged toward the cigarette pack, hesitated. "I don't see how it can matter after all these years," he muttered, staring intently upward, as if there might be a message emblazoned across the night sky, encrypted, ready to decode.

"Confession's good for the soul," I said.

"You don't look any more like a priest than you do a cop," he said.

I held my tongue.

"Albert Ellis Albion," MacAvoy said with contempt, tossing the name into the air as though it were a coin that might come down heads or tails.

I remained motionless, practically holding my breath. Heads or tails. Talk or keep silent.

"Bastard didn't do it," MacAvoy said, throwing pebbles onto the sand. He wasn't trying for distance but a few made it into the water with tiny rainlike splashes. "Oh, he did plenty, our little Al-Al, but he didn't kill Thea."

I waited. He tossed more pebbles, harder, aiming at the water now, sidearm, trying to make the rocks skim the surface.

"You coach him for his confession?" I asked after five long minutes had passed. "Did you write it out for him?"

MacAvoy said nothing. He threw a pebble at a long-legged seabird. It squawked hoarsely and hopped away.

"Must have been a lot of pressure coming down," I said sympathetically.

"Damn Camerons." He gave up on the pebbles, sat perfectly still. "Girl fuckin' killed herself. Walked into the ocean, further north, some ritzy private beach. Walked in, didn't walk out. People she was with, hell, they're probably too classy to report it. But no, the Camerons can't leave it like that, can they? Tarnish the family's sterling reputation, now, wouldn't it? Must be something wrong with a family, one of the dear girls headed for the looney bin, another one kills herself, don't you think? Bad for the political branch of the family, so we have to rustle up some poor turkey who's gonna earn himself a Murder One anyway. Not just any ordinary junkie killer. A confessor, you know?"

"You did what the Camerons wanted?"

"Not just me, missy," he said indignantly. "Write it down. Quote me on it. Everybody did what the Camerons wanted. Mayor to police chief on down the ranks, couldn't kiss-ass fast enough. What did it matter if some pervert—and he was a killer, mind you, caught red-handed—got an extra life sentence tacked on, long as they could have their little girl's body buried in consecrated ground, prayed over by a bishop?"

"Was there a body?"

"Sure there was," he blustered. "In the ocean. Off Marblehead."

"Oh, yeah," I said. "And then there was that girl who got drunk and fell off the boat. Too bad."

"Yeah. Too bad."

"Heather Foley's body has never been recovered, Mac."

"Happens."

"Two-day delay between the time the coroner gets a female body and the time he declares it Thea Janis's corpse."

"That happens, too. The man must have been busy. He's dead, now, so I guess you'll have to take the matter up with someone else."

"I'm taking it up with you, Mac. Must have been a regular free-for-all, a circus. Both families identifying the same body."

"Don't know a thing about it," he said.

"I hear the Foleys were in pretty regular touch with the Swampscott police."

"Did you? Some families are like that. No luck. Sons always in trouble. Then the daughter drowns." He yawned enormously. "I'm getting tired of all this yapping."

So. He knew the Foley boys had been in trouble with the cops. He was exaggerating his own ignorance.

I said, "Did Al-Al lead the police to his victims?"

"Well, they found him standing over the Evans girl. He showed 'em where he'd left another. God knows how many women that lunatic cut up."

"But not Thea?"

He stared out at the deep blackness of the ocean, an ocassional whitecap catching starlight. "I told him to say he threw her body into the sea. There, that's what you want to hear, isn't it? She was dead, after all."

"What makes you so damned sure she killed herself? She could have walked away. People do it all the time."

"Fifteen-year-old girls? Stark-naked? Those clothes in Marblehead, they were hers, all right."

It was in the Marblehead file that the erased notation on the margin had first caught my eye.

"I thought the clothes were never physically linked to Thea."

"Well, you know, they couldn't do then what they do now. Take a strand of hair and DNA-type the root. Who'd even heard of that?"

He was staring hard at the outgoing tide.

"What?" I said.

"There was a ring, a silver band, engraved with her initials. It was there when Franklin Cameron, her dad, came to see the clothing the first time. Gone when he left. And we were told to scrub it off the records."

That would account for more erasures.

"Now why do you suppose we were told to make that ring disappear, girl?"

I knew the right answer—because the ring confirmed identity, confirmed suicide—but it bothered me all the same. Everything about MacAvoy's confession bothered me. It seemed canned, prepared. I wondered if he'd spoken to any of the Camerons since my first visit.

"Are you Catholic?" he asked suddenly.

"Half," I said.

"Practicing?"

"No."

"Me, I was born and bred Catholic. Fed Catholic.

You know, the Camerons sent a priest to see me, their family priest, old geezer, must have passed long ago. Father Martin. Yes, Father Martin. He talked to me about sin, venial sin and mortal sin, and what's the age when you're truly responsible for your actions, and he got me so confused that it seemed they were right and I was wrong. I just wanted to do my job, close the case."

I nodded. "You figure the priest visited the medical examiner, too? He a religious man?"

"All I know is I did the damned Camerons a favor. I encouraged a man to confess to a crime, turn a suicide into murder. And do you think they were grateful to me for it? Treated me like dirt. Sergeant I was then and sergeant I stayed. I never got another promotion after that case. I didn't think it would be like that, sitting in the squad room with the other cops thinking I was bent, when all I'd done was a favor, something a priest practically ordered me to do."

I pretended to accept his lie.

"And that's why you hate the Camerons," I said.

"They used me. They'll use you, too, girl. Sorry, sorry. Girl's what I grew up with. It's hard to change."

I'd have felt better if he hadn't thrown in that last apology. He was damned good, but he was a barefaced liar. Had he concocted the suicide tale himself or had Tessa briefed him? Franklin, before he died? Garnet?

Between them, the Camerons had constructed several lines of defense: First, simplest, innocent Thea was murdered by Albion; second, only if required, Thea killed herself and MacAvoy helped set Albion up to play patsy.

Problem: Neither take seemed worth the kind of money the Camerons had shelled out to MacAvoy.

"There was a funeral," I said conversationally. "Who's really buried in Thea's grave?"

He shifted, rubbed his knee.

"All I know is she's buried in sanctified ground. There's a tomb, and the case is closed and cold as my bones in January."

She, not Thea, not Dorothy.

"So why would someone pretend to be Thea now?"

"Rattle some skeletons in the Cameron closet," he suggested with satisfaction. "It would have to be someone close to the family."

"Or someone close to the investigation," I said.

"Nix that."

"The other daughter, Beryl, the one 'headed to the looney bin,' you ever interview her?"

"No."

"Why?"

"I saw enough crazies on the street, thank you. I didn't have to check out the ones in padded cells."

"You remember her doctor's name?"

"You don't ask much," he said ruefully. "Why in hell should I?"

"Was it Andrew Manley? Guy who died in Marblehead last night?"

"Sorry," he said. "That's enough. That's all. I'm a tired old man. Leave me in peace."

"I could," I said quietly, "if you'd tell me the truth."

"I've told the truth."

"You told me a good story, Mac. Not the truth. There's a difference."

"Get away from here."

"I especially like the part about the grieving father removing the silver ring. You make that up yourself?"

"What would you know about any of it?" he asked.

"The Camerons aren't fools. Six hundred and fifty thousand dollars is way too much to pay a cop to turn a suicide into a murder."

"Six hundred and fifty—what are you saying, girl?"

They must have paid even more, to account for the boat and the Cape properties.

I said, "Of course, it's not too much to pay for a murder. Did Franklin Cameron pay you to kill Thea?"

"Murder? You've lost your senses."

"You're going to have a hard time explaining away that real estate, Sergeant. On your retirement? You shouldn't be slapping down any twenties on bar tables. The cottage is a good cover, and so's the 'I hate all Camerons' routine, but it's not enough. The money, and the file erasures, and the simple fact that you got total control of the case all scream cover-up."

He had a grip on my arm. "Are you saying I killed someone? I never drew my weapon on duty except once, and then I never fired it."

"Too bad you got greedy."

"And you're not working for money, I suppose." He rose to his feet slowly, an old bull elephant, a rogue. He grabbed me by the arm, tried to get a stranglehold on me. I let him walk me a few steps into the tide. I wasn't going to hit him unless I had to. He was an old drunk. His strength had deserted him. His fury I could handle.

"I want the truth," I said.

"What's truth, anyway? An old whore, there's truth for you."

"What did the Camerons pay for?"

"Concealing a suicide."

"The truth, dammit." I recited the nine-digit number. "What does that mean? Why did you erase it off Thea's file? Why?"

I wasn't sure if it was the number or the tide. Mac-Avoy took a wavering step and collapsed. Goddamn, I thought, he's having a heart attack! For a moment we both splashed around. I righted myself, turned to find him.

He had a gun pointed at my left eye.

43

Time settled over us like a blanket of dust. I had all eternity to notice that MacAvoy didn't hold a matte black pistol in his two-handed grip. Black, I might not have seen the details. Moonlight glinted off the stainless steel finish of the big SIG-Sauer automatic. Maybe that's how he spent the money, I thought, buying expensive guns.

I smiled at him, my best effort. It must have looked ghastly.

"Your whole career, you never shot anybody," I said, keeping my voice rock steady. "You're not going to start with me, are you?"

Deliberately, I turned the last sentence into a question. Keep him talking.

"Why'd you have to mess with it? After all these years?" he asked.

"The nine-digit number, the one you erased, what's it mean?"

"Can you swim?"

"No," I lied, letting my tone and my breathing register panic. "Not well."

"I'm a crack shot," he said. "Maybe you oughtta just swim out to sea, keep going till I can't draw a bead on you anymore. Give you, like, a sporting chance."

"I'd never make it," I said, hoping he'd give me the opportunity. The water felt cool and murky. I lifted one foot, then the other. My sandals floated free. I took inventory. My clothing was light, nothing that would weigh me down. I'd hate to soak the miniature tape recorder. My S&W 40, at forty-one ounces, was centered in the small of my back.

MacAvoy said, "Too bad this didn't happen twenty-four years ago. Your body could have been mistaken for Thea's. The family wasn't fussy about a likeness."

As he spoke he waved the gun, motioning me away from shore. The water was up to my rib cage. I wondered how good a swimmer he was. The tide was sucking us both deeper.

He started to laugh, possibly the beer catching up. The gun barrel didn't waver.

"What's funny?" I asked mildly.

"What some people pay for," he said. "That's funny. The way some people think that more money than a guy ever dreamed of—more than he could even imagine —is peanuts. That's fuckin' funny. People and money."

He wasn't drunk, but he was happy. He'd flashed the gun, but now that the shock value had worn off, I didn't believe he'd use it. The man acted like he wanted to talk; maybe he needed the weapon in order to feel he was in control of the situation.

I encouraged speech with another question.

"You thought the Camerons offered too much?" I asked.

He was facing the shore. I was staring out to sea, considering the tide, feeling the ocean rhythm, praying for a sudden crashing wave. Undertow. Riptide.

"The damn number you're so interested in," Mac-Avoy said teasingly. "It's a cross-reference, to a missing persons file. What do you think about that?"

He sounded so full of himself, so boastful. I thought of all those nights at the bar, when he hadn't been able to one-up his cronies. A rich man, a clever man, a man who had to walk down to the beach to get drunk alone, so he wouldn't spill his secrets.

"I don't understand," I said.

"I didn't kill anyone. Don't you see? Yeah, I got Albion to confess to another one. Big deal. What did he care? What did it matter, where he was going? For the Camerons, Dorothy's disappearance wasn't such hot stuff either, you know? The big deal for them was this: *Two* people disappeared the same day! Dorothy Cameron and the family gardener, some no-account bum named Alonso Nueves. I was paid for Albion's confession, sure, but mostly I was paid to make damn certain that nobody ever connected those two disappearances. That's the God's truth."

He started laughing again.

"Better their daughter should be dead, you know? Better a Cameron girl should get *murdered* than to run off with a fuckin' gardener."

"Put the gun away," I said. "Mac, face it, you're a cop, not a killer." I wasn't afraid of him. There's a tension in someone's face, in their arm, in their whole being, before they pull the trigger. MacAvoy wasn't even breathing hard.

The bright light on shore shocked both of us. A deep voice boomed, shouting against the roaring ocean waves. I couldn't understand a single word.

For a moment the ex-sergeant stood frozen. Then he drew the wrong conclusion.

"Goddamn you, you set me up!" he muttered, and all the murderous energy he'd been lacking poured through his body, an almost visible impulse from brain through spine to shoulder, racing down his arm toward his trigger finger.

I filled my lungs and dove to the side, kicking for the sandy bottom. I expected a shot, sudden pain, but none came. I kept moving my arms, kicking my legs until I had to breathe or burst.

When I surfaced, I tried not to gasp for air, to inhale quietly.

I was much farther out to sea than MacAvoy. He'd chosen to target the beacon on the beach, firing round after round. If I could swim nearer . . . My hand closed on the S&W 40 in my waist clip.

I couldn't swim with the gun in my hand. Its weight unbalanced my stroke. I tucked it back in my clip, slid underwater.

There was no light, no sound. No way to gauge my progress.

This time I surfaced badly, close to MacAvoy, but not close enough to grab him.

"Bitch!" MacAvoy yelled when he saw me.

He gazed at the light on the beach, at the moonlit sky. He didn't point his gun at me. Suddenly he turned, opened his mouth, stuck it in, deep, so that most of the barrel disappeared.

"No," I screamed. The noise was soft, a gentle pop.

I got the full back-lit effect. The sudden jerk of MacAvoy's head, the recoil that dropped his arm and gun into the sea. The back of his skull opening, leaking blood and coral. I could close my eyes, I thought, and still see it, over and over.

I made a retching noise, grabbed my gun, and aimed at the light. Anger flooded me. Whoever the hell was on shore—the Windbreaker Man, DEA, the police, a mob hit man—had scared MacAvoy into the long silence, and he'd never tell me more about the man who disappeared with Thea Janis.

"Stop," screamed a voice. "Don't shoot. I'm hit. I'm on your side."

On my side. Right. So why was I the one who pulled the ex-sergeant's bloody corpse out of the sea? Why was I the one holding a dead man and wishing I could remember the words, the all-important words of my father's religion? All I could mumble was "Our Father who art in Heaven, Hallowed be Thy name, Thy Kingdom come, Thy Will be done." I said it twice, three times, four. It wasn't absolution. I couldn't have granted absolution, but how I wished I could recall the Latin words.

44

Thank God for full moons. I finished dragging Mac-Avoy's remains onto the sand, fully appreciating the term "dead weight" as I rolled him out of the water. Slowly, I approached the beacon, a huge battery-powered flash, the type used to warn drivers away from major accidents. He was on the ground, moaning: Mr. Windbreaker, Mr. Denim Jacket, leaking blood from a leg wound.

I found that I had MacAvoy's SIG-Sauer in my hand. I didn't remember retrieving it. It felt slightly heavier than my 40. The stainless steel glittered.

What kind of harebrained idiot stands next to a light and yells at an armed man holding a prisoner in the ocean? A sniper lurks in the background, wears black, uses an infrared scope and a target piece. Silence and stealth are his weapons.

"Who the hell are you?" I demanded.

He clamped his lips, so I delved into his pants pocket, and extracted a battered wallet. Driver's license for one Ralph Farrell. MasterCard for same. I compared the driver's license photo with the drawn features of the man on the ground. Ralph Farrell, all right. A total stranger.

"Talk," I said, waving MacAvoy's piece.

"Get me to a hospital, Carlotta."

"As soon as I know how you know my name, and not a second before."

He said nothing. I walked away.

"Carlotta!"

"You could bleed to death," I said through gritted teeth. "Hell, I might shoot you myself."

"Keith Donovan," he said faintly.

"What?"

"I'm an investigator. Mainly bodyguard stuff. Keith Donovan hired me. He said you were in danger. A threatened mob hit, but he knew you weren't taking it seriously. I told him a blind tail wouldn't work, especially with a pro, but—"

"But he paid you," I said, blood roaring in my ears. Donovan.

"How long has this been going on?" I asked sharply.

"Lady, will you fuckin' take me to a hospital? And put the damn gun down."

"When did he hire you?"

"First of the month."

Before I'd even known that Thea Janis and Dorothy Cameron were one and the same. Before Paolina's father had disappeared.

"Who told Donovan about the hit?" I asked.

"I don't know. How the hell should I know? I'm bleeding here, lady. I saved your fuckin' life."

My hand shook. I could have killed Ralph Farrell, Donovan's goddamned unsolicited answer to my imagined cry for help.

For a brief moment, I wished I had. Considered it. Easier to explain to the cops. With two corpses, I could spin a fine tale: MacAvoy kills Farrell, kills himself. I'd never used my gun.

Fini.

We were at the end of the earth, on the ocean, in a quiet cove. Nobody'd heard the shots. I could have left MacAvoy, his gun beside him, walked away clean.

Farrell was groaning, making like MacAvoy'd hit a major artery, and he was watching his life's blood flow onto the sand. I knelt to get a better look. It was a clean, in and out wound through the fleshy part of the calf. I managed to rip the lining out of his sweat-stained windbreaker, fashion a pressure bandage.

"Can you drive?" I asked. "Where's your car?"

Nothing but a shiny upturned face. Not even a grunt.

I had to bundle Farrell into my car, get him to a hospital. He was loath to enter without me. Seemed to think he'd done something terrific. Ought to get a reward.

I said, "That old man wouldn't have killed me. I was never in any danger."

"Sure," Ralph Farrell muttered. "He just pulled his gun to show off."

I dumped him on the doorstep of the nearest medical center, told him to tell the cops any fantasy that appealed to him.

"Oh, I will," he said.

"Remember," I said. "This gun is registered to a dead man. If they let you go, trot back to your employer. Tell him I will be in touch. Tell him he did the wrong thing. Tell him I could have fucking killed you."

"You're angry."

"Tell him that, too."

I drove back to the beach. I was finding too many corpses. I wasn't linked to the one in Marblehead. Yet. Could I afford to get tied to this one?

Could I leave him here, the crooked old cop who'd taken his pension in real estate instead of respect?

Did I have a friend on the Marshfield squad?

Nope.

Did I have a friend on the Boston squad?

If my numbers really matched the tag on an old missing persons file, I might.

I dragged MacAvoy's body further up the beach, staggering under the weight of him, avoiding his ruined head with my eyes and my hands. I keep a coil of rope in the trunk of my car. I tied one end tightly around his legs, tied the other to a piling behind the old stone wall, relic of an ancient pier. Probably the same piling he'd used to tie off his six-packs.

I opened my shirt and ripped the tape off my bra, stared at the soaked mini-recorder. The spindles had stopped turning. I hoped it was the end of the side, not irreparable water damage.

I left the recorder on the seawall, crawled down the beach, curling into the salt water, inching deeper until it covered me, washing away the blood and stink. When I thought of all the answers MacAvoy could have given me, all the secrets lost in bright blood and tissue, floating out to sea, I could have cried. I'm not sure I didn't. I splashed my face. It was all salty water. An infinite wash of tears.

For whom?

For MacAvoy, making his final move so suddenly I couldn't stop him. A crooked cop.

For Thea lost long ago? For near-speechless sedated Beryl? For a mother with no daughters? For an unmourned, forgotten missing man, possibly the sole innocent, and the way they'd all come together twenty-four years ago and spoiled their lives forever.

After I'd retrieved the recorder and rubbed MacAvoy's SIG-Sauer with sand and hurled it into the ocean, I called Mooney from a gas station.

45

Home is where they have to take you in, no matter how battered, bruised, or broke. I don't have that kind of home. I have friends. I have Gloria. I have Mooney.

He met me at a rest stop on Route 3, dropped off by an unmarked unit. Found me barefoot and shivering at a picnic bench, elbows on the table, heels of my hands pressed into my brow. He coaxed me into my car, fiddled with the heater. He waved the officer in the unit off to Boston, then listened to everything I had to say— no interruptions. He waited a few minutes, as though he were chewing and digesting each word.

"It wasn't your fault," he said.

That's what I should have said to MacAvoy: *It wasn't your fault.* Universal absolution.

"What do you mean, it wasn't my fault?"

"You want to take credit, go ahead. But MacAvoy messed with the records, MacAvoy took Cameron money. What with you out there asking questions, he was probably thinking about the end of the road, keeping his piece in his pocket when he went beer drinking by the ocean. You sped up the action, that's all."

That's all. I swallowed a lump as big as a goose egg and tried not to see the ocean water change color around MacAvoy's misshapen head.

"You got something on tape," Mooney continued.

"I'm not sure," I said, reluctant to display my drowned recorder. "At first, MacAvoy was giving me nothing but crap, a fairy tale about how he got this enormous reward for making Thea's suicide look like murder."

"And that's not what this is about."

"Did you find the cross-reference, the file that wasn't supposed to figure in Thea's disappearance?"

"MacAvoy never threw out a sheet of paper in his life."

"You found it." I almost stopped shivering.

"The Cold Case squad had it. Sooner or later, maybe in a hundred years, someone might have linked it to Thea."

"Why didn't MacAvoy destroy it?" I asked. "Or take it home, put it in a safety deposit box, so he'd have a stronger hold over the Camerons?"

"He couldn't destroy it, Carlotta, because it's cross-referenced twice, the second time to the FBI. I've got a call in to Gary Reedy."

I rubbed my head. It felt heavy, logy, like I was waking up the morning after a high-octane bash.

"We ought to be heading back," Mooney said. "Want me to drive?"

"No. I can handle it," I said automatically. I flicked on the headlights, put the Toyota in gear. Route 3 was practically empty. A few dark trucks hustled along in the middle lane.

"Have they heard from Marissa?" I asked. "Is she still missing?"

"Daily newspaper readings. On tape. She's okay so far. They're renegotiating, a new price, a different rendezvous."

"Reedy seems to be handing you more information."

"When he feels like it. Back to tonight. You said this guy, Nueves, the gardener, disappeared the same day as Thea Janis."

"That's what MacAvoy said. The exact day. MacAvoy was paid off to make sure the two disappearances were never linked."

"You figure they ran off together? This Alonso Nueves and Thea Janis? That it would have been some kind of political bomb?"

I said, "I don't figure it at all, Mooney. Six hundred thou is too much to pay just to name suicide murder. It's way too big a payoff to keep newspapers from speculating that your underage daughter ran off with a guy who's not listed in the Social Register."

"Doesn't make sense," Mooney agreed.

"Dammit, Mooney, I blew this. I should have given MacAvoy to Internal Affairs. If he'd had the chance to come clean, he might not have killed himself . . ."

"Carlotta, if you can't drive straight, pull the damn car over. You win some, you lose some. If it went down like you said, you're not doing jail on this. You even have a witness."

"Some witness."

"Get over it," Mooney said through clenched teeth.

A shiver ran down my spine. "I've got blood on me, I've still got his goddamned blood on me. I—"

I coasted into the breakdown lane, and we sat. He looked at me once. His hand moved, like he wanted to hold me, comfort me, but I was stiff and miserable, chilled with salt water and failure.

I let him drive me home. That's how bad I felt.

"Mooney," I said as I opened the door. "You know how MacAvoy seized control of the case, years ago."

"Yeah."

"Can you do that? Since it's so spread out, over time and space. Dover, and Marblehead, and Marshfield. Weston."

"State police will have something to say about it."

"But they know you. And with the FBI connection, they may want nothing to do with it."

"I may want nothing to do with it."

"Mooney."

He shrugged. "They might give me some time with it, hoping I'll fall on my butt."

"You won't."

"Why's that?"

I was starting to feel less like a killer. More like a cop.

I said, "You know Marblehead's searching for a young guy in the Manley death, the one they're calling a tramp—"

"Seen hanging around the Marblehead shack. Yeah. What about him?"

"How are you at lying to the media?"

"I love it."

"Tell them there's been a break in the case. Tell them you've got the guy in custody."

"Just for the sake of lying?" he asked.

"Why not?" I said.

He yanked out a cellular phone, dialed a number, spoke briefly.

"That ought to make the morning editions," he said.

We sat on the front porch waiting for a unit to come and fetch him. As we spoke I noticed a light in Donovan's house.

I took a brief inventory. Had I left a nightgown, underwear, anything I cared about at his house? Would I go there again?

How had he learned about the supposed mob hit? Had Mooney betrayed me? Set Donovan up? Mooney would know I could never go back to a man who didn't respect my ability to protect myself, to live my own life, make my own choices.

I swallowed and stared at Mooney. I couldn't ask him. I needed him too much.

"Mooney," I said. "Do you think you can wangle an exhumation order?"

"I doubt it," he said. "Why?"

"Something MacAvoy said, about the Camerons not being too choosy with the body. And a girl named Heather Foley, who drowned right before the Camerons' Mount Auburn Cemetery funeral extravaganza. At first, Heather's family maintained the body was hers. The ME went against them. Heather's body has never been recovered."

"Some never are."

I could tell he was interested. Mooney doesn't believe in coincidence any more than I do.

"Who's buried in Thea's grave, Moon?" I asked.

46

I woke well past three the next afternoon, feeling sandy, waterlogged, and uneasy. My sheets were twisted and tossed on the floor, like I'd fought with them during the night. I had trouble deciding on a pair of shorts, a simple shirt. My hands moved awkwardly, as though they'd swollen from the heat. I fumbled, matching holes and buttons incorrectly, cursing repeatedly. Finally I tossed the clothes in a heap, yanked on an extra-long T-shirt, and headed downstairs.

Sunday. Sunday afternoon. A mere week ago "Adam Mayhew" had called, begging for an appointment. Now he was dead. MacAvoy was dead. I swallowed phlegm, ran for the bathroom, brushed my teeth twice, then scoured my hands so thoroughly I might have been mistaken for an obsessive-compulsive and hauled off to Weston Psych.

Newspapers were stacked on my desk. My message machine blinked red. I navigated the straits, made it to the kitchen, swigged orange juice from the carton.

Roz must have done groceries. I ate half an English muffin smothered in peanut butter. It felt fine going down, but landed in my stomach lumpy and indigestible.

I studied myself in the hall mirror, climbed the stairs, and tried dressing again, consciously choosing an image. Not the navy power suit. Easy slacks, shapeless top. Vest. Yes. If I tucked in the shirt, the vest added a touch of professionalism. I shook out my hair, looped it through a stretchy band. Nothing fancy, just sufficient to keep its weight off my neck, its curls under control. I hadn't selected my role yet, but I had determined my destination.

Swampscott.

My target was one Edith Foley, called "Edie" by the public relations cop Roz had snookered into divulging her address. Edie Foley, Heather's mom. I studied Roz's notes: Divorced. Ardent churchgoer. Catholic mother of eight, once upon a time. If I asked her how many kids she had, what number would she recite? Do you stop being a mother if your child dies?

I shuffled business cards. Reporter, real estate agent, Avon lady, product survey specialist. I wound up tucking eight possible identities into my wallet. Improvisation is often the key.

My car was starting to feel like home. Behind the steering wheel, I relaxed a bit, regaining confidence. *I can handle Boston traffic. I can always drive a hack.* I wasn't keen on listening to the news. I shoved tape after tape into the boom box. Every song sounded mournful, a tale of death and sorrow, death and sorrow, over and over again.

Swampscott is south of Marblehead, too close to crowded Lynn for the wealthy. Oh, I suppose there's some snazzy oceanfront property, some developer's dream acre, but the Foleys lived near the Lynn line—the most crowded section of town—in a clapboard house that gave ramshackle a good name. The streets—Eastern, Maple, Cherry—had generic names, and the town had the look of all sunbleached August New England towns. Nothing to lift it out of the summer doldrums. No ocean view. No breeze.

I spent twenty minutes observing the house. Patches on the roof. Negligible weedy lawn. Overgrown bushes. Two window screens missing, one slashed. No screen at all on the front door, which opened and banged shut with amazing frequency. Lots of people living there, or stopping by. Maybe all those kids had grandkids now, pressed Edie into nonstop child care service.

I hadn't seen the splendor of the Camerons' Marblehead house up close, but I'd practically taken the deluxe tour of their Dover palace. I could no more imagine Tessa Cameron setting foot in this not-quite-slum than I could imagine the Queen of England naked.

So many people coming and going, maybe Edith Foley wouldn't care who I was. Maybe she ran a licensed day-care, in which case I could be practically anybody from the state righteously poking my nose into her business.

I could be one of her neighbors with a complaint about the noise. Hell, poor woman probably got complaints all day.

I decided to drive for a while, search for steeples. I

noted two, one Episcopalian, one Catholic: Saint Aidans.

I remembered passing a bakery, homed on the smell. Bought a ring of something gooey, studded with summer fruit. Paid for it with Andrew Manley's money. This time I parked around the block, so she wouldn't see my car.

New neighbor makes friends, part one.

The doormat said, "Howdy, stranger!" I didn't think they sold those east of the Mississippi. Native New Englanders aren't known for their outgoing ways, their friendliness.

I knocked, carefully balancing my string-tied white bakery box.

"Hi, hon, yer a tall one, what yer got there?" Her hair, what was left of it, was white and poked from her scalp at odd angles, like coconut sprinkled from a can. My Edie, according to research, had to be the same age as Tessa Cameron, but this was an old woman, her skin leathery and tough.

"Do you live here? Are you Edith Foley?"

"Sure am." She focused on the box hungrily. "Did I win a raffle?"

See what I mean about improv skills?

She wore a silver cross around the neck of a much-laundered flowered housedress that buttoned down the front, stretching over ample hips.

"At Saint Aidans," I said helpfully, hoping she worshiped nearby.

"I don't b'lieve I entered that raffle," she said.

Oops.

"Somebody must have entered for you," I said cheerfully, not missing a beat. "One of your kids, maybe an unknown admirer."

"Joseph," she said immediately. "My oldest boy has such a sweet tooth. He'll be around anytime, beggin' for a slice. Now, come on in, hon. You'll git sunstruck standin' out there."

If I decide to turn bad, watch out. It's so easy to gain entry. Why so many crooks get caught baffles me. Or it used to before I became a cop, started meeting actual perps. Imagine all the kids in your high school who couldn't make it past tenth grade, who thought flipping burgers offered a brighter future than frog dissection. Marry them off young, to each other, give them lots of kids they can't afford to raise. There's your basic prison population, with a few add-ons for drug dealing and out-and-out racism.

Edie said, "You marched this down from Saint A's in this heat, hon? Aren't you a sweetie? Take a load off. Don't mind the cats."

The opening and closing door hadn't signaled the entrances and exits of persons, but of felines. At least seven stretched their necks and regarded me with unblinking eyes. From the stench, seven did not account for half the cats who roomed with Mrs. Edith Foley.

"Live far?" Mrs. Foley said, breezing in with a tray bearing two spotty glasses of something yellowy, and the fruit ring, still in its pristine box. "Have some lemonade?"

"Thanks," I said, trying not to sneeze. Everything in the living room was floral, ruffled, bowed, and worn, covered with cat hair and dust. Flowered chintz furniture next to flowered mismatched drapes. Jumbles of oversized busy-patterned pillows. Lacy antimacassars. A riot of defiant femininity gone wrong.

Every surface was littered with cat statues, chew

toys, family photos in Plexiglas frames, grocery store magazines, stacks of mail.

"Live near here?"

I realized that Mrs. Foley was asking for the second time. Stunned by the decor, I'd failed to answer.

"Over on Cherry," I said quickly, tuning my voice to her down-home accent. "Just moved in. Renting a room till I get back on my feet. The folks at church have been real nice to me."

She sat, eyes wide with curiosity. I helped her clear a place for the tray, which wasn't easy, but it let me ask questions about the photos as I moved them.

"You in this one?"

"No, child, that's my boy Harry, second oldest, and his wife. They got two little boys now."

"Isn't that swell?" I said miserably, starting to work out a back-story about my troubles, one that might lead to a sharing of confidences. If she was going to get me to talk, she was going to have to trade tales of woe.

It was easy to pretend to hold back tears because I was actually swallowing the sneezes provoked by the dust and the cats.

"Oh my dear," she said. "Have you, um, suffered a loss?"

"It's silly," I said. "I really shouldn't—"

"Now, hon, the best thing in the world is a good cry and a talk with a stranger. I know what I say, believe me."

"It's just that picture, those cute kids. I've had my share of trouble. First, my husband up and left me—" This was true enough. That Cal had departed some years back with my blessing Edie didn't need to know. "But I worked regular and I tried to keep my life straight till my daughter, my little girl, died—"

Every time I say something like that, I'm tempted to spit over my left shoulder, pound a piece of solid wood to avoid the evil eye. If anything happened to Paolina—

The part about the dead child seemed to skip by without leaving a ripple in the water. Edie fastened on the husband who'd departed. People hear what they want to hear, that's for sure.

"Hon, I know just how that is," she said sympathetically. "My man walked out of this house over twenty years ago, left me with seven boys to raise up on my own."

"Seven," I echoed. "My goodness, you just can't tell anything about folks by lookin' at them, can you?"

One thing I learned as a cop is that people tend to confide most readily in people who sound like them or look like them. It was obvious that Edie hadn't been born in Swampscott, or anywhere in New England, not the way she talked, not with the "Howdy, stranger" welcome mat. I couldn't place her accent, except that it was more West than Midwest. I don't do the Professor Higgins bit, but I could parrot her own words back to her, broaden my A's, drop my G's, sound like I'd grown up in her neck of the woods.

It's a music thing. You've got to have the ear.

She sipped lemonade, opened the box, oohed and ahhed over the pastry. Went down the hall in search of a knife and plates. I shooed a cat off the tray while eagerly looking for a picture of a girl, a young woman, an old picture. Most showed Mom and the boys.

Aha! A small table to the left of a dinky fireplace had the look of a shrine. Covered with a paisley shawl. Candlesticks. Statues of various saints. There. A five-by-seven that practically shouted high school yearbook shot.

Heather had done her hair up for the occasion. She'd worn a white Peter Pan collar, a choker of fake pearls. Her smile was her best feature, open, honest, a little bit reckless. Young.

I heard Mrs. Foley shuffling down the hall, but I didn't return to my seat. One of the cats had already usurped my chair, and I wanted Edie's reaction when she saw me studying her daughter's photo.

"We've got something else in common," she said, a catch in her voice. "I used to have a girl too. I always think my life changed the minute Heather died. Good luck to bad in the wink of an eye."

"That's just how I felt when my Wendy died," I said. I wasn't going to use Paolina's name.

"Oh, hon," she said consolingly. "You're still plenty young. You can have more kids if you want, if you can take it. My family was almost grown when Heather died, but I truly think her dad, Harold, wouldn't have lit out like he did if she hadn't passed. I never saw anything hit a man so hard. Took care of all the arrangements, and then raced out of here like he had a fire in his belly he couldn't put out."

"Your girl was older than mine," I said. "Pretty too."

"Age makes no difference," she said. "You love them to pieces, that's all."

"Your girl died, just like mine, and then your husband walked out, and look at you. You survived. I'll bet that's why the folks at Saint A's thought I oughta deliver the cake. Do me some good, make me stop feeling sorry for myself, feeling like I'm the only one gotta cross to bear."

She didn't see the cats wiggling their tails across the

fruit goo. I wasn't planning to eat. I mean, my cat's okay. He's a loner and so am I.

I wished I'd sent Roz to do the interview. But Roz, with her hair, with her earrings and rings and fingernails . . . I don't think she'd have hit it off with Edie.

"You have any other kids?" Edie asked me.

"Wish I did. Just the one girl. My poor Wendy," I said, automatically thinking of Paolina, and hoping we could turn the conversation back to Heather before Edith Foley came to her senses. So far the woman hadn't even asked my name.

Such is the power of a white bakery box.

"A girl is such a gift," Edie said. "My boys, God, I love 'em so, but they never really understand, you know? It's like they'd help out if they could, but they haven't got a clue. I've got granddaughters now, two of 'em named for my Heather."

"She was real cute. She get sick?"

"Oh no, hon. It was one of them accidents. Boatin' accidents. There's gonna be an article about it in the *Tab*, you watch for it."

She was still in touch with the police department.

"Won't that make you feel bad?" I asked. "Somebody raking up the past like that?"

"No, hon. You of all people should know that's one thing people never get straight. I talked to the priest about it, got me so riled. The minute you lose a child, people, even friends, figure it's like you never had her, never watched her grow up, never miss her. I know it's just they don't know what to say, but it's hard to credit. They don't mention her in your hearing anymore. Makes you nuts. You feel like you dreamed the whole thing, like maybe you never had a girl. That's why I keep Heather's picture right there. So everybody knows I don't forget."

"Does it still hurt as much?" I asked. "I know that's real personal, but I guess I'm trying to figure if I'll still miss my Wendy so much after years have past."

"Oh, hon, forgive me. When did she die?"

"It's been two years and six months. Leukemia, they said, the very worst kind. I put all her stuff in a box and I still haven't opened it."

"You will," Edith said imperturbably.

"And, you know, you're right. Nobody ever talks about her with me. Makes me lonely."

"You can talk about her with me," Edie said.

"You said you lost your girl twenty years ago?" I switched topics quickly. I didn't think I could conjure a realistic version of made-up Wendy's final days, not in front of Heather's mom.

"More than twenty, and then my husband left three weeks later, right after we thought they'd pulled her body out of the sea. I thought I'd about die myself. And then I was relieved, you know. I could bury her, and know where she was, know she's in the graveyard behind the church, bring her flowers in the springtime."

"That's a comfort," I agreed. "I bring Wendy lilies-of-the-valley."

"But it wasn't her," Edie continued. "My husband said the body was so swole up, he couldn't rightly tell, and some other folks had the dental records or something like that to prove it was their baby and not mine. Heather never ever came back to me, but I still go to the churchyard. We put a memorial stone, and I pretend she's there. Doesn't do no harm."

I nodded solemnly.

"It's hard to believe your husband just left like that. He write you a note or anything?"

"Did yours?" she asked.

"Well," I confided, "I guess he didn't need to. He was messing around with my best friend, and I found out and all."

"No kidding?"

"He wanted me to take him back," I lied, "but I got my pride."

"Good for you, gal."

I recited something I've never believed, mentally attributing it to one of the faceless, nameless churchwomen at Saint A's.

"Well, you know what they say, when God closes a door he opens a window."

She gazed at me with none of the scorn I felt my remark should have earned, but with a questioning look, as if she was trying to remember which window the Lord had opened for her.

"You know, I just about told a lie back when I said all my luck went with my husband and my girl."

"Really."

"I mean, he left town, and she drowned, that's plenty of bad luck right there, a whole lifetime's worth, but the good luck was with my boys. Two of 'em were in pretty big trouble then, gonna do jail time, it seemed. And that just melted away. Charges got dropped."

"Your husband leave you any money for child support?"

Surely she'd kick me out, refuse to answer such a personal inquiry from a total stranger.

"Yeah," she said thoughtfully, "he was real decent about that too, didn't clean out our accounts like I'd expected, so I guess I shouldn't complain. Have some of this cake. It looks so good."

She shoveled a huge slice onto a too-small plate. It quivered and threatened to slip over the side. I nibbled a mouthful of air. I wanted to shout questions at her. Had a cop named MacAvoy spoken to her husband before he'd left town? Had strange men in fancy suits come by? But I'd gone and lied my way into a sticky situation and I was just going to have to sit out the visit, listening and complaining in an alien voice.

I glared at a cat as it tried to take a swipe of cream cake.

I'd extricate myself somehow, plead church work, an incipient headache. Faint, if I had to. Stop by the police station on my way home. Check the Foley boys to see if they had current records or sealed juvie files. Ask if anybody remembered the exact charges they'd faced twenty-four years ago, and why the threat of jail had suddenly evaporated into thin air.

I wondered where Mr. Harold Foley, Heather's father—who'd misidentified his daughter's body—had gone, whether he might be a very rich man, like MacAvoy used to be.

Or perhaps a very dead man, like MacAvoy was now.

47

The Swampscott force was not as gullible, not as trusting as Edith Foley. I should have brought them cookies, doughnuts. The gossipy public relations cop was not on duty and the small force didn't have time to spare on ancient dropped charges, even if they did involve the numerous and often troublesome Foley clan. Charges were made and dropped all the time. Hadn't I read Miranda?

Well, yes, I had, but I'd wanted something a little more concrete, names and places, and dates. Dates, foremost.

It was dark by the time I quit waiting for a friendly cop with time to spare and ventured home. I hesitated, holding my keys, decided to try the back door. I wanted to see whether it had been fixed. I'd given Roz instructions and cash. If the two-by-fours were still holding the door in place, I'd take great pleasure in kicking the whole shebang down.

Maybe if I vented my anger in door-kicking, I wouldn't charge into Donovan's house, tell him precisely what I thought of his stupid overly protective gesture, hiring a gumshoe to guard same. I could almost hear his rationalization: You'd never have let me if I'd told you. Right. But that didn't make secrecy the answer. A secret bodyguard was worse than no bodyguard. A secret bodyguard could get killed. Mistaken for a mythical mob hit man.

Instead of kicking the door I almost tripped over the tiny girl as she ran from under my back porch. She'd been hiding near the garbage bins. She smelled like she might have dined from one.

"Pix?"

"Yeah. I need to talk to you."

"Talk."

"There's somebody at the shack needs you."

"The shack burned down," I said.

"Near the shack, on the beach."

"Alonso?"

"Can you come?"

"Is it guarded?"

"Not now. *Can you come?*"

"Yeah."

"Now? It has to be right now."

"Get in the car and crank down the window."

"Food?" she asked.

"We'll stop on the way."

The door had been repaired. Pleasantly surprised, I rang the bell three times, then another three till Roz opened up.

"What?" she said indignantly. "You forgot your damned key?"

"I'm in a hurry. Messages."

"Thanks for getting the door fixed, Roz. And Paolina called."

"Whoa. She's not allowed to use the phone at camp."

"She said a counselor drove her into town to pick something up. I don't know."

"What did she want?"

"I guess she's not having that great a time. Wanted to know if you could come out and get her."

"Tonight?"

"Yeah."

No telling when Pix might decide to take it on the lam again.

I said, "Can't tonight. If she calls again, tell her I'll make it soon. Isn't Friday the last day? See if she can hold out five more days."

"Will do."

"And, Roz?"

"Yeah?"

"Get my thirty-eight out of the closet."

"Is it loaded?"

"I hope so. It's more useful that way."

Roz, for all her skills, doesn't like guns and doesn't drive. I could have asked her to track down one of her boyfriends who did, drive up to New Hampshire in the middle of the night, but the way Roz looks, let alone the way most of her guys look, would any camp counselor release a girl of Paolina's tender years into her care?

Tender years.

The years hadn't been tender to Pix. Nor had the brief time since I'd seen her. She'd acquired a nasty bruise on one cheek, a split lip. She wasn't talking about how they'd happened. At a Route 1 McDonald's, she squeezed two Big Macs and a large order of fries into her tiny frame, slurped a chocolate shake so gelatinous the straw made sucking sounds like a swamp.

I drove, listening to tapes I'd jammed into the boom box. Trying to soothe myself with timeless blues.

"Got a mortgage on my body, lease taken on my soul," sang Robert Johnson, dead at twenty-eight.

I couldn't get my mind off Woodrow MacAvoy. What would they write on his tombstone? What verse of Scripture had Edith Foley chosen for her daughter's memorial?

"Leave your car here," Pix said, as we passed a small realty office with an unlit parking nook. I remembered passing it before. It was about half a mile from Marblehead Neck, off Ocean Avenue.

"Why?"

"It's safer."

"Alonso can stop running. I know a cop who'll make sure he's treated well."

"I can't bring anybody but you."

"I promise."

"You can't bring a car."

"Pix, are you trying to set me up?"

"You fed me," she said. "I don't set up anybody gives me money, drugs, or hamburgers."

I believed her.

We walked the causeway side by side. Her legs had to work hard to keep up with my stride.

"Is any of the shack still standing?"

"Not much. Use the steps from the lane. Did you bring a flashlight?"

"Yeah."

"You left your gun in your car?"

I'd left the forty locked in the glove compartment.

"Am I going to need one?" I asked.

"No. I promise."

She didn't seem to expect my promise in return. I withheld it. The .38, my old Chief's Special, felt fine in its waist clip.

The ground around the burned shack was churned with footprints, gouged with the spray from heavy hoses. I had to watch my footing on the uneven approach. Smoke no longer rose from the scattered boards, but the smell of fire was strong, acrid. A throat-closing stench. Yellow "Do Not Cross" tape marked the shack as a crime scene.

I heard a noise, the faint, throat-clearing announcement of another human presence. I spun to face it.

The woman seated on a nearby rock wore a wide-brimmed hat. For a moment I had the foolish urge to ask Pix if this was the "real woman" with whom Alonso was currently sleeping.

Too old, I thought dismissively.

I studied her more closely. Dear God, it seemed like I'd known her all my life. I'd seen two versions of her face, aged and thin, aged and fat.

It was her eyes I recognized. Only her eyes.

"Pix," I said.

"I didn't lie."

"What about Alonso?"

"She wants to help. I believe her. I told her about you. Did I do right?"

"Yeah, Pix. Go over and sit on the steps now. Okay? Warn us if you see anybody coming."

"You think Alonso will be back?"

When I didn't answer, she walked away.

48

She sat like a woman carved from rock. A hundred questions burned my throat, but I kept silent, ceding her the opening, letting her begin, so I'd get some idea where her thoughts were headed. Part of me was afraid she might fade into mist. I fought off the impulse to touch her, to feel solid flesh.

Slowly, she removed her hat. Her hair was gray, steel to Beryl's yellowed white. No one would have confused the two sisters now, one bloated with medication, the other . . . merely average. Unremarkable.

All that was unique and beautiful in Thea, she'd made deliberately plain. Either that, or she'd changed so completely that her reckless beauty had evaporated. Her hair, vaguely curly, was an unstyled clump too heavy for her thin neck and sharp features. Tortoiseshell glasses hid the angle of her brow. She held her head low. Her chin seemed less pointed, less remarkably small. If she'd had plastic surgery she couldn't have looked more different, and yet her features were the same. Under a short-sleeved khaki jacket, her breasts swelled, camouflaged but large for her small-boned body. All fire and color drained from her, Dorothy Cameron seemed plain as salt.

"Hello," she said, glancing around as if she'd expected a larger audience. "You must be the detective. Carlyle."

Her calm words floated on the mist and I shivered. It was the dampness of my clothes, I told myself, not the flicker of dread, not the sensation of hearing the voice of someone returned from a watery grave.

"You know who I am . . . who I was." There was no lift at the end of the sentence. No question.

"Yes," I said, when it seemed nothing else would follow unless I replied.

"I understand the police are holding my son."

Mooney must have gotten the word out quickly.

"Alonso," I said.

"Yes. I'm willing to deal: My freedom for his."

I said, "The police want him for murder. I doubt they'll find your offer attractive. Running away isn't in the same league."

"Oh, they'll want me," she said.

"What makes you so sure?"

"Because *I* killed Andrew Manley." She nodded at the police tape. "Here. Friday night."

"How long after he phoned me?" I asked.

"Don't try to trip me up. I can answer all your niggling questions," she said scornfully.

"Give it a try. Before we go to the police. Listen, Thea—"

She closed her eyes. "Call me Susan. Susan Gordon. I've been Susan Gordon most of my life."

"Why did you kill Andrew Manley, Susan Gordon?"

"Because he never listened to me. He never believed in me. He didn't trust my talent, because of Beryl. He assumed I was unstable, because of her. He should have seen through all that, though all the—" She came to an abrupt halt.

"Why kill him *now?*"

She sucked in a deep breath, regained control. "Because revenge is a dish best eaten cold," she said.

"You've come back for revenge," I echoed.

"And to make sure nothing happens to my son."

"You ran away from Avon Hill because you were pregnant?"

"Oh no." She shook her head, smiled crookedly. "What a foolish girl you must think I was."

"I don't think you were foolish."

"Then grant me good reason for what I've done," she said with the first hint of anger I'd heard in her voice. "I disappeared. I did it well. Because I had no other choice."

I swallowed. I found her simple presence astonishing. Carved from rock. Edges worn away by the sea.

"You named your son for a gardener who disappeared," I said, "disappeared the same day you did."

"It's not unusual to name a boy for his father." I thought she smiled but it might have been a trick of the light. "Since I'd killed the man, it seemed the least I could do."

If she'd killed the gardener, that would have been

worth the payoffs, worth turning MacAvoy, worth using Heather Foley's timely disaster.

Waves broke on the rocky shore, retreated into mist. She murmured, " 'Silenced for what they did to you, worse, far worse than caged for acts of rage.' " She shook her head, alarmed, as though she'd just realized she'd spoken out loud. "Excuse me. Susan has no poetry. Susan speaks plainly."

Does Susan speak the truth?

"Do you have a key to the house?" I asked.

"No."

"Do you know a way in?"

"Why?"

I didn't want her sitting on a rock by the sea. I'd already lost one life to the Atlantic.

"I didn't mean to kill him," she said. "I paid for his death with my gift. I paid."

I wasn't sure if she was talking about Manley or about Alonso Nueves, gardener. Alonso, the Cuban day-jobber at Avon Hill, the romantic dreamboy of the Weston Psychiatric Institute. The man in Beryl's cherished photo. Her lover, too, perhaps.

What would a man of Franklin Cameron's stature have thought? Have done? His precious daughters and the gardener?

"Let's talk about it in the big house," I said gently. "Aren't you cold?"

"Cold? No." She folded her arms, rubbing them with her hands, her motion negating her denial. "I won't go into that house."

"Why?"

"Why should I? Don't you trust me?" The shadowy smile again.

"With what?"

"With my life, with my life, with my life."

I was starting to get angry with her verbal tricks. I said, "You're playing for Alonso's life, aren't you? Your son's life."

"Can you arrest me?"

"I can make a citizen's arrest, take you to the nearest station house. I can advise you to see a lawyer. I hope you have your details straight about Manley's death. I hope you have an eyewitness."

"Why?"

"Because your boy was seen on this stretch of beach. His motorbike was in the shed."

"Circumstantial," she said dismissively.

"But convincing," I said. "And I hope you have proof about Alonso Nueves, too. Because I know the cop who's handling this, and he's going to want more than your sacred word of honor that friend Alonso didn't take a hike that day."

She was staring at the big house, her mouth moving. No words came out.

"What?" I asked.

"Have they kept it shut? Have they installed an alarm?"

"It's been closed since you left. I don't know about alarms, but I could give the place a once-over."

"If we can get in, I can show you proof," she said.

"But you don't have a key."

"There used to be a way, through a window with a loose jamb. As kids we crawled through, into a sink, so we never got hurt."

"Show me," I said. "Pix?"

No answer.

I'd told her to stay put.

But she was gone. She couldn't help by fetching tools, getting a crowbar from my trunk.

First I checked the house for signs of a system. Almost everybody's got one these days, those little glowing keypads by the side of the door, the red and green lights. The Camerons, bless them, had the kind I know best.

"Unless we're unlucky and this is the particular window they've wired, we ought to be able to do it." I kept my voice optimistic. If I'd deserted a beautiful home on the seaside, I'd have driven heavy nails through the ground-floor window jambs.

The rich are different. Once Thea had pointed out the window, one of fourteen identical slits, it went like clockwork. She helped me remove the screen. Her nails were clipped short, unvarnished. No nonsense, like her clothes. She moved like a woman in a dream. I rarely took my eyes off her.

"The lock's broken. The top half of the window should slide right down," she said. "We may have to tap it or something."

Oil would have been nice. A hammer, a screwdriver.

Even as I thought about the items we lacked, the sill groaned and gave, sinking twelve inches.

"You first," I ordered Thea. "Clear space for me, but don't move around. If you see a glowing red light on the wall, don't, I repeat, *don't* walk in front of it."

Her face grew even paler. "Don't leave me in there alone," she said.

"The sooner you go, the sooner I follow."

She slipped off her sandals like a veteran housebreaker. She went in backward, feet first.

Don't think I had no qualms about following. For the first time, I envied cell phone owners. I could have called Mooney, gotten his scalding advice. I didn't want to crawl into an unlit basement with a confessed murderess.

But, dammit, I did want to find out what Thea'd hidden there so long ago.

Head first? Feet first? I followed Thea's example.

Sometimes the riskiest moves turn, in a tick of the clock, into the most ridiculous. Inside, I flicked on my flashlight to discover Thea and me cowering in a huge old double sink, one woman to each compartment. We exchanged glances, mine wry. This didn't look like the boogeyman's hideout to me. But Thea's eyes hid no smile. They stared blankly across the room. I held up my flash. When she saw the huge white freezer chest, she gasped.

"You'll see," she said, starting to unfold herself.

"Wait," I said.

"Why? You got me in here. I want to get out as fast as I can."

"Unless you know the four-digit code, we have to crawl under the motion detector. See the red light on the left wall? It's between here and the freezer. If that's where you want to go, crawl."

"What if we—"

"Set off the alarm? You get your choice—identifying yourself as a member of the family, or running like hell."

"Great," she muttered.

"I don't think we'll have to," I said soothingly, lifting myself out of the—thank God—empty sink. "I've seen this system before. To set it ringing, you pretty much have to walk straight through a beam, and the beams aren't wide. You ought to tell the family to upgrade."

The floorboards were wooden. Heavy planks, six-by-tens, worn smooth, dusty as hell.

"Keep your tail down," I hissed as we slipped under the beam, Thea doing the baby crawl, me going army-style, hands and elbows, dragging my legs.

"Okay," I said. "Up."

Thea said, "Is it locked? The freezer?"

"If it is, I hope you have the key."

"Try the door," she said impatiently, looking away.

"What's inside?"

"Whatever remains of a man after twenty-four years in a freezer," she said firmly. Then she swallowed.

I assumed the door would be locked, so I gave it a halfhearted tug. It opened. Nothing tumbled out. I shone my flashlight on wrapped packages tagged "spareribs." Ice cream cartons. Frozen lemonade in yellow cans.

"Well?" she said.

"You can look," I said. "I don't think you'll find it too upsetting."

I was wrong.

"Oh, my God," she said. "Where could he be? They could have buried him anywhere on the estate, towed him out to sea."

"I don't think so, Thea."

"Susan," she said automatically, still stricken by the contents of the freezer.

"Susan."

"They'll never believe me now."

"Who's they?"

"The police."

"The other 'they.' The ones who moved the body."

"None of your business," she said.

49

I tried to find Pix on the way back to my car. Couldn't.

I urged Thea/Susan to confide in me all the way to South Boston. *Nada.*

I ushered her in the front door of the D Street station house. No camouflage beyond her hat. No cameras. Who would link her to a woman dead twenty-four years? Under the harsh fluorescents, I could see the lines age had dealt her. She held herself beautifully erect, walked with a measured tread dominated by a statue-like passivity. To me, she seemed like a figure in a Greek tragedy—all parts played, all oracles read, all actions come full circle. Clytemnestra, having dealt the inevitable blow, waiting, waiting, waiting for Orestes.

No choice, no choice, everything about her seemed

to echo. No choice. I followed my path. I did it well. It led me here. Inevitably here.

I willed her to run, rail, curse, do anything but walk like a sheep toward slaughter.

Thea Janis, child prodigy, returned runaway, marched into the interrogation room, sized Mooney up with a single cool glance before sinking into a chair. She tapped her foot while I brought him up to date.

"Do you wish to confer with an attorney?" he asked immediately.

"Where's my son?" she said.

"Do you want an attorney? You can call your own lawyer, or we can provide you with one."

"No."

"Are you aware that anything you say may be used against you in a court of law?"

"I expect it to be."

"You waive your right to an attorney."

"I waive all rights. I've killed two men. I wish to clear my conscience and my soul."

"Conscience" and "soul" made Mooney uncomfortable. I could tell by looking at him.

"Can a matron search her?" I asked quietly.

"Why?"

"Look, Mooney, I don't want anything else to happen tonight. She could have a knife, pills, a gun."

"You didn't search her on the way in?"

"I wanted it strictly legal."

"Okay."

As we waited for a female officer, Mooney rummaged through a pile of papers. I glanced at them. MacAvoy's spidery handwriting was familiar from Thea's file. Page after page in MacAvoy's hand fluttered past. Had he left a secret legacy?

Thea seemed eager to begin. "Do you use a stenographer or a tape recorder?"

"You should confer with an attorney," Mooney said.

"I don't agree. I killed Alonso Nueves on April 8, 1971. That's the day Thea died. I remember it well."

Mooney flicked the tape recorder on, gave his name and mine, the date and time. For the record, he repeated his question concerning an attorney. Thea affirmed her decision to speak without counsel.

She glanced at the tape recorder with affection before beginning, a storyteller at heart.

"My name is Dorothy Cameron. I once wrote a book under the name Thea Janis. Thea, Dorothea, was my own name, but Janis I chose deliberately, because of the two-faced life I already led. My name proved prophetic. I have lived for the past twenty-four years as 'Susan Gordon.' I believe I made up the name although I may have known a Suzanne Gordon when I was a child. I don't recall."

"Would you like something to eat or drink?" Mooney asked.

"No. On April 8, 1971, I had an argument with Alonso. He was a traditional man, an older man. He thought he owned me. He didn't know I was seeing others, sleeping with others. He thought because I was young, I was inexperienced. I was anything but inexperienced.

"I told him I was pregnant, and that I planned to abort the fetus because I was uncertain of the father's identity. At first he didn't believe me. I showed him the suitcase I'd packed. My doctor's appointment card. Told him about the trick I'd played on my family to get time, at least one night away from home to recover. He went berserk. He hit me. Ironic, really: He hit me so hard he could have caused the very thing he most wished to prevent, but, well, I find people to be unpredictable except for the ones I write about, the characters who exist in my head. He hit me and I hit him back, which surprised him. I think it shocked both of us. We were in the greenhouse behind the Dover estate. I'd met him first at Avon Hill. I helped him get a job at the Weston Institute when he had trouble at the school. It was my fault, you see. He was fooling around with an underaged student. That was me. I had certain contacts. I used them, and I kept seeing him and several other boys and men as well. Teachers. Gardeners. Psychiatrists."

"Like Dr. Manley," I asked.

"Never Dr. Manley," she said. "Not in that sense. Please, don't interrupt. I thought the boys could teach me, I suppose. I had a lot to learn. Every boy, every man I slept with was so different, secretive, bold, tentative, proud, worried that I wouldn't be satisfied, positive I'd beg for more. And yet, in the moment of passion, they were all the same. Released. Abandoned. I thought I'd study them, learn everything I could. I was analytical, in control. I was not passionate. I saw it as a job, to learn these things. I didn't think of myself as wanton or wild or wicked. I was a recorder, a camera, a writer.

"I knew Alonso had not been faithful to me. He talked of seducing girls at the institute, how easy it would be. Possibly my own sister, who sometimes stayed there overnight, even then. When he was asked to leave the institute, without telling Daddy, I arranged for Alonso to move into the empty apartment over our garage. It was extremely convenient. I felt I'd done so much for him.

"When Alonso hit me, something snapped. That's the only way I can describe it. A flood of anger opened up, a rip in the universe filled with blood and smut and fog. I'd never been hit before. Never. There'd been rough sex, yes. But I always knew what was coming after the first time, and his violence astounded me, frightened me. There were tools in the shed and I hit him with a trowel, with anything I could reach, but I specifically remember the trowel. It was sharp, triangular. He didn't move. I kept hitting him. Then I knew I'd killed him—and that my father would never be Senator Cameron and my mother would never forgive me. And it seemed to me that keeping my mother and father from realizing their ambition was a worse sin than killing Alonso, because he'd hit me. He'd hit me."

She seemed angry and outraged all over again.

Mooney turned off the tape recorder.

"What are you doing? I have more to say."

"I need to get another cassette."

"I want to talk about Manley now. He should have helped me all those years ago, but all he cared about was sidling up to my mother, seducing, screwing my mother. He never cared about Beryl or me. I'm not sorry I killed Drew Manley."

"There's a technical problem," Mooney said smoothly. "Don't worry, we'll let you confess to your heart's content. Carlotta, can I see you outside?"

"May I keep talking?" Thea asked, almost desperately, as though the sound of her voice was the most important thing in the universe, as though once she'd started, she couldn't stop. She grabbed the recorder. "Maybe there's still a little room on this tape."

"Go ahead," Mooney said with a shrug. "Here. Here's paper. Why don't you write what you need to say?"

Thea seemed grateful, but I knew something was wrong. That's definitely not the way the interrogation game is played.

"What is it, Moon?" I asked as soon as he'd closed the soundproof door.

"MacAvoy left a trunkful of papers at his place. In the attic. Fancied himself another writer, a true-crime novelist, the next Joe McGinniss, who knows?"

"Do you believe her?"

"I don't know what to believe. According to Mac-Avoy, Alonso Nueves was strangled. Bludgeoned as well, messy. But for cause of death, MacAvoy insists he was strangled."

"Was there an autopsy? I don't understand."

"No autopsy," Mooney said. "Just observation."

"Observations from a dead man," I said.

"Worth a lot," Mooney observed, tongue firmly in cheek.

I said, "There could still be an autopsy."

"How?" he asked.

"Thea might help," I said.

"Ah. Then let's ask the dead woman," he said.

I stared at him, wondering how he'd read my mind. For the first time, she was the dead woman to me. Not Thea, not the vibrant girl of fourteen, the collective wet dream of Avon Hill. I thought about skin cells and how quickly we lose and renew them. I thought about snakes, growing larger, leaving their shed skins behind.

I thought about myself and who I'd been at fourteen and fifteen.

Was any of that part of me left?

Any residue of Thea?

Perhaps in the young Alonso. Wherever he might be.

50

Long ago, Mooney and I used to team up for a game called "good cop, bad cop." At first, we'd taken turns, alternating sweet and sour, but it soon became clear that I owned the rogue role. Something about Mooney's choirboy face makes him a natural-born good guy.

But since she already knew me, had reason to trust me, Mooney thought I should play the "good cop" role.

I felt miscast.

"Sorry," Mooney informed her bluntly as we reentered the interview room, "but it's not going to fly. I don't have time to waste. Confessors! Geez, it's nothing to be ashamed of, trying to save your kid. I'm sure we'd all try to cushion our own kid's path, if we could. But your boy crossed over the line, lady, way over it."

He started gathering pens, notebooks, and tape recorders, as though he were in a hurry to get home.

"But I killed Andrew Manley," she said, sitting bolt upright. "You haven't heard the details, taken my statement."

"Try this," Mooney said harshly. "By me, you're about as credible as that woman claimed to be Anastasia, daughter of the friggin' Czar of Russia, all those years. Yapped about it till the day she died—how everyone had stolen her birthright—and then a couple forensic scientists did some DNA testing, and guess what? Phony as they come. You should know this: If you're a fake, we can find out."

"I know."

"Keep up on that sort of thing, do you?" Mooney taunted, "bad cop" all the way.

"Mooney," I said reasonably. "Before he died, Dr. Manley came to me with some stuff about recovered memory syndrome. I did some reading, and believe me, after twenty-four years, she could be off on a few details."

"Details!" Mooney snorted.

"What does he mean?" Thea asked.

I went on as if no one had interrupted. "She could honestly think she hit the guy with a trowel. Kept hitting him with it, until he bled to death. She could have blanked out on the part about strangling Nueves—"

"What do you mean, strangling him? Who told you that? He was a big man. I couldn't have gotten my hands around his neck. I couldn't have killed him with my hands." Thea stood, clasping the edge of the table for support. Her words came faster. "Dr. Manley and I never spoke about those memories, not the killing memories. I never forgot killing Alonso, not for a single moment, not a single detail. I never will. I can hear the rattle in his throat. I can see the blood—"

"Prove it," Mooney said scornfully.

"I can't," she murmured, staring at me like I could help her if only I had sufficient desire.

"If we had his body," I said carefully, "there are tests that could be done, even now, to show how he'd died."

"We don't have a body," Mooney said to me, explaining it slowly as though to a child. "And we're not going to get one, understand? The Nueves guy did a flit, could be anyplace. She's using him for credibility, so we'll let her testify that she killed the shrink, get her kid off the big hook. But it's too late. Her kid was at the scene—"

She looked him over from head to toe, slowly. Then, with ice in her voice, she said, "What exactly do you want?"

"What do you mean?" Mooney returned.

"I'm fairly perceptive," she said, with an edge to her voice. "Since the two of you returned from your hallway conference, you've been behaving quite differently. You obviously have an agenda. You want something from me. Stop fooling around and level with me."

Moon lifted one eyebrow, stared at me. We must have been rustier at the game than I'd thought. On the other hand, it's seldom you bring in a perp half as sharp as Thea Janis.

After a pause, I led off. "We need you to request an exhumation, to sign an exhumation order."

"And who, pray tell, would you like to dig up?"

"Dorothy Cameron," I said, "also known as Thea Janis."

"That might get my family in an uproar—and I don't

want them told about me, understand? How would it help me?"

I said, "It might help your son."

As she thought it over, I could almost hear the gears spin. Without the concealing brown spectacles, her eyes were enormous. How could she bring herself to wear them day after day, like blinders on a racehorse?

"Where do I sign?" she said.

Quickly Mooney motioned me out of the room.

"Don't try any more tricks," Thea advised as he shut the door.

"I'll have to get a judge's approval," Moon said urgently. "It's not like we're going digging tonight."

"I know."

"Where are we going to keep her?" he said. "If I arrest her, I've got press coming out of my ears, national TV. Can you take her?"

"No way. Someone's already tried to crack my house, searching for her notebook."

"Who?"

"Possibly her kid. Possibly Manley's killer."

"Which means you don't think they're one and the same."

"Whatever, she's not coming home with me. What about you? Your mom would love the company."

"I assume that's a feeble attempt at humor. How about Gloria?"

"No," I said. "Gloria's not up for guests yet. We could stick her in a hotel."

"Sure," he said, "with what money? And what makes you think she wouldn't waltz out the door?"

"Don't you have any federal witness protection bucks? Couldn't you put a guard on her?"

"No extra money, no extra men," he said. "Come

on, Carlotta, if they've already tried your house, it could be the safest place. Roz can bodyguard her."

"I thought you were concerned about a mob attempt on my life," I said. "Aren't you worried she might get in the way?"

"Oh, that," he said coolly. "Turned out to be bunk, like you thought. Just a punk trying to plead."

So that's how I got Dorothy Cameron as a houseguest. The digs would definitely not be what "Thea Janis" had been accustomed to, but "Susan Gordon" seemed to require less splendor.

51

Mooney didn't trust her one bit. He shadowed us home in an unmarked car. I half expected her to make a run at a traffic light, but she never moved. I doubt she noticed our honor guard.

"Do you have another car?" she asked. No big deal, like she was asking questions for the census bureau.

"No," I said. "And you are not to take this one. If you'd like to visit anyone, I'll drive you."

I made a mental note to call Gloria, make sure no cabs picked up at my house without my knowledge.

Time passed. I didn't play the radio or the boom box. I wanted her to feel free to chat. Some people can't take silence. Thea wasn't one of those.

It seemed hours before she asked, "Did Drew Manley really talk to you about recovered memories?"

"Yes."

"Why?"

"I don't know. He seemed unsure himself. He kept trying to talk, then running away. I think it was very important to him, but he didn't know where to begin."

She twisted her hands in her lap.

"Why are recovered memories important to you, Thea?" I asked.

"Who said they were?" she snapped.

Then there was just the engine, running a little ragged, racing at the stoplights. Tuneup time.

"Maybe he didn't deserve to die," she said eight minutes later.

For the rest of the drive, no matter what I asked, she maintained her silence like a shield, staring straight ahead as though she could see the horizon three thousand miles away.

There are lots of rooms in my old Victorian. When times are tough I can rent them to Harvard students. Times haven't been that hard lately. I've gotten used to having only one tenant: Roz.

I chose Thea's room with care. No telephone. No jack for a telephone. No lock. I didn't give a damn for her personal privacy. She was either too exhausted to fuss or beyond such niceties. The room had no windows that overlooked trees, drainpipes, or porches. Straight down to unwelcoming cement a floor below. Not a high enough drop to kill you, unless you had a lucky fall. Her purse had been searched at the station house, so I wouldn't have to worry about her shooting herself—or me—in the night.

Her door, like most bedroom doors, opened inward. She could fashion a lock by shoving a chair underneath the door handle. I couldn't do the same.

Instead I woke Roz, climbing to the third floor with dread. If I found her with Keith Donovan . . . talk about the end to a perfect day.

She was home, asleep, alone. A minor miracle. She opened her eyes and snapped on the light as soon as she heard my tread. I don't know if it's the karate training or a natural sixth sense. No one sneaks up on Roz. Together we carried one of her futon mats downstairs. If Thea had plans to flee, she'd have to step over her watchdog.

Roz was sufficently awake to haggle for a higher fee, so I figured she could handle the job.

It must have taken me all of two minutes to fall asleep.

The phone rang. With one eye still glued shut, I rolled over and stared at the illuminated dial of the bedside clock. Four A.M. The phone chimed again.

Tessa Cameron's accent sounded more ragged than regal. I wondered if she'd been drinking, steadily downing Martini after Martini, since hearing the news of Drew Manley's death. Once I recognized her voice, I guess I was expecting her to rant on about how I'd failed in some way, failed to keep her lover alive.

"The kidnapper," she whispered, startling me. "He just called. Garnet insists he will take the ransom alone. He will not tell the FBI where he is supposed to make the—what you say?—the drop."

"Yes," I said, struggling to sit, to make sense of her words. The floorboards felt cool under my bare feet.

She continued, "I pick up the extension, very carefully, between rings, the way I see the federal agents do, so I know where Garnet will bring the money. You must go as well. Meet him there. Watch out for him."

"Garnet knows about this?"

"No, but of course he does not know! You will go for me, because I paid you."

"You paid me to find a fraudulent manuscript," I protested.

"And have you done so?"

I thought of the notebooks Pix had described, the ones the missing Alonso had protected so vigilantly.

"I think I know where the book is," I said.

"Good. Then I pay you more, to make sure Garnet is not hurt."

"That's all?"

"All?"

"You're not hiring me to catch the kidnappers. You're not hiring me to get the ransom back."

"Just to see that my boy is not hurt."

"When is the rendezvous?" I asked.

"In one hour, so we have no time for foolishness. The man who calls, the one with the voice like a machine, he knows Garnet already has the money. The kidnapper wants to give him no chance to think, to plan."

"Where?"

"Underneath the Harvard Bridge. On the Boston side."

One of the few areas of town that wouldn't be deserted at five in the morning. The Charles River Esplanade comes to life early, crowded with runners, joggers, Rollerbladers, cyclists, all rushing to finish their exercise regimen before the workday begins. Run, race home, shower quickly, get to work. The urban Boston schedule.

"I'll be there," I told Tessa Cameron, hanging up before she could tack any provisos onto my mission.

I yanked on underwear, tried to fashion a running

outfit suitable for the fancy Back Bay. I settled on gray to blend with the gathering light. My sleeveless gray knitted shirt could be worn as an overblouse, hiding the gun at the small of my back.

I called Mooney at home, woke his dread mother, who threatened me before agreeing to wake her darling son.

"Jogging clothes," I said to Moon. "Corner of Commonwealth and Mass. Ave. within the half hour."

"Anything else?" he said, as if I were making a reasonable request at a reasonable hour.

"Binoculars," I said.

52

"**O**kay," Mooney said, bending and stretching in exact imitation of my runner's warm-up, "first thing, assume the FBI's got people all over the place. Half the joggers are agents. If you see a weather 'copter, that's gonna be full of agents."

"I don't know," I said. "According to Tessa, Garnet refused to tell them anything."

"Why would he need to tell them when they've got his phone tapped?"

"Are you sorry I woke you?" I asked.

"That brings up a question: What do you think of this kidnapping? First you figured it was the real thing, and Garnet was trying to hush it up. Then you called it a phony, with Garnet using it to move cash. How about right now, this minute?"

"Not a clue." After a deep breath, I repeated, "Are you sorry I woke you?"

"No way. The drop's going down in my jurisdiction, no state lines have been crossed. It's my case."

"Shall we mingle?" I asked.

Mooney elevated an eyebrow to show he was intent on deliberately misunderstanding me, adding sexual overtones where none were intended. Then he grinned, and we jogged the single short block to the river in companionable silence, trotted briskly down the green-painted wooden stairs at the right of the bridge.

"I admire your sweatband," I told him. To tell the truth, I couldn't figure out what it was, maybe his aging mother's chin strap. We'd both dressed and driven quickly. Our reward: twenty-five minutes till opening curtain, according to Tessa Cameron. I wanted time to sort the civilians from the troops, if possible.

"No friggin' FBI," Mooney said softly. "I don't recognize a soul. Maybe the kidnapper used some kind of code."

"A code the FBI couldn't break? Come on."

A biker whizzed by on a blue Diamond Back so shiny it must have just come from the showroom.

"Personal," Mooney said. "Like the kidnapper talks to Marissa, says to Garnet: Take the money to the place we went on our second date."

"And *Tessa* would know that? Garnet would tell his mother where he went on a date?" I asked.

"Go ahead, scoff," Mooney said. "Maybe Mama squeezed it out of his chauffeur, or his valet. Or his nanny."

"He's forty-two," I said. Mooney increased his stride.

It was still easy going, although running is not my

sport. My wind's okay from volleyball and swimming. I'm not saying I was comfortable. My gun bumped up and down. The binoculars smacked my chest.

I kept checking my watch.

"Figure the kidnapper will show?" I asked Mooney.

"Kidnappers are after money," Moon replied. "That's what the Bureau preaches. But kidnappers panic easily, and when they're scared, they kill. So we want to identify the kidnapper, follow the kidnapper, if we can. We do not mess with the kidnapper."

"Gotcha."

"Make sure you do, Carlotta, because whoever picks up the cash could be a gofer, some guy who got spotted a twenty to deliver a bag from Point A to Point B. We nab him, we've got zip, and the kidnapper kills Marissa."

"And we get shot at sunrise by the FBI."

"They won't have to wait long," Moon said. "Geez, I'm thirsty."

"Maybe we can use that tree as a vantage point. It's got location. Good climbing tree." There aren't a lot of hefty trees along the Esplanade. Mainly spindly Japanese cherries, donated by Boston's Sister City, Osaka, and planted as a gesture of goodwill. Pretty enough, they're too young to climb, too short to offer much in the way of camouflage.

"I don't climb trees," Mooney said.

"I do."

A full-breasted blonde with a royal scarf tied at her throat charged past on Rollerblades. The scarf matched her plunging bikini top.

"Think she's FBI?" I asked Mooney.

"Are you going to climb or comment on the passersby?"

"Maybe I should have worn green," I said. "To match the tree."

"Shhh. I'm gonna try the radio."

I wondered who Mooney'd bribed to get the broadcast frequency for the FBI.

"It's dead quiet," he said. "This isn't right."

"They could have changed frequencies."

"See anything?"

"No."

"Not even other bird-watchers? FBI could have commandeered a building with a view."

"Without telling the Boston police?"

"I wouldn't put it past them," Mooney said.

I dangled in the crotch of a sturdy maple and watched the sun rise over Beacon Hill, glinting on the golden dome of the State House. I was shielded by sufficient branches to make good use of my binoculars. My eyes worked while my mind worried at a sequence of events that had played out twenty-four years ago April. What might MacAvoy have told me if he'd lived another five minutes?

To earn truly big bucks, MacAvoy would have had to know where the real skeletons were buried . . .

"Mooney," I said, "how's the exhumation order coming along?"

"It's August," he grumbled. "My pet judge is on vacation."

"Make another pet. It has to happen soon. As in now."

The sun was rising quickly, almost blinding to the east.

"There he is. Garnet," I said. "At three o'clock and closing. Carrying a duffel bag."

"Not very sporty," Mooney commented.

Garnet had made no effort to blend. In his pinstriped suit and knotted tie, he could have been hot on the campaign trail. He seemed to be alone, but half the feds in Boston could have been following.

"Where do you think he'll dump it?" Mooney asked softly.

"I don't know. It might be a direct hand-over."

"Too risky."

"Yeah," I said, "but he can't leave the bag on the ground and skedaddle. Half these Rollerbladers are do-gooders who'd race three miles to return it. In that getup he looks like he'd offer a fat reward."

"We should have brought Rollerblades," Mooney said. "Dammit."

"Or a boat," I said, glancing at the dawn-lit Charles. "The kidnapper could be a sailor."

"Dammit."

"Get on your radio and see if Beacon Hill can spare a couple bicycle cops," I said. "If I have to, I'll trip a skater and steal his blades."

While Mooney was speaking into the radio, I saw him, saw *them*. I started my descent faster than I should have, skinned my elbow on a stray branch. In seconds I was tugging at Mooney's shirt.

"Look!"

"What?"

Two people approached Garnet, one on foot, one on blades. In spite of the added height of the blades, the pedestrian was taller. Thin and muscled, he carried a well-stuffed camper's backpack like it weighed nothing. They were heading outbound, Garnet in, toward the city. Each party in the threesome seemed aware of the others, pacing themselves, so they'd pass underneath the bridge at the same time, the two strangers splitting to flank Garnet.

"Don't try anything," Mooney cautioned.

I had the scene centered in my field of vision. I was trying to remember every detail for later Identikit use. Ears, eyes . . .

"Mooney," I said excitedly. "The Rollerblader's a girl. Short hair tucked into a cap. Blond. Shit."

"What?"

"I've only seen her once, but I swear to God, it's Marissa. It's Marissa goddam Cameron! Garnet knows it's her. Look at his face."

"Stop jumping to conclusions!"

"She's not built like a man, Mooney!"

"The first guy could have a gun on her."

"From in front?"

"Stockholm Syndrome," Mooney muttered. "He could have turned her, like Patty Hearst. She could think he's on her side."

"My God, look at his fucking ears, Mooney. *You can move on him.* You've got a legit warrant."

With that parting shot, I took off. Not fast. Just like the rest of the joggers, pacing myself for a burst. I wanted to get close enough to lunge, to knock Marissa Gates Moore Cameron on her cute little fanny.

It had never been a real kidnapping.

Mooney moved next to me.

"Alonso's the guy," he said, no question in his tone.

"Wanted in Marblehead. He looks exactly like his mother."

"Extortion for past wrongs?"

"We'll ask him when we nail him," I said. "I'm going to bump Marissa off her blades. Cover the guys. Get backup."

I knew Mooney'd already taken care of everything, called in both silent-approach and siren cars. I just couldn't help myself.

Moon picked up the pace.

The Harvard Bridge passes low over the path, a half-moon shape, sudden darkness in its shadow.

I hadn't counted on the moment of blindness, coming in from the sun. Garnet must have seen me.

"Run!"

I'm sure it was his voice.

"Hold it," Mooney said. "Boston police!"

Marissa moved just as I lunged. She had a good long stroke and I was lucky to grab her by the skate blade. She fell headlong on the grass, wrenching her leg away from me, kicking at me with her heavy footgear.

The marked units arrived, sirens screaming. Uniforms jumped out, guns drawn. There was yelling. I stayed frozen, hanging on to Marissa's blades till a young cop ordered me to my feet.

Everything was going like clockwork. Until Garnet Cameron refused to press charges. Point-blank refused.

Mooney had to let him go, let Marissa go. It took Garnet five minutes to persuade Marissa not to level assault charges at me.

Garnet would not allow the police to open the duffel. He held grimly to its strap.

Marissa made a grab for Alonso's backpack. I was ready to tackle her again, but Mooney got there first.

"My clothes are in there," she offered lamely.

"Then we'll return them to you," Mooney said, "once they've been examined."

"Oh, Garnet," Marissa cried, apparently losing her admirable composure, "are you all right?"

It would have been more convincing the other way

around, but I got the feeling she was coaching him, feeding him his lines.

"Darling," he said, "I'm so glad you're back."

Alonso shot her a killing look. If he'd had a gun, she'd have been dead on the path. I was glad two policemen held him at bay.

Marissa, now openly weeping, clutched her husband's shoulder. Almost reluctantly, he squeezed back.

With the voice of a man in command, Garnet said, "That backpack is my wife's property. I insist on its immediate return."

"No way," Alonso said. "No fuckin' way!"

"If it belongs to your wife, Mr. Cameron, we'll return it in due course," Mooney said, with full marks for politeness.

"I don't believe you have any reason to hold this young man," he said, referring to Alonso. "I said I wouldn't be bringing charges. I have my wife back. I don't want to create a public—er, the campaign and all . . ."

Mooney smiled. Then he formally arrested the young man. On a John Doe warrant issued in Marblehead. Patted him down and stuck him in the backseat of an unmarked unit, ordered the driver to take the suspect to Area D. The backpack traveled in the trunk.

As soon as it disappeared, Garnet and Marissa hailed a cab. Neither said a word of thanks to me or Mooney or any other cop.

"Mooney," I said.

"What?"

"First, you might want to have somebody follow the cab, make sure it doesn't head straight to the airport. If it does, be ready to hold them as material witnesses."

He gave hurried orders. Another unit screeched away from the curb into Storrow Drive traffic.

"Material witnesses to what?"

"I'm not sure. You can always say it was a bureaucratic snafu."

Mooney said, "Yeah, like I need the bad press."

"Mooney, think about it. Did Garnet look like a man deliriously happy to have his wife back, his campaign on track, his money saved?"

"No on all counts."

"Did he look like he'd willingly trade his wife and his dough for Alonso's backpack?"

"Now that you mention it, yes. So what's in the backpack?"

"What I was hired to find in the first place," I said. "Thea's novel."

"A novel? This is about a *novel?*"

"Moon, please, if there are notebooks in the backpack, may I read them?"

"They're police property," he said automatically.

"Yeah, but is someone going to read them right now? The minute they're ticketed and placed in the property office?"

"You know how it goes," he said. Which meant no.

"Let me sign them out. Please, Mooney."

"We'll give them a look," Moon said. "Together."

53

Mooney and I sat shoulder to shoulder, baking in his overheated office. It was barely nine o'clock and I didn't want to contemplate what new heights the temperature would reach by afternoon. Mooney had no office window and the station had no air conditioning; it wasn't worth thinking about.

It takes time to read. Just as it had taken time to book Alonso Gordon, run a records check on him—no previous convictions—print him, take him to a holding cell. He'd claimed indigency, so a public defender was currently sought.

It takes time to remove notebooks from a backpack, sort through them, arrange them in order from two to thirty-eight.

Takes time to digest dense poetry, prose. The story

seemed to be Beryl's, the daughter called "b," the one who could perceive snakes twining under the dining room table, but couldn't hear the hum of insects.

I'd already given Mooney the gist of the first chapter, the one buried beneath kitty litter. He was not familiar with the "magical realist" school, and I could tell he felt that put him at a disadvantage. It made him read more closely, reluctantly removing his glasses from his desk drawer, perching them on his nose.

I have to admit that what intrigued me most were not daughter "b" 's searing nightmares. What I found most compelling were the errors—the places where Thea had written "i" instead of "her," slipped into first person for a long narrative or a short poem, only to drag herself back to third person, to "b" 's unusual world.

The first chapter had been a much easier read. The second was choked with rewrites, cross-outs, changes. I wondered if Thea had written the first draft of this, her second novel, long ago, if something had recently oc-curred to make her start work on it again.

I thought I might have found the trigger: a newspa-per clipping from the *Seattle Daily News,* barely a col-umn-inch long, stating that Garnet Cameron, son of the late Franklin Cameron, had announced for governor of Massachusetts.

Was that small mention enough to drag Thea to her forbidden memory books? Was the tantalizing sight and smell of paper enough to send her to the store for fresh ink?

During the revision process had she found her fre-quent slips into first person curious? Curious enough to ask a therapist about, a therapist who might have mentioned the possibility of recovered memory syndrome, of long-repressed memories coming home to roost?

I reread a passage, glanced at Mooney to see if he'd completed it yet.

"at night i emerge and merge, a butterfly jettisoned by her cocoon, uncontrollable, uncontrolled. passion while not fruit can bear fruit. the monitors stalk. monitors of aisles of bedrooms nile monitors would be more welcome than these aisle monitors, snapping at bare toes.

"giggling in delight at unexpected hairy places, fuzzy animals delighting in passing fluids, warm and silky fluids, back and forth back and forth through the night."

That would seem to be Beryl's story. Except for the initial "i." Beryl spending the occasional night at Weston Psych, with "monitors." Thea had been a day student at Avon Hill. But "monitors" seemed more a school word than a hospital word.

The heavy knock at the office door startled both of us.

"Maybe they found a PD," Mooney said, as in public defender.

They hadn't. Gary Reedy had found us. He ignored my presence. If I'd been a cockroach crawling the floor, I'd have commanded more attention.

"Lieutenant," Reedy snapped, "any reason you chose to leave the FBI out in the cold this morning?"

"Agent Reedy," Mooney returned smartly, "considering the credibility level of our sole witness, I thought you'd prefer to have the Boston police handle it." He applied his big cop shoe directly to the toe of my sandal. Just a little pressure, but a definite warning. The way he did it, I couldn't even maneuver my other foot around to kick him. I could feel my cheeks redden. I stared hard at the table.

Reedy said stubbornly, "It was Marissa Cameron's hair in that box. We had it DNA typed, matched with strands from her hairbrush. And it was cut with a blunt knife. What kind of woman goes around chopping off her hair—"

"Have you seen Marissa's new hair-do?" I asked.

"Yes."

"It wasn't hacked off with a knife."

"You have a theory," he said, looking at Mooney but talking to me, the "gangster's moll." It must have cost him in the pride department.

"Newbury Street," I said.

"What?"

"A cab left her at the corner of Newbury Street. Send agents out with her photo—a new one with short hair —and you'll probably find that she rented or borrowed a condo from a Back Bay friend, lived there with Alonso. She must have used a dull kitchen knife to saw off a few locks of hair. I doubt Alonso approved; in my experience, men are long hair freaks. She conned him into delivering the box, then went to the nearest hairdresser with a tale of woe. Newbury Street is crawling with hairdressers. Some, you don't even have to make an appointment. She could have told them anything— her nephew was playing with the scissors, her niece put chewing gum in her hair."

Gary Reedy leaned his back against the door and sighed. "But, the thing is, was she ever really kidnapped? Do I file charges against her? Against her husband?"

Mooney asked, "What do they say?"

"What do you think? That the Bureau made a hash

of the whole thing, and thank God she's home, and if I so much as open my mouth, I will find myself minding the store in—"

"Butte," Mooney and I chorused.

"The Bureau doesn't even have a substation there anymore," Reedy said, "but you get the idea."

I said, "I think she was Garnet's plant in the enemy camp at the start. I think it began as extortion, these notebooks for money. The kidnap might have been Marissa's idea, so she could keep tabs on Alonso, make sure the notebooks didn't wind up on some publisher's desk. We may have all seriously underrated little Marissa's desire to be governor's lady."

"She was supposedly ready to divorce him. There was a rumor he'd be leaving the race."

"Got him some pretty decent coverage, didn't it?" I said. "But maybe I'm just getting cynical in my old age."

"But have you talked to the suspect. He seems to genuinely feel that she—uh—cared for him. Certainly she slept with him. She doesn't seem cast in the Mata Hari mold," Reedy objected.

"Neither did Mata Hari," I said, "which is why she was so successful."

"Hmmm," said the FBI's Special Agent in Charge.

"Want my opinion?" I asked. "I think Marissa fell for him, for Alonso. Not so hard she wasn't looking out for number one—herself—at all times. I think she'd have gone with whoever made the big score. If it looked like Garnet was going to lose the race, and Alonso got lucky with money, I think she'd have stuck with him. She's probably composing a tale for the *National Enquirer* even as we speak, and I guarantee, it will be genuine sob stuff, and she will come out quite a heroine. Expect to see her on *Oprah* within the week, whatever else happens."

Reedy frowned. "Thanks," he said to Mooney as if I'd been entirely silent. "Anything I can do for you?"

"Thanks," Mooney said, "not at the—"

This time I kicked him. "The exhumation," I said.

"Yes," Mooney said. "You might be able to expedite an exhumation order—"

"That would depend—"

"It concerns a case that already involves the Bureau—"

Mooney's phone trilled. He gave it a sizzling glance —*how dare you interrupt me?*—then answered, giving his name and nothing more. He nodded at me.

"Take it in the corridor, line two."

"Thanks."

I exited and took to the hall phone. "Hello, Carlyle here."

It was Roz, speaking quickly, whispering. "They're going to kick me off this phone in a second. I'm with Thea—that's who it is, right, the one I drew the pictures of?—and she's at Weston Psych, threatening to batter the doors down. Can you get the hell over here?"

"Why'd you let her out?" died on my lips. Thea was there. How and why no longer mattered.

"It will take me half an hour," I said, already plotting the quickest route. "Can you control the situation till then?"

"Yes."

"Think we need a cop?"

"No," Roz said. "Gotta go."

Honestly, why do I ever believe her?

54

Since I'd already seen Beryl once, and Security recalled that I'd been duly approved by Garnet, my arrival was greeted with general relief. From a distance I could hear Thea's voice, raised in shrill argument. No wonder Security regarded me fondly; can't have guests shrieking in the looney bin. Distinctly lower class.

Jannie, the aproned attendant, confided, "We must have called Mr. Cameron seven times, but no one's answering his phone. We've left messages everywhere."

"It's fine," I said, calmly assuming an authority I didn't have because it seemed no one else was willing to shoulder the burden. "Beryl Cameron's sister has returned from an extended vacation and wishes to see Beryl. I'm certain that if Dr. Manley were here, he'd have no objection. Dr. Manley's assistant could remain present during the entire visit, or if Thea finds that unacceptable, you might move Beryl to an observation lounge equipped with one-way glass. You have those, I assume? Both Beryl and Thea know me, and while I have no degrees in psychology, I'd be happy to monitor the meeting, so that nothing in any way violent or upsetting could occur. I'm sure the Cameron family, whom I represent, would agree that the institute would be behaving in an entirely responsible manner."

Well, I did still represent Tessa. It's just that I sounded so unlike myself, I had to bite the inside of my cheek to keep from smirking.

A security man in an impeccable suit frowned and said, "There's a woman with Miss Cameron—"

"Oh yes," I agreed, pursing my mouth in distaste. "Dreadful, isn't she?" No way to get chummy faster than to claim a common enemy; I knew Roz would do the same for me in similar circumstances. "The woman can wait in my car. Or if you'd prefer she leave the property entirely—"

"I would," he said, sounding relieved.

I was glad Roz couldn't hear his disapproving tone. If she had, she'd have practiced karate kicks on his ears, and he'd have fired his Taser, and God knows what kind of free-for-all would have erupted.

As it happened, Roz listened amiably enough to my request; she ought to, I figured, after letting her charge get this far from the house! I told her, in no uncertain terms, to clear out. I also blinked my left eye twice in quick succession: an established signal. She'd wait in the car, on alert.

Jannie once again played wardress. Thea—dressed in the same loose shift and khaki jacket of the night before —and I waited for Beryl in the ground-floor sunroom they'd tried to pawn off on me before. An ornate mirror covered most of the right-hand wall. One-way glass indeed. I wondered if the room was wired for sound. Plenty of space to lay wire under the thick carpet. Potted palms and sofas, thick with cushions, in which to hide microphones.

Thea was keyed up; I couldn't have kept her from talking if I'd tried.

"Did you read my first book?" she asked, apropos of nothing, without saying hello, without seeming to notice Roz's dismissal, the change in personnel or surroundings.

"Nightmare's Dawn?" I said. "Yes. Twice. I can't say I enjoyed it. I admired it. It seemed very painful, very real."

"The new book doesn't measure up," she said in a half-swallowed whisper, as though she could hardly bring herself to mention a fear she'd clung to so tightly and so long.

"Why do you say that?" I asked.

"I tried," she answered despairingly. "I wrote. But it was never the same after everyone knew who I was. I felt exposed, like film left in the sun, blank and empty, stunned by the light. I wrote, but I ripped every page to shreds. I made confetti, flushed it down the toilet, so no one would know I'd tried and failed. I panicked."

She stared at the plush carpet. One thumb and forefinger circled the other wrist, squeezing the flesh like a handcuff. I looked at Jannie. No sign of Beryl. I wondered if they were stalling, trying to neutralize us until Garnet Cameron answered his phone.

Jannie indicated a central table, surrounded by four graceful chairs, inviting us to sit. If I were going to plant a bug in the room, I'd have used the underside of the table, or perhaps the huge cut-glass vase that served as a centerpiece.

Thea didn't give Jannie so much as a glance. She said, "I kept my notebooks wherever I went. I always wrote, but I could never show my work. It was as if that part of my life was over, covered with glass, dusty, locked away. The first notebook was filled, the first chapter written over twenty years ago. It was Beryl's story. I was afraid to write my own."

"Everyone loved your writing," I said soothingly, because she was starting to pace and frown, and I didn't want to give the staff any reason to call in a major headshrinker, advise Garnet or Tessa that one more family member could do with an extended rest.

Thea said, "That was the problem. *Nightmare's Dawn*. They loved it, they loved me, they wanted me to keep writing the same book over and over. I was so young and everyone expected so much. Before I ran away, when I couldn't write, I started to dream about killing myself."

Jannie stood straighter. She seemed to make eye contact with someone beyond the mirror.

"Do you know the story of Thomas Chatterton?" Thea continued. Jannie relaxed.

"No," I said.

"He was a poet, a prodigy. Today, he's regarded by some as a precursor to the entire Romantic movement. Born in 1752."

"That's a while back," I said, because she seemed to expect comment.

"His work was never appreciated, and in order to live he became desperate enough to attempt a literary fraud. He invented a fifteenth-century monk, Thomas Rowley, and wrote a series of Rowley's poems that he then 'discovered.' The dead monk's poems were all the rage of London and so was Chatterton. Until the deception was made public."

"What happened?"

"Chatterton was banned from literary society. Two years later, living in squalor, he ate rat poison. A genius at fifteen, dead at seventeen. . . . There aren't many tales of prodigies who live happily ever after. I couldn't find any."

"Is that why you wrote a will?"

"I had one thing of value, the book I'd written in a joyful spurt—a week, maybe a month at most. I gave it to Beryl. It seemed, at the time, like a whim, but it wasn't. I wanted her to have it because . . . because I'd ruined her life."

I spoke softly. "Exactly how had you ruined Beryl's life? Had you plagiarized her work? Is part of *Nightmare's Dawn* really Beryl's?"

"Of course not! I ruined . . . I have to talk to Beryl first, to Beryl."

"Your will wasn't valid," I said after a brief pause. "You were underage."

"I didn't really think I'd die," she said.

"You must have had money as well. A trust fund?"

"Whatever, it was probably divided between Garnet and Beryl."

"You don't seem to care."

"There was always a lot of money when I was growing up."

"Did you arrange to take some with you when you ran?"

"Three thousand dollars," she said ruefully. "I didn't know anything about money. I thought it was a fortune until I discovered what it could buy. I've learned poverty, if nothing else." She got to her feet, took a step toward Jannie. "What's keeping my sister? You promised."

I got between them, took Thea's hand, walked her back toward a chair. I said, "I thought your second manuscript was very fine. It's uneven. There are chunks of dazzling imagery. You need to work on it."

"But I'm not a child genius anymore," Thea said. "Not 'talented for my age.' "

"Just a writer," I said. "Just a poet."

She swallowed audibly. "Thank you," she muttered faintly.

"You write the occasional poem still?" I asked, thinking about "berlin, *now.*"

"An act of madness, darkness. I tuck it in my footlocker, lock it away as quickly as I can, afraid some horrid Pandora will escape, and now she has, escaped forever—"

Beryl entered, alone, in a wheelchair that she worked with her hands. It hadn't occurred to me that she'd lost the ability to walk. Maybe she hadn't. Maybe her weight made the wheelchair necessary. Certainly she wouldn't have been confined to bed so long her legs had atrophied. Not at WPI.

Thea saw her and began to weep, deep sobs starting in her gut, welling uncontrollably. Ugly tears. I passed her a box of tissues and she blew her nose.

Beryl didn't give any sign of recognition. I didn't know if anyone had prepped her for the meeting or if they'd sent her to the sunroom cold, to observe her reaction.

Thea dropped the Kleenexes, not even looking for a wastebasket. She lowered herself to her knees, mumbling, stumbling in her haste to speak. "I'm sorry, Beryl. So sorry. You were right. You were right, and I was afraid to say you were right, and so they put you here. 'Silenced for what they did to you, worse, far worse than caged for acts of rage.' I've come back, and I'll be put in jail for what I did, for killing, but I don't know how to free you, Beryl. I don't know what they've done to you." Her speech became more rapid, her voice loud, angry.

"What have you done to my sister?" she screamed at Jannie. "She wasn't like this. She could speak, she could laugh. She could dance and sing, and play the piano. Do you know that? She played better than Mama ever did. Other children liked her best, always. My father liked her best."

Thea was on her feet now, menacing, backing Jannie into a corner. "What have you done to her? I want her medical charts! I want to see what that idiot, Manley, did to her, did to her so he could have my mother when my father died. He'd have done anything Mama said. And Tessa would have said anything Franklin wanted her to say!"

"Dorothea!" Beryl's croak of a voice commanded our attention. "Dorothea," she repeated slowly. "Why are you come from the dead?"

"I was never dead."

"Yes, you were. We buried you, Thea. I wore white, not black. Mama made me wear white."

"Beryl!" Thea grasped her hand. "I'm not dead. I've come back for you. To tell them that you always told the truth."

"Why? Why now?" Beryl patted her nightgown and I could hear the faint crinkle of paper. She must have kept her sister's words near her since she'd found them in the photo box.

Thea's voice sank to a whisper. "I didn't know before. Honest to God, Beryl, I didn't know. Manley promised me he'd help me explain to you if I came back, and now he's not here."

"Is this about recovered memory, Thea?" I asked.

"Yes. Yes, that's what he called it. He said that when Daddy came to your room, *you* were there, *you* remembered. But I learned to go to another place in my head, to pretend so deeply that it never happened, that after a while I could just go away in my mind, and then it truly never seemed to happen. So I wasn't really lying when I told Mother that Daddy never bothered me at night, and that you were making the whole thing up. Even when you tried to kill yourself, taking all Mama's pills, I thought, 'She's just crazy.' I'm so sorry . . ."

"When?" Beryl asked.

"What do you mean? When did I remember?"

Solemnly, Beryl nodded her head.

"When I started to rewrite your book, Beryl. I'd been writing about you, and the stories you told me, stories I didn't believe, about Daddy tying you with birthday ribbons, and I realized I'd written 'tying me'—not 'tying her,' but 'tying *me*'—I erased it so fast, but then I *knew*, and I felt so sick inside I couldn't move or talk. It clawed at me, that 'I,' that 'me.' I couldn't write without 'I' or 'me' coming out. It was as if my hand was not in control any longer. I put the notebooks back in the footlocker, and I locked it tight, and I didn't look at them again. I wanted Thea to stay dead then, more than ever, because I didn't want to remember." She was breathing quickly now, talking fast and low. I hoped she spoke too softly for audio equipment, if they were using it, but in a first-class joint like this one, they probably had stuff that could catch the faintest sigh.

"Aren't you Thea, Dorothea?" Beryl asked, shaking her head back and forth, back and forth. "I wish you were her. I wish you were."

"Yes, dear, I am, but I've been somebody else for a long time, so long that I have a grown son. I have another life, a quiet life . . . I had a quiet life. But I couldn't stop the remembering. Not once it started."

I heard a man's voice then: Garnet, calling, racing through the hall, coming closer.

"There's another way out," Thea said to me. "I won't see him. *I won't.*"

Before I could stop her, before I had any idea of her intent, she seized the fat crystal vase, shook half the flowers on the floor, and thrust the leaded ball away from her, hard and fast, with hands and elbows, like a volleyball pass. It crashed through the mirror, destroying a vast section of phony wall, revealing an adjoining room staffed by a lone white-coated technician, frozen in his chair.

Then she had me by the hand, and we were smashing through the opening she'd made, racing through the small observation room, out a nearby door, down a path lined by late-flowering shrubs.

Roz had the presence of mind to start the car when she saw us running toward the lot.

I'd had the presence of mind to grab the spool of tape off the machine operated by the astonished open-mouthed man in the lab coat.

As soon as we were safely on the highway, Thea whooped and hollered in victory. Roz and I joined her. I think I'll always remember that one unexpected glimpse—Thea as she might have been, with laughter in her eyes and color in her cheeks.

Maybe she knew there wouldn't be much to celebrate at the end.

55

The message light burned on my answering machine. Tessa Cameron's querulous accented voice demanded to know what had occurred at the drop site. Instead of phoning, I reluctantly wrote her a refund check, stuck it quickly in an envelope, licked the stamp. Roz ran it to the mailbox before I could waver.

I couldn't satisfy Tessa, couldn't prove Thea's notebooks fraudulent. Nor could I return them; they were evidence in at least one murder trial.

I could ignore Thurman W. Vandenburg's plea for information about Carlos Roldan Gonzales, Keith Donovan's request for reconciliation. I suppose I could have used a good psychiatrist for Thea, but Donovan and I no longer shared that precious and rare commodity, trust. Without it, we had no future, and I didn't want to talk about it, talk about it, talk about it endlessly, until he twisted my words and put me in the wrong—unbending, unloving, unforgiving.

There are things I don't forgive, it's as simple as that. In myself. In others.

Mooney's recorded voice jerked me back to the here and now. The exhumation of Dorothy Cameron's grave would occur at 10 A.M., Tuesday, August 22, tomorrow morning.

I phoned the station and he was there, answering crisply, with his name and nothing more.

"Mooney," I said, "how'd you get it scheduled so fast? I thought—"

"The FBI moves in mysterious ways," he said.

"The Bureau?"

"Don't ask. Just be there. With Thea. She signed the application; she has to attend."

"Who else are we expecting?"

"The Camerons know. They're trying to get a last-minute injunction forbidding the 'desecration' of Thea's grave."

"Will they?"

"No. I'm planning to bring Alonso Gordon as my guest."

"Alonso couldn't have anything to do with these deaths—so long ago—"

"I know that, Carlotta."

"So you're trying to stir up a commotion, Moon. Is that what I'm hearing?"

"Yes."

"I can see where you'd need a break," I said. "You can't keep Alonso locked up for Manley's death if his mother's going to keep saying she did it."

"Right," Mooney said. "I can't charge anybody, and I've got a political tiger by the tail. I want out."

"So we go hunting at Mount Auburn," I said.

"Find out the truth," Mooney said.

An old whore, there's the truth. That's what Mac-Avoy had told me, before he'd blown his brains out.

"Bring a lot of cops, Mooney," I said.

"I'm going to read you Alonso's statement," he said, as if he hadn't heard me. "I'd like you to write it down, maybe leave it on your desk. I wish you had a fax."

"I don't. Let me understand this, you want me to leave it lying around so that his mother can see it?"

"I never said that."

"I have a pen," I said. "Low tech. It may take a while."

Mooney read it slowly, repeating words, spelling occasionally.

" *'My mother always told me my name was Alonso Gordon, but I believe I'm Garnet Cameron's son. I believe that because I found these papers in my mother's footlocker, this old thing we've always had. I never knew my father. My mom never even told me his name. I always thought there was something about my dad in that old locker, but it didn't seem to matter until recently, when I found myself at odds and ends, without real work.*

" *'I stole the key and opened the locker. There were all these notebooks and they reminded me of stuff I'd read in high school. And there was an article about Garnet Cameron running for governor. I think my mom stole those notebooks, maybe, but I don't want to get her in trouble. Like, maybe she was a servant in the Cameron house and the kid, Garnet, got her pregnant, so she stole something he really valued, in case she ever found herself in need of some ready cash.*

" 'Well, I was in need of cash, and she'd said she couldn't help me, which really pissed me off, you know? I mean, I'm this rich guy's son. So I took off. I came to Massachusetts the hard way, working cross-country, odd jobs, you know? And I read those notebooks and they're like about really awful stuff that I think happened at the Cameron house a long time ago. I figured even if he wouldn't accept me as a son, he'd pay for that book.*

" 'Then I met his wife. Just one of those things. I knock on the door and he's out and his wife's there and she looks like every dream I ever had. And I tell her my story and she believes me, every word I say. And she says she's got a better idea. For getting money, 'cause she says Garnet's real tight with a buck.*

" 'She says go ahead and try the blackmail bit, but if he doesn't come across she'll meet me in a day or two and I can call and say I'm holding her, kidnapping her. She says he'll pay two million for her. Two million!*

" 'And that's what I did. I asked for money to keep a secret, and if that's against the law, I broke the law. I sure didn't kidnap Marissa. She came to me. And I think she wants to be with me. I don't understand what this is all about, tell you the truth. I never went to see the doctor. I did call him on the phone, 'cause my mom said he was somebody who'd help me. He told me about the shack, and I stayed there for a while with this kid, Pix. But I never even saw the doctor.*

" 'I wish my mother was here.' "

"Is that a true confession?" I asked Mooney. "He actually uttered that last line?"

"Leave it on your desk, and bring Thea tomorrow."

The phone clicked. I was tempted to call back. Instead I summoned Thea, told her about tomorrow's scheduled event, and abruptly excused myself. I went to the bathroom, spent a long time washing my face and hands, noisily splashing water, cooling off from the car journey, filling my palms with tap water, drinking it, a dangerous habit with Cambridge water.

By the time I returned she'd read it. I could tell. She sat in my desk chair, collapsed by the weight of his ignorance.

"He believes Garnet is his father," she said to me, a wild look in her eyes.

"He doesn't know who you are," I responded.

"Yes, he does. I'm his mother. He knows me."

"Not as Thea Janis. Not as Dorothy Cameron."

"Listen," she said. "I did the best I could. I wanted him to have as little to do with that family as possible. I gave him the best father I could—I don't want him to know about Thea Janis."

"Okay," I said mildly.

"Promise," she said.

Sometimes I have to make promises I know I can't keep.

This one kept me awake late into the night, remembering Thea's poem.

> perhaps as penance,
> i must walk,
> barefoot and holy,
> through snow-wax camellias

I could remember no more, but I was afraid. I slept badly, woke at sunrise, sweating. It would be a scorcher of a day.

56

They do an extremely discreet and dignified exhumation at Mount Auburn Cemetery. Impossible, really, to differentiate it from a funeral, unless you happen to be in the know.

The cemetery was closed to casual passersby, the iron gate barred. The green canvas tent raised over the Cameron plot was totally correct. Striped would have been too festive, spearmint too springlike. The grass-green tent was large and opaque. No one could see the feverish activity within, the two sweating gravediggers first removing Thea's marker, then measuring a six- by two-foot rectangle in the soil, carefully cutting away the sod, hefting their shovels, dumping the mounded earth into wheelbarrows. The cop observing, taking notes. The man from the Medical Examiner's office, waiting.

The old caretaker seemed to recognize me. "You'll see," he said flatly. "Told ya there's a body in that grave."

Rows of black folding chairs had been set along a pathway. Due to an inconveniently located birch, there seemed to be a dividing aisle—bride's side, groom's side —or Cameron side, cop side, in this case. Most FBI agents stood, it seemed, including Gary Reedy.

The trick was keeping Thea away from her renowned family. Not from her son, Alonso, who attended under guard, wearing a cheap blue lightweight suit, obviously provided by the public defender, and manacles that restrained his wrists and feet. Thea had greeted him with a kiss, assured him that everything would be all right. Alonso sat like a man in a dream, sniffing the fresh-mown lawn, unaware of his surroundings at first. Slowly his eyes moved down the row of chairs, came to a full stop at Marissa's.

She was wearing bright campaign yellow, sleeveless and clingy, her hair tucked under a wide-brimmed straw. He couldn't have seen her face. She'd chosen her hat well.

Garnet straightened his tie for the umpteenth time. He couldn't keep his eyes off Thea. He made no approach; after the scene at Weston Psych, he must have realized his sister would run to avoid him. Tessa Cameron looked utterly bewildered in her widow's weeds. I wondered whom she'd donned the black silk shirtwaist for—her lover, Drew Manley, dead four days, her "lost" children?

Tessa studied Thea carefully, standing, and pivoting on spindly heels. Saw the steely hair, the undistinguished profile, the utter plainness of the pretender to the throne. Yet, there was something, some memory that kept Tessa turning her head in her daughter's direction. Tessa seemed, I thought, beyond all else, puzzled.

The digging took two hours and twenty-seven minutes, with several breaks, during which the rhythmic noise would abruptly halt, and the audience hold its collective breath. When they finally struck the metal casket, it pealed like a muffled church bell. Tessa shivered. I searched the area for Edith Foley, for a man who might be one of her sons. No. There'd be no need to involve them yet. I was glad I wasn't a Swampscott cop, glad I wouldn't be bringing the news to Edie's house.

"Tell me," Thea said, clinging to my arm.

I knew what she wanted to hear; we'd been through it before. "It's simple," I said. "They had to have a murder so you could be buried in holy ground."

"Yes," she said, her fingernails nearly piercing my skin. "My mother was—is—so religious, so Catholic."

I tried to pry her hand from my elbow.

"And they had to have a body," she continued, prompting me, urging me to speak.

"So they could bury the gardener."

"The man I killed," Thea said, "with a trowel. The first man I killed."

I nodded. Her stubborn commitment was past argument. She saw her duty clearly: The way to save Alonso was to claim Manley's murder; the way to claim Manley's murder was to admit Alonso's.

"It should be over soon," I said.

Mooney tapped me on the shoulder.

"Time to toss some tinder on dry brush?" I whispered.

"They're opening the casket," he announced.

Garnet stood, clearing his throat. "If it's a question of identity," he said, "I believe proper procedure would dictate taking the casket, unopened, to a mortuary or funeral parlor of the family's choosing—"

"To the Medical Examiner's Office," Mooney corrected. "It will eventually be conveyed there."

I left Thea with Roz—Thea's protective lioness, as if she needed one with all the attendant cops and son, Alonso, too—and entered the stifling tent. The smell hit like a clenched fist. I backtracked blindly, reaching for the tent's opening fold, retreating into the sunshine, gasping for air.

"Here," Mooney said, offering me a rag. I took it gratefully. He'd soaked it in turpentine. Chanel wouldn't have made a dent.

Back inside, it took my eyes a moment to adjust. The tent kept out more sun than I'd expected.

"There is one skeleton," the man from the ME's office was saying into a tiny tape recorder, "consistent with a female body of less than twenty years."

"The casket," Mooney said. "Is it extraordinarily heavy or high?"

"No."

"In your opinion, could it contain a secret compartment?"

"No."

"A second corpse?"

"No."

I could make out Garnet to one side, handkerchief pressed to his nose.

Mooney said, "Then keep digging."

The gravediggers looked at each other in astonishment. From where I stood, I could see the tops of their heads, but their boots were lost in the blackness of the pit.

"Hey, now," one of them said, "that's enough. If we

got to dig out another, it'll be after lunch and not before."

"I'm sorry," Mooney said. "I didn't mean you. You're finished for the day. Two forensic anthropologists will be taking over." With a few grunts the diggers heaved themselves over the side of the gaping hole.

Two of the men I'd classified as FBI entered the tent, one black, one white. The white carried a large toolbox. Both donned headgear reminiscent of miners' hardhats, with front-mounted flashlights. I would have liked to inspect their toolkit. From where I stood I could see small handbrooms, a tiny trowel, toothbrushes, tweezers.

The black man surveyed the ground, knelt, and let a handful of dirt sift through his fingers. He said, "It would be best to winch up the casket, place it on a trolley, and remove it, rolling the cart along the uncut turf. If the rest of you will now leave the tent, we could work more easily."

Garnet, scuffing at the dirt with a wing-tipped toe, said, "I don't intend to move without some sort of explanation."

Mooney, ignoring Garnet completely, said, "He couldn't have been buried far under the casket."

"What the hell are you talking about?" Garnet snapped.

The black forensic anthropologist said politely, "Gentlemen, would you mind moving this outside?"

So the conflagration took place outdoors in the shimmering heat, ten sunny days after Andrew Manley had come to me about a manuscript written by Thea Janis, living genius, long presumed dead.

It began with the sudden exodus from the tent, but the seed had been sown as soon as Garnet left Tessa's side. When her son abandoned her, Tessa had hurried off to inspect the opposition. Marissa tried her best to hold the older woman back, to keep mother from daughter. No use. Tessa, seemingly struck mute, placed a gloved hand under Thea's chin, tilted her face to the sun.

"Mama," Thea said. Just the one word with a faintly foreign pronunciation.

Tessa began babbling in Italian. She lost all color in her face. I was afraid she would faint.

"Mama, I'm sorry," Thea said defiantly, for my ears, for Mooney's ears, but most of all for Alonso's. "I didn't mean to kill Drew Manley. I know you cared for him."

Tessa turned away, stumbling, walking past Thea's chair onto the closely clipped grass. After four quick steps, she faltered, stopped. No place to go.

Alonso said, "Wait a damn minute. *Mama*? If she's your mama, then— Mom, what are you saying?"

Thea rose and put a hand to his lips. "It's okay, darling," she said. "It's a relief. I'm guilty. I have nothing to hide now. You'll be free to go soon. I don't blame you for any of this. Just go home. Promise me that."

He looked at Thea, then at Marissa, thinking perhaps of other promises, kept and unkept.

"We have something here!" The voice from the tent seemed far away, muffled.

Mooney stared at me, lifted his right eyebrow. I took a deep breath. I didn't want to blow my one planned line, my lighted match, as it were.

"Thea," I asked, "was your brother Garnet present when you killed Alonso's father?"

"When she what?" Alonso demanded.

I knew he was chained hand and foot, still I feared

he might hurt his mother, who glared at me with hatred in her eyes.

"No," Thea said. "No!"

"She never told me who my father was," said Alonso. "I assumed—" He stared at Garnet, looked away. "She said, just another guy on the road. A one-night stand. She wasn't even sure of his name. After a while I stopped asking. I never stopped wondering."

"He was a gardener," I said, holding out the photo Beryl had loaned me in exchange for her sister's words and pictures. He took it, his eyes glued to the image of the man who might well be his father. "I think he loved your mother," I went on, "and possibly your mother's sister, and I don't think that sat well with the family, their well-bred daughters and a gardener."

Alonso's mouth worked. He swallowed, said, "You killed him because—"

"Bitch!" Thea screamed, staring at me. "Take me to jail, anywhere, away from here! This isn't what I wanted. Alonso, I never meant to hurt you. I killed Dr. Manley for you."

"You didn't know where Manley was." Alonso spat the words at her like they were poison. "Tell me about my dad."

"Who knew where Manley was?" I asked quickly, shoving words into the gap.

"Marissa," Alonso said. "She took me to this incredible house. She said if I asked for it, it would be mine. They never even used it. Can you believe that? A family so rich they'd leave a house to rot? A mansion on the ocean. I grew up in trailers, in other people's garages. Mom took in laundry, for chrissakes."

Thea bowed her head. "That was only for a little while, Alonso. Only a little while."

"Long enough so I was the maid's kid, all through school. 'Wash my sheets, Alonso.' And then, all of a sudden, I thought I came from a family with a fucking mansion on the ocean. Money to burn." He gazed at his mother questioningly, but she turned away, refusing to meet his eyes. "I guess I do," he murmured to himself. "Guess I do."

"Did you tell him that, Marissa?" I asked.

"I may have told him the family was well off," she said, glancing down at her nails, totally in control.

Alonso used his voice as a weapon, a crude cutting tool. Elevating his chin, he stared at Marissa as if he could see past the brim of her hat. Slowly, he drawled, "Hey, cutie pie, after your little 'kidnapping' adventure, did you tell your dearest husband exactly who you'd been to bed with, what a great lay I was, how much better than he ever was, how much you got off on it? You know, the stuff you said you'd tell him if you got the chance? Or did you holler 'rape' instead? Is 'rape' why I know about that cute little star tattooed on your cute little butt?"

A flush crept up Marissa's cheeks. Her mouth worked for a moment before she drew herself to her full height. Her voice was tight enough to quiver when she finally spoke. "You'd think the police would keep him quiet!"

Garnet snorted. "Why silence the ring of truth, Missy dear? I do hope you had one hell of a time, because you know, it's going to cost you—"

Weakly, Tessa said, "Children—" She must have meant don't quarrel or don't squabble in public, but she couldn't take her eyes off Thea's face, couldn't raise her voice above a whisper.

She walked back toward Thea then, stiff-legged on the uneven grass, an old woman.

"How could you?" she asked in her crow's voice.

"How could you?" Thea answered.

"How could I what? I don't know what you're talking about."

"She's crazy, Mother," Garnet said.

Thea ignored him. "You never heard me cry at night? You never heard Beryl weeping?"

"Children cry."

"Especially when they have bad dreams, Mama." A single tear rolled down Thea's cheek. "Remember how we always had bad dreams?"

"Not you. Never you. Beryl had nightmares. She was a difficult child, always."

"It must have been difficult for her, being the sacrificial lamb. Don't you remember her dreams? About Father? And about Garnet," she finished slowly.

"*You* never had those dreams. It was only Beryl—"

"I lied, Mama. I forgot."

"And the dreams were never about Garnet," Tessa insisted. "About Franklin, yes. Beryl was afraid of her father. She was a fearful child."

Tessa tried to touch her daughter, wipe away her tears. Thea drew back warily.

"They weren't dreams. You had to know that. What could Father have said to you? That it took him an hour to tuck in his daughters at night? That he was working late? Our room was almost right above your room. Did you lock your door? Take more sleeping pills? Turn on the radio? A little soothing music to block out our cries? *Beryl always told the truth.* She didn't need your pet psychiatrist. We didn't need Dr. Drew—you never believed us."

"You agreed with me, Thea, that nothing had happened!"

"I repressed it! I couldn't deal with it, so I made it go away. *But you lied!* You said Garnet and Dad weren't even home, and bad little Beryl made it all up to get attention."

I said, "When Drew Manley first hired me to find Thea, he was excited, elated as a child. The next time I saw him, he was destroyed. A broken old man who *knew*, in this one case, that he'd done far more harm than good. Today, more psychiatrists give credence to children's tales of abuse. They make sure the kids see a physician. They search for physical evidence—"

Mooney emerged from the green tent and cleared his throat. Such a small noise, but it turned us all around as if our bodies were on strings.

"There is another skeleton," he said. "It appears to be that of an adult male. Unearthed sixteen inches beneath the casket, lying in soil."

"This is absurd—" Garnet spluttered.

"Calm down. You might want to know that the remains are consistent with having lain in the ground for twenty-four years—"

"Twenty-four years!" Garnet scoffed. "What about twenty-six? Thirty? Fifty?"

"The forensic anthropologists can more accurately date the remains at their laboratory."

"This is ridiculous," Garnet said, drawing himself up to his full height. "Surely we're not responsible for whatever was in the earth before we buried Thea!"

"For now," Mooney continued, "I can say positively that the hyoid bone has been recovered, snapped in two, a clear indication of strangulation."

Quickly I said to Thea, "Was Garnet with you when

Alonso died? Were any of his friends there? Because *you* didn't kill him, Thea."

"Susan," she spat. "I'm Susan. I'm nobody."

"Thea," I said, "you hit the man because he hit you, but you didn't move him from Weston to Marblehead. You didn't strangle him when he came to. You may have helped shove his body in the freezer in the Marblehead basement, but you didn't bury him."

"I didn't strangle him! I hit him with a trowel! I told you. I told the police. I told everyone!"

I said, "He was alive when someone drove him out to Marblehead. You must have had help. You couldn't have carried him by yourself. You didn't drive. He was alive when you took off your clothes and buried them in the sand and dove into the sea."

"Garnet," she said. Two syllables and all the accusation in the world. "What did you do to me? What have you done to me?"

"It was Father," Garnet countered, never taking his eyes from Thea's face. "Dad killed him. Once he knew you were pregnant, there was no stopping him."

"Dad wasn't there!"

"It was a lifetime ago. Maybe you repressed it, Thea. How can you remember? For sure?"

"I remember, Garnet. I remember so well. I remember every moment of my last day on earth, Garnet. And you were the only one. You sold my dreams for yours. You took my reputation for yours. You took my talent and my voice, and everything I had. You stole my life—"

"I had to protect Father."

"Two with one stone," Thea said bitterly. "That's your gift, Garnet, your only gift: killing. You killed Beryl's soul, you and Father. You killed Alonso—you were always jealous of him, I see that now; you must have been jealous of every other man I slept with. *Did you think you were so special, Garnet? Did Daddy give me to you? Were the rights supposed to be exclusive?* When you finished Alonso off, you conveniently got rid of me, convinced me I had to disappear, die. *Was I getting to be a problem, Brother dear?* You must have killed Drew after I spoke to him, after he guessed the truth about what you and Father had done to Beryl and me, and then you set up my son to take the blame. Just as you set me up so long ago. I'll see you dead for that. I'll kill you."

"Take him to court instead," Mooney said.

"Oh yes," Garnet said lightly. "Do. Judges and juries adore tales like this. Institutionalized witnesses, twenty-year time gaps, recovered memories! At the moment recovered memory syndrome may have some scientific credence, but it's a day-to-day thing. Go ahead. Let's do this in court."

"They won't need to, Garnet," I said softly. "It's over. Once you're accused, what will you do? Keep running for governor while your sister tells her stories, the way only Thea Janis can spin a tale? Face it, Garnet. You're no one. When you killed Alonso, you might as well have killed yourself—"

I could have gone on speaking, but he was walking, walking quickly down the path. With all the cops present you wouldn't think he'd have been able to get to his chauffeured car, order Henry out into the lazy stream of afternoon traffic.

But he did.

Later, the chauffeur said he thought it odd for Garnet to order him out to the old Marblehead house, to raise the glass divider. He especially thought it strange when Garnet opened the rear window, tossing his cellular phone to the pavement, where it shattered on impact.

But Henry was accustomed to obeying orders.

He pulled over on command, saw Garnet walk around the back of the old Ocean Avenue property, barefoot. He'd left his tie and briefcase in the car, and his city shoes, socks neatly rolled within. So curious was Henry that he followed, at a distance.

Garnet set a steady pace, shedding clothes as he walked, his shirt, pants. He flung his key chain into the sand, the motion almost joyous. His underwear followed.

When he ran into the sea, it was no more than knee-high, but he started swimming immediately. Swimming straight out from shore, letting the waves break over his head, never looking to the left or the right, never looking back.

Henry said he never thought Mr. Garnet intended to kill himself until his head was a tiny dot, far away, tossed on the waves, gulls reeling and calling in the air.

57

In Thea's second novel, the character named "d" sleeps with her brother, and bears a child by him. I wondered if Alonso had read it closely, understood what he was reading. I'd watched his eyes move at the graveyard, searching first his uncle's face, then the photo of his long-dead namesake.

Fiction? I hoped so. I recalled Thea's taped confession—she'd told Alonso Senior she was uncertain who the father was.

I hoped Alonso Junior would never hear that particular tape. He looked too much like his mother, like his uncle.

Better he shouldn't know. Maybe his mother was right when she said she gave him the best father she could.

I spent most of the night in Mooney's spartan office, listening to uninformed brass criticize him via telephone. According to various "superiors," he should have immediately issued an all-points on Garnet Cameron, initiated a high-speed car chase through five cities and towns, endangering pedestrians and drivers alike. I sat nearby, offering quiet support with my presence, rolling my eyes whenever the phone rang. Supplying doughnuts and coffee.

I thought he'd done the right thing. A trial would never have resolved the issues at stake. Garnet's death might make reconciliation possible, once Tessa finished grieving. If she ever did.

About the FBI: Alonso Nueves Rojas, subject of the elusive missing persons file #902869432, itinerant gardener, was a Cuban national under FBI surveillance. Ten years after the Bay of Pigs, Cuba was a hot spot for the Bureau. They'd traced Nueves as he made his way north from Miami, deciding whether to approach him as a prospective counterintelligence agent. Although he'd once fought for Castro, he now declared himself an anti-Castro patriot. The Bureau had inconclusive paper concerning his whereabouts on November 22, 1963, the day Kennedy died. The FBI hadn't made up its collective mind, friend or foe, when Nueves abruptly disappeared.

That was all. That was why MacAvoy had been afraid to dump the Nueves file entirely, perhaps why his shaky eraser had failed to obliterate the number. Simple fear of Big Brother FBI.

Gary Reedy got to stamp "Case Closed" on #902869432. He was a happy man. He shook Mooney's hand when he left, actually smiled at me.

58

It was over, but I didn't feel like celebrating.

Tessa'd found her lost child, but at what cost? Her peace of mind . . . her lover . . . her son . . .

We finished up late Tuesday night—all the charges and countercharges, the handshakes, the stares of enmity. I'd put in a lot of night driving lately, but I knew I'd never sleep. I didn't see how a last long haul could hurt.

I got in my Toyota and headed north in a drizzle that grew heavier as I traveled, north to New Hampshire and Paolina.

I wondered whether Thea would keep writing. I doubted she'd publish her second novel, even if she continued to revise it. Despite its promise, it had brought such pain. Shoved too many faces, both innocent and knowing, into the unforgiving truth.

As to truth, I couldn't plumb the depth of her talent. Maybe she *had* lost the gift. A prodigy's talent is often like that. It doesn't mature with the person, just stays as it was. Thea's words echoed: "I'm no longer 'talented for my age.'"

I found myself driving faster the closer I got to Paolina's campsite. Turning up the music, singing along with Les Sampou on "Sweet Perfume," trying to shut down my thoughts.

Paolina must have been scared or she wouldn't have called, wouldn't have begged me to pick her up as quickly as possible. But I'd had Pix in the car, another child clinging to me for help. Roz had answered the phone. Had Paolina willed her voice calm, not to worry me?

Some things can't be undone. Thea had said it, screamed it as the police continued to search for Garnet's body.

What if I wasn't there? Wasn't there when Carlos Roldan Gonzales came for Paolina?

Some things can't be undone.

I heard the phrase with every swipe of the windshield wiper across the rain-splattered glass.

I don't think I took a breath till I saw her, lying on her left side, curled tightly into a sleeping ball. The girls slept six to a cabin, and I had to tiptoe for silence, and bend at the same time to allow for the low ceiling. The counselor on duty had given me permission to wake her, take her home. The counselor had said she'd been fine—active and happy—until last week, until a phone call.

But campers weren't allowed to receive calls, I'd protested.

"He said it was an emergency."

An emergency.

Paolina wakes slowly, full of stretches and yawns and small secretive smiles. She squirmed into clothes laid ready at the end of her bed. Ready for what?

She didn't speak till she was beside me in the car, her tote and backpack in the trunk, her farewell letter written, weighted by a rock to the long kitchen table where her summer friends would find it when they woke.

Paolina talks when she's ready. Five minutes or five hours. Or not at all.

The rain beat steadily on the roof.

When she spoke her voice was guarded. She could have been talking about archery practice or a soccer game. "My father called," she said, her face turned away, staring into the darkness outside the passenger window. "My real father."

Usually she called him Carlos. Since she found out he existed. "Father" had always been the man her mother had married, a Puerto Rican absentee who'd given the family legal-immigrant status and not much else.

"He wanted me to go with him," she said.

Dear God, I could have lost her. The thought was an alarm clanging in my ears. How had he known where she was?

"He changed his mind," she said softly. I couldn't take my eyes off the narrow road, couldn't tell if she was hiding tears of sorrow or relief.

I waited, but she seemed to have run out of words.

"Did you want to go?" I said, trying so hard for nonchalance I could barely spit out the question.

"I'm . . . not sure. But he didn't give me the chance. I'm not sure."

"I'm sorry I didn't come sooner," I said.

She fell asleep with her head resting against the window. I reached over to reassure myself that her seat belt was fastened.

When I turned the car into the driveway, she woke again, and helped carry her things up the walkway. We peeled off our damp rain gear in the foyer. The red light flashed on my message machine.

Carlos Roldan Gonzales's voice, his deep sonorous accented voice, dominated the room.

"Little one," he said, as if he knew Paolina would be with me, listening, "I am sorry if I disappointed you. I will come when it is safe. It may seem foolish, perhaps, in your country, but I have enemies who may have learned of you, who would not hesitate to use you to get to me. I don't want you hurt, *querida*.

"Señorita," he said, his tone changing to speak to an adult. "Take care of her. She will be safer with you. For now."

I knelt and held her in my arms till she wriggled her protest.

What would I do if Carlos came for her? What would I do if she chose to go with him?

To lose my brilliant child.

The next day, Wednesday, because I felt rich with Paolina beside me, granted permission by her mother to stay with me till camp's official Friday end, I hired myself to find a tiny blond girl named Pix.

I put an ad in *The Phoenix* begging her to call. I signed it "Alonso." I sent Roz into all the best-known Cambridge and Somerville squats. I went myself, tacked up a hundred posters on bulletin boards and walls, drawn by Roz, copied by Xerox. I offered a generous reward. I tracked her through the Missing Children's Center, through the prison and probation systems, through the Internet.

I never found her.

> perhaps as penance,
>   i must walk,
>   barefoot and holy,
>   through snow-wax camellias

Pix visits my dreams. My penance, perhaps.

Afterword

He said, "She has a lovely face;
God in his mercy lend her grace,
The Lady of Shalott."

ALFRED, LORD TENNYSON

AUTHOR'S NOTE

The poetry herein attributed to the fictional Thea Janis
was actually written by Nancy Linn Pearl in the summer of 1963. It is used with the consent of the poet.
Because I needed a poem as evidence of Thea's current
liveliness, I attempted to capture Nancy's early style in
"berlin, now."